SEA OF
AKERI

KINGDOM OF
VENDA

ATERR

MARABELLA

SANCTUM

TEUX

GREAT RIVER

FALWORTH

KINGDOM OF
DALBRECK

REUX
LAU

CRUVAS

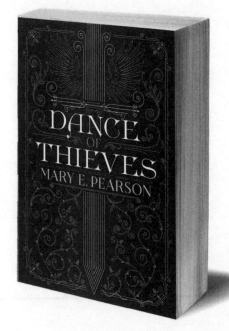

VOW OF THIEVES

VOW
OF
THIEVES

NEW YORK TIMES–BESTSELLING AUTHOR OF THE REMNANT CHRONICLES

MARY E. PEARSON

Henry Holt and Company

NEW YORK

Henry Holt and Company, *Publishers since 1866*
Henry Holt® is a registered trademark of Macmillan Publishing Group, LLC
120 Broadway, New York, NY 10271 • fiercereads.com

Library of Congress Control Number: 2018955720

ISBN 978-1-250-16265-6

Our books may be purchased in bulk for promotional, educational, or business use.
Please contact your local bookseller or the Macmillan Corporate and Premium
Sales Department at (800) 221-7945 ext. 5442 or by email at
MacmillanSpecialMarkets@macmillan.com.

First edition, 2019 / Designed by Rebecca Syracuse

Printed in the United States of America

1   3   5   7   9   10   8   6   4   2

For Dennis and the vows you made and kept

The youngest ones ask me questions.

They want to know about the world Before.

I am the oldest. I should know.

> *Did you fly, Greyson? In the sky like a bird?*
>
> *Yes. With my grandfather.*
>
> *How?*

I wasn't sure. I was only five, but I remember looking down, watching the ground disappear, my grandfather weeping as he held me in his arms.

I never saw him weep again.

After the first star fell, six more followed.

There was no time for weeping after that, or explaining things like flying.

There was only time for running.

Tai and Uella crawl into my lap.

> *Will you teach us to fly?*
>
> *No. I will teach you other things.*

Things that will keep you alive.

—**Greyson Ballenger, 15**

CHAPTER ONE

KAZIMYRAH OF BRIGHTMIST

A DUSTY BEAM OF LIGHT WORMED ITS WAY THROUGH THE STONE, and I leaned in, hoping to steal some warmth. I was a thief. It should have been easy, but the warmth eluded me. How long had I been here? Five days? A month? Eleven years? I called out to my mother and then I remembered. *That was a lifetime ago. She is gone.*

The narrow beam came only after long spells of darkness, maybe once a day? I wasn't sure, and even then it didn't stay for long, sneaking in like a curious onlooker. *What have we here?* It pointed at my belly now, my shirt stiff with dried blood. *My, that doesn't look good. Shouldn't you do something?* Was it a laugh I heard as the beam faded away? Or was it a quarterlord taunting me?

I wasn't dead yet, so I knew that the knife plunged into my belly had at least missed anything vital. But the wound wept yellow, and my brow was feverish, the filth of the cell seeping in.

My dreams seeping out.

Rats rustled in a dark unseen corner. Synové hadn't mentioned them.

I remembered her telling me about her dream. *I saw you chained in a prison cell . . . You were soaked in blood.* I remembered her worried eyes. I remembered dismissing her fears. *Sometimes dreams are only dreams.*

And sometimes dreams were so much more.

Where is Jase?

I heard a rattle and looked up. I had a visitor. He stood in the corner studying me.

"You," I said, my voice foreign to my ears, weak and brittle. "You're here for me. I've been expecting you."

He shook his head. *Not yet. Not today. I'm sorry.*

And then he was gone.

I lay down on the floor, the chains jangling against the cobbles, and I curled tight, trying to ease the ache in my gut.

I'm sorry.

An apology from Death?

Now I knew. Worse things than dying still lay ahead for me.

CHAPTER TWO

KAZI

Two Weeks Earlier

JASE WALKED THROUGH THE DOOR AS NAKED AS A PEELED ORANGE.

I soaked up the view as he crossed the room and snatched his trousers up from the floor. He began to pull them on, spotted me watching, and paused. "I can hold off on this if you'd like to take advantage of my vulnerable position?"

I raised a discerning brow. "I think I took quite enough advantage this morning. Get dressed, *Patrei*. We have miles to cover today."

He pasted on a dejected frown. "As you command."

I knew he was ready to be on his way too. We had made good time, but between the trip to Marabella and now our trek back, we'd been gone from Tor's Watch for over two months. He pulled on his shirt, his skin still steaming against the brisk air. The tattooed wing on his chest glistened in a soft fog. Our lodgings had afforded us a hot spring. We had soaked miles of travel from our skin last night and again this morning. It was a luxury neither of us was eager to leave behind.

I walked to the window while Jase finished dressing. The manor was mostly in ruins now, but hints of its greatness shone through, intricate blue-veined marble floors that still had some shine in hidden corners, towering pillars, and a ceiling that once held a painting, bits of cloud, a horse's eye, and a beautifully rendered but disembodied hand gracing the broken plaster. Was this the home of a ruling Ancient? Aaron Ballenger himself? The opulence whispered like a dying swan.

The surrounding grounds were sprinkled with crumbled outbuildings that seemed to extend for miles. They hadn't withstood the ravages of falling stars and time, forests now pulling them back into the earth with their gentle emerald fingers. Even the manor, nested high on a rocky ledge, wore a leafy headdress of trees and vines. But at one time, long ago, it must have been perfectly beautiful and majestic. Whoever had once wandered these halls probably thought it would be perfect forever.

Before we left Marabella, the king's aide, Sven, had drawn out a northern route for us that paralleled the Infernaterr. The map included multiple shelters and even a few hot springs. It was a slightly longer route, but one he said would be less affected by weather. We were heading into the stormy season, and the Infernaterr exuded a permanent warmth. We had traveled fast and far in three weeks, and if we kept up our pace, we had less than a handful of days until we reached Tor's Watch. As we drew closer to home, I heard the excitement rise in Jase's voice. He was exuberant about the changes we would make.

We had a plan. He had things to do. I had things to do. And we had things we would do together. Even though I had fears about our return, I was mostly exuberant too. I could finally admit that I loved Hell's Mouth. It hummed in my blood like it had that first day I rode into it. Only this time I wouldn't be an intruder looking for trouble. I'd have trouble riding right beside me, and I would be a part of it all, helping Tor's Watch to become something more.

It was all we had talked about our first week on the trail—staking out the boundaries for this new tiny kingdom and revising the rules of trade. Any lingering hopes anyone entertained of taking over the arena and Hell's Mouth would be quashed—especially once they learned that Tor's Watch's sovereignty was to be formally recognized by the Alliance. It was to become the thirteenth kingdom. Or the first. I smiled, thinking of Jase's audacity in the face of the queen's generosity, to insist on being named the first.

My role as liaison was not just an honorary position. I was still Rahtan, and most important, I was still in the queen's employ. She had given me duties to perform to ensure the smooth transition of power. She also believed the presence of a representative from a major kingdom would carry weight and add stability as the changeover took place, and warned me that resistance could come from unexpected places.

She had given me an additional mission—to be my first priority when I reached there. I had told her about the youngest scholar's final guilt-laden words: *I'm sorry. Destroy them.* While we'd believed all the documents burned, where there was even a fragment of doubt, there was a mountain of concern.

Secure those papers, Kazimyrah, and if you can't safely send them to me, destroy them. We have no idea what information the scholars escaped with after the fall of the Komizar, or what they have developed since. We don't want these papers to fall into the wrong hands if there's even the slightest chance for a repeat of the carnage—or worse.

Worse?

There was only one thing worse than the Great Battle. The devastation.

Only a handful had survived, and the world still bore its scars.

I promised her it would be the first matter that I addressed.

She also asked me to send a history book or two if there were any to spare. *I'd like to read more about this land. Greyson Ballenger was a brave leader.*

So very young, but determined to protect his charges against scavengers. It doesn't always take an army to save the world. Sometimes it takes just one person who won't let evil win. It is heroes like Greyson and those twenty-two children who inspire me.

The queen, *inspired*. She didn't seem to grasp that she inspired most of the continent. She inspired me. She made me see myself differently. She saw me as someone worth saving, in spite of my rags and past. She inspired me to be more than what others expected of me. I dared to believe I could make a difference because the queen had believed it first. Even when I landed our whole crew in prison, she didn't give up on me.

And now, with some pride, I knew she counted on me.

I imagined that by now Gunner had found the mysterious papers and would be trying to decipher their secrets. But regardless of what they contained, Gunner would be required to hand them over to me—no matter how loudly he protested. Tor's Watch would forfeit the recognition of the Alliance if the Ballengers didn't comply. In any event I had my own means to make him hand them over. Nothing would stand in the way of me keeping my promise to the queen, or in the way of Tor's Watch becoming a recognized kingdom. It wasn't just Jase's dream, it was mine too. And it could be that by now the papers had been brushed aside while Gunner was consumed with other matters, like preparing for Jase's return.

Jase had sent Gunner a message saying he was on his way home and he had good news to share. That was all he was willing to tell him. As energized as Jase was by the prospect of Tor's Watch becoming a recognized kingdom at last, he wanted to explain everything personally, and not have Gunner impulsively announcing things to everyone that Jase—and the queen—weren't ready to publicly share. He also didn't mention that I would be with him. That would take some personal explaining too, more than a short note could convey. But at least for now Jase's family knew he was well and coming home.

The message sent by Valsprey would reach the Ballengers through the same circuitous black market route as all their messages did—first to the Valsprey handler in the Parsuss message office, where the Ballengers secretly had someone on their payroll. The queen had raised her eyebrows at this revelation, and Jase promised that little transgression would be remedied too. Of course, as a new kingdom that would soon be receiving trained Valsprey of their own, there would no longer be a need to pinch the birds from other sources. The king said we could expect the handler with Valsprey to follow on our heels within a few months.

I heard the scuff of footsteps on the gritty marble floor behind me, then felt Jase's heat at my back. He still radiated the warmth of the springs, and as he drew close, he rested his hands on my shoulders.

"What are you looking at?" he asked.

"The perfect beauty. Things lost. Us."

"Us?"

"These past weeks have been—"

I didn't know how to finish, but I knew there had been something in these days together that I didn't want to lose, something that was pristine and almost sacred. We'd had no outside influences to come between us. I feared that might change.

"I know, Kazi. No one knows more than I do." He brushed aside my hair and kissed my neck. "But this isn't an end. It's just the beginning. I promise. After all we've been through, nothing can pull us apart. I'm afraid you're stuck with me now."

I closed my eyes, breathing in his touch, his scent, and every word he spoke. *I promise.*

Things had changed between us in a way I hadn't thought possible.

Only now did I understand the unbearable weight of secrets. You can never know their true burden until they've been lifted from you. These past weeks we had been swept up in the near-giddy lightness of truth.

We shared everything freely, no longer stumbling over our words. As much as I thought I knew about Jase, I learned far more—all the day-to-day details that had shaped who he was, from the mundane to the agonizing. I discovered more about his vulnerable underside, his worries as his father lay dying, and the new responsibilities that had so recently fallen upon him. He had thought it would be years before he had to shoulder the weight of being *Patrei*, but at nineteen, all the decisions were suddenly up to him.

He told me a secret he had never shared with anyone else—about his sister Sylvey and her last pleas to him, his guilt over denying her, refusing to believe what Sylvey already knew—she was dying. Even after four years it was still a raw wound for him, and his voice cracked as he told me. It helped me to see myself better—the impossible choices of a fleeting moment—the regrets we bury deep within us, the things we would do differently if only we could have one more chance, if only we could rewind a moment like a card of yarn and weave it into something else. *Run, Kazi, run for the stick. Jam it in his groin, bash in his nose, smash his windpipe.* Why didn't I? One different choice might have changed everything. But my mother's voice was strong too. *Don't move. Say nothing.*

For Jase it was the opposite—he hadn't listened. The last look in Sylvey's watery eyes before she closed them forever still haunted him. He hesitated when he shared what was perhaps his darkest secret of all, that he had stolen her body from her tomb and buried her at the base of Breda's Tears in the Moro mountains. It was sacrilege in Hell's Mouth, in all of Eislandia in fact, to desecrate a tomb, a crime punishable by death. Not even his family knew what he had done. I tried to imagine the torment he must have gone through as he traveled alone with her wrapped corpse slung over his saddle on a dark mountain trail.

Other truths were harder to share—they surfaced in layers—some buried so deep they were only a vague ache we had learned to ignore. We helped each other find those truths too. *How did you survive, Kazi? Alone?* He didn't just mean, how did I eat or clothe myself. I had already told him that. He meant the day-to-day loneliness of having no one to turn to. It was inconceivable to him. I didn't have an answer because I wasn't exactly sure myself. Some days it felt like all that was left of me was a hungry shadow, a thing that could disappear and no one would notice. Maybe believing that was what helped me slip away so easily.

Though our truthfulness was a heady elixir that I wanted more of, the closer we got to Tor's Watch, the more I felt the weight of new secrets creeping back in. I had concerns about Jase's family that I didn't want to share because I knew he would dismiss them. He was the head of the family, the *Patrei*, after all. They would listen to him. But could hatred really be erased by a command? And his family's hatred toward me had been visceral. It consumed them to the core.

I will gouge your eyes out one at a time and feed them to the dogs.

This was the "family" I was returning to. It wasn't just Priya's threats that worried me, but the gulf of broken trust I wasn't sure could be bridged again, not even for Jase's sake. I had seen Vairlyn's gutted expression as I took her son at knifepoint. I would always be the girl who had invaded their home, the girl who had lied and stolen from them.

Even the sweet innocence of Lydia and Nash was probably tarnished now. It would have been impossible to keep the details of Jase's disappearance from them. There was also the matter of Gunner and his cruel taunts when he knew what Zane had done to *my* family. It didn't matter if he was Jase's brother. My hatred for him hadn't eased in these past weeks. I couldn't pretend that night was forgotten any more than they could.

"I know how much your family means to you, Jase. I don't want you to be caught in the middle or be forced to choose sides."

"Kazi, *you* are my family now. There is no choosing. You're saddled with me forever. Understand? And so are they. That's how families work. Trust me, they will come around. They loved you already. They will love you again. More important, they will be grateful. The Ballengers let their guard down. I have no doubt we'd all be dead if you hadn't intervened."

He had assured me before, recounting details of infamous past slaughters visited upon the Ballengers, and on this matter I had no doubt either. Jase would have been first. Kill the strongest and then move on to the rest. What would it have been? An unexpected knife in his back when he stopped in to check on Beaufort's progress? It was imminent, that much I knew. Beaufort had expected his plan to come to fruition in only a week before I had intervened. More supplies had been ordered. Production was set to begin in earnest. Additional metalsmiths were being sought out to help Sarva fashion two dozen more launchers. But Jase's family only knew what they saw, not what might have been, and they had witnessed my betrayal—not Beaufort's. His plan to dominate the kingdoms—that would only be my false claim measured against his grand promises to them. I knew Jase would back me up, and yes, maybe that would be enough, but I wasn't certain. I didn't understand all the emotions and complexities of a family, and I worried that maybe it was too late for me to learn.

"I've never had a family before, Jase. I may not be good at—"

"You have Wren and Synové. They're like family."

A sharp tug pulled inside me when he mentioned them. I missed them already, far more than I'd thought I would. We were used to being separated for short periods as we went on different missions, but our beds in the bunk room, in a neat row together, always awaited our return. This time I wouldn't be going back. These past weeks I had often wondered where they were and how they were doing. Wren and Synové, I supposed, were the closest thing that I had to family. They would lay their lives down for me, and I for them. We had become sisters in a very real sense, but we never said the word. Family was a risk that you might never recover from, and we led dangerous lives by choice. Justice burned in us, like a brand seared into our skin the day our families were taken from us. The unsaid words between us were our safety net. Jase's family was a solid unit, all of them the same, always together. I wasn't sure I could be part of that kind of family.

"And you had your mother," he added. "She was your family, no matter how short a time you two were together."

We had already talked about my mother. Even the oldest, most painful secrets were not held back between us. Lines deepened around his eyes when I told him, and I wondered if the telling was as painful for him as it was for me, his own regrets piling up beside mine, wishing his family had never given the Previzi safe haven—or employed them.

"It will all work out," he promised and kissed my earlobe. "And it all doesn't have to happen overnight. We have time. We'll ease into all the changes."

Which meant he knew there would be difficulties ahead. "Ready to go?" he asked.

I spun to face him, scrutinizing him from head to toe, and sighed. "Finally dressed, are you? Once I've settled in as magistrate, I'm going to have to rein you in, *Patrei*."

"So today it's magistrate? Yesterday you were Ambassador Brightmist."

"The queen left the roles to my discretion, depending on how you behave."

"Plan to arrest me?" he asked, a bit too eagerly.

I narrowed my eyes. "If you don't toe the line."

"If you weren't so impatient, you wouldn't be saddled with me now."

I laughed. "Me the impatient one? I seem to remember it was *you* who pulled the twine from Synové's package."

Jase shrugged, his eyes wide with innocence. "The twine practically unraveled on its own. Besides, I didn't know what was inside or what a simple red ribbon could lead to."

We hadn't even made it through one full day on the trail before he wanted to open Synové's going away gift for us.

"Never trust Rahtan bearing gifts," I warned. "What you don't know can get you into trouble, *Patrei*."

"But trouble is what we do best together." He gathered me into his arms, his eyes dancing with light, but then his playful expression turned serious. "Are you sorry?"

I felt myself falling deeper into the world that was Jase Ballenger. "Never. Not through a thousand tomorrows could I ever be sorry. Trouble with you makes me glad for it. I love you with every breath I will ever breathe. I love you, Jase."

"More than an orange?" he asked between kisses.

"Let's not get carried away, *Patrei*."

The words I had refused to even think before came surprisingly easy now. I said them often and in a hundred ways. Every time our lips met, every time my fingers raked his hair. *I love you.* Maybe part of it was a fear, fear of jealous gods and missed chances. I knew more than ever now that chances could be wrenched from your grasp in an instant, including chances for last words, and if there were to be any final words between Jase and me, I wanted them to be those.

My mother's last words to me had been desperate with fear. *Shhh, Kazi, don't say a word.* That's what I always heard first when I thought of her, the fear.

We went downstairs to where Mije and Tigone were stabled in what might have once been a long, open dining hall. Indeed, it still was, the floor thick with clover, which both horses had effectively mowed down. We were headed into windswept plains where grazing would be harder to come by, so I was glad that they had eaten their fill.

We saddled up and left, and as we rode, I relived the magic of each day, determined not to let these weeks roll into oblivion. I kept track of where we had come from and where we were going, so no unexpected turn could push us down an uncharted path again. And throughout the miles I memorized every word between us so they could never be forgotten.

"What about us, Jase? Will someone write down our story?"

"What do you mean?"

"Like the hundreds that are on the vault's walls, and the ones in your bookcases."

An amused smile pulled at his mouth, as if it hadn't occurred to him and he was intrigued by the thought. "We will, Kazi. You and I. We'll write our own story. And it will take a thousand volumes. We have a lifetime ahead of us."

"That's a lot of trees."

He shrugged. "We own a mountainful, remember?"

We. Everything was we now.

We wove our dreams together like armor. Nothing could stop us now.

CHAPTER THREE

JASE

"A BUTTON?"

I laughed as Kazi described the full-cheeked blustering quarterlord howling at the end of an alley like his nose had been cut off.

"Why risk so much just to steal a useless button?" I asked.

Her smile faded, her gaze serene, her fingers moving across her palm as if she still held the prized button in her grasp. "It wasn't useless," she answered. "Sometimes you have to remind yourself that you're not power-less. That you have some measure of control. That maybe your skills aren't good just for filling your own stomach, but also for making others consider theirs. If a thief could steal a button straight off his belly in the middle of the day, how much more might they take from him in the dark corners of the night?" She chewed on the corner of her lip, her eyes nar-rowing. "I know he didn't sleep well that evening, and that gave *me* the sweetest sleep ever. Sometimes you need to own one whole day. Maybe that's what makes you brave enough to face another."

I was still trying to understand her world, what she had been through, and the resolve it had taken for her stay alive. "Brave? You're the bravest person I've ever met." I looked sideways at her. "Of course, the most scheming too."

She squeezed the seed from the date she was nibbling and threw it at me, hitting me directly on the chin.

I rubbed the spot. "A schemer with good aim?"

"Says the Grand Schemer himself, but I'll take the compliment," she said and looked ahead again, her shoulders swaying gently with each of Mije's hoof falls. She was silent for a long while before she asked, "Will you tell them I was a thief?"

My family. I knew that was what she meant, but I sidetracked the question.

"Was? You still are a thief. I count my fingers every night before I go to sleep. But let's not make them call you Ten."

"Jase."

I sighed. Truth between Kazi and me was one thing, but with my family, it was another. I'd have to talk them down from a furious ledge before I told them anything. I knew they would listen, but it would be hard for them to go from seething to open arms with just a few words. Not when their home had been invaded and their prized investment— and their *Patrei*—had been stolen from them by someone they thought they trusted. "Yes, I will tell them. Whenever you're ready. Though it might be a good idea to dispense one truth at a time. Slowly."

She grinned. "Agreed. I suppose we don't need to hit them with everything at once."

"Of course, you realize once you tell Lydia and Nash, they'll want you to teach them everything you know."

"We'll stick to juggling and coins behind ears for now. Shadows are a bit harder to master."

"Don't forget the silent signals," I reminded her. "They would love using those at the dinner table."

She smiled. "Already on my list of priorities."

Even before she was on her own, she had told me she and her mother had developed a silent language between them to survive the streets of Venda, because there were often risky moments when they had to remain silent. I had a few subtle gestures for my crew, but I was surprised at how many signals she and her mother had. A flick of the fingers meant *smile*, a tucked chin, *watch, be ready*, a rigid hand, *do not move*.

I told her stories about my childhood too, the trouble us older children would get into. She laughed, both appalled and amused. I told her about one hot summer when we were particularly bored. Our antics involved ropes, pulleys, and snatching hats from unsuspecting people passing below us on the boardwalk as we stalked them from high up in the tembris trees.

"A thief in training? No wonder that shopkeeper called you one of the untamable Ballenger brood."

I shrugged. "We gave the hats back, but got a scolding from our mother. She said if we put half as much work into our studies as we did our pranks, we'd all be geniuses. But when she thought we weren't looking, we saw her shoot our father an approving nod. They both thought we were quite clever."

"Yes," Kazi conceded. "Clever as little foxes stealing eggs from the henhouse."

⸻

The forest had grown thicker, and the peculiar chirps of striped squirrels sounded overhead, disturbed by our presence. We fell into silence, and my thoughts drifted back to Beaufort, as they frequently did. Kazi and I had discussed him together many times, but we'd come to no conclusions.

Dominion over the kingdoms.

But how?

Yes, Beaufort was developing powerful weapons, but he had no army to use them. He came to Tor's Watch empty-handed, rags on his back, and his hat in hand. He and his group were a pitiful sight. Even if he was working with one of the leagues and he armed every one of them with the launchers he had developed, he still couldn't bring down an entire kingdom, much less all of them.

Was Beaufort delusional? Trying to speak his lost dreams of power into truth? If so, Kardos and the rest all had to be as mad as he was. But Sentinel Valley was no delusion. The mass graves were sickeningly real. Maybe it took madmen to concoct such schemes.

"Do you think this is Ogres Teeth?" Kazi asked.

We passed a row of broken columns rising up in the middle of the forest, their purpose long lost to the world, but they looked like they might be the ruins Sven had described to us. There were so many vestiges of another time in this forest, I pulled out the map and checked it again to be sure.

"Yes," I answered. "This is it."

You asked me why an open world frightens me, Jase? Because it gives me nowhere to hide.

According to the map, we were headed into another one of those open worlds soon. I think it bothered me more than it did her. I was used to solving problems, fixing them one way or another, and this one I couldn't fix. I couldn't undo the past and take away what had been done. Her fear weighed on me. I had already studied the map, trying to find any way around it, but there was none.

We turned on a switchback, and the mountains and forest ended abruptly. We found ourselves on a high trail, looking out at an endless plain that was a strange deep red. In the distant north the harsh land of Infernaterr shimmered like a silver sea lapping at its shores.

"Whoa, Mije." Kazi stopped and stared at the vast emptiness. It was our third time having to cross an empty landscape that offered no shelter.

I watched her eyes skim the miles, her chest rising in quicker breaths.

"You don't have to be afraid of Zane anymore, Kazi. He's in the family's custody. They won't let him go."

She blew out a disbelieving huff. "You so sure? Gunner seemed willing enough to trade him away the last time I saw him."

"I promise you, Gunner won't let him go." I wished I could tell her it was because of what Zane had done over a decade ago to her and her mother, but that wasn't why he would hold him. Zane had a connection to the labor hunters that had descended on Hell's Mouth and stolen me and other citizens away, and for that Gunner would never let him leave Tor's Watch—at least not alive.

I watched her focus on the horizon, on some tiny point in the distance, probably imagining a busy town full of shadows and dark corners and how only a flat landscape lay in the way of her getting there. Her chin lifted. "I'm not that powerless six-year-old anymore, Jase. I'm not afraid of Zane. I guarantee, he's the one who's afraid of me now. He's the one looking over his shoulder, waiting for a door to open and for me to walk through it. He's the one who's afraid to sleep at night."

I had no doubt of that. I'd seen his expression when he saw her that last night in Tor's Watch—when he saw *her* looking at *him*. Her eyes had glowed with a primal hunger, with the ferocity of a Candok bear that couldn't be stopped. And yet I'd felt her heart pound beneath my arm when I pulled her close at night and a wide-open sky pressed down on us.

"But I've seen you—"

"Still struggling to sleep out here in the open? I know." Her expression darkened, her brows pulling together, as if she was perplexed by this too. She sighed. "I can't quite shake it. For now, I suppose, it's a part of who I am. My mind reasons that there's nothing to be afraid of, but something inside me I can't control reacts differently." I heard the confusion in her voice. She turned and looked at me. "I'm not sure how long it will take to convince my heart to stop racing every time I'm confronted with no place to hide. Maybe a lifetime. Are you up for that?"

"That's a lot of riddles."

"I still have a few in me."

I did too. Like how many of my brothers would it take to hold me back from Zane when we got home again? How would he ever answer my questions with my hands around his throat? He stole Kazi's mother. He left a six-year-old child to die on the streets of Venda. My pulse raced hot thinking about him, but I knew Zane wasn't mine to finish. I had only cultivated a few months' worth of hatred for him. Kazi had eleven years. Her anger trumped mine by a long shot.

Zane would be left for Kazi.

After she got her answers.

———————

We made our way down to the plain quickly, the soil so red it looked like it was drenched with ripe cherries—or blood. Every part of this continent held new surprises. The landscapes we had passed through had been both breathtaking and tedious, and sometimes jarring. The most jarring was Stone Canyon, which Sven had marked clearly on the map. *Go around if you'd rather. Most do. It's a sight you won't forget soon, but it is the shortest route.* Kazi and I had opted for the shortest route, but every nerve I possessed prickled as we traveled through it. Tigone and Mije both stamped in protest. Even they could see the stones weren't just stones, and wind whistled eerily through the canyon like a stream of voices.

Sven said legend claimed that one of the stars of the devastation had sent molten rock spraying like a fountain. Ancient peoples were caught midstep as they ran to get away. Huddled crowds were grown together as one rock, forever anchored to the cliffs that rose above them. Distinct, horror-stricken faces sometimes emerged from the mass. There was no erasing this part of history. Faces frozen in time lined our path, and they were a grim reminder of how quickly the world of the Ancients had changed. Maybe how quickly all of our worlds could change.

In comparison, the red plain we traveled across now seemed almost tranquil, and if it took a few dozen riddles to get Kazi through it, or more Ballenger legends, I was ready. I wondered sometimes if, as we rode in silence, she was busy composing her next riddle. She never seemed to lack for one when I asked. I, on the other hand, didn't have a knack for composing them and had struggled mightily with the single one I had given her. But that one seemed sufficient for her. She asked for it over and over again.

Say it again, Jase.

But you already know the answer.

But it's an answer I will never grow tired of.

And maybe I never tired of telling it to her. I fingered the red ribbon tied to my saddle. *What is it for, Kazi?* Not since that first time I had seen her staring at my bare chest had I seen her face flush warm. *Tell me.* But in my gut, I think I had already known, and if gifts like that ribbon meant trouble, it was the kind that I wanted.

Kazi cleared her throat to gain my attention. "All right, here you go, *Patrei*," she said. "Listen up. I won't repeat myself."

Composing. Just as I thought.

> "I have two arms but not a bone,
> I can't be hurt with knife or stone.
> I have a head but lack a face,
> I don't need eyes to match your pace.
> I'm shifty, a thief, a trick of the eyes,
> My robes are made of mystery and lies.

I am short, I am thin, I am monstrous and tall,
But when midnight comes, I am nothing at all."

"Let me think." This time I wasn't stalling for a kiss. I was stumped. Arms with no bones? A head but no face? I was mulling it over when something else caught my attention.

We both halted our horses and looked into the sky. "Valsprey," Kazi whispered, almost as a question.

We'd seen it at the same time. A white speck in a blinding blue sky flying toward us, its massive wings gliding through the air, majestic and unearthly all at once. A wild bird? It seemed unlikely that it was a trained messenger bird, considering our location. It rapidly got closer, flying low enough that I could see the black slash of feathers above its eyes. It was a wondrous sight out here in the middle of nowhere, and it commanded our gazes. Then, suddenly, it violently catapulted backward as if hit by something. A spray of feathers exploded in the air, and it spun out of control, plummeting to the earth.

"Down!" I yelled, leaping and pulling Kazi to the ground with me.

Someone had shot it out of the sky.

We weren't alone.

CHAPTER FOUR

KAZI

JASE HOVERED OVER ME, HIS HAND PROTECTIVELY PRESSING ON my back. Mije and Tigone pranced nervously on either side of us. Jase stood quickly, grabbing our quivers and bows from our packs, and dropped back to the ground beside me. We scanned the plain. There was nowhere for someone to hide. Where had the shot come from? There was no doubt the Valsprey had been shot from the sky. No bird changed its direction that dramatically then fell to the ground without something making it happen.

"I didn't see an arrow," Jase whispered. "Did you?"

"No. Nothing."

But if not an arrow, what? A stone from a sling? But I didn't see a stone either. A predator? But a Valsprey was large, with a five-foot wing-span. To take one down, the predator would have to be far larger, something like a racaa. There had been none.

We both eased up a bit on our elbows, looking for someone to emerge from a hole dug in the plain, but no one emerged. We finally stood, back to back, both of us nocking arrows, synchronizing our turns as we searched and waited to see something. The only thing that greeted us was the quiet hush of a gentle breeze sweeping the plain.

We went to where the bird had fallen, a white twisted splotch on the crimson landscape. One of its broken wings angled skyward as if hoping for a second chance. There was no flopping or lingering last movements. The bird was dead, which was no surprise. But as we neared and got a closer look, something about it was wrong.

"What—" Jase said.

We both stared at it.

The bird was quite dead. But it was clear it had been dead for weeks.

Its eyes were sunken leathery holes, and its ribs poked through decayed paper-thin skin, its breast mostly featherless. We both looked around, thinking there had to be another bird somewhere else, but there was none. *This* was the bird we had seen fall from the sky.

A trick of the eyes?

Carried here by some baffling wind current?

We guessed at possibilities, but none made sense.

Jase nudged the dry carcass with his boot, flipping the bird over. A message case was attached to its leg. It *was* a trained Valsprey, after all. I bent down and pulled the case from its leg, then picked at the thread that sealed it shut. It came apart, and a small piece of parchment unfurled in my hands.

The words I read wrested the breath from my lungs.

"Who's it from?" Jase asked.

"I don't know."

"Who is it for?"

I stared at the note, wondering how it was possible, but somewhere deep inside, I knew. Sometimes messages had a way of finding people. *The ghosts, they call to you in unexpected moments.* This wasn't a message sent by a Valsprey. It was sent by a different kind of messenger. I held it tight, not wanting to give it to Jase.

"Kazi? What is it?"

No more secrets, we had promised.

I held the note out to him. "It's for us," I said.

Jase took it and read it carefully, several times, it seemed, because he just continued to stare at it. He shook his head, his lips paling. He blinked as if trying to clear his vision, trying to make the words reorder themselves into something that made sense.

> *Jase, Kazi, anyone,*
> *Come! Please! Samuel is dead.*
> *They're banging the door.*
> *I have to—*

In an instant, his expression went from lost to angry. "It's a hoax. Some kind of sick hoax." He crumpled the paper in his fist and whipped around, scanning the landscape again for the perpetrator. "Come out!" he yelled. Only a haunting whine of wind answered back.

"Do you recognize the handwriting?" I asked. It was a desperate scrawl, written in haste. It didn't seem like a hoax.

He looked at the message again. "I'm not sure. It might be Jalaine's. We have Valsprey at the arena . . . The office door there is . . ." He paced, shaking his head. "I had Samuel working there while his hand healed. He—" Jase grimaced, and I could almost see his thoughts spinning out of control, while mine were leaden, plummeting to one conclusion—

"Samuel is *not* dead," Jase growled as if he had read my mind. "Jalaine overreacts. She thought I was dead once when I fell out of a tree and the air was knocked out of me. She ran to tell my parents and caused a panic." He scanned the landscape again, thinking out loud. "Maybe Aram wrote it, or maybe someone we don't even know, someone trying to trick you, to convince you to release me. Maybe they didn't get the message that I was coming home and think you're still holding me? Or maybe—" He stopped midthought and his shoulders slumped. He leaned forward, resting his arms on Tigone's back like it was the only thing holding him up. "Samuel is not dead," he said again, but this time so quietly only a ghost could have heard him.

I looked past him to where the bird had been and saw Death hunched over, his back bowed, lifting a body from the valley floor. He looked over his shoulder at me, and then bird, body, Death, they were all gone.

Who wrote the note, how it managed to get to us, or if it was even true became secondary questions. Getting home was what mattered now. We stopped at watering holes only for the sake of the horses. For us there was no rest until the evening when darkness closed in.

I looked back at the long path we had trampled in the sandy soil, a crooked line on the red landscape. Dying rays of sun puddled in our tracks.

We built a fire in silence, gathering twigs and sticks and breaking off branches from a dead bush. Jase wrestled angrily with one branch that refused to break free. "Dammit!" he yelled, yanking furiously.

I reached out and touched his arm. "Jase—"

He stopped, his chest heaving, his nostrils flared, his eyes still fixed on the brittle bush. "I don't know how it could happen," he said. "Except for his hand—" He turned and met my gaze. "Samuel was strong and sharp-eyed, but his injured hand—" His voice caught.

Was. Samuel *was*.

"It will be all right, Jase. We'll figure it out together." Every word I uttered was hollow and inadequate, but I wasn't sure what else to do. I felt pathetically useless.

He looked away, and his chest rose in a slow, deliberate breath. He raked back his hair and squared his shoulders, and I could see him stitching back together whatever had come undone inside him, refusing to give in to despair. I opened my mouth to speak, but he shook his head and walked away, rifling through his gear. He pulled out his ax and in one fierce swing parted the branch from the bush.

"There," he said and threw the conquered wood onto the fire. Sparks danced into the air. He turned his attention to the dead stump, hacking away at it with the same ferocity. The noise was bleak in the emptiness, and every *whack* juddered through my bones.

"Jase, talk to me. Please. Do you blame me? Because you weren't there?"

He stopped mid-swing and stared at me, the fury draining from his face. "You? What are you talking about?" He lowered his ax to the ground. "This is not your fault, Kazi. This is us. Ballenger history. This is what I've tried to tell you all along. It's always been the wolf at our door. Our history's been riddled with violence since the beginning, but not because we want it that way. Now we finally have a real chance to end it. No more power plays. No more black markets. No more paying taxes to an absentee king who never does anything to improve the lives of people in Hell's Mouth. Lydia and Nash are going to grow up differently than I did. They're going to have different lives, ones where they're not always having to watch their backs. They won't need *straza* trailing them everywhere they go. Our history is about to change. *We* are going to change it, together, remember?"

I nodded, and he pulled me into his arms, the bush forgotten.

The wolf at the door. I couldn't help but think of Zane.

My history was about to change too.

est we repeat history,
Let the stories be passed,
From father to son, from mother to daughter,
For with but one generation,
History and truth are lost forever.

—Song of Jezelia

CHAPTER FIVE

JASE

THE WINDS HOWLED ACROSS THE PLAIN LIKE A FORLORN BEAST.

Kazi and I burrowed close together in our bedroll, the blankets pulled over our heads, sharing each other's warmth. Her sleep-filled breaths were moist against my chest.

Do you blame me?

I knew what silence could do, the fear and doubt it could sow. I used it with calculating purpose on prisoners, letting the long ticks of silence twist their imagination into something hideous and painful. I used it on traders and ambassadors to push a negotiation in my favor, making them think I was about to walk away. I used it on Zane to produce Devereux's name. I never meant to use it on Kazi, but I had been consumed, feeling my denial fade with every mile we traveled. I wrestled with the fact that the note could be true. The silence Kazi heard was only fear trapped inside me. But how was she to know that? I knew firsthand how silence had pushed me to a breaking point when my father wouldn't speak to me.

Give it time, Jase, Tiago had told me. *He didn't mean anything by it. He's blind with grief right now.*

Tiago's words had meant nothing to me.

My father had burst through the front door, yelling for my mother. The news of Sylvey's death had reached him. He'd been away, chasing down the perpetrators of an attack on our farmstead. He had stomped through the hall, muddy, dripping with the wet of a storm. I tried to stop him at the foot of the stairs to explain, and he shoved me aside. *Get away from me!*

As the following days went by, all energies were focused on my other brothers and sisters who were still sick. Micah died. The rest recovered. The fears I had wanted to share with my father stayed sealed up inside of me, especially once I stole Sylvey's body. My father couldn't have known the guilt his silences had helped fuel. But Tiago did. *Give it time*, he repeated days later when the whole house could hear my parents arguing.

If I had been here—

You couldn't have changed anything!

I would have—

You are not a god, Karsen! Stop acting like one! You don't have a cure for the fever! No one does!

We should have had more healers! More—

For the gods' sakes, Karsen! What's done is done! What matters is what we do now!

Their screams had cut through me, colder than the icy wind that howled outside. It was true. He couldn't have changed the outcome. But what about me? Could I have changed the outcome for Samuel? I shouldn't have put him on at the arena, but I had thought the arena office was secure. We had well-armed guards posted because too much money traded hands there. Who had attacked him? Or did it happen somewhere else? An angry trader in a back alley? Another mysterious crew like Fertig's waiting on a deserted trail? Where were his *straza*?

"You're awake," Kazi whispered, her voice drowsy.

"Shhh," I said. "Go back to sleep."

"What are you thinking?"

My arm tightened around her. "I'm thinking how much I love you."

"Then I'm glad you're awake. Tell me again, Jase. Tell me the riddle . . ."

She mumbled a few more incoherent words and drifted back to sleep, her cheek nestling into my shoulder. I kissed the top of her head. My breath, my blood, my calm.

We were in the foothills, the sun warming my face. A sense of hope stirred in me, like we were back on course, back in the familiar, and no more dead birds would fall from the sky onto a bloody and barren landscape. We had returned to a world of reason I understood. Still, just in case, we altered our path so we'd approach Tor's Watch the back way, through Greyson Tunnel, as a precaution. It was the longer route, but if a league was stirring up that much trouble, they would likely be in town, and we had no *straza* with us.

Kazi's lips parted with a sudden small gasp.

"What is it?" I asked, immediately scanning the landscape.

She smiled, wonder filling her face. "I just realized, Hell's Mouth won't be the only city within the borders of your new kingdom. There's another one."

I knew every hill, valley, and gorge of Tor's Watch. "No," I replied. "Hell's Mouth is the only city. That's it."

"There's the settlement."

The revelation sank in. It wasn't exactly a city yet, but it was within the new borders I had declared. I whistled out a worried breath. "What will Caemus think of that?"

"I don't think it will be a problem. In fact, I think he'll be fine with it. Now, Kerry, on the other hand, may take another swing at your knee-cap when he learns you're his new sovereign."

"I'll be sure to wear my tall boots next time I visit. What about your queen?"

"She's grateful for what you did, Jase. You already know that."

I did. She had expressed it again when we'd had dinner with her and the king. "But that was before she knew that her settlement would be under my rule. I don't want any complications that will jeopardize—"

"It's going to need a name. Any ideas?"

"That should probably be left to Caemus."

"True." But she went ahead and tried out several anyway, her head cocked as she listened to their sounds on her tongue, her dreams as full as my own.

CHAPTER SIX

KAZI

GLINTS OF AUTUMN SLIVERED THROUGH THE TREES, SHAKING
the few sparse leaves with one last quiver as if saying good-bye. Winter
was impatient, already frosting the early mornings in white. I wondered
what Tor's Watch would look like in winter. The dark towers would be
striking against a white, snowy landscape.

Today we would arrive. Jase thought it would be just before nightfall, but even darkness closing in could not stop him. He sat forward in
his saddle as new vistas came into view, eager, scanning the horizon as if
he expected to see someone he knew, his skin itching with the closeness
of home. Tonight we would be sleeping in beds at Tor's Watch. We would
be eating dinner at the family dining table. Our new life would be
beginning.

The yearning stirring in me came as a surprise. Maybe Jase's unflag-
ging belief that this was just the beginning was taking hold in me too. I
was eager for what was to come, but at the same time, a swarm of nervous bees hummed in my chest. Somehow, I would have to fit into a

close-knit family that shared a history and traditions. And there were other worries.

We'll get our answers soon, Jase had promised, because uncertainty was a worm that ate through both of us. We both desperately wanted to know the meaning of the note and what had really happened to Samuel, but my stomach twisted at the thought of Zane. It wasn't that I was afraid of him, at least not afraid of what he could do to me anymore. Natiya and Eben had taught me all the ways to kill someone, even without a weapon. I was far better trained than Zane. But I was afraid of what he might tell me.

I had been terrified the night that I asked him about my mother. In an instant I became a child again, my bones turned to liquid, the uncertainty I had punched down for years suddenly alive. And now I would have to face that moment all over again when I faced Zane. That fear had warped into a new question—could the answers be worse than not knowing?

Just kill him, Kazi, I told myself. *It's what you always planned to do. Kill him and be done with it. You don't need answers.* I had lived with doubt for this long—I could live with it forever. Justice was all I cared about. Answers wouldn't change anything. My mother was gone.

How can you be certain she's dead?

Jase's question had been as fragile as a robin's egg in his palm. He had held it out carefully to me, as if the shell were already cracked. Of course, I couldn't be certain she was dead. Not really. I had never seen her body, but I had taken a dream and molded it into a conclusion somewhere along the way, a carved piece of puzzle that fit into the shape of my life.

I had been certain, for so long, that one day she would find her way back to me, or if I only looked a little harder, one day I would find her. And then one bitter winter, when many Vendans had died already, I was curled up, shivering in my hovel, blue with the cold, thinking I might be next, and I heard a noise.

Shhh.

It was only wind, I told myself.

Kazi.

It was only my rumbling belly.

Shhh.

I was so cold already, frozen to the marrow, but I raced outside anyway, searching, desperate, not wanting to be alone, the snowflakes whirling in cutting blades, drifts numbing my feet, wind whipping at my face, and then . . . there was a curious calm. Against the startling white that made the empty streets of Venda unrecognizable, I spotted something.

Had it been a shivering frozen dream? Delirium fueled by hunger? Even then, none of it had really seemed real. How could I explain to Jase something that even I didn't understand? I saw my mother, her long raven hair trailing in a loose braid down her back, with a crown of fresh green vines woven atop her head, like the kind she used to weave for me on holy days. She was spring in the middle of a harsh winter. She turned, her eyes warm amber pools, looking into mine as if trying to send me another one of her silent signals, her lips mouthing my name—*Kazi, my beloved, my* chiadrah—and then she turned and walked away from me, but now someone was beside her. He looked at me too. Death. She looped her arm through his and then she was gone. But Death lingered a moment longer. He looked at me, then finally stomped his foot in warning, and I ran back to my hovel.

Maybe you saw what you needed to see so you could move forward? Jase suggested.

I had mulled that possibility over in my head countless times since then. Had it only been the desperate loneliness of a girl finally letting go? She had already been slipping away from me for months and years, my guilt rising as my memory of her faded, and that guilt would spike a renewal of my search for her.

Maybe seeing her that night was her message to me to stop waiting for her to return. So I would stop looking.

Except some time after that, I began looking for someone else.

One way or another, I couldn't quite let go.

Since that night I had seen Death many times—and that was no dream. Maybe he had always been there, and in the busyness of trying to survive, I simply hadn't noticed. Or maybe once a dark door has been opened it can't be shut again. Now in unexpected moments I heard the warning whispers of ghosts, and Death took pleasure in taunting me, pushing me. He became like a quarterlord I was determined to beat, and the prize was my life.

"Apples!" Jase called out suddenly. He was already steering Tigone to the low branches of the trees, plucking ripe red apples as he went. He tossed some to the ground for the horses and gathered more in the folds of his cloak before he dismounted. He bit into one, slurping up its goodness, then shrugged. "I called them first, but I might be convinced to share with you."

I looked down at him from my elevated position. "For a price, I suppose?"

He grinned. "Everything comes with a price."

I rolled my eyes. "Of course it does." I slid off Mije and ambled toward him. "But even for an ambassador?"

"First it's an apple. Next thing you know, you'll be wanting your own office."

I wrinkled my nose. "A little office for an ambassador? Oh no. I had my eye on one of those big fancy apartments at the arena. Top level."

"Those are quite costly, I'm afraid." He circled his arm around my waist and gave me a bite of his apple, then kissed me, the sweet juice wet on our lips.

"Well, *Patrei*, just what might it cost me?"

His brows rose. "I think it's better if I show you."

We kissed again, banter still playing between our lips as he pulled me to the ground. I knew the lightness, the play, the laughter were his gifts to me, a promise that no matter how close we were to Tor's Watch and whatever challenges it held or objections his family voiced, we would not lose the perfect beauty of these last weeks. It would not change anything between us. He didn't need to say the words again. I felt them in every kiss. This was just the beginning.

It was as if Mije sensed we were near. Without a nudge, he picked up his pace, eager for his rest and fresh sweet hay, which the Ballenger stables always had in abundance. Jase had been right about the timing. The sky was striped with purple, dusk closing in fast as we headed for the back entrance at Greyson Tunnel. A shimmering black cloud, alive with bats heading out for their evening meal, streamed above us.

Jase looked at me, the dusky sky flecking his brown eyes with soft light. "Stay close beside me," he said. "I don't want Priya taking a crack at you. She has a temper, in case you hadn't noticed."

"Priya? A temper? *Noo*," I mocked. "I never would have guessed." I could handle Priya, but I really didn't want to. I wanted to make our transition back into Tor's Watch as uneventful as possible, and not antagonize the family any further.

"By the time we make it through the tunnel, the news will probably already have reached the house. I wouldn't be surprised if the whole family is waiting on the front steps for us."

He said it as a complaint, but I knew that was exactly what he was hoping for. The *whole* family—including Samuel. That if the note was written by Jalaine, it had been a hasty overreaction, another case of panic that held no truth. That's what I was hoping for too, though the prospect of confronting his whole family on the front steps in just minutes snatched the breath from my chest. I knew I had to get it over with. Deal with their anger and move on. We had a plan. They would be part of it.

We finally rounded the last copse of trees and emerged on the open slope that led to Greyson Tunnel. The towering black silhouette of Tor's Watch loomed before us against the evening sky.

But something about it was wrong. Very wrong.

Jase pulled back on Tigone's reins, staring. I stopped too, trying to make sense of it.

The skyline had changed. The silhouette made no sense.

Between the spires of Riverbend and Raehouse there was a gaping hole, as if a hungry monster had taken a bite out of it. The center black spindle of the main house was gone, and as my eyes adjusted to the shock, I noticed there was more that was gone.

The wall.

The front fortress wall near the entrance to Tor's Watch—the solid rock wall that was four feet thick—had a cavernous gap, and jagged piles of rubble spilled down the mountain. The guard towers were gone too.

"This can't—" Words froze on Jase's lips. A shocked second passed and then he bolted toward the destruction.

"Jase! Stop!" I shouted. "It might not—"

A powerful whir split the air. And then another. Arrows. I circled in place, trying to see where they were coming from.

Jase heard them too and pulled back. He was about to turn Tigone around when an arrow struck his thigh. He grimaced, still trying to turn, and another pierced his shoulder, sending him recoiling backward. Tigone reared.

I still couldn't see where the shots were coming from. It seemed to be from everywhere. I raced toward Jase. *"Baricha!"* I yelled at Tigone. *"Baricha!"* The command for "run," but the arrows kept whirring, and Tigone reared again, uncertain which direction to turn.

Jase was yelling the same to me: "Run, Kazi! Go back!" Then another arrow hit him in the chest. In a split second, two more lanced his side. He slumped forward.

"Jase!" I screamed as I reached him.

No arrows had struck me. They were only aiming for the *Patrei*. His eyes met mine, hazy. "Go, get out of here." His last words before he fell forward on Tigone.

Dark cloaked figures descended upon us from all sides, surrounding us like yelping hyenas, shouting strategies to one another. *Get him.* I pulled a knife with one hand and my sword with the other and rolled from Mije, landing on my feet swinging, taking down the first cloaked figure that was already reaching to pull Jase from his horse. I doubled back, swinging at one coming at me from behind, slicing his head off, and yelled, *"Baricha!"* this time to Mije. He followed my command and galloped back toward the forest. Jase lay lifeless over Tigone's withers. I rolled to avoid the swinging blade of a third attacker, jerking my knife upward to slash his hamstring, then stabbing him between the ribs as he stumbled forward. I shoved his body aside and prodded Tigone's hindquarter, slapping her with the broad side of my sword, as I shouted, *"Baricha!"* again, praying she would follow Mije before more of the attackers closing in could grab Jase.

It worked. Tigone barreled through the cloaked figures, knocking three of them down. But almost in the same moment, I was caught from behind, a hood flying over my head, the world fully black now. My weapons were wrested from my hands, but I continued to fight and heard a snap like a melon cracking open when my boot connected with the firmness of someone's skull. I pulled my small boot knife free and stabbed backward over my shoulder into the face of whoever held me around the throat. A scream split the air and the arm fell away, but as I reached up to yank off the hood, a fist punched into my belly, and a sharp pain doubled me over. I was thrown to the ground, and a knee pounded into my back, pinning me to the rocky ground.

The voices erupted in a new frenzy. How many were there? They had been lying in wait for us. An ambush. They knew we were coming. Who else knew Jase was coming home besides Gunner?

"Stay down, bitch!"

"After him!"

"She killed Iersaug!"

"That way! Go!"

"Bloody hell!"

"He won't get far!"

"Stay with her! I'll get him!"

"Search the grounds for others!"

I heard the fading gallop of someone chasing after Jase. I struggled against the weight that had me pinned. *Run, Mije. Deep into the forest where it is dark. Please, by all the mercies of the gods, run. Don't stop. I can't lose him.*

My head swam, nausea striking as my arms were jerked behind my back. They tied my wrists and legs with rope. The ground beneath me was warm and wet, and I smelled something—the salty tang of blood. *Mine?*

It was only then I realized that the fist that punched me had held a knife. And just before the chaos faded and the darkness deepened, I realized something else.

I recognized one of the voices.

It belonged to Paxton.

CHAPTER SEVEN

JASE

MY EYES WOULDN'T FOCUS. MY HEAD WHIRLED, OR MAYBE THAT was Tigone still circling in terror. I caught glimpses of Kazi fighting, Mije galloping, the distant fortress wall, a forest of trees as the world spun around me. And then I couldn't see anything at all.

This?

This was how it would end?

Maybe it already had. But my hand. My fingers. They held something. *Kazi? Where are you?*

My fingers ached. My arms. They burned with fire. *Hold on, Jase.* I had something in my grip. Tigone's mane? The reins? I squeezed tighter.

"Kazi—" I couldn't draw a breath. My chest. Then everything went cold. Frozen.

My fingers slipped. Horse, saddle, air, sliding past my hand. I fell, slamming to the ground. The arrow lodged in my chest jammed farther into my body. A burning jolt knifed through me, every part of me on fire again. Gurgling breath rattled through my lungs. A scream rolled from my throat, like a dying animal. I heard galloping, a horse getting closer. Footsteps. Rustling. They were close. I tried to roll to my side, crawl, get away, my fingers digging into a moldy bed of leaves, but no more breaths would come. I coughed blood, saltiness filling my mouth. This. This was how it would end.

Run, Kazi. Go—

Kazi—

The greenhouse. Please—

I love—

The Dragon will conspire,
Wearing his many faces,
Deceiving the oppressed, gathering the wicked,
Wielding might like a god, unstoppable.

—Song of Venda

CHAPTER EIGHT

KAZI

"LIKE THIS, KAZI. PUT YOUR HANDS HERE."

I feel his hand in mine, warmth against the cold, Jase teaching me the jig, the way the Ballengers dance it. His face glows as we twirl around an empty, crumbling ballroom that once held ancient kings and queens and the most powerful people on the continent. And for this night, it still does. It seems our feet don't touch the ground. They all watch us, ghostly, willing it to never end, leaning forward the way ghosts do, wishing, remembering.

"Do you hear that, Jase? They're applauding us."

He looks up at the empty balconies and smiles as if he sees and hears them too. "They're applauding you."

Would my memorized steps impress his family? Was I nimble enough? Graceful enough? Enough of anything? Because I did want to impress them. I desperately wanted that. To show them I knew how to do other things besides steal their Patrei. Show them I could learn to be part of a family.

He spins me, lifting me into the air, the muscles of his shoulders flexing beneath my hands, then he lets me slide downward between his arms until our lips meet. The music we imagine together beats against our skin, the air, the swooning murmurs of those watching, Jase's boots tapping our promises into place, unassailable, enduring—

A crash jarred me awake, a door slamming into a wall. The ballroom we danced in vanished. I was back in my small dark cell, my dream dissolving in a quick gust, my arms cold again. Heavy footsteps clipped the cobbles in the hallway outside my cell door. I tried to use them as a measure for the passing days. They came as regularly as the taunting beam of light, but I was still uncertain how much time had passed. Some days were worse than others, delirium getting a strong foothold, it seemed, all the way into my soul. I fought against it. Sometimes it was Jase who brought me back from the edge. His voice reached through the darkness. *Go with the current. Just a little farther. Keep going. You can do it.*

Had it been five days? Ten? Maybe far more. One dark day rolled into the next with no beginning or ending. The footsteps grew louder. Soon I would hear a faint *plop*, followed by the skitter of rats as a hard roll was dropped through the tiny opening at the top of the door. I had to hurry to get the meager lump of food before the rats did. It was all they fed me. One roll a day. Strangely, they wanted me to stay alive. But they wanted to keep me weak too.

They were afraid of me.

I had killed three of them, that much I knew—and maybe at least one more after I was captured. All the lessons from Natiya, Eben, Kaden, and Griz had become second nature in that chaotic moment when we were attacked. My desperation to save Jase had exploded through me like a hot flame. Every nerve blazed with one goal. Saving him was all that mattered. Had I? Had he gotten away? I couldn't fail again. Not this time.

Where are you, Jase?

I told myself he had made it into the cover of the forest. I told myself a lot of things, every day bolstering myself with a new possibility when both fear and logic shook me with their cold hands. *Five arrows. One in his chest. The chances of surviving that—*

I told myself that a hundred arrows couldn't stop him, not even one in his heart, that he had made his way to someone for help. I held on to that thought, fast and tight, like a rope keeping me from plunging off a cliff. But who would help him? Where would he go? Had our attackers breached the walls of Tor's Watch?

The *thump, thump, thump* of the arrows still vibrated in my throat, steel piercing his bone and flesh again and again. Blood ran everywhere. A familiar voice crept in, my own, whispering cruel thoughts that had haunted me my whole life. *Sometimes people vanish from our lives and we never see them again.*

No! I argued with myself and struggled to my feet. I pushed the lid off the water barrel and cupped some water into my hands. It had an earthy, ripe taste, like cider had once been stored in it. The barrel hadn't been refilled since I was thrown in here. Maybe once the water was gone I would be too. I leaned against the wall and slid back to the floor, out of breath from the small effort. My festering wound throbbed, my brow was on fire, and yet I trembled with cold. I didn't know much about injuries, which only now surprised me, considering the life I had lived. Even my two months in a Reux Lau prison cell hadn't resulted in any injury. Had my mother made a wish upon a wish stalk? Many wishes to protect me? Maybe now they were all used up. *My* chiadrah. *Is she coming? Is that her I hear walking closer?* I swiped my hand over my sweaty brow. *No, Kazi, that was before. You're in a cell now, and Jase is—*

There was shuffling outside the door as my captor paused and slid open the lock on the peephole. But this time there were two sounds, first the soft *plop* of the roll and then a second sound. A firm *slap*.

Something heavy hitting the ground. I pulled in a breath, bracing myself, then crawled on all fours toward the door, the chains on my ankles rattling behind me. I pressed on the wound, sticky ooze wetting my fingers.

"Cowards!" I screamed, pounding on the door before the footsteps retreated. My daily response was proof that I wasn't too weak or dead yet. That I would kill them all. *I would.* And Paxton would be first.

But the burst of anger against the door took more energy than I had to spare, and I collapsed against it, dizzy with pain, then fell in a heap to the floor. *One more day, Kazi. Make it one more day.* How could I steal keys from my jailors if they never opened the door? How could I do anything when I grew weaker by the minute? *Jase, where are you? I have to know.* Maybe needing to know was all that kept me going. I still needed to be there for him. Which meant eating.

I reached out, feeling for the roll, and my fingers closed around it. I could live on a single measly roll far longer than they could imagine. *As long as it takes.* My stomach was no stranger to emptiness. I had years of experience at this. I tucked the roll in my shirt and felt for the second item I'd heard fall. Had I imagined it? Dreams and delusions were my constant companions in this devilish place.

My hand touched something soft. I snatched it up and examined it with my fingers. Knotted cloth? A handkerchief? I squeezed. It contained something pliable. I sniffed. Sweet. Food? Some sugary delicacy? A trick? I unknotted the cloth and dabbed my finger into the thick sticky paste, then tapped it to my tongue. Honey—laced with leafy herbs? This was not food. It was medicine. A poultice to leach away infection.

Medicine, from one of them?

Maybe at least one person on the other side of that door wanted me to live. Someone who was afraid too.

More medicine came the next day, and the next, and next. Some of it I ate. I guessed that it couldn't hurt and might actually help. The oozing stopped. My brow cooled. My mind cleared. The wound seemed to be shrinking, the skin weaving itself back together. An extra roll was also dropped each day—with a chunk of cheese hidden inside. I eagerly devoured it, but I was still weak from days of being chained and starved. And darkness. Complete soul-sucking darkness. It seeped into my bones like a numbing liqueur.

My benefactor didn't reveal himself, but each day I felt the fear through the door, dread that I might call out and reveal him—or her. I sensed they were taking a great risk for me. Who was smuggling medicine and extra food? Who wanted me to stay alive?

I heard the daily signal that food was on its way, footsteps, and I knelt near the door, ready to retrieve my roll and medicine, when I noticed a rumble. A different sound. Many footsteps. The rumble grew louder, and the door flew open. My hand shot up to protect my eyes from the piercing brightness. I squinted and blinked several times, trying to adjust to light I hadn't seen in days, maybe weeks, and finally I saw what appeared to be a squad of guards crowding outside the doorway. All heavily armed.

"Get to feet," one of them ordered. "We go for walk."

"And if too weak to walk, we drag you."

"By hair."

"Your choice."

I looked at my half dozen captors, uniformed soldiers, all with shaved heads, tall, hard, and muscled, looking like they'd been carved from the trunks of giant trees instead of being fashioned from flesh. Three of them were a head taller than the others. There was something unnatural about them. Their skin pulled tight and their eyes were dull, like worn pewter plates. Soldiers? They spoke Landese with a strong accent that I didn't recognize.

I winced as I pushed up from the ground, holding my side, forcing strength into muscles and bones that shivered with weakness. I steadied myself against the wall. "I'll walk."

CHAPTER NINE

KAZI

CLINK. CLINK. CLINK.

The chain jumped along the cobbles behind me, monotonous musical notes filling the grim air. The guards made me walk in front of them. The floor was cold and damp against my bare feet. The long musty passage we lumbered through still gave no hint to where I was.

"My gods, she stinks," the guard behind me complained.

Good, I thought. *Get a nice long whiff, asshole. It might be your last.*

I reached up and fluffed my hair, hoping to release more of my rotting cell perfume. I was immediately butted in the back with a halberd and sent sprawling to the ground. I hunched as I fell, trying to protect my gut.

"No sudden moves!" he yelled. "Keep your hands at sides!"

Another guard mocked him for being so jumpy. "Can't you see she can barely walk?"

"And half your size!" Another one laughed.

"She's Rahtan. They can't be trusted."

I gathered my breath and what paltry clues I could. Jumpy. Sensitive noses. And they distrusted Rahtan. So they weren't entirely stupid. But they had the stature of tree trunks. I wasn't sure any of my tricks could bring them down. I managed to get to my feet again, using the wall as support, my hands shaking from the exertion, sweat springing to my chest. I turned to face them, focusing on each one after the next. Since I was sure introductions weren't imminent, I tried to catalog their distinguishing features: *broken nose, black teeth, divot in forehead, no neck, hairy knuckles,* and *scar eye.* I also noted which accoutrements hung at their sides, the usual course of weapons, but also some that were unique, regional—a region I didn't know. These soldiers were from somewhere other than Eislandia.

There were no keys hanging from their sides that were readily visible, but an ax that might break my chains hung from No Neck's belt. Which of them had shot Jase? Maybe all of them, but then I remembered— *no*—the voices I heard during the attack didn't have accents. And the man whose head I had parted from his shoulders had white hair and a beard. These were not the attackers who had stabbed me, but they must be in collusion with them. Just how many cutthroats was I dealing with? And what did they want?

"I apologize for the stink," I said, trying to get them to loosen their scowling lips. "I guess I forgot to bathe this morning, and it's been a very long day. Or has it been two weeks?"

Broken Nose, the smallest of the bunch, grinned. Divot Head glared.

"I'm Kazi. Such a pleasure to meet you all. Do you have names?"

They weren't amused. "Shut up!" Black Teeth snapped. The names I bestowed would have to stand.

"Move," No Neck ordered. "The general is waiting to question you. But bath first. He don't want to smell your stink either."

His accent. The familiarity struck me. Two of the men in Fertig's gang of raiders had called to each other and sounded like these soldiers. What accent was it? And who was this general? The one who had attacked Tor's Watch? We reached a bath chamber, and Scar Eye dug deep into a vest pocket to produce a key that unlocked my leg chains, then shoved me inside and told me to hurry. I had five minutes, and I had better come out smelling like roses. Black Teeth laughed like it was an impossibility. Scar Eye didn't smile. His expression never changed.

Alabaster sconces lit the chamber with warm flickering light. The chamber wasn't what I expected. Soap? Fluffy towels? Fresh, clean clothes folded on a settee? A large copper tub with steaming water? Shoes? Was this a bribe? Who was this general with the sensitive nose? I almost felt like I was being courted—if not for the stab wound and scowling guards. More likely I was being prepared for something, and I doubted it was anything good.

I peeled off my clothes and then, very carefully, the sticky poultice from my wound, getting a good look at the one-inch puncture for the first time. The skin was puckered, angry, and a portion of it still oozed. Leftover pieces of honey and herbs clung to the stained skin around it. The hot water stung as I eased into the tub, and the strong soap stung more. I scrubbed gently and quickly, wincing as I cleaned around the wound. At the same time, my eyes swept every corner of the room, searching for anything that might be used as a weapon. There was nothing. The only possibility was breaking off a leg of the settee to use as a club, which would not be a quiet endeavor, nor highly effective against their long halberds. But then I noted the edge of the tufted settee. Decorative nails held the fabric in place. Still worthless against halberds and swords, but they might be useful at some point.

"One more minute!" No Neck shouted through the door.

I quickly hopped out of the tub, dried off, and threw on the shirt and trousers that had been left for me, then worked and pulled at the fabric on the settee to pop out the nails.

"Enough time!" The door flew open.

I sat on the settee, my back to the guard, the loosened nails between my legs. "I was just putting on my shoes," I said.

"Hurry up! No fast moves."

I palmed two small nails and shoved them into the hem of my shirt as I bent over to slip on my shoes.

I noted the chains weren't returned to my feet. Maybe they deemed me weak enough to be little threat.

"Are we going to see Paxton?" I asked as I walked ahead of them again.

"Quiet!"

"The general?"

"I said no questions!"

And no fast moves. They were a wary lot. There would be no juggling, at least not with oranges, to distract them. One advanced ahead as we climbed a narrow stone staircase. I had barely moved in days, much less climbed flights of stairs. Halfway up, the exertion made my head swim. If not for the extra food and medicine I had received, I wouldn't have even been able to make it this far. My knees shook. On the next step I stumbled and had to grab the wall to steady myself. It forced the soldier behind me to stop short, and he cursed as he ran into me. I fell against him and he pushed me away. The rest of them chuckled. I was exactly as they wanted me to be. Weak and at their mercy.

"Stupid clod!"

"Not much of a soldier now, is she?"

"Scrawny weakling."

"Keep moving!" another shouted.

I did. I put one foot in front of the other, pulled in one breath after another. Weakness didn't stop me from being a soldier. Maybe it even made me a better one. I knew how to use everything, even a momentary stumble.

The soldier's tiny push knife now hung heavy in my pocket.

We emerged into an expansive room busy with activity. Soldiers were hunched over tables, and their fingers followed lines on what I guessed were maps. Others wheeled large steaming kettles to where lines of more soldiers waited. My cheeks ached with my first smell of real food. Hot parritch, sweet corn muffins, smoked meats. Even my knees turned warm and wobbly with the scents wafting through the air, as if they recognized food too. When I saw a fat ham sitting on a table near the kettles it took all my self-control not to bolt for it. Hairy Knuckles was sturdy, well fed, and indifferent to the abundance of food. He led the way without lagging.

I searched the room, looking for people I might recognize, like Paxton, or any of his muscle-bound *straza*. But then my eyes settled into the *details* of the room. They suddenly blossomed, all of them out of place. The high-timbered ceilings, the enormous iron chandeliers hanging from them, the heavy tapestries covering the walls with hunting scenes and picnics, racaa, and tembris. It was a beautiful, well-appointed room, with stuffed couches along walls and beautiful woven rugs on the floors—not a soldiers' barracks.

At one end of the room were ornate sideboards loaded with fine dishes, and on the far wall was a painted crest—*the Ballenger crest*. My throat went dry. *This was their inn*. We were in the rambling dining hall of the Ballenger Inn, but there were no Ballengers. No Gunner, no Priya, no customers, only more soldiers who looked like the ones who escorted me, at least a hundred of them. *I'm in Hell's Mouth*. What madness was this? Who were these people? This was not just Paxton and his league of thugs I was dealing with. Had Paxton joined forces with others? Had they taken over the whole town?

The missing spires of Tor's Watch and the gaping fortress wall burned behind my eyes. A sour taste rose in my throat. What had happened while we were gone? The words in the note skipped through my head. *They're banging at the door.*

My steps must have slowed, and No Neck gave me a rough shove forward, his knuckles digging into my back. Above the din of voices I heard shouting.

"He was riddled with arrows, for gods' sakes! No more excuses! Find him! Today!"

Jase. Whoever was yelling had to be talking about Jase. Which meant he had gotten away. My first full breath in days filled my lungs.

Divot Head grumbled and shook his head. Black Teeth sighed. Neither appeared to be eager to reach the angry voice, and yet that appeared to be exactly where we were headed. We turned at a large center pillar and walked toward a smaller dining room that adjoined the main hall. The wide arched opening gave a clear view of several people inside, including the one who was shouting. His back was to me, but his hands waved in fury. I spotted Oleez in the middle of the room, her distinct silver braid trailing over her shoulder. Beside her was Dinah, a timid girl who helped Aunt Dolise in the kitchen. They gathered up dirty dishes at a long table that ran down the center of the room. Oleez spotted me too. Her head bobbed slightly and then her expression grew sharp, and she looked away. Was it fear or hate I saw in her eyes? Her message was clear: *Don't speak to me.* Was I just another enemy in the midst of many more?

"Go on! You too! Get out of here!" the man seethed. "Don't return until—"

"General Banques?" Broken Nose called meekly. "We have the prisoner you asked for."

His back still to me, the man stopped yelling. His shoulders squared and his head jerked slightly to the side as if his neck had a kink—or he was trying to tamp down his anger. He remained still, seconds ticking away, then finally turned, his expression icy and calm, a stark contrast to who he had been just seconds earlier. This was a man who loathed being caught unaware in a moment of unrestrained wrath. He wanted to present some other kind of image to me—an image of complete control—but the sheen of sweat on his pale forehead betrayed him. He shot an almost imperceptible glare at Broken Nose as a warning. *Don't sneak up on me.* Another clue. Someone was new to this job, either Broken Nose or General Banques. Maybe both.

His cool gray eyes crept over me, trying to intimidate me before he ever spoke, every blink calculated. His upper lip lifted. He was tall and I guessed in his mid-thirties, or maybe the creases around his eyes weren't from age but ingrained anger. His hair was thick and black and slicked back with balm.

I returned his stare. Something about him was eerily familiar. Maybe it was his voice, the tone—

"So you're the one who—" He let the thought dangle. The one who *what*? "You're not what I expected," he said, stepping closer. He nodded to Black Teeth and No Neck, and they both grabbed me by my arms. Really? I was starved and weak and recovering from a knife wound, and though I may have wanted to leap at him, I had already expended all of my energy just walking to meet him. Even Rahtan were human and had their limitations. I made a show by taking a long look at the hands gripping my arms, then turned back to him, raising my brows. Coward much?

"You're one of Paxton's lackeys, I presume," I said.

He smiled. "I'm in charge here."

"And you are?"

"It doesn't matter who I am. I know who you are. A co-conspirator with the Ballengers—"

"Conspirator to what? You have no—"

He reached out and clutched my neck. Rage pulsed in his fingers. *Die tomorrow, Kazi. Whatever game he's playing, learn it. Jase still needs you.* And now it seemed other Ballengers might too.

"Listen carefully," he ordered. "Unless you tell me exactly what I want to know, you'll face a rope just like all the other conspirators we've already hanged. Do you understand?"

Already hanged? My mind sprinted like a gazelle, trying to grasp what he was saying. Was he mad? Ballengers? Had he executed Ballengers?

"I thought that would get your attention."

I resisted swallowing. Resisted drawing in a breath. I met his stare. *Blink last, Kazi.* Push lightly. Attempt to bring him back to reality. I began to recite kingdom protocol.

"You are in violation of Alliance treaties by—"

He pulled me away from the guards and slammed me up against the wall, his grip on my neck tightening. "Where is he?" he hissed. The room quieted in an instant, and I struggled to breathe. Everyone was watching now. "You yelled a command to his horse! To both horses! What did you say?"

"Run," I rasped.

He loosened his grip. "Run where?"

"Anywhere. Just run. Get away. I don't know where they went."

Which was true. And while I thought he saw the truth in what I said, he was not pleased by this news. It was as if I was his last hope of finding Jase. Maybe that was why they finally pulled me from the cell. Their other efforts hadn't panned out. His nostrils flared, and his eyes widened, making him look crazed. His fingers tightened on my neck again. If he couldn't find Jase, my neck would do. I guessed that I could take him down—I'd only have one shot at it—but I knew that I would die in the process. I was too weak and surrounded by too many to fight them all off.

"We found him!" a voice called.

The general released his hold on me, and I gasped for breath. His interest shifted to someone else in the crowded room. I recognized the voice and turned. Paxton and three other men wove their way through soldiers. Paxton's appearance had changed dramatically. He wasn't his usual cool, polished self. His normally neat ponytail was oily and tangled and his clothes rumpled and dirty. A sheen of gritty sweat coated his face. As he pushed through the milling soldiers who had pressed closer for a better look, he spotted me. His steps faltered for a moment, but then he pushed past me too. He threw a sack on the table. "At least we found what was left of him. It looks like he fell down a ravine and animals got to him before we did."

Another man confirmed Paxton's story, saying it appeared that a pack of hyenas had gotten to him.

Banques left my side and looked at the sack on the table. "This?" He lifted the sack and turned it upside down. A swollen, blood-smeared hand fell out, landing with a thud on the table. Oleez gagged and turned away. Several of the soldiers blanched.

I leaned back against the wall, sweat springing to my palms. "No," I said. "It's not him. That is not his hand. That is not the *Patrei*'s hand." The words clanged over and over again in my head. *It is not him.*

"Really? How can you be so sure?" Banques replied, his tone suddenly turned sickeningly sweet. "Come, take a closer look." I didn't move. He crooked his head to the side, looking it over. "I agree, it's in pretty bad shape, but I guess that's to be expected with animals fighting over it." He pulled a handkerchief from his pocket and flipped the mutilated hand over, then smiled at Paxton. "At last. Well done, men." Paxton's attention turned to me, stone steady, silent, none of his usual cocky replies rolling off his tongue, but his last warning months back at the arena skipped through me again: *Tread carefully, cousin. Remember, everyone is not always what they seem to be.* Paxton had hunted down his own kin? Was he more vile than I had even imagined?

"No," I said more firmly. "You're wrong. And you will be answering to the *Patrei*. He is the law of Hell's Mouth and—"

"Not anymore." Banques picked up the hand carefully with the handkerchief and tugged at one of the fingers. "Here, it's only a cheap piece of jewelry to me. You can have it. Call it your trophy." He gave the bloated finger another strong yank, pulled something free, and threw it at me. It clinked across the floor and came to rest at my feet. Something gold. I stooped to pick it up but then couldn't stand again.

I held the ring in my palm.

A gold signet ring.

Jase's ring.

This is just the beginning, Kazi.

I promise.

We have a whole lifetime ahead of us.

Saltiness swelled in my mouth. My teeth clenched and the soft flesh of my cheek was crushed between them. The floor of the room tilted. I stumbled to my knees. *Animals got to him.* The light went dim. Voices warped, my ears pounding with unintelligible words. I looked up at Paxton, but my eyes wouldn't focus. His face was a blur, and then hands gathered under each of my arms, lifting, dragging me, but I couldn't see where we were going. It was all a cold muffled haze, like I had fallen deep into a river, no words, no breaths, sinking, and I couldn't find my way back to the surface, and there was no one there to reach down and pull me up.

Greyson writes our names in large letters on the wall, all twenty-three of us. It looks big and important. Permanent. He writes our ages too. The youngest is only three.

Greyson says, *We are strong, but together we are stronger.* Every day when I look at all our names together, I feel taller, smarter, stronger.

—Razim, 12

CHAPTER TEN

KAZI

"LEAN BACK AGAINST ME. I'VE GOT YOU. GO WITH THE current."

Jase's arms wrap around me, holding me tight, righting me every time I dip below the surface. "I've got you, Kazi. Feet forward. Just a little farther. You can do it."

"I can't, Jase, I can't without you."

I feel myself sink, go deeper, not caring, not wanting to breathe. Letting go. It is easier to let go, give in, everything about me numb and heavy. I watch air bubbles slip from my nose, my mouth, bright spheres against the darkness, swirling upward like shining strands of white pearls.

"You can do it, Kazi. Go with the current."

"Not without you, Jase," I whispered. "Not without you."

"You're awake?"

The pearls vanished, and I gasped as I sat up. An apple-cheeked woman sat in a chair in the corner of the room. She rose and lifted a tray from the table beside her. "Broth," she said as she came toward me. "King's orders. He wants you to eat and get your strength back."

I looked around the beautifully furnished room. Where was I? Had it been a dream? I instinctively assessed the woman and my surroundings. She was unarmed and there were no guards, but my will to run was gone. I felt the swollen flesh on the inside of my cheek with my tongue. It wasn't a dream. What did it matter? Run where? To whom? Into what other nightmare?

Her jumble of words were just coming together in my head.

"*The king?* The king is here?"

"He'll explain. I'll let him know you're awake." She set the tray down on the bed beside me and left.

I felt for the push knife in my pocket, and the nails I had pulled from the settee. They were gone. Was she the one who took them? I sat in the middle of a four-poster bed, surrounded by luxurious linens. Was I in a room at the inn? I stared at the glistening bowl of broth. Instead of feeling hunger, bile swelled in my throat. I swung my feet over the bed, but with one step, my legs collapsed beneath me and I fell facedown onto the floor. Jase's ring tumbled from my palm, the clink of gold ringing in my ears again. It was a sharp sound, a knife running under my skin. *Deeper*, I thought, *cut deep*. I wanted to die. I wanted to sink into the floor and disappear, but old habits and rules surfaced.

Tomorrow, Kazi, die tomorrow.

"No," I choked. "Not this time."

Pain rumbled through my chest, and I inhaled sharply, struggling to hold it back. *Don't, Kazi. Don't. He is not dead.* If I sobbed, it would be an admission that it was real, but my chest tore open anyway, a flood of dying sounds pouring out of me, and it seemed there was no question, *I was dying*. I had taken a risk and lost. Everything I had finally allowed myself to feel these past months spilled through the room, disappearing. There would be no tomorrows, not ones that mattered. I was empty, and I would never be full again.

Make a wish, Kazi, one will always come true.

My wish had already come true, and the jealous gods snatched it away, just like they had taken away my mother. There would be no more wishes, no more stars, no more anything. I lay there, staring at the ring just out of my reach, the floor icy against my cheek, too afraid to get up. I couldn't do this again. I couldn't drag myself back to a place where I cared to go on.

The ring glowed on the floor, reflecting all the light the world held, the shine of Jase's eyes, the glint of his hair in the sun. A ring that was not just a ring. The general had called it a worthless piece of jewelry, but he was wrong. It was the reworked gold of countless *Patrei*s. Its worth was not in its scratched metal but in its history and honor. Its promise. *I made a blood vow to protect them, Kazi. And the* Patrei's *vow is his family's vow.*

I forced myself to my feet and retrieved it. My hand shook as I slipped it on my finger. "You made a vow to me too, Jase. You promised me a lifetime of—" My voice broke. I had also made a vow, that I would keep him safe always. And I had failed.

The door opened, and the king walked in. Just as the woman had said. King Montegue, the bumbling King of Eislandia who didn't know Hell's Mouth from his own ass. But he'd apparently managed to find it today.

He stared at me, his eyes dark and deep, contemplative, a hesitation in his step. His oafish grin was gone, but neither was he the sly king I had glimpsed at the arena. His shoulders drooped. He appeared to be a very tired king. He raked back his hair, unruly like the first time I met him, loose strands falling forward.

"This was not how I hoped to cross your path again," he said. "I am truly sorry. I know you've been through a terrible ordeal. I'm afraid General Banques can be crude and harsh, especially after everything we've been through. I've spoken with him. I apologize for his treatment of you, but these are very hard times."

My mind was fuzzy, still trying to navigate through something thick and suffocating. I spun the too-large ring on my finger. Hard times? I finally looked up, "*Why* are these hard times?" I asked. "What have you done? Why is Banques hanging people? Who is he hanging?"

Why have you killed the Patrei? But that was a question I couldn't ask aloud. It was an impossible thought.

The king glanced at my untouched broth and sighed. "You deserve answers, and you'll get them. But first you do need to eat."

"I can't—"

"Please." He came over and took my hand, gently nudging me forward. "I have a lot to tell you, but it will take strength to hear it all. You'll feel better once you eat. I promise. And I understand you were wounded. I've called for our healer to come take a look." He guided me to the chair and table in the corner, then brought the tray of broth to me as if he were a servant.

He sat on a stool opposite me, his eyes creased with concern, waiting for me to lift my spoon.

It will take strength to hear it all?

I didn't want strength. I wasn't sure what I wanted. I used to know. I wanted what Jase wanted. A home. A family. Answers. Did any of that matter anymore? Would answers bring Jase back to me? I'd thought I wanted certainty, that it would be freeing, but now certainty was the anchor that pulled me under. I stared at the broth, still drowning, lost, that girl wandering the streets again, weak and not sure where to turn.

"Please," the king repeated.

Go with the current, Kazi. Keep your head up.

I picked up the spoon and ate.

I had almost finished the bowl and was ready to hear the explanation he promised me, when there was a tap at the door. He stood. "I'm sorry. That's probably the healer. I'll give you two some privacy. I'm sure she'll need you to disrobe."

"But you said—"

"I'll be back. As soon as she's done."

If someone could be the opposite of General Banques, the king was that person. He was soft-spoken, and his movements were quiet, pensive. Apologetic. Had something sobered him since our first meeting? *These are hard times.* Did he really comprehend what was going on here? A tyrant was on the loose, hanging people. Was this another case of the king being oblivious to whom and what he ruled?

As he left, the healer entered, a woman I had never seen in Hell's Mouth before. Somehow I was expecting, or maybe hoping, to see Rhea, the healer who had treated my dog bites.

This woman was pinched and angled, with a stout leather bag clutched in her fist. I realized she might become suspicious when she saw how well my wound was healing . . . unless she was the one who had slipped me the medicine? A healer. Of course. Who else would know about a poultice to treat an oozing wound? Who else would even know the likely state of a wound without examining the patient?

"Thank you," I said, hoping to prompt some admission from her.

"For what?"

"For coming, of course. Treating me."

She looked down at me, her lips tight against her teeth, and offered a curt reply. "King's orders." She rummaged roughly through her supplies, a hiss escaping through her teeth.

Was it me she didn't like? Or was it the king? Or maybe it was the whole state of affairs outside the inn. How far had this madness spread?

"Who was hanged?" I asked.

"Traitors," she answered. "Now show me your wound. I have other duties to attend to besides the likes of you."

The *likes* of me? She stared at me as if I were a roach crossing her path and she was the high queen of everything. Did I have something written on my face? Street trash? Vermin? Or was it just Vendans she disliked? Those mysterious barbarians who wore tethers of bones at their sides? I was used to insults, some even from my own countrymen who looked down on me. When you are on the lowest rung of society, you are a comforting reminder to those just a bit above you that life could always be worse, that they are not you. The healer's movements were sharp, efficient. She was here unwillingly at best, and certainly not my benefactor.

I lifted my shirt, and she gave the wound a cursory glance before applying stinging tincture and a bandage. Her hands were rough and the wound still tender, but I hid a wince behind a clenched jaw. She scribbled something out on a piece of paper, then frowned as if she remembered something. "I'd rather not have to come back. Do you know how to read?"

My shoulders pulled back. "I'm afraid only in three languages," I replied. "Fluently, that is. Five altogether." It was only a small stretch. "*Caz ena*, beetch?" I added.

Her brow squiggled for a moment, uncertain what I had said, but I was sure that the unsettling familiarity of at least one word confounded her. She put the piece of paper on the table along with a small vial of tincture and left. I watched her walk out the door unaware that her bag of remedies was one small item lighter.

When the door banged shut, I looked at the scalpel in my hand, not sure why, at this point, I even took it from her bag. A habit of survival? On the streets of Venda, I had never passed by an easy steal. It all added up to something that could help me survive for one more day. Even if it was something I didn't want, it could be used for trade later. I couldn't trade this scapel for anything, and a thousand slit throats wouldn't give me back Jase.

An ache gnawed beneath my ribs, like an animal trying to escape. I remembered my last frantic seconds with Jase, but they only amounted to disconnected glimpses that I couldn't put together. What had been my last words to him? *Stop? Run?* Those minutes had been stricken with fear and anger. *Rewind it, Kazi. Make it all different.* One more chance. But the moment was gone. Someone had stolen the last words I wanted Jase to hear from me. *I love you. I will always love you.* I had tried to save him. I had fought for all I was worth, but it hadn't been enough.

I turned the scalpel over in my hand. It gleamed sharp and deadly. It was meant to slice flesh so cleanly you barely felt it. I nicked my fingertip, and a bright red bead bloomed against my skin.

A blood vow. And the Patrei's *vow is his family's vow.*

The bead grew larger, like a glistening red ruby, and I lifted my finger to my lips, rubbing the warm blood across them, tasting it with my tongue. The saltiness, the centuries of vows, the promises. And Jase.

You are my family now, Kazi.

I wiped the blood from the scalpel and slipped it beneath the chair cushion for safekeeping. This weapon would not be taken from me.

The *Patrei*'s blood vow was my vow. Protect at all costs.

And I had nothing left to lose.

CHAPTER ELEVEN

KAZI

INSTEAD OF RETURNING TO SEE ME HIMSELF AS HE'D PROMISED, the king had me brought to him. But not before I was given another change of clothes, curiously complete with leather vest, high boots, and a weapon belt—minus the weapons. I looked almost like a real soldier again. My escort was unarmed. The king had a very different regard for my talents than Banques and his goons. As I padded forward, a fog ebbed in and out around me. It wasn't hunger, but memories and words I couldn't flush from my head. I squeezed my eyes, trying to make horrific images vanish. *Animals got him.* I made myself focus on a distant point down the hall. The faraway point was all that mattered. It kept the world from turning upside down.

The guard stopped at a door, and I was led into what appeared to be the king's private dining room, the drapes drawn against the bright of day. Tall candles glowed atop golden candlesticks on a table set for two.

The king turned as I entered the room, his hand absently pressed to his side, and I wondered if there was a pocket inside his vest that held treasure—or were his ribs simply aching? *These are hard times.* Had he been injured? His eyes swept over me, and he smiled. "I see they brought you proper clothes this time. Good. You deserve to look like the premier soldier you are."

"You mean the premier soldier who was stabbed, starved, and held in a dark cell for countless days?"

He grimaced. "Fair enough, but if I could explain." He pulled a chair out for me to sit.

I shook my head, refusing his offer.

"It was a mistake," he said. "They didn't know who you were."

"I screamed it through the door every day."

He looked down and sighed as if dismayed. "Prisoners scream a lot of things, I'm afraid."

"Why do you have prisoners? Why are you here?"

He stepped from behind the chair, walking closer to me, taller than I remembered. "I mean no disrespect," he said, "but if you don't mind, that's a question I would like to ask. Why are *you* here? At the arena I saw you slug the *Patrei* in the jaw, and then shortly after that, you arrested him at knifepoint and hauled him back to Venda to face trial for harboring fugitives."

"At knifepoint? How would you know that last part?"

"Oleez, a servant who was there, told General Banques about the confrontation."

Had Oleez been there that night? I didn't remember seeing her, but she could have been hanging back in the shadows. It would explain her sharp look in my direction.

I studied the king. He was an enigma. Different. He was still the tall, broad-shouldered king I had met at the arena, though more well-groomed now, and with an air and presence about him I hadn't seen before. It wasn't his clothes or how he carried himself—it was his demeanor that had changed. The king before me was brooding, almost meditative, his words calm and even. Thoughtful. Where was the clueless buffoon who shrugged and grinned and tapped his fingers together like a child? Was it the hard times he had mentioned that made that king disappear?

"I'm here because I had orders from the Queen of Venda to escort the *Patrei* back to his home," I answered, still uncertain how much truth was safe to share. "She said I had overstepped my bounds by arresting him. There was no evidence he knew who the fugitives were that he harbored. Some of them didn't even have warrants."

"So hunting down fugitives is what you were really here for all along? Not treaty violations?"

I nodded.

Color flushed his neck. "And you didn't think to tell me?" His eyes were hard steel looking into mine, and his words clipped. "I *am* the king, after all. But maybe you only saw me as a simple farmer shopping for Suri." He looked away and a deep breath filled his chest as if he was trying to shake the resentment I'd heard in his tone. But where there was resentment, there was awareness. He wasn't completely oblivious. He knew how others viewed him and his reign.

"Please," he said, walking back to the chair. He pulled it out a little farther. "I thought you should have a more substantial meal. You have some catching up to do."

I eyed the chair, and then him. I remembered the luxurious bath and the fine bed linens and didn't move. "Why am I feeling like a goose being fattened up for a holiday dinner?"

He sighed. "Did you ever stop to think that maybe I'm trying to make up for overstepping *my* boundaries? For the egregious break in protocol? For being busy with other matters and not paying attention to who was taken prisoner and how she was treated?"

Had he only been juggling—and dropping a few balls in the

process? I knew from Jase that Montegue had become king unexpectedly a few years ago when a draft horse crushed his father. He was only a little older than Jase, who would be—

An angry fist grabbed my heart and shook it. I still expected Jase to walk through a door. I couldn't stop thinking of him as alive, busy, vibrant, taking care of what needed to be done, already scouting out borders, drawing up new trading rules, explaining to his family about me. None of that was going to happen. I felt myself being pulled under the current once more, everything about me unsteady, trying to breathe. I reached up and felt his ring on my finger.

Don't fight it, Kazi, lean back, feet forward.

His voice, so clear in my head. So close. So determined.

The king's eyes remained fixed on me. Curious. And, strangely, patient.

I walked over to the chair and sat, but it felt more like I was collapsing into it. Every word, every effort, drained me. Jase was not coming through that door. Not through any door ever again. *He's alive, Kazi. He has to be alive.* My head ached with the battle going on inside. I had lived through this battle before. I couldn't do it again. Did anything the king had to say even matter?

Head up. Breathe. Jase pulling me up again and again.

"Explain," I said.

"Please, let me serve you first." He lifted a silver cover from a dish and spooned some perfect, tiny roasted potatoes onto my plate that were delicately coated with herbs, and then beside them he set three boiled quail eggs. He drizzled a smoky golden sauce over it all, making it look like a piece of artwork rather than something to be eaten. It made me want to laugh. It was a glaring contrast to the grim news coating my mouth.

As he returned the silver cover to the dish, he hesitated, spotting my hand on the arm of the chair. "You're wearing the signet ring?"

"Your general pulled it off the—" I blinked away the sting in my eyes. "He gave it to me. He called it a trophy."

His brows pulled down and he shook his head. "He shouldn't have done that. I can dispose of it if you'd like?"

I stared at the ring. Dispose of it? *It's only a cheap piece of jewelry to me.* Did either the king or his general have any idea of the history this ring held? *It's been in my family for generations. Once it's put on, it never comes off.* I spun it on my thumb.

"Are you all right?" The king stared at me, waiting for my answer.

"I'll keep it."

He sat opposite from me and explained that almost two months ago, Hell's Mouth had come under siege by miscreants who raided businesses, burned homes, and preyed on its citizens. He was in Parsuss, and by the time news reached him, the lawlessness was out of control. A league run by a fellow named Rybart was conducting an all-out war, trying to gain control of Hell's Mouth and the arena. Citizens were panicked. Some were dying. Worse, the Ballengers were doing nothing to help them, instead demanding more protection money first.

Impossible. Jase would never do such a thing—but would Gunner? I already knew he was impulsive and short-tempered. Trying to blackmail me to send a letter to the queen had been his idea. And I would never forget how low he had stooped when he held Zane out to me as a bribe. But would he break the Ballenger vow to protect the town and hold the citizens hostage for more money? Surely the rest of the family wouldn't allow him do that.

"It seems they had to find some way to finance their latest illegal endeavors," the king went on. "As you are aware, they'd been harboring fugitives for some time, but it was for a very specific purpose. They conspired together to build weapons. They had stockpiled quite an arsenal."

"But that's not possible. There were no weapons. Beaufort said—"

"They were there, all right. Luckily one of General Banques's advance squads of soldiers found the stockpile in a Ballenger warehouse and confiscated them. There was some damage done to the town in the battle for retrieval, but we used the weapons to eliminate Rybart and his ruffians. That's what the army's using now to protect the town."

My mind reeled with a different truth. I knew what I had heard. Kardos had complained that Jase had taken their only working weapon, and we had arrested them before their arsenal could become a reality. There were no weapons, except for the one prototype that Sarva had fashioned—*one* weapon—and Jase had taken and hidden it. Who had made additional weapons? Had it been Rybart's league all along, working with Beaufort to terrorize the town and turn them against the Ballengers? And now a whole army was—

That was another thing that made no sense. "But you don't have an army," I said. "How can—"

"I do now. I needed one quickly and had to hire private militia. My advisors recommended it and—"

"*Mercenaries?* You have hired mercenaries roaming the streets of Hell's Mouth?"

"I've been assured they are professional qualified militia, and really, I had no choice. You have to understand, there was a war going on here. As I mentioned, property was being destroyed. Citizens were dying. I had to do something. It's costing me a fortune, but Paxton assures me that profits from the arena will help me recoup some of the expense. If not, I will have no fields to plant next season."

Everything had spun out of control. "You've taken control of the arena too?"

"Someone had to. Too many citizens rely on it for their income. If the arena fails, so does the town."

"And the Ballengers? Where are they?" I asked. "Are they the prisoners you spoke of?"

He shook his head. "As soon as they knew their scheme had been uncovered, the whole clan managed to retreat into that vault of theirs in the mountain to avoid arrest. They won't come out, and there's no reaching them without blasting our way in, and that might bring the whole mountain down on them. We don't know exactly who all is in there, and I really don't want innocents to die."

"You can't blast through a mountain of solid rock."

"The weapons we confiscated are frighteningly powerful. Some are handheld, but a few are similar to ballistae. They're not like anything we've ever seen. We don't know what the Ballengers planned to do with them. My one fear is that some papers have gone missing. I'm afraid the Ballengers may still have the plans in their possession in order to build more. We need to find those papers."

"I burned the plans."

He set his fork down and his chin lifted slightly. "So it was you who did that? I saw the burned-out workshop."

"How did you know it was a workshop? Did Oleez tell you that too?"

"No, it was another servant. Several of the staff were left behind when the Ballengers fled. We've taken them in and given them work to help make their lives normal again. That's what we're trying to do with the whole town. We mostly have it back under control now." He sighed and took a long drink of the wine he had poured. He added more to my untouched glass, filling it to the brim. "The problem is, the Ballengers have a few loyalists," he explained, "and those few keep stirring up more trouble, making it harder to calm nerves. Commerce is suffering. Livelihoods diminished. Some citizens are afraid to go about their business as usual. I can't blame them. The few violent loyalists are keeping the whole town hostage. I understand their loyalty. It's all they've ever known, but the Ballengers have sealed their own fate. Their reign is over, and my loyalty is to Hell's Mouth, to get it back on its feet again. What the townspeople need is some sort of conclusion. A finality to this horrible mess, so they can move on."

He looked down and scooted a potato across his plate, examining it like it held the answer to his problems. "I may as well say it right now. I need your help. I'm ashamed I didn't tell you up front." His gaze rose to meet mine, the candlelight flickering in his pupils. There was a weight in them, something that made him look younger, a boy king who was overwhelmed. "This is all new to me," he finally admitted. "I'm trying to step up and do what I should have done all along. Be the leader my subjects have always needed me to be, even the ones in the far reaches like Hell's Mouth. Maybe if I had done it sooner, none of this would have happened."

His dark eyes never left mine, searching my face like I held some coveted key that would fix everything.

"What do you want from me?"

He was direct. "Tell the town that the last *Patrei* is dead. But say that Jase Ballenger was found guilty of crimes against the Alliance of Kingdoms and executed in Venda by order of the queen. That justice has been served."

CHAPTER TWELVE

KAZI

I STARED AT HIM, UNABLE TO LOOK AWAY. SAY THAT JASE WAS executed in Venda? Was he serious? His eyes remained fixed on mine, unflinching. Long seconds passed as I tried to absorb why he would want me to tell such a ludicrous, evil lie.

"But we both know that is not what happened," I finally answered.

"Is the truth really better? Torn apart by animals? Tell the town he was a scavenged meal in his last valiant effort to return home? I don't want to make a martyr out of him like the first Ballenger—the mythic man who died saving the last remnant of humanity. That only begs for the loyalists or another Ballenger to rise up with more self-righteous violence. This senseless war could go on forever. Is that really what anyone needs? For the good of the town, it's best that this chapter of history be closed for good. Seeing him as a convicted criminal who was served justice by the Alliance would do that—especially hearing it from the queen's own guard who witnessed the execution. It will be done and over with. It's the kindest truth, and will help the town let go and move forward into a new era. I'm only asking you for the sake of the people. They've been through so much, and the seer has already predicted a bitter season coming. We don't want a starving winter ahead of us. The people need closure." He reached out and squeezed my hand. "Can you help me give them that?"

I looked at his hand clasping mine. Large, warm, gentle. I slowly pulled mine free. "Closure," I repeated, a placeholder for the storm whirling in my head.

He nodded.

"I'm wondering . . . just how did you know the *Patrei* was returning?"

"He sent a message."

"A message that you intercepted?"

"The man in the message office who had been on the take from the Ballengers turned it over to us. He wanted the bloodshed to end too."

"And that's when you ordered the ambush."

"The last thing we needed was for him to rouse more violence in the town. Or bring commerce to a halt again. Revenue was just beginning to pick up again. Too many have been hurt already. We didn't know you would be with him." There was no denial in his answer, only justification. He had murdered Jase.

I stood and wandered around the room, feeling the wobble of my knees and the shallowness of my breaths. The wound in my gut stabbed again, reminding me I was weak. I was nothing. The king was right. Food. I needed food. Strength.

I felt Jase's arm's around me, holding me, keeping my head above the water.

Steady.

I've got you. I promise.

I turned to face the king.

I smiled to reassure him.

Juggled the words in my head into the perfect order, then stacked them into a neat pile. These were the things I knew how to do, the things that were second nature to me while everything else swirled wildly out of control.

I needed control.

"I do see your point," I said. "The town does need to move forward. Into a new era." I walked back to the table, the king's plate empty, mine still full. I remained standing and stabbed a quail's egg and ate it, then stabbed one of the tiny potatoes. I ate it too and washed it down with a long sip of wine, draining half the glass. Some of it dribbled down my chin, and I wiped it away with the back of my sleeve. Heat and reckless-ness rushed into my fingertips and toes. "One thing surprises me, though, Your Majesty. You're a gambler, aren't you? I wouldn't have expected it."

"No," he replied uncertainly, "I never gamble."

"I killed at least three of your soldiers, and yet you took a chance that I wouldn't kill you the minute you stepped into my room earlier." I looked around the empty dining room, my hands raised in a question, the fork still in my hand, acting as a pointer. "And here? No weapons? No guards, even though you just admitted murdering the *Patrei* of Hell's Mouth, the true ruler that my sovereign entrusted me to return to his home. Yes, you're a gambler, a foolhardy one perhaps." I leaned forward on the table. "Or maybe you're just a very *stupid* one."

His chin lifted. Angled.

The sly king. Ah, there he was. Back again. Slinking out from the shadows. All he needed was a little prod.

My gaze burned into his. "You're nothing but an opportunist who moved in on an unstable situation for your own gain and employed wolves like Paxton and Truko to help you get it. All you care about is your newly acquired wealth at the arena. You think you can tell me you are respon-sible for orchestrating the ambush of the *Patrei*, without benefit of trial, and I will just lie and do your bidding?"

He pushed against the arms of his chair and slowly stood, the sly king unfurling, taller, imposing, in control. No juggling. Not caring. He was fully exposed. His skin seemed to stretch tighter across his face, his cheekbones sharper, his eyes darker and deeper.

"I wanted to give you the benefit of the doubt. Your vacillations between kissing, attacking, and arresting the *Patrei* left me with some doubt about which side you were really on. Vendan soldier—or traitor to the Alliance in league with the Ballengers? I guess I have my answer now."

He stepped toward me, and I jerked the fork in my hand upward, a warning.

A grin lit his eyes. "You think you're going to kill me with a pickle fork?"

"You'd be surprised at the creative places I know to shove a simple small fork. I'm not saying your death would be quick. On the contrary, it would be ugly and slow—maybe something like being torn apart by animals."

I swallowed, the last few words clawing in my throat.

"I didn't order that part," he said. "That was fate, ordered by the gods." He took another step toward me. "Put down the fork. You know that I'm stronger and could overtake you easily."

"And yet here we are," I replied. "I'm the one holding a pickle fork, and I can see the veins rising in your neck. Your pulse is racing. There are many kinds of strength, Your Majesty. Maybe you should become acquainted with them all instead of dwelling on your biceps and that useless muscle between your ears."

The door to the dining room flew open, and his cronies rushed in.

"I should have known," I said. "Listening in?"

They slowed when they saw the fork in my hand. They began to spread out. "Not behind me," I warned. "In front of me where I can see you—unless you want me to plunge this fork into the king's throat immediately." I was closer to him than they were to me, and I was still a lethal yet unknown factor who had killed at least three of their soldiers.

"Stay where she can see you," the king ordered.

I really had no plan beyond this moment. Wren would hate this. No escape. No juggling. But if I were to die, the king would die first. Of that much I was certain.

They created a half circle in front of me, and I eyed each one carefully. Banques, Truko, Divot Head. And Paxton. My eyes rested on him the longest. My only regret was I couldn't kill them all.

"Put the fork down," the king repeated. "You'll never get out of here alive."

"Maybe that was your greatest miscalculation. That I ever planned to."

"Don't be foolish," Paxton warned, edging closer. "The king might have a position here for you, one that could be lucrative. He's very generous. You're looking at this all wrong. Don't make a rash decision."

I glared at Paxton. "You just might be the worst of them all, you worthless pile of dung. You're a Ballenger too."

"Barely," Paxton answered. "My family was cast out generations ago."

"Let's show her," Banques said. "Show her why she should agree to your proposition."

I felt the numbing heat of the wine in my belly, wishing it could numb far more. "I will never agree to any proposition."

Banques smiled. "Oh, I think there's something that might change your mind."

"Maybe I'm a bit of a gambler after all," the king said, stepping forward, unafraid, "and the best gamblers always hold back a bit of negotiating gold."

I stared at him, his eyes like hard glass, and icy fingers clutched my spine. Was his bumbling, oafish manner just a part of the façade he had carefully groomed for years? *Suri. Such is the life of a farmer king.* I remembered his shrug and clownish grin. That was not remotely the man who stood before me now. There was awareness in his gaze, and a swagger in his stance. He knew what I was thinking, and it seemed to energize him, the sly king at last taking center stage.

"Go," he said. "Look out the window. There are other guests here at the inn whom I think you know." He nodded to Truko.

Truko was a hulk of a man with unruly hair and wiry black brows always pulled in a scowl. His eyes were wide and unblinking. When I had told Jase about one of my rules of survival, *blink last*, he was amused, laughing that it was one of the things he hated about Truko—the man never blinked. Jase never knew what was going on in his head. As I met his frozen stare now, there was nothing amusing about it. His steps wheezed against the floor as he plodded to the window and whisked back the drapes.

This was no bluff. I knew before I even lowered the fork or walked to the window that the king had won. That Death had seen all of this coming and that was why he shook his head at me.

"Go," the king repeated. "See who is out there. I think you'll be surprised."

CHAPTER THIRTEEN

JASE

IT WAS THE SOUND OF WATER RUSHING OVER STONES. A SUCKING, gurgling noise like a tide rushing out. It came again. And again. It ebbed and rose with the stab in my chest and then I realized it was not stones and water I heard. It was my own breaths, liquid, wet, the sounds of me trying to breathe.

There were other sounds, distant, garbled voices, but those didn't matter.

Only the stones, the water, the next breath.

Write it down, before you forget.

And each day we do.

But we can only write about Now.

Before is already gone, except for the nightmares.

Every night we must comfort the younger ones.

All they know of Before is the After.

They are afraid it will happen again, that our new family will be torn apart.

That is the reason we hide in here, Nisa cries.

She is right.

I am afraid too.

My grandfather believed in me.

I try to believe like he did, but some nights, after Nisa is asleep, I cry too.

—Greyson Ballenger, 14

CHAPTER FOURTEEN

KAZI

THE WINDOW LOOKED DOWN ON A SMALL ENCLOSED courtyard. A guard stood in each corner. Long swords hung at their sides. In the center two children played, rolling a hoop back and forth to each other. Oleez sat off to the side. She saw me looking down from the window, but her expression remained blank.

Someone took the fork from my hand. Paxton, I think. I didn't resist. The message was clear, and the king held the winning card. Do as he said, or there would be consequences. There was no changing his mind. I felt like I had been caught, a quarterlord passing sentence, and a fingertip was about to be snipped. I couldn't talk my way out of this one.

The king came over and stood close behind me. His chest was fire at my back. He pushed the drape back farther. "They look happy, don't they? They've actually become very fond of me. I give them attention, presents. More than he ever did. They're quite content. Trust me on this."

I could barely absorb his nonsense. I only imagined their faces as I told a crowd that Jase was a convicted criminal who had been hanged. "Don't make me say it in front of them. I don't want them to hear."

"They have to know about their brother sooner or later," Banques said. "They've mostly forgotten him already. They'll take it well."

"Please," I said.

The king stepped away and said to Banques as he left, "Explain to her the rules of the game. Make sure she understands them, then return her to her room."

A game? This was no game. The outcome was already assured. There was only one winner.

With the king gone, I turned to Banques. "You can't do this. This violates everything that the Alliance—"

"This violates absolutely nothing," he snarled. "I will remind you that this is the Kingdom of Eislandia, and Montegue is its rightful and true ruler. It is not only under his jurisdiction to rule and protect as he sees fit, it is his moral duty to ensure the peace for his citizens. He is doing his job and doing it well. He does not take the advice of a thief or barbarian soldier, especially not one who is sympathetic to the Ballengers, who brought about this carnage in the first place. We are still trying to stamp out a war and restore order and must use every means at our disposal for the good of all."

Every means? He glanced down at the children, then glared at me, his hand curling into a fist in like he wanted to smash it into my face. He warned me to be silent while he explained everything. The rules, it turned out, were easy to remember. They were nearly all the same.

1. If you ever leave as much as a small bruise on the king . . .

2. If you ever leave a bruise on any of his cabinet or soldiers . . .

3. If you are ever found outside your room without an approved escort . . .

4. If you ever steal so much as a hairpin . . .

5. If you ever lie to the king . . . one of the children will die, and you will be forced to choose which one.

"Understand?" he asked.

I nodded. But I would slit my own throat before I would choose between Lydia and Nash.

CHAPTER FIFTEEN

JASE

THE TIDE, THERE WAS A RHYTHM TO IT.

In.

Out.

It was winning. I felt it pulling me under.

Blackness. It was all I knew. And silence. Had I stopped breathing? But the pain was still there. The pain was everywhere.

I had to be alive.

Burning. Wet. My skin, my lips, everything on fire.

Hell. I had to be in hell. And I couldn't find my way out.

He's coming to.

Bloody saints. Not now. Keep him quiet.

I tried to reach up, to feel my eyes, to see if they were open, because I still only saw blackness, but the slight movement ignited a red-hot poker stabbing into my shoulder. I groaned and a hand pressed hard over my mouth.

"Shhh," a voice hissed. "Unless you want to die!"

I was still because I couldn't move. I couldn't reach up to push the hand away. I heard something creak over my head. A wooden floor? Muffled voices.

No love lost between us and the Ballengers . . .

. . . burned us out . . .

If any were here, we'd be the first to hand them over . . .

Good riddance, I say.

If you do see him, you're to report it immediately.

I heard the sound of horses riding away, and the hand lifted from my mouth.

I felt myself slipping again, falling back into some dark cave. "Who are you?" I whispered.

"Kerry."

"Kerry of Fogswallow?"

"How many Kerrys do you know?"

Only one. A small child was able to hold me down.

———◦◦◦———

The heavy scent of burning tallow stirred me awake. When I opened my eyes, a candle flickered in a glass lamp and shadows shifted on walls. Barrels lined the room, and there were rushes scattered across the floor. I was lying on a pallet. Caemus sat next to me on a milking stool. Shadows filled the hollows of his face. None of it made sense. What was I doing here? What had happened to me? And then, bit by bit, the black fog rolled back. We had been attacked. Kazi and I—

I tried to rise, but instead I sucked in a sharp breath, coughed, and pain shot through my chest.

"Hold on, there," Caemus said, gently holding me down. "You've barely got one foot out of that underworld. Don't go stepping back into it."

"Where am I?" I whispered.

"The root cellar. Lucky thing you dug it. Don't know where else we'd hide you." He poured water from a pitcher into a cup. "Here," he said, bringing the water to my lips. I struggled to drink. Even my tongue ached. It was dry, coated, and salty. My lips were cracked, and I shook with the effort of lifting my head, even with Caemus's help.

He set the cup aside. "That's enough for now. We didn't think you were going to make it at all. You've been in and out for days now."

I couldn't remember any of it. "Where's Kazi? Why isn't she here?"

And then the fog rolled back a little farther. *Baricha.* I had told her to run, to get away, but instead she jumped from her horse and fought them, beating them away from me, ordering the horses to run. She killed one, and then another, and then a fist—a fist punched into her stomach—but I couldn't move. I couldn't get to her. I couldn't do anything. I had never felt more helpless. *Baricha.* Tigone ran into the forest. Metal flashed, voices shouted, the world faded in and out. Pieces were all I could remember— slamming to the ground, footsteps, someone lifting me.

"He only brought you."

"He? Someone brought me here? Who was it?"

"I don't know. It was dark, the middle of the night. He didn't say his name, and it was hard to get a good look at him. I think he wanted it that way. He told me to take care of you—to do my best, but not to call a healer. He said they were watching all the healers, following them. He tried to give me coin for your safekeeping, but I wouldn't take it. Before he left, he wiggled your ring off your finger. Said he needed it, and I didn't argue, seeing as he was trying to save your life."

They.

They were watching healers.

"Who are *they*?"

"I don't know. We haven't gone back since the fires. We're making do with what supplies we have here. It's too dangerous in town."

He had to tell me twice. Maybe three times. I was still drifting in and out, trying to grasp his details. Taking sips of water. Coughing. Still feeling like I had a foot in an underworld that didn't want to let me go.

He said that about two months ago there had been a bad fire. The north livery burned down. All the horses inside died. The next night there was another fire and then a raid on a caravan. More trouble came after that, but he and the rest of the settlers had stayed away, afraid of being hit on the trail, not to mention that since five Vendan soldiers had absconded with the *Patrei*, Vendans hadn't exactly been welcome in town. Except for a hurried trip to get some medicine at the apothecary, they hadn't been back. Caemus mostly kept his head down, not wanting to be noticed, but from the little he gathered from whispers at the apothecary, it seemed the Ballengers had been running everywhere, trying to stop whoever was stirring up the mayhem before an army had marched in and taken everything over.

"*An army?*" I asked. Each new bit of information he gave me seemed to twist into something more impossible. "What army?"

"I don't know, but I heard there's a lot of them. I got a glimpse of a few as I rode in."

An army from where? A neighboring kingdom? Or had the leagues joined forces? I thought about Fertig's gang and Kazi's observation that they were well trained.

"And Tor's Watch?" I already knew the answer. I had seen the broken spires, the walls. But I still couldn't understand *how*. Our defenses were impenetrable. Our walls, our guards, our vantage point, and the steep grade leading to Tor's Watch—an army with a dozen ballistae couldn't breach our walls. Our archers would take them out before they were even in range. "How did they bring down the wall?"

Again, he said he didn't know for sure, but he said they had weapons unlike anything he had ever seen. "Word is, the whole nave of the temple is gone and that one shot brought it down. The apothecary's wife said they did it just to get everyone's attention. It worked. No one's challenging them now."

This was not an army coming in to rescue a town. It was an invasion. Paxton, Rybart, and Truko. It had to be. They had joined forces.

I was afraid to ask, but more afraid not to. "What did the weapons look like?"

"That was the strange part," he said. "They weren't that large. They carried them on their shoulders." He went on in some detail. They sounded exactly like the launchers Beaufort was designing for us—the ones we never got.

"What about Kazi? Do you know where she is? Do they have her?"

He shook his head. "Don't know. The man who brought you didn't say, and like I said, we haven't been back to town."

But I did know. They had her. She was their prisoner. That was the only way Kazi wouldn't be here beside me. Unless—

I remembered them swarming over us, black shadows moving over the dark hillside.

"I have to get to—" I leaned over on an elbow, trying to sit up, then fell back, unable to breathe. Caemus cursed, saying I was going to break open the wounds that Jurga had stitched shut.

"You're not going anywhere. Even if she is in town you wouldn't be any help to her, not with the shape you're in. And not with just one of you, and hundreds of them."

"But my family. They could—"

"They're not helping either. They're all hiding inside that mountain of yours. I know that much."

The vault. And that meant it was really bad.

"I have to get to them. They'll know what we were up against. They'll help me find—" But then I felt the black fog rolling back in, and my eyelids eased shut against my will. I was afraid I might not open them again, afraid that this time the underworld might pull me under and not let go.

The cellar, the musty air, the pain, everything slipped away.

CHAPTER SIXTEEN

KAZI

I WAS RETURNED TO MY ROOM AND LEFT ALONE IN MY "FINE" accommodations for two full days. I was told I would be summoned when they were ready for me. My door wasn't locked. It felt like a test. But there was no worry that I would leave. I cracked it open and peeked out, but I didn't dare step through it. Food was brought to me in abundance. More clothing. More medicine. But no came one to speak to me—or give me more rules. The waiting and wondering and being able to do nothing drove me to near madness. *Summon me, for gods' sakes!*

My hours were filled with a thousand questions. Who had been hanged? How many had died? How could there be a warehouse of weapons? Was Gunner truly responsible for all the carnage? Had he blackmailed the town for more money as he let Rybart pillage it?

But the *Patrei's* vow was his family's vow, and as much as I hated Gunner, I couldn't believe he would do this. Though he *was* impulsive. He had lied to the town and said the queen was coming.

On the other hand, as much as he hated the idea, he did help rebuild the settlement. Jase's promise was his promise too. And surely Vairlyn would never allow—

A cloud of locusts batted in my head, details flying around in a mad, scattered mess. I couldn't sort out the truth. I searched for solutions, one thought crashing into another. Ultimately, only one thought rose above the others again and again—I had to get Lydia and Nash out of their grip. That was the most important thing. But my skills as thief and soldier offered me nothing. Stealing a tiger or even Beaufort was one thing, but stealing two small children who were under heavy guard was another. And where would I take them? The city crawled with enemy soldiers. Tor's Watch was destroyed and abandoned. There was only one of me and hundreds of them. And there was the possibility they wouldn't even come with me. I remembered Gunner's and Priya's last bitter words. Had they poisoned Lydia and Nash against me? Everything pointed to failure, and failure carried too great a downside. If I could get a message to the queen—

But the arena had been taken over too. *Traders.* I could slip a message to a trading caravan. But when? I was under heavy guard, and even a trading caravan might be sympathetic toward the king, and then, if my treachery were discovered—

This violates nothing. It's within his rights.

I felt the same panic as I had that day when I spit in the queen's face, useless, lost, a bird with plucked wings. The world I knew how to navigate had disappeared. I had to follow the rules Banques laid out. It was my only option.

As bad as the panic and questions were, at times it seemed they were all that saved me from another kind of madness. *Jase.* He was gone. It was a crushing thought that would slam into me unexpectedly and rob me of what little sanity I had. Only thinking of how I could save Nash and Lydia allowed me to shove the madness away.

On the third afternoon, guards knocked loudly on my door and told me the king required my presence. I had been summoned. They told me specifically what to wear. My mind raced once again as Black Teeth and Broken Nose escorted me to another wing of the inn.

"Here," Broken Nose said, stopping at an open door and nudging me inside.

The king's chambers bustled with activity as if last minute preparations were being made. A bevy of nervous servants hovered around him, adjusting his baldrick, lacing boots, buckling breastplates, filling scabbards with knives and swords. He seemed to drink in the attention, and I guessed this was all new to him. But it was clear there was an urgency too, a rush to slip the king into another new persona.

His head turned as I entered the room. He waved me over and gave more orders for servants to "prepare" me. A long sword and dagger were slid into my weapon belt. There was no worry that I would use them. It had been clearly outlined what would happen if I made the slightest aggressive move. Any weapon was useless to me. However, I did note these were dull. Very dull. They were more suited for beating dust from a rug than for stabbing anyone. But when sheathed, they certainly gave the appearance of strength.

"What are you staring at?" he asked, though it had to be obvious. He was dressed in full military regalia. The black leather pauldron on his shoulder gleamed with polish. "Don't be so surprised. Of course I'm a soldier. I've been under Banques's tutelage for years now, and it's not an exaggeration to say he's the finest swordsman on the continent." A farmer under the tutelage of a swordsman? For years?

He paused to look at himself in a mirror, tugging on his tunic and adjusting the baldrick across his chest. "And I think it's fair to say, too, that the student has now surpassed the master." He turned to look at me, his expression solemn. "I'm the leader and protector of my kingdom. I need to convey that in my attire, to inspire confidence."

He painted an imposing and impressive picture. No doubt Synové—and maybe any girl in Hell's Mouth—would swoon over his transformation. His dark hair was trimmed and combed, a single strand falling forward as if he had just swung a sword. His cheeks glowed with a fresh shave, and his leather breastplate was cut to accent his wide shoulders. Every detail conveyed strength, leadership, and a message that this was a king who was fit and able to lead.

I didn't respond and he paused, waving away a servant who was tending him. He stepped closer to me. "I'm not the monster you think I am. I am a just ruler and have to listen to my advisors. That is what they are paid for."

"Using children as hostages is vile. Your advisors are vile. And if you listen to them, that makes you vile too."

"That's easy enough for a bystander to say. Words and lofty accusations are easy, aren't they, when you haven't watched people die? You don't run a troubled kingdom beset by marauders where hard decisions must be made every day—and I have made one. Sometimes sacrifices must be made for the greater good."

I couldn't restrain a deep roll of my eyes. "Is that another gem your well-paid advisors vomited into your hands?"

His dark lashes fluttered, and his eyes ignited with fury.

"I'm sorry," I said. "Does bruising your delicate ego count as a transgression too? Will the children now suffer for it?"

He stepped closer, his face inches from mine, his chest heaving. "Rybart preyed on the town, pillaging and burning it while the Ballengers and their henchmen blackmailed it for more protection money. Those are the facts! And *I* am the King of Eislandia." He lowered his voice so only I could hear him. "*You will show me respect,*" he hissed between clenched teeth. "*Do you understand?*"

This was no show. The man who had courteously pulled out a chair for me just days ago now fumed with hot rage. He had stepped into the role of powerful monarch in a ravenous way.

"Yes, Your Majesty," I answered cautiously. In that moment, looking into his dark eyes, I was afraid that bruising his ego might be what mattered most of all. I was usually good at judging temperaments, knowing just how far I could push, but this king seemed to be many different people, and I didn't understand even one of them.

He looked away, grabbed a paper from a table, and handed it to me. "Here, Banques prepared this. It's what you will be reading to the town. Read it word for word. We have to leave soon, before the last bell rings."

Servants swarmed in again, making final adjustments to his uniform. One young woman fussed over him, picking away imaginary threads. I wasn't sure if she was afraid of him or completely enamored, but when he turned his back, she quickly fluffed her hair with her fingers and smoothed out her bodice, and my question was answered.

When he was satisfied with his appearance, he shooed her and the other servants away and studied me—from the sword hanging at my side to the long, tailored woolen jacket that servants had dressed me in. His inspection was slow and searing. He finally nodded as if pleased. "Yes, you look like you just rode in, maybe a bit gaunt from the journey. We'll fill out those cheeks with a tasty celebration afterward. Trust me, this is all for the best. Let's go share your news."

He pulled my hood up to cover my head and took hold of my arm firmly but gently, leading me to the door, playing the role of a soldier king leading a respected messenger of a foreign monarch to share the important news of the *Patrei's* execution. A new era was beginning.

The entourage gathered in the large foyer of the inn. Just before we emerged onto the street for the procession to the plaza, I was pushed forward to walk with Banques and two soldiers, while the king hung back. More soldiers filled the space between us, but I glimpsed Lydia and Nash being brought to him. Nash ran happily into the king's arms. The king lifted him up, holding him on his hip with one arm and grabbing Lydia's hand with the other. Lydia's smile was more reserved, but it was there, and somehow it stabbed me with stinging jealousy. She should be smiling at Jase. Oleez stood off to the side. She smiled at the king, and they shared a few whispered words. She avoided my burning gaze, though I know she felt it.

Banques called for the entourage to move forward, and we proceeded out the front door of the Ballenger Inn. I eyed Banques as we walked—the king's tutor for years? What else had he been teaching him besides swordsmanship? But mostly I wondered who was really in charge, the king or Banques?

I thought I had known what to expect, a town confused by the sudden change in power. A town wondering where their *Patrei* was. A town waiting for something to happen. Anything.

But it already had.

The first thing I saw was the damage. The remains of a building that once housed a pub and apartments stood abandoned, splintered timbers poking out of the rubble like broken bones. A little farther down, an eight-foot crater gouged out half the cobbled street. Wagons maneuvered around, pretending it wasn't there.

But the damage was the least of it. When I looked up, I saw soldiers stationed overhead. Everywhere. They manned the skywalks and roofs like birds of prey, their dark cloaks waving in the wind. How many mercenaries did he hire? Where did he get the money? The power astounded me.

The soldiers on the ground carried the usual types of weapons, swords, halberds, and such, but the ones on rooftops or skywalks were equipped differently. Slung over their shoulders were shiny metallic weapons, each about four feet long. I had never seen anything like them before, but I was certain these were the launchers that Jase had described to me. From their vantage points, they saw everything—and they were strategically out of reach of anyone who might try to overcome them and seize their formidable weapons. This wasn't a town that was being protected. Rybart and his men were dead and gone. Now it was a town that had been invaded, and these soldiers were there to squelch any opposition.

A pervading grimness hung in the air. The sky was gray with winter. Frost dulled the windows and cobbles. Even the people were gray, their cloaks pulled tightly about them against the cold, their faces shadowed by scarves, hoods, and hats as they went about their business. A few heads turned as I passed, curious, but unable to get a good glimpse of me beneath my hood.

A bell rang out. Last bell. The clang shivered through my teeth. People stopped what they were doing and headed toward the plaza. By order of the king? Or from genuine hunger for news? Some sort of hope? The hope I could not give them.

I turned the corner and was stopped by the sight of the temple, another gaping hole in the city. Only the bell tower and the altar remained standing—the rest was rubble. The broken statues of saints stared heavenward. The air was punched from me, and I stared, not quite believing it. It had been the beautiful focal point of the entire plaza, its white marble walls casting an ethereal glow over everything. Now, instead of a sanctuary, it looked like a passage into hell. Jase had told me what his launcher was capable of—and it was not this. Unless Beaufort hadn't been honest about what it could do. And of course, Beaufort was not honest about anything.

"The temple was a rat's nest for loyalists. It had to go," Banques explained. "It will be rebuilt when the last of them are gone."

I had been so consumed with the temple I didn't see what was above me—not until Banques glanced up. I followed the line of his sight and immediately turned my head and gagged. He grabbed my arm.

"Steady now," he whispered. "Remember, you're being watched, and you are the messenger who brings news of justice." He lowered his voice. "Most important, remember who walks not far behind you. Take a deep breath now, and walk up those stairs with your head held high. Play your role respectably, as you should have done in the first place."

My stomach churned as I climbed the steps to a platform overlooking the plaza. When I reached the top, I was surprised to find Garvin standing there. His eyes combed the streets and the approaching citizens.

"You're working for them?"

His head dipped in acknowledgment. "Nothing personal. Someone else is meeting payroll now."

"And that's all it takes? A weekly wage?"

He shrugged. "It's all business."

"I suppose I should expect as much from someone who sells starving tigers to butchers."

He grinned. "So you did recognize me after all those years." He nodded like he was pleased that he wasn't so forgettable after all.

"I mentioned your name to the queen. She said it was a pity I didn't haul you back too. Something about trying to slit her throat?"

He shook his head. "That was only business too. A hired job. She took it too personally."

He turned back to the streets he was eyeing. Looking for whom? Ballengers who had once employed him? I had to resist the urge to throw him over the rail.

Banques nudged me forward, and when I turned, I found I was now eye level with at least a dozen bodies that hung from the high branches of the tembris. I tried to force back the bile rising in my throat. The body closest to me was gray, his face covered with frost, small icicles hanging from his chin. I didn't recognize him and began to avert my eyes from the rest, but not soon enough. A sick saltiness swelled inside my mouth. Hanging just past him was a body I recognized. Drake. One of Jase's *straza*. *Of course he was a loyalist. It was his job to be loyal!*

I skimmed the other faces, afraid of who else I might find hanging, but more afraid not to look. Three bodies over from Drake I recognized another one. It was the dressmaker who had measured me for clothes. Her eyes were still open, sightless. My nails dug into my palms.

"She was hiding agitators," Banques explained, as if that justified it. "We give every citizen a chance to cooperate and do what's right. She chose not to, which made her a Ballenger accomplice and a danger to other citizens. Our job is to restore order and to make everyone feel safe again."

I turned and looked at him. His voice again, *familiar.* Each syllable made the hairs on my neck rise. I knew him, but I didn't. He went on, giving all the justifications. His story was almost word for word like the king's, a repeated narrative, like an awl working wood, deepening a groove until it became a truth of their own making. *We are keeping the town safe.*

If they repeated it often enough, did they think that would make it true? That I would be fooled? That it would wash the blood from their hands?

"This is no way to protect a city," I said. "You're nothing but opportunists here to seize its wealth."

He waved his hand, dismissing my accusation. "Let's hurry this along, shall we? It's cold and it's getting late. The people want to go home. Let's not keep our good citizens waiting."

The king walked up the platform steps behind us with Nash still in his arms and Lydia at his side. Nash and Lydia didn't seem to even notice the hanging bodies, or maybe they had become numb to them. What horrors had they already endured? Neither looked my way, as if they had been instructed not to, or perhaps before the city was seized, the family had made it known to them who had taken Jase away. Maybe they didn't look at me because they couldn't stand the sight of me.

The three of them moved to the opposite end of the platform, and the king set Nash down just in front of him, resting one hand on Lydia's shoulder. He addressed the crowd, telling them that a premier soldier of the Queen of Venda had arrived with news that would help them to move forward, news that would close the door on the troublesome times they had been through. Better times lay ahead. His voice was assured, the timbre promising, his expression genuine, a small crease of concern deepening between his brows, and then with a motion of his hand, he deferred to me, inviting me to step forward.

Banques indicated that I should go out onto the skywalk where the citizens could get a better view of me. The wood planks creaked beneath my feet. When I got to the center, I turned and pushed back my hood so they could see me. A low murmur rippled through the crowd. *That soldier. The one who took the* Patrei. Maybe the last time they saw me I was juggling oranges outside the mercantile, or I was kissing the *Patrei* in front of the apothecary. Or maybe they saw me slugging him at the arena. I was a mystery to them.

The wind whipped at my hair, and the air fogged with my breath. This was hardly the same city it had been just months ago when it had been full of color, and noise, and light, and warmth. Now it was a dreary sea of long woolen cloaks. Scarves covered noses and mouths, and only bare slivers of eyes looked up at me. Was it because of the harsh weather, or did they want to hide their identities? I wondered how many loyalists stood among them, still waiting for the *Patrei* to return. I saw the tired slump of their shoulders, and the gloom in their downcast faces. The paper the king had given me shook in my hands. How could I do this? Tell lies about Jase? Tell them in front of Lydia and Nash?

I gave the king one last pleading look. *Don't do this to them.* His head angled slightly to the side, unrelenting. He placed a hand on Nash's shoulder, pulling him closer. Was it a gesture to comfort Nash, or was it a warning to me?

I looked back at the crowd. I read the words. "Citizens of Hell's Mouth, I bring you news of Jase Ballenger." Each word floated in the air, unreal, untrue, impossible, and yet they came from my mouth. *Jase, I need you.* This couldn't be happening, but it was. "The former *Patrei* of your city will not be returning," I went on. "He was arrested and delivered to the Queen of Venda and a tribunal court of law to be tried for crimes against the Alliance of Kingdoms. He was found guilty by that court and sentenced to hang by a rope until dead. I witnessed his confession, his prayers to the gods for forgiveness for his crimes, and his subsequent execution. Jase Ballenger is dead."

A low, muffled moan, impossible to pinpoint, rolled upward, and then a cry and someone fell to their knees. Soldiers on skywalks and roofs lifted the launchers, ready. Soldiers on the ground moved in closer.

Banques motioned for me to continue.

I spoke louder, trying to rise above the murmur. "The rightful and true ruler of Hell's Mouth, King Montegue, is restoring order and working to make Hell's Mouth greater than it ever was. The Alliance and I both urge you to help him keep your city safe by turning in traitors. As you can see, innocents do not suffer under his rule."

I paused and looked over at Nash and Lydia, and the armed guards standing so close to them. The king nodded for me to go on. "Only the guilty who have put you all at risk will suffer a penalty," I said. "If you know of any other Ballengers or sympathizers in hiding, you are called to turn them in or risk being charged with crimes against the kingdoms yourself. It is time for Hell's Mouth to move forward and embrace a promising new future."

There was a noticeable lull, a stillness settling over the plaza, and then a voice screamed out, "*Murderer!*"

Almost at the same time, something struck me and my head exploded with pain. I fell back, catching myself on the rail. A rock tumbled over the planks.

There were more shouts and then a resounding hush as the crowd shifted, absorbing whoever had called out. Soldiers moved in, trying to find the perpetrators, but in a fluid sea of gray, they were lost as the crowd dispersed.

I reached up and felt my head, and when I pulled my hand away, there was blood on my fingers. I looked back at Lydia and Nash. Their faces were blank. Any emotion about the news I had delivered was buried deep beneath some new hardened armor they had never worn before. The king lifted Nash again and pulled Lydia close, saying it was time to go. Nash nestled his head on the king's shoulder, but his gaze turned toward me. The intense hunger in his eyes carved a hole in my gut. Was it hunger for revenge that I saw? The fire in them made him look just like Jase. I watched them all depart down the stairs in a tight knot. Lydia never looked my way, but I knew she missed nothing. She heard what I had said about her brother.

Banques handed me a handkerchief for my head. "Well done. Believe it or not, it went surprisingly well. There might be a place in this kingdom for you, after all. The *Patrei* and his whole lawbreaking family will soon be forgotten."

I stared at him as I pressed the cloth to my temple and imagined how

I would kill him. There were slow ways. Eben had described them to us on dark nights around a campfire. Ways the Rahtan were no longer authorized to use. Ways he had learned from the Komizar that were far slower than a pickle fork. Ways I had never dreamed of using before, thinking them depraved. They didn't seem so anymore.

I stare at the spears. We have pulled apart bed frames and sharpened the ends. I threw one today, past the gate at a screaming scavenger. I felt strong and powerful. I missed him and he picked it up and ran away. Now he has a spear to use against me. I think his aim is better than mine.

—Greyson, 15

CHAPTER SEVENTEEN

JASE

I SAT ON THE EDGE OF MY PALLET, READY TO STAND FOR THE FIRST time. It was a milestone.

"Don't be such a baby," Kerry scolded. "Stop grimacing. You want to get up and pee on your own, or not?"

I did. I forced the grimace from my face. "That better?"

He grunted. Kerry had become my nursemaid, sitting with me, washing me, feeding me—and regularly berating me. He showed me no mercy. Sometimes I wondered if it was his revenge for the post holes I had made him dig. Four days ago, he started giving me weights to lift so I would regain my strength. The sacks of potatoes he handed me couldn't have weighed more than five pounds each, but the strain of lifting them burned all the way down to my thigh, where one of the arrows had struck. My arms shook as I lifted them. *You're turning to flab*, he had chided as he squeezed my upper arm. If Caemus was within earshot, he would counter, *Leave him be. He's doing just fine*, much more sympathetic than my warden. But I was frustrated with my progress, and in some ways, I appreciated my relentless taskmaster. I had to get out of here and find Kazi. If they were holding her—

It was something I couldn't allow myself to think about for too long, but there was still no word. Caemus had finally taken a chance and gone into town—maybe just to keep me from crawling there myself. With soldiers on every corner, he had to keep the hood of his cloak up, his head down, and his words few, but there was still no word or sign of her. Or of my family. I asked him what he did see, and he said nothing but grim-faced soldiers, and as far as news went, it seemed that everyone was tight-lipped and afraid to talk. The town had gone unusually quiet. He was afraid to pry for fear of drawing attention, but he did overhear a shop-keeper grumbling that Paxton and Truko were running the arena now.

It was like being hit with another arrow. I shouldn't have been sur-prised. We knew someone was challenging us, and I had always suspected one of the leagues was behind the fires and raids. But now they had names. I never seriously thought they could pull something like this off—or even that they would try. Yes, they grumbled. We grumbled. But we all made money and we had fallen into a comfortable—if rocky—routine in our dealings, until they began working with Beaufort. The Ballengers them-selves had financed this takeover. Zane must have been their go-between. How long had they been planning this? I would kill both Paxton and Truko if they had harmed Kazi. And I wouldn't make it quick. I didn't need a powerful weapon to—

Caemus's description stopped me. I remembered him saying one shot brought down the nave of the temple. Was he mistaken? *One?* The launcher I tested was powerful. It could take down a man with accuracy at two hundred yards, probably three men if they were standing close together, but one shot couldn't take down a temple. I remembered the destruction in Sentinel Valley and Beaufort's boasting about dominion over the kingdoms. Was Hell's Mouth the starting point for his campaign?

The Ballenger histories described in detail the rubble the town had been made from. Centuries of rebuilding transformed the wreckage into the wonder it was today, but now someone like Beaufort and his conspirators could hold it hostage and return it to the rubble it had once been? And there was an army to carry out his plans. That part still didn't add up.

"Ready?" Kerry asked, handing me a crutch he had fashioned for me.

It had taken me over a week just to get to the point of sitting up. I had no shirt on, but had bandages wrapped around half of my upper body. Paxton and his crew had been determined to kill me.

"Hold your breath, and I'll help you to your feet." I used the crutch as leverage, and Kerry tucked his fingers beneath a bandage and pulled. The pressure felt like a bull sitting on my chest. I clenched my teeth.

"Kerry! What do you think you're doing?" Jurga yelled. She was frozen halfway down the cellar steps. We were both in trouble.

"He's got to get up sooner or later."

"He's right," I said, coming to his defense. "I have to get my strength back." Words poured out of me then, desperate words I didn't even know were there. "Kazi is alone, maybe hurt, they're holding her against her will, my family's in hiding, the town's overrun, and when they all need me the most, I'm here helpless. I have to get stronger, I have to go."

Jurga listened to me, wide-eyed. I felt like a child begging for the impossible, even though I knew it was not something that either Jurga or Kerry could give me.

I blinked, trying to clear my vision. "I have to find her."

Jurga stared at me, her mouth pursed like she had sucked on a lemon, then she looked long and hard at Kerry. "Come on, help me get him up these steps. A little sunshine will do him good."

The first several days, I never strayed far from the storage shed, always ready to retreat back inside if a warning signal of riders came, but none ever did. It was like they had stopped looking for me, which meant they probably thought I was dead.

It wasn't only Kerry who put me through my paces. The other settlers took turns as well, walking me in circles around the shed and helping me to ease back down on a bench when I needed to rest. Eventually they took me a little farther to view their finished homes that I had never gotten to see. They showed me the raised foundations, the wooden floors that they never had before, the supplies that filled their shelves. They invited me in, they fed me, they added bones to my tether that I now wore the same as them. *Meunter ijotande*, they would say. Never forgotten. Day by day, I learned more of their language. I was ashamed that I had ever protested the rebuilding of the settlement, and was glad for the extra work we had put into it. Glad for my blood vow and alms. There was so much I didn't know back then, that I knew now. Things I never would have known if not for Kazi.

"Another set," Kerry ordered. His eyes gleamed. He loved watching me suffer. But I was getting stronger. He had me lifting buckets of water now—only half full—but the pain in my abdomen had at least become tolerable, or maybe I was just getting used to it. How much longer before I'd be ready to leave? But I knew there would be no second chances. I had to get this right the first time. I had to be strong enough to do what I needed to do. I turned my frustration into work—more sets, more food, more walking.

When we finished my daily regimen, I usually sat on a bench in the sun and read to Kerry. The teacher we sent had brought books, some filled with legends of other worlds far from Tor's Watch, but the ones he liked best were the ones I told about the Ballenger history and Greyson, who was little more than a child himself when given the task of keeping everyone safe. Kerry's eyes glowed with admiration and intense curiosity, maybe the way mine had when my father first told them to me. I didn't embellish. I didn't need to. The truth was astonishing enough.

"How do you know all these stories?" he asked.

"I've written them down—every one. It was part of my schooling. I have a whole library of Ballenger history at my home. Someday I'll show you."

Home. If it was still there.

If anything was there.

Who will write our story, Jase?

We will, Kazi, and it will take a thousand volumes. We have a lifetime ahead of us.

Last night more of the fog had rolled back. A glimpse. A fist going into Kazi's stomach—but there was a glint of light too. What was it? I couldn't stop worrying about what I hadn't seen and didn't know.

"I'm going with you when you go to find her," Kerry said as if he knew where my mind had wandered. His chin jutted out, cocky and determined. Unafraid. His fingers absently rubbed his scarred arm. I guessed that whatever monsters were out there, they might not be any worse than the ones he had already faced. No wonder he liked hearing stories about Greyson. Like the first *Patrei*, Kerry didn't let his young age hold him back from what needed to be done.

"We'll see," I answered.

I had an army of two, and one was a seven-year-old child.

CHAPTER EIGHTEEN

KAZI

YEARS AGO, WHEN I STOLE THE TIGER, IT WAS NECESSARY FOR me to employ a different tactic from my other thefts. I needed help and had to procure the favors of many. Of course, I made sure no one ever knew exactly what purpose their favor served—it was important that they weren't implicated—but I knew that many guessed. That was how the whispers began. *It was Ten. Ten stole the tiger.* And then others would scoff at the notion. *That scraggly strip of a girl wrestle a tiger? She'd be nothing but a nibble in the beast's stomach by now. Besides, why would she?* And still others would speculate about more malevolent culprits. *They say a circle of devil's dust was found in the storage shed. A demon ate the beast whole.*

Bribing the tiger was the first order of business. It turned out that getting the tiger's trust was the easiest part. By the fourth afternoon, his nose twitched when he saw me coming with a morsel of meat tucked in a ball of dough. But all the other steps—from decoy wagons, to distracting brawls, to heavy sleep elixirs, to black devil's dust—those steps multiplied one after another. *Trade this for that, and that for this,* and then someone would decide it wasn't enough and they needed more. Sometimes I had to trade with people I despised, smiling and jumping through their endless hoops. I got through it by always remembering the end goal, what it was all for—a chained beast with haunting amber eyes.

I ended up hiding the tiger right beneath the butcher's nose in a storage shed behind his shop that he only went in once a week to sharpen his cleavers and knives. And then I went back and spirited the animal out in the middle of the night once the streets were deserted. A planned distraction drew the butcher's attention away—along with most of the *jehendra*—for no more than half a minute. He had moved only steps away from his shop front, but that was all I needed. It was the escape route I spent the most time working on, finding the darkest, most assuredly deserted streets, the places that gave me somewhere to duck if I had to, finally walking one route seven nights in a row to be sure it held no surprises, something that might startle a tiger and make him roar.

Today my eyes had never stopped scanning the streets, the trees, the shadows, but I only felt my spirits sink lower with every step. There weren't enough bribes or enough favors in the world to evade the soldiers on every street and rooftop. Not to mention I had no favors to offer in the first place and, most important, no one to offer favors *to*. Except, perhaps, the person who had secretly passed me the medicine in my cell, but even they were too afraid to come forward.

As soon as we returned to the inn, my head was tended, and then I was escorted to the private dining room at the inn for the "celebratory" dinner the king had promised. Apparently he agreed with Banques that the delivery of the news had gone well. I guessed that a rock thrown at my head was of little consequence to them, nor the ringing pain between my ears, but maybe other addresses to the crowd had drawn a barrage of rocks. In comparison, my injury was trivial—or maybe the whole point was to shift anger to someone else—me. In that case, I guessed the day was a roaring success. The word *murderer* still ate away at me, and the things I had uttered about Jase remained foul in my mouth, but I'd had no choice. I would do it again, and no doubt, Banques had plans for more of these addresses from me until the last of the resistance was stamped out.

The same positive sentiments about the day were repeated by guests. Apparently none of them thought that corpses hanging from trees in the middle of the town plaza were anything to be bothered about. I didn't recognize any of the attendees at this intimate dinner gathering, and I wondered if they had come from Parsuss—the king's own loyal followers— or if they were Hell's Mouth citizens who turned with the tide as easily as Garvin did.

Everyone seated at the long table fawned over the king and Banques, treating them like true saviors. The four women were elegantly dressed, as if we were attending a grand party, their faces painted with powders in a way I had never seen before, and their necks and wrists adorned with glittering jewels. The room was a thief's paradise—if only rules didn't have to be obeyed.

Each guest laughed and smiled and hung on every word that spilled from Montegue's mouth. Halfway through dinner, one of the women, who had already drunk too much, danced around the table and conveniently fell into his lap. The hair piled atop her head fell loose, and more fawning ensued. *Your Majesty* this, *Your Majesty* that, followed by a slurred feigned apology and a protracted kiss on his lips. He soaked it up like a dry sponge, his lips stuck to hers for a good half minute, his hands roaming over her hips, until Banques finally cleared his throat, reminding them we were all there watching.

Throughout dinner, Montegue had glanced at me numerous times, expecting what, I wasn't sure. To join in the praise? I contemplated it. At some point I knew I had to backtrack and gain his confidence, pretend that I'd been won over and was ready to take "a place" in this new kingdom, as Banques put it. Pretend that I was one of Montegue's admirers. I knew how to do it. This was my specialty. Even the wary were not impervious to flattery—because they deserved it, after all. It was all about making them believe. But the timing had to be right. It was a delicate matter that had to be carried out smoothly, like sliding a razor-sharp knife beneath the thin skin of a fish to separate it from the flesh. And I was not feeling delicate nor smooth right now. Instead I was a miserable jumble of hesitation and second-guessing.

Why was this so different? I remembered trembling with fear the first time I engaged a quarterlord, certain that my intended larceny blazed in my eyes. I'd had to lock my knees to keep them from shaking. The quarterlord was huge and powerful and intimidating, and I was none of those things, only a disgusting six-year-old bug to be crushed and forgotten. But I hadn't let that stop me. Hunger had already honed a sharp edge within me. In spite of my fear and knocking knees, I'd found a way to disarm his suspicions and make off with two juicy figs. I glanced up at Banques and Montegue. *Think of them as quarterlords, Kazi. Play them. Feed their egos. Earn their trust. Throw them crumbs, then hook them behind the gills like openmouthed fish.*

And then cut their throats.

But this game had a different risk. Back then, I only had myself to lose. Maybe that was what had made me bold. Now I was playing for far more than one dirty street urchin's life. I was playing for Lydia's and Nash's freedom—and their lives. I was playing for Jase, and the vows I made to him and, by default, his family. His blood vow was mine. And I had yet another vow—to the queen. Find the papers and destroy them. *You can juggle all that now, can't you, Kazi? Just don't drop an orange. Not a single one, or you're done.*

Laughter erupted around the table. Something Montegue said was apparently quite entertaining, and I had missed it. I was failing miserably. Another glance from him. Expectation shimmered in his eyes. Was I shaming him with my silence? *Grovel, Kazi. Smile. Juggle. Compliment the bastard. Make him believe. You can do it one more time.*

I searched my mind, trying to think of one small thing to add to the conversation, the first seed to plant, but only hatred bubbled up.

Such a creative use of the tembris, Your Majesty. How did you get all those nooses up on those high branches?

Nice work of demolishing the temple.

So convenient that the corpses aren't stinking yet. I guess the cold weather helps. The gods must be with you.

"The stew is quite good," I commented. "My compliments to the chef." The tinkling of crystal and laughter around the table came to a dead stop. They were the first words I had spoken. I made eye contact with Montegue. "And my compliments to His Majesty for choosing such a fine menu." It was pathetic, I knew. It was not my smoothest moment. I had to do better.

The compliment seemed to eat away at his concentration. After a few minutes, he leaned back and set his napkin beside his plate, done with his meal.

When the foolishness around the dining table grew tedious, the king announced we were finished and leaving for the arena. A carriage was brought around because the evening was cold. "We" included Banques. Oleez and the children were called from their rooms to join us. Everywhere he went, they went.

"What do you think of it?" The sweet earthiness of wine was on his breath. His hair was disheveled, and his eyes, glassy.

It was just the two of us in the Ballenger apartment. He had dismissed Banques, Oleez, and the children to go check on some other quarters he had acquired. He sauntered around with a wineglass in one hand and running his other down marble pillars, or peering up at the high ceilings and chandeliers. His boots clicked heel to toe, deliberate on the polished floors like he was tapping out ownership. "Far more elegant and fitting for a king than the inn," he mused. "And more secure too. I'm having the bedchambers refurbished and then we'll move over."

We. I didn't know whom that meant.

When I didn't answer, he paused from his inspection of a drape panel and faced me. "Are you still upset about the children? I promise you, I did ask them, but they continue to refuse to speak to you."

"If you'd just let me—"

"I'll ask again tomorrow. Maybe they'll change their minds, but I'm afraid the Ballengers poisoned them against you. It may take a while. You need to give them the time they need. They're only children."

His concern appeared genuine, and yet he used them as leverage against me? I wondered if the threat to harm them was only a hollow one crafted by Banques to make me comply. "Would you really kill them if I stepped out of line?"

His brows rose with interest. "Do you plan to step out of line?"

"No."

"Then it's a moot point, isn't it?"

"Maybe so, but it's a terrible pressure to live under minute by minute, afraid that I might do something inadvertently that could bring them harm."

He grinned as if amused, letting the brocade drape slip leisurely from his grasp, and turned to face me fully. "Rahtan are quite well trained, I understand, and you don't strike me as the kind of person who does anything *inadvertently.* I'm sure you needn't worry."

"But I do."

"You did threaten to kill me, remember?"

"With a pickle fork."

The grin that had twisted the corner of his mouth now lit his eyes. "One you claimed to be quite skilled with."

"I won't deny that," I answered cheerily, to fuel his amusement.

He took a sip from his glass and shrugged. "My point is made." He walked over to the window and stood beside me, setting his glass down on the deep marble ledge. "I'm sorry about your head today. It was one disturbed heckler. He'll be found."

"And hanged?"

"That will be up to Banques."

"Do you take responsibility for anything? You *are* the king."

He didn't answer, but maybe that was answer enough. He leaned forward on his elbows, looking out at the arena, lit with flickering torches—more of his new domain.

"At the end of the week we'll be going to Tor's Watch," he said. "I want you to speak to the Ballengers. Convince them to come out."

"Speak through the door of the vault? They can't hear anything through that."

"But—"

"I've seen it. The door of the vault is three feet thick and made of solid steel, and it's surrounded by solid rock. Not even a ghost can squeeze through it."

"There has to be a way. How do they get fresh air?"

I didn't know how much he already knew, but I did remember one of the rules, *if you ever lie to the king.* I avoided lies and chose my truths sparingly.

"There's a ventilation system that was created by the Ancients. I wasn't told how it works. I only had a brief tour."

He turned and looked at me, his eyes narrowing. "A tour given by the *Patrei*?" There was resentment in his tone, as if Jase had usurped a personal right of his.

"Yes," I answered.

For such a simple piece of information, he took a long time to absorb it. "What about another way out?" he finally asked. "Is there another door?"

"No, I didn't—" Jase's words tripped through my head unexpectedly. *Every good stronghold has more than one way out. Otherwise you could be trapped.* Why hadn't I thought of this before? Was it possible that Jase's wisdom applied to a vault built by the Ancients? Maybe that was where he had learned it in the first place.

"I never saw another door," I answered. Which was true, but how were they getting food? They'd been trapped in there for over a month. The hole in the roof of the cave Jase called the greenhouse was a hundred feet up. Things like Candok bears and snakes sometimes fell through, but nothing went back out. Were they foraging in there like the first Ballengers did, braving whatever animals had fallen in? And perhaps eating them?

He stepped away from the window, gulping back the last of his wine. An angry line pinched between his brows. "They can't stay in there forever. They'll have to come out eventually."

He shifted awkwardly on his feet, setting his glass down, then turned suddenly, pressing his hands against the wall on either side of me, pinning me between his arms. He looked at me, and I wasn't sure if he wanted to kiss or kill me. His eyes blazed with a fire that I couldn't read. I could almost see a battle going on in his head. *Stand your ground. Blink last, Kazi.* My heart sped, but I returned his stare, waiting him out to see what he would do.

He leaned closer. "I'm still a little confused about you and the *Patrei*," he said. "The last time I saw you at the arena, you punched him in the face, and you didn't hold back. He had blood running from his mouth. That was no mere lovers' quarrel. It looked like you wanted to kill him. And then, it's my understanding that you arrested him in a very violent encounter. But your reaction on learning of his death seemed to indicate that you cared for him? Just what was your real relationship with the *Patrei*?"

Our real relationship? I worked to keep the panic from my face. If he knew the truth about Jase and me, who and what we really were to each other, he would throw me back in a cell and never let me out. My head ached as I tried to block out thoughts of Jase, terrified it would all be plain in my eyes.

Montegue pressed forward so his thighs brushed mine. Heat radiated from his body. "Or maybe you're undecided yourself?"

I tried to recall everything he might have seen, and also what others might have told him—especially Garvin and Paxton. "I bided my time with him out of necessity. It was my only way into Tor's Watch."

His face tilted slightly, pushing closer, his eyes dusky, swallowing me. "So, you were using him?"

"It was my job. I don't regret it."

"A loyal Rahtan. And that's all it was?"

"He was an interesting pastime while I searched out Beaufort."

"But then you valiantly tried to save him, even risking your own life."

Someone had been reporting my every move to him. Since I couldn't tell him why I risked everything to save Jase, I embraced the lie instead, letting it become part of me fully and completely, a vow written in blood. I let rage spark in my eyes.

"I was charged by a very angry queen to return the *Patrei* to his home," I snapped. I brushed his arm aside, freeing myself. I strutted to the sideboard and poured myself the glass of wine I had refused earlier, then whirled to face him. "I was not happy about the journey back here," I said, my tone thick with resentment. "The *Patrei* threw it in my face for every mile we traveled. He seemed to find it endlessly amusing that I had been chastised by my own queen and reminded me that I had over-stepped my boundaries. Often. I was *minutes* from fulfilling my mission and being rid of him for good when we were attacked. Of course I valiantly fought for him! If I failed in my mission—" I looked down, drawing out the effect.

"If you failed, what?" he asked.

Every swallow, every flash of my eyes, was a morsel. Every word and inflection mattered. Spinning. His eyes were transfixed, forgetting the rest of the world. *Take your time, Kazi. He is waiting. Watching. Swimming closer.*

"If I failed, I might as well not return home. I would face severe . . . *consequences.*" I cleared my throat as if the difficult memory were stuck there like a bone. "I had already been on shaky ground with the queen," I continued. "Unfortunately, we'd had several run-ins. She thought I was too . . . independent." I chugged back a gulp of wine. "So yes, of course I was angry, and valiant, and desperate. Not to mention I was stabbed, starved, and jailed. When the *Patrei*'s hand fell from the bag, it was the final confirmation that my career as a soldier, the job I had brutally trained and worked for, for almost half of my life, had been yanked from my grasp. Gone. I would have no position in the Rahtan to return to. The queen had made that clear. So now that you know what was at stake for me, I imagine under similar circumstances you might be angry and fight for all *you* were worth too."

Even he, in his limited knowledge of Venda, knew of the Rahtan and their elite status. He nodded as if he agreed but then added, "Except your queen was wrong. The *Patrei was* guilty. He knew he was hosting a fugitive, and he conspired with him."

"I'm afraid the queen only deals in hard evidence, and I had none. Besides, she had what she really wanted anyway—Beaufort—the man who helped orchestrate her brothers' deaths."

His lips rolled tight over his teeth as if he were weighing whether it all added up. "Yet the *Patrei* still wanted you after your betrayal?"

His eyes were expectant. Garvin had told him something, maybe sharing a conversation he'd had with Jase about me. Maybe Jase had revealed to Garvin that he loved me.

"Yes, he did want me. Very much. I'm afraid my initial charade worked a little too well, or more likely, I was just another challenge for him. The *Patrei*, as you may know, had an ego the size of a mountain and was not one to accept defeat."

He walked over and took my wineglass from my hand and set it on the sideboard behind us. His pupils had grown to onyx moons.

"And how do I compare to the *Patrei*?" he asked, his voice husky.

My stomach jumped to my throat. "What do you mean?"

"Am I smarter? More desirable?" He stepped closer. "If he was only an assigned job for you, then you won't mind if I kiss you. In fact, you'd probably be glad for it. A king is a quite a step up from a *Patrei*, isn't it?"

Kiss him, Kazi. Do it. It's only a dry morsel of bread to draw him closer. Gain his confidence. But something tugged inside me. Was it the memory of Jase's lips on mine? *Do what you have to do, Kazi.* But the tug pulled harder. A familiar whisper. *Listen, Kazi. Hear the language that isn't spoken.* I felt like a quarterlord's eyes were fixed on me from afar, watching, waiting for me to slip something in my pocket, and then pounce. Something was off. The king wasn't swimming toward me, like a lured fish, but around me. *He is the one with the hook in his hand, ready to catch me.*

His face turned and dipped down, his mouth drawing close, but at the last second, I turned my head. His lips brushed my cheek instead, and a small chuckle rippled from his chest. "Well played, soldier," he whispered, still pressing close. "I wouldn't expect you to change your feelings toward me instantly—especially since I cost you your hard-earned job. I respect that even. I'd hate for you to use me the way you used him." His tone was thick with insinuation. He stepped back, leaving me room to breathe again. "And in truth . . . we both know the stew was only mediocre tonight, don't we? Never lie to me again. Not even about stew." His stare pinned me in place. He was far from the clueless, bumbling king I had once thought him to be. But what else was he?

When we got back to the inn, just as we were parting, he asked, "Can Rahtan resign their positions?"

"Yes," I answered uncertainly. "I suppose so."

"Good. Then the problem of your position is solved. You work for me now. You can rest assured, you'll have a far more illustrious career in the Montegue ranks. Your career isn't over, it's only just beginning."

It was announced two days later—after Banques had reiterated the rules to me. He didn't want me getting any "independent" ideas like the ones that had supposedly turned the queen against me. This time when I reached the platform in the plaza, Montegue didn't stand apart from me. While Banques hovered over the children nearby, Montegue reached out and pulled me close to his side, his hand at first lightly pressed to my shoulder, but then it slid to my waist. Was he trying to imply something to the crowd? Or testing me for absolute allegiance?

From the far side of the platform that looked over the plaza, the corpses that still hung from the tembris caught my eye. They watched me. Their heads turned. Their eyes were sharp, waiting expectantly. Was I foe or friend? I blinked, and their gazes were once again dull, dead, but I heard their hearts, the unified thump, hoping for something to happen.

Montegue told the gathered citizens that I would be staying on and lending aid to get the town back on its feet, that my assistance would be invaluable, though he didn't say exactly what I would be doing. I wondered myself. He nudged me to back him up and repeat his words, which I did.

The announcement was met by the crowd with a low rolling murmur that I imagined to be the word *murderer*. I was lower than a scavenger in their eyes, lower than vermin, but Montegue was pleased with their reaction. He imagined it to be a different word. I saw relief in the momentary drop of his shoulders. He interpreted the murmurs as approval, and there were no rocks thrown, no shouts. He stood for a moment, still, gazing out at the crowd. His chin lifted, as if he was soaking the moment in, his chest growing with accomplishment.

"They're forgetting the *Patrei*," he whispered, almost to himself. "Moving forward. Soon they'll only remember me, as it should have been all along." But I sensed it was more than just progress he wanted. That while he hated Jase, some part of him wanted to *be* Jase. Power was only part of it. He wanted to be loved, the way Jase had been loved. The way Jase was still loved.

It is not natural, Greyson says.

It is a trick, Fujiko counters.

We stare at the circle of trees growing from piles of rubble. Even from high on the cliff that looks over the valley we see them change daily.

Magic, I say. *It is some sort of magic.*

—Miandre, 15

CHAPTER NINETEEN

JASE

My stomach quivers oddly. How can I be nervous? But I am. I am a lot of things I never expected to be. I want the moment to be perfect.

"We don't have to do this now. Unless you're ready?"

"I've been ready since the first time I kissed you, Jase Ballenger."

I smile. "I doubt that."

"Almost the first time," she concedes. "But I am ready now. We'll take it slow."

She reaches out and pulls my shirt free from my trousers. I help her lift it over my head.

Her fingertips brush along my chest as if she can feel the feathers of my tattoo.

I swallow, wondering how slow I can take this.

She looks up at me, and I am lost in golden pools.

I remember the words she said to me just minutes ago.

I want to grow old with you, Jase.

Every one of my tomorrows is yours.

I bend forward, my lips meeting hers.

Bound by the earth,

Bound by—

"We're ready for you."

I startled awake. Caemus was staring down at me. "Still needing naps?" he asked.

It was his way of saying I wasn't ready.

"I wasn't sleeping. Just thinking."

He snorted. "Oh. Is that what that was?"

"I'll be right up," I said.

He turned and started back up the cellar steps. Maybe I wasn't one hundred percent yet, and sometimes I was dragging by the afternoon, but if I spent one more day wondering where Kazi was, I would go insane. My dreams wouldn't sustain me. I needed her. I needed to know she was safe.

I pulled off my shirt so it wouldn't accidentally get stained with dye. The settlement had already worked hard enough to pull together clothes for me. I didn't want to ruin a good shirt that had come off someone else's back.

Caemus stopped halfway up the stairs and turned to look at me. "You talk in your sleep," he said. "But I already knew. I figured it out when you were here building the settlement. You two seemed inevitable. That's how it is with some folks."

I kept my eyes fixed on the shirt in my hands. I couldn't talk about this. "I told you, I'll be up in a minute." I snapped the shirt out and began folding it, carefully creasing the sleeves, pulling on the collar, making sure everything was even and perfect. I shook it out and folded it again.

Sometimes you have to remind yourself that you're not powerless. That you have some measure of control. Maybe that's what makes you brave enough to face another day.

"I know what you're going through, boy," Caemus said. "I had a wife once. It wasn't quite the same. I'd had her for a lot of years, and then a water snake bit her. In a matter of hours, she was gone. It didn't matter how hard I held her or how crazy I got with wanting her back. It didn't change a thing. Sometimes people leave us forever and there's no getting them back."

My neck flashed with heat. His words were too similar to something Kazi had once said about her mother. *She's dead, gone, Jase. She's never coming back.* But I still saw it in her eyes, the small sliver of hope she couldn't extinguish. She was afraid to believe, but it was still there, like a saved wish stalk tucked deep in her pocket.

I shook my head, rejecting Caemus's insinuation.

His voice turned more sober than it already was. "No one saw or heard anything about her when we were there, and trust me, a Vendan stands out in Hell's Mouth, especially a Vendan soldier."

"She's alive, Caemus. I know she is. She's a survivor."

His lips rolled over his teeth, like he was chewing on the thought. "All right," he sighed. "If you believe it, I think it must be true. I just want you to remember there's other people who need you. You have to keep your head on straight. Don't go doing something crazy, something that's going to get you killed. That won't get her back."

I nodded. "I don't plan on getting killed."

"No one ever does."

He turned and trudged up the rest of the stairs, and I stared at the folded shirt on my bed, at all the angles that didn't line up. I knew other people needed me too. It gnawed at me every single day. The town, my family. Hundreds of people I had vowed to protect. Blessed gods, did I know. My father had drilled it into me since the day I was born. Duty. But if it took something crazy to save Kazi, that was exactly what I would do.

CHAPTER TWENTY

KAZI

"IT'S NOT FAIR. MAKE HER SHARE IT WITH ME!"

Lydia held a fisted hand over her head while Nash jumped for it and complained loudly to Oleez.

I stood at the rail of Gods Pavilion, near the entrance to the grave-yard, watching them argue. Montegue scheduled a stop here on the way to Tor's Watch to soak his feet. There was a bubbling hot spring that the marble pavilion had been built around, and at the center three descend-ing circular steps surrounded the steaming pink water. It looked like misty clouds at sunset, and besides its reputed curative qualities, breathing the steam was supposed to impart the blessings of the gods. Though Montegue used the word *strength* instead of *blessings*.

I heard him speaking quietly with Paxton and Truko about revenue at the arena and ways to increase it. He wanted more money—and soon. Truko tried to explain that revenue always went down in the winter months as crops were fewer and weather discouraged travel. I wondered at the urgency in Montegue's voice, the way he lowered it and hissed his words through clenched teeth. *Find a way to increase it.* With so much at his disposal, why did he need more—and quickly? Was it only to help the citizens as he claimed? Or was he worried about the seer's prediction of a starving winter?

Banques had instructed me not to speak to Nash and Lydia on the way here—apparently neither of them wanted to be anywhere near me, and I had to ride several paces ahead of them between Paxton and Truko, with a buffer of soldiers just behind us. But when we turned at a switchback, both of the children had their eyes fixed on me.

Nash rode on the same horse in front of Montegue, while Lydia rode with Banques. As young as they were, Nash and Lydia were both competent riders. They used to have their own horses. Now, wedged in saddles with Banques and Montegue, the real reason they didn't ride alone was suddenly obvious. *He is using them for protection.* Revulsion burned inside me.

Even with all the soldiers that surrounded Montegue and Banques, they still feared a loyalist might be hiding high on a bluff or just off the trail. No one would risk shooting one of the Ballenger children with an arrow. An unstated threat was there too. Hurt the king in any way, and what would happen to the children? I wasn't the only one who had to follow rules.

How long before the last loyalist was pummeled into submission and the king didn't need them for protection any longer? And he was using me as part of his plan to make the town comply. Once Lydia and Nash ceased to be an asset, would they become a liability? A threat to his monarchy? Would they only become more Ballengers who might one day rise up and exact their revenge against him?

But then I watched Montegue laugh as he lifted Nash down from his horse. He ruffled his hair and told him to go play with his sister. *They've actually become very fond of me. I give them attention, presents. More than he ever did.*

Fifteen minutes hadn't passed when an argument broke out.

"Give it, Lydia!"

It wasn't like Nash to complain, especially over a common eyestone, nor like Lydia to withhold it. They were always the best of friends. I watched their bickering with interest. Oleez was only mildly trying to settle the squabbling, as if she didn't really care, and Montegue became increasingly irritated with the noise, his brotherly façade cracking.

"I can help you find another," I blurted out. "There's sure to be some over by the wash." The children stopped arguing and stared at me, a fiery gleam lighting their eyes. Banques's head swiveled with a start. I had spoken to them against his orders. "Only with His Majesty's permission of course," I added.

Montegue weighed the thought for a moment, then looked over at Lydia and Nash. I knew that sending them and their squabbling over to the wash and out of his earshot was tempting for him.

"Will that solve your problem?" he asked them.

Nash shrugged unenthusiastically. "I guess."

Lydia frowned. "As long as she doesn't touch us," she said, her face pinched with convincing disgust. My throat throbbed. I knew what I saw in her eyes, *the juggling, the hatred, the show*, the performance expertly spun in every breath and blink. She was someone I recognized—a survivor.

Montegue was eager to get back to his conversation with Paxton and Truko. He nodded to two soldiers assigned to follow the children as they played around the graveyard. "Stay close," Banques instructed them, then shot me a warning glance, a reminder of the rules of the game. I wasn't in the inner circle of trust yet.

But I was getting closer.

The king had pressed near to me again this morning after an announcement. He stared at my lips. The ones Jase had kissed. The lips he believed the *Patrei* had wanted but couldn't truly have. A riddle filled his eyes, and the answer was just out of his reach.

"Did you love him?" he had asked.

For the first time in my life, I was grateful for my years as a starving orphan. Grateful I'd learned to smile and juggle and pretend I didn't care about a sour crabapple within arm's reach as a quarterlord scrutinized every move I made. Grateful for my artful shrugs and indifferent sighs. Grateful that I had learned how to size up a mark and how to patiently feed their fantasy.

Everything inside of me ached with Jase. I would never stop loving him. But my answer to the king was a quick smirk. I threw off his ridiculous question like he was a child asking if the moon was made of cheese, just enough insult to cure him of the notion. And it was a notion he wanted to toss away. The same way he refused to hear *murderer* murmured through the crowd, but heard *long live the king* instead.

We knelt at a dry wash near the creek. Oleez joined us sifting through the piles of pebbles. Lydia and Nash continued to argue, but when the guards became bored and stepped away, Lydia managed to whisper to me, "I'm sorry."

"Me too," Nash said.

"You have nothing to be sorry about," I whispered back. "I'm going to get you out of here and back to your family. I promise. You just have to be patient and keep doing what you're doing."

"They've had no choice," Oleez explained, her voice hushed as her eyes darted to both sides to make sure no one was within earshot. She said she had been in town shopping with the children when the attack came. Their *straza* were overwhelmed by soldiers who descended on the town like mad, swooping bats, sending everyone scattering for their lives. She and the children were captured. They'd been targeted by Hagur, an arena employee who had been tailing them, knowing the attack was coming. In the event of an abduction, the children had always been coached to go along with their captors until help came to free them, to do whatever was necessary to survive. Oleez confessed it was not a plan she ever thought would come to fruition. She reached out and protectively brushed the hair from Lydia's eyes.

"What about Rybart?" I asked. "Was he preying on the town as the king said?"

"Someone was. I don't know if it was Rybart. But it was as bad as it's ever been. Businesses torched. Raids on caravans. The Ballengers were pulled in all directions."

"Is that why Montegue had to send in troops?"

"So he claims, but the troops came as a surprise. Mason had just hired on more crews to patrol. It had been quiet for a few days, which is why I even came to town with the children. Then the troops roared in. Everything started exploding around us. They say the family escaped to the vault. They're blaming everything on them. They—"

"Finish up down there!" No Neck yelled. "The king's putting his boots on!"

Oleez shot a worried glance at No Neck. "Some of these soldiers, like that one, they are not of this world," she whispered. "There is something not right about them." I had wondered about them too.

"Coming!" I called back.

"I hate the king," Nash hissed.

"Someday I will kill him," Lydia concurred.

"No," I said firmly. "I will take care of that in due time. You just keep doing what you're doing. And those things I said about your brother—" My throat swelled, and this time it was Nash who comforted me.

"The king made you say those things about Jase. I know." His voice was tiny and wise, and I had to stab my nails into my palm to keep from choking.

"We knew none of it was true," Lydia added. "Our brother isn't dead. He's the *Patrei*. He's too young to die."

I pulled in a deep breath, trying to keep from crumbling. They were survivors, but still children.

"Where is he?" Nash asked. "When is he coming?"

I looked at Oleez. She had seen the mutilated hand bearing the signet ring too.

"Kazi?" Lydia prodded.

I cleared my throat, forcing the wobble from it. "As soon as he can," I answered. "Jase will come as soon as he can."

———⁂———

The call to depart had come. The weather had turned and snow had begun to fall. Lydia and Nash ran ahead, following on Oleez's heels, multiple shimmering eyestones clutched in their fists.

As I passed the Ballenger family tomb, I paused, staring at the tall scrolled pillars. I stepped closer. *Ghosts . . .* I felt their slumber, the ones who had let go and rested. I felt the gentle beat of their hearts, their peace—but I felt the others too—those ghosts who were a gathered sigh whispering over my head, restless, an ageless breath still anchored to this world, the ones who, for some reason, couldn't let go.

They were shimmers of light, cool fingers brushing my arms, lifting strands of my hair, curious, remembering, hoping—reliving moments, wishing for a second chance—much like the living. *Shhhh.* It was only a breeze whispering through the pines if you didn't know. If you had never looked Death in the eye, you likely couldn't recognize it at all.

The large tomb held numerous crypts, but I knew one of them was marked with the name of an occupant who wasn't even there. It was not her breaths I heard. Instead, she was buried at the base of Breda's Tears, the moon and sun as her companions. I was the only one Jase had ever entrusted with the truth of the empty crypt. He had gone against everything he ever had been taught and the law of the land, to grant the last wish of his sister.

I marveled at the lavish and enormous memorial, the one that had frightened Sylvey so much as she faced death. Carved twelve-foot angels bearing scowls and holding swords larger than a man guarded either side of the entrance, their features daunting and imposing. Their deep-set eyes followed you wherever you moved. A richly sculpted eagle graced the cornice above, its enormous claws gripping a fluted ledge, its glare casting a timeless warning to those who approached. An abundance of chiseled fruit draped in leafy marble garlands wound through the spaces between. The details were intricate, right down to the pebbled skin of lemons. In Venda the dead were buried in unmarked graves, sometimes with a clump of thannis laid on top that quickly tumbled away in the harsh winds.

Either come in or go away.

I stepped back, startled by the faint voice.

There was no going in. The stone door was eight feet high. I remembered that at Karsen's funeral it took two large men to push it shut. How did fifteen-year-old Jase ever do it by himself in the middle of the night? Desperation? Maybe. Desperation could make you incredibly stupid or incredibly strong, or maybe both.

I pressed my cheek against the door, the smooth stone cold against my skin, my eyes stinging. *Jase.* My heart said he wasn't dead. This was not his realm. *He is alive.* But my head told me something different. The clink of his ring on the floor when Banques threw it still made my throat swell. I closed my eyes, trying to will away the pain, banishing thoughts of rings and remembering my vow to Jase instead.

Kazi . . .

My eyes flew open. The sound was close, warming my ear, as if it straddled two worlds. I stepped back from the door, angling my head, trying to hear more.

I didn't know . . . I swear I didn't know. I'm sorry.

The voice drifted away on the wind, *shhhh*.

"On your horse! The king is waiting!"

And with No Neck's order, I left the voices behind and went to face the new ones that were waiting for me at Tor's Watch. How many of them might be dead too?

CHAPTER TWENTY-ONE

JASE

JURGA, ERIDINE, AND HÉLDER HOVERED OVER ME, WATCHING while Caemus brushed another line across my forehead.

"A little more over there," Jurga said, pointing to my temple.

It was a group effort, making sure he closely followed the sketch I had made for him. Kbaaki designs were very specific, and a lot of people in these parts were familiar with them. It had to be believable. It covered half of my face.

"I still think it's too early for you to go," Caemus grumbled as he dabbed more dye on my face.

"I can walk. I can ride. It's time," I answered. And if I could get to it, I had at least one weapon and a bag of ammunition waiting for me. That would get Paxton's attention. And if I could reach that one weapon, I could get more.

"Turn your head," Caemus ordered.

Since I was probably the most recognizable man in Hell's Mouth, it was necessary that my appearance be dramatically changed. The heavy furred cloak, boots, and hat would do a fair job. The thick muffler that would cover the lower half of my face would help more, but if it was removed, I still had to look like someone else. Kbaaki designs were striking. It was hard to even see a face when looking at the swirl that circled an eye.

"That's it," Hélder said, nodding in approval, comparing Caemus's work with my sketch. His wife, Eridine, concurred.

"And now the ring," I said.

Caemus winced.

"You sure?" Eridine asked.

I was going to be crossing hillsides that were probably crawling with the soldiers of this so-called army. Kbaaki almost always wore decorative jewels in their left brows as a defense against hostile spirits. Jurga had a tiny earring that would do the job. It was another detail to convince anyone I might see—and a distraction to keep them from looking too closely at me.

"I'll do it," Jurga volunteered, taking the needle away from Caemus. She didn't give me any warning. She just pinched my brow and jammed the needle through. A rumble rolled through my chest as she fished the earring through behind it. I had already learned there was a lot of iron behind Jurga's meek façade—and now I knew there wasn't an ounce of squeamishness to go with it.

Eridine dabbed at the blood. "That should do it," she said. "I doubt even your own mother would know you now. Just be sure to keep that chest covered."

With the frigid weather, there wasn't much chance of me going shirtless, but her point was made. The tattoo on my chest was a dead Ballenger giveaway. She also instructed me to avoid washing my face or the dye would fade faster. If I was lucky, it would last for two weeks. Hopefully I wouldn't need it that long.

Jurga held up a small mirror. Half of my face swirled with dark black-blue ink, the other half broken by a single swirl around my eye. I barely recognized myself. I practiced my halting Kbaaki accent. "Gets out of my ways, you lowlanders. Gives me rooms to breathe."

Eridine and Hélder chuckled.

"It might work," Caemus conceded.

I was about to try out another line when the door of the shed flew open. Kerry slammed it behind him and leaned over, gasping for breath. "Riders!" he croaked. "Hurry!"

I may have had some of my disguise in place, but finding a Kbaaki hunter in a Vendan settlement would be suspicious, not to mention that my chest, with the Ballenger crest, was exposed. I jumped up from the bench, and Hélder hurried to slide aside the plank that led to the root cellar. Before I could reach it, the door flew open again, crashing back against the wall. I turned and stared at the armed intruders. They looked as shocked to see me as I was to see them.

"You lying devil! What the hell have you done? Where is she?"

Wren flew at me, slamming me up against the wall, her *ziethe* circling my neck. "I told you to watch her back or I'd come after yours!"

"Give him a chance to speak, Wren!" Synové reasoned, then looked at me, her blue eyes blazing. "Talk, you snake, and make it good!"

"I don't know where she is," I said. "We were attacked. I'm going after her, so either kill me or get out of my way."

By now everyone was talking, trying to calm Wren and Synové down. They had come across the ruin in the forest where Mije and Tigone were hidden. They saw the blood staining Mije's saddle and assumed it was Kazi's.

"They were ambushed, girl! Put your weapon down!" Caemus ordered.

Wren's eyes glistened, glaring into mine. Her hand shook with the strain. She finally lowered her *ziethe* and turned away.

Synové burst into tears. "I know where she is. She's chained in a cell."

And then, between sobs, she told us about her dream.

Hold on to to each other because that is what will save you.

    Out of many you are one now. You are family.

I look at our put-together family.

None want to be here any more than I do.

We are all different. We argue. We wave our fists.

But we hold each other too.

We grow together, strong like the circle of trees in the valley.

—Greyson, 16

CHAPTER TWENTY-TWO

KAZI

Tor's Watch hadn't been my home. Not yet. Not truly.
When I had been here before, I had only been an interloper, an imposter
wheedling my way past defenses. I'd been a soldier with an agenda, hiding
beneath a false premise. I only saw a fortress that overflowed with
secrets, and viewed every room as a potential hiding place. But still,
even then, though I tried hard not to, I had seen the beauty of it, that it
was a living testament to the devotion that had made the Ballengers
who they were. It was like a perfectly cut jewel, and I had wondered in
reckless moments what it would be like to be a part of it, sometimes settling into a chair in the empty dining room when I was sure no one was
looking, imagining that it was always saved for me, the chair next to
Jase.

When I had crept down hallways, my hands sweeping the walls, I
had felt the centuries in every block of stone and wondered which generation had cut it and set it into place. I had seen the hard-won history
that was recorded on Jase's bookshelves. On the vault walls I saw the

scrawling desperation of the original patchwork family, children who were sewn together by dire circumstance and somehow made it work, children who had, against all odds, survived. I felt an unexpected kinship with them.

This was the home and history that Jase had loved and made a vow to protect. This was what made the destruction before me all the more devastating. A dizzy wave of nausea struck me when I saw the fallen spires in the glaring bright of day. The hideous gaping hole that—

There's a room on the third floor. It has a view that reaches to the horizon— and it's away from everyone else. I think it should be ours. You can decide.

The room that would have been ours.

It was gone now.

I pushed the thought away and buried it deeply, for fear the weight of it would snap me in two like a piece of tinder. I buried it with all the other things that would never be ours.

A jagged line of stone scarred the center of the main house. Spires on either side remained untouched. Inside the front gates, all of Tor's Watch was transformed. The arbor that had once been heavy with flowers was barren with winter, and armed soldiers were the ones beating a path through it now. The king ordered Paxton to take Oleez and the children to Raehouse while he took me to the vault. I shot Paxton a condemning stare—Lydia and Nash were his kin—but it was an empty warning. He knew the rules I had to abide by. His gaze met mine, unmoved, his expression hard, his thoughts probably set on his lucrative rewards. He jumped at the king's orders like a boneless bootlicker. A hot coal smoldered in me, and it took every bit of my strength not to fan it. I had to gain the king's confidence, to make him believe his words and logic were winning me over. And gaining the king's confidence meant not digging out Paxton's eyes with my bare hands. I tossed a smile at him as he left. I guessed it worried him more than my glare.

I was grateful when we descended into the tunnel. It was the most unchanged. Here there was no summer or winter, no broken stone blocks tumbled in my path, only torch-lit darkness and the musty scent of despair, and that was a scent I was used to.

The armed entourage marched ahead of us toward the vault, their heavy boots echoing through the stone cavern. I wondered what had happened to the poisonous dogs that were kept at the far end of the tunnel. Killed by the king's men? Or perhaps the family had taken them into the vault? That thought lifted me. I would love to see them loosed on my current companions, even if I was bitten in the attack.

Why Montegue thought my voice would make a difference I wasn't sure. Did he think that the word of a powerful distant kingdom could penetrate impossibly thick steel? Or maybe he was simply grasping at anything. Desperation can make the most calculating logic flee. Impatience burned in his expression and steps.

After I'd spent ten minutes calling to every possible Ballenger, my pleas only met with the persistent silence I had expected, Montegue screamed, pounding on the massive door, sweat beading on his forehead. His fury caught me by surprise. He turned away, combing the hair from his eyes, his face a knot of rage.

I looked at the expressions of the stoic guards holding long, sharp halberds in case the Ballengers emerged. They showed no surprise, and I wondered how many times this scene had already been played out. How many times had he pounded on the door and how many threats had he already hurled? If they were trapped, why did he care so much? They weren't going anywhere. He could starve them out.

"I am the King of Eislandia," he growled, almost to himself. "They're going to regret this." He stomped away, ordering me and the whole entourage to follow.

By the time we reached the T of the tunnel and turned down the next one, his heaving breaths had slowed and he had regained his composure.

"We need those documents," he said calmly.

"You mean the plans for the weapons? I already told you, I destroyed them."

"There are others. Different documents. Ones that were in the scholars' quarters. They're missing."

My scalp prickled. The papers in the scholars' quarters? Was he talking about the ones Phineas had told me to destroy? How would he even know about those, especially if they had disappeared? How could he—

A cold weight settled in my stomach. I quickly composed a few words, trying to keep them casual. "There are papers and ledgers all over Tor's Watch. How would you know if a few were missing?"

"A servant told me."

I looked sideways at him, my pulse speeding. "Oleez?" I asked, forcing my voice to remain even. My head pounded like drums at the gallows as I contemplated even the smallest lie. "I think she was the one who was responsible for cleaning their quarters."

"Yes, Oleez told me they were missing. She noticed as she was straightening up one of the studies."

Oleez was in charge of the main house—it consumed her days. She never went to Cave's End, much less to straighten papers, of that much I was certain, and then I thought about another piece of paper—the one I had stolen at the arena from the king's vest pocket. I chewed on my lip, then took a chance and cast my net a little wider. "What makes you think the papers are important? Did . . . Devereux say something?"

His steps slowed and his brows rose in a question. "You're on a first-name basis with General Banques now? He must have taken a liking to you, after all. Count yourself lucky."

I molded my face into indifference, but my mind reeled. *Devereux was Banques?* I was fishing, but I hadn't expected this, not to find my game so far up the chain of command.

Zane had said it was Devereux who gave him money to hire labor hunters. Devereux *Banques.* The so-called general was doing the dirty work of stirring up trouble? He was sneaking around back alleys, preying on the citizens of Hell's Mouth and the Ballenger family *months ago.* Before he was a mighty general, he was just a lowly back-alley thug with a satchel full of cash.

And he worked for the king.

Images flashed behind my eyes, doubts and pieces falling into place—using labor hunters and fires to create unrest and keep the Ballengers scrambling, choosing a settlement site that would antagonize the family, attacking settlers in the dark of night to implicate the Ballengers and bring down the wrath of the Alliance, the assault by Fertig and a well-trained gang that sounded alarmingly similar to these hired mercenaries, and finally, Beaufort looking back over his shoulder expecting someone to come to his rescue. He was waiting for the king—the sly king who feigned innocence at every step, the king who wanted respect and wouldn't incriminate himself by rescuing a criminal. The king who was a more cunning liar than Beaufort and Banques put together. The cold weight in my stomach turned to ice in my veins.

We had caught the wrong dragon.

Montegue stopped walking and looked down at me. His eyes were clear. Knowing.

It was too late to backtrack, to pretend that I hadn't figured it out. That would be a lie, and he would know.

"Leave," he ordered the guards. He watched them scuttle away, leaving us alone, then turned back to me. His perusal was suffocating.

"It was you all along," I said. "It was you conspiring with Beaufort. Not the leagues. No one knew about those papers in Phineas's room.

Not even Beaufort. He thought everything was destroyed by the fire I set."

A flame lit Montegue's eyes. He was proud of this information.

"But Phineas had a little secret," I said. "A side deal he shared with you—copies of the plans."

"No . . . not copies," he answered slowly, his tone cryptic. "And far more than a side deal." He leaned against the tunnel wall, staring at me, his head angled to the side like he was trying to see inside mine. "Beaufort had offered the continent to me . . . while Phineas offered me *the universe*." He pushed off from the wall and walked toward me, everything about him changing—his shoulders wider, his eyes liquid black, sucking me into their darkness. "You see, the poor man was burdened by being the youngest and lowest ranking of the group—pushed around by the others—but he was also, by far, the most brilliant. A creative mind like his comes along only once every few generations. I recognized that and knew he was eager for a chance to prove himself. I gave him that chance."

I stepped back as he approached, but my shoulders met the tunnel wall. "All of this, everything you've done, none of it was ever about restoring order," I said. "Just the opposite. You were the architect behind it all."

He stopped in front of me. Too close. "How does that make you feel?" he asked. "Does it impress you?" The light of an overhead torch flickered across his features, and his thick lashes cut a shadow under his eyes.

Horrified? Sick? But the answer had to be one he wanted to hear. "I can't help but be impressed, but mostly it makes me feel stupid that I didn't see it before."

It was the right answer. He smiled. "If it were obvious, I wouldn't be much of an architect, would I?"

Priya's office was now the king's. It seemed he had laid claim to some prime space in every place the Ballengers had previously owned. He was like a wolf marking territory—the inn in town, the apartments at the arena, and here at Tor's Watch, the very serene and ordered office of Priya, the heart of the numerous Ballenger businesses.

He told me more about the side deal he had struck with Phineas—the one that offered him "the universe." Phineas had had a theory, but he didn't want to share it with the others. If it played out, his agreement with the king was that he would no longer be under the thumb of Torback or the others. He would have the freedom to pursue his own studies. "He had an intense curiosity about everything and felt stifled by them. His mind never rested. I promised him that freedom."

"Except that Beaufort murdered him to keep him from talking."

He shrugged. "Phineas's mind was strong, but his courage weak."

I didn't tell him that as Phineas lay dying, he pleaded with me to destroy his papers. "Before Phineas died, he said the tembris told them. What did he mean?"

His eyes brightened. "Haven't you ever wondered about the tembris? Trees that reach to the heavens, taller than any others on the continent? Phineas wondered. I did too, from the first time I saw them. They're unnatural. Not of this earth. They look like something fashioned for the gods. And the way they grow in that neat circular fashion, almost as if something had marked where they should grow. Perhaps where a fiery star had exploded into the earth?"

He went to the window that looked out on the Ballenger gardens. "And what about the racaa? Did you know they're identical to sparrow hawks except for their size?" He turned to face me. "Phineas knew that. And then there's the matter of the eight-foot giants who roam the continent. Men and women twice the girth and two heads taller than everyone else. But it's not just about size. It's about passion too. We've all heard stories about the devastation, the raging of seas that refused to calm, the shaking of the ground that swallowed cities whole, the fury of the mountains that bellowed smoke all the way to the sun. Passion that reached all the way into the belly of the earth."

He reached into his vest and pulled out a tiny vial. He removed the stopper and tapped a small amount of its brightly glittering contents into his palm, then blew on it as he swept his hand through the air in a circular motion. Instead of the sparkling dust falling to the ground, something else happened. The crystals swirled, and his small puff of air became more—a strong wind that whirled about the room. Papers ruffled and fell to the floor. Wisps of my hair lifted from my shoulders, fingers of warm air circled my arms, then swept across my lips, suddenly hot and stinging. Montegue held his palm out, and the crystals returned and condensed just above it, following the circular movement of his hand. The wind ceased and the crystals sprinkled back into his palm in a tiny pile as if he had spoken a command to them. He carefully tipped his palm and returned the crystals to the vial.

I felt like a child watching a clever sideshow, trying to find the hidden strings. What had just happened? This was not simple sleight of hand.

"What is that?" I asked.

He smiled and looked at a shimmering fleck of crystal still in his palm, then licked his fingertip and dabbed the tiny grain to pick it up. He stared at it, mesmerized. "The magic of the stars," he answered. "*Desire.* An element thrown to earth by the gods themselves that can reach into everything that exists and understand its need—what drives it. It imprints on whatever it touches. Grow, eat, burn, hunt, explode, conquer. Its entire purpose is to make things more than what they were, like a fish buried in a cornfield to make plants grow taller and stronger. What farmer doesn't want that? The magic of the stars can make anything bigger, better, and more powerful."

"That's what's in the munitions?"

He nodded. "That's what opened the door. The star element is released with heat and fire. You can see what it does to just a small amount of the black powder. But Phineas managed to distill the element to its purest, most powerful form—making it possible to unleash the magic of the stars for *everything*. Everything and everyone is driven by something. This drives it more. Imagine the possibilities. Creating unstoppable armies, controlling wind, rain, fire, crops, the *seasons*. Maybe even day and night. The possibilities are limitless."

Fire. I recalled a strangely scorched hillside on our way here. The edge of the forest was burned in an unusually straight line, as if it had been controlled.

"We already experimented on a few soldiers. The results were astonishing. If only we had more."

My mind immediately sprang to Fertig's iron grip, and his soulless eyes that had terrified me as he tried to choke me to death. He was driven by a crazed desire. Was he one of the "astonishing" soldiers? Sickly dread slithered through me like some dark poisonous creature. *No Neck, Divot Head, Scar Eye.* Their hands were like Fertig's—and their eyes—as if something had crawled inside of them that wasn't quite human—or maybe it had just made the inhuman part of them greater.

"This," Montegue said, patting his vest where he had returned the vial to an inner pocket, "is all I have left. So you can see why those papers are so important. I *will* have them."

At any cost. He didn't need to say the words. They were clear in his tone.

Phineas offered me the universe. Was Montegue mad? Did he really believe he could control the universe?

He walked over to me, the stray grain of stardust shining on his finger-tip like a tiny, perfect diamond. He held it close to my lips, studying me, and I feared he might try to put it in my mouth.

"Do you want to see what it's like?" he whispered.

I didn't respond, but he smiled as if he could hear the wild rush of blood pounding through me.

"No," he said, retracting his offer. "Every grain is precious, and I don't know what your true desire is. Yet."

True desire? What was he talking about?

And then he licked the grain of dust from his fingertip.

I wasn't exactly sure what happened next, but the light in the room seemed to change as if it all came from him. The hunger in his eyes ignited like a wildfire, and in one step, he had pinned me against the wall. His hand slipped around my waist, and his face pressed close to mine. "I wanted to kill you," he whispered against my cheek.

His breaths were heavy, instantly hot, like a furnace had raged inside of him all along just waiting to be let loose. *Kill me or kiss me?* Now I knew. *Kill.*

"The minute you were captured, I wanted to kill you, more than I had wanted to kill any Ballenger." He lifted my chin so I had to look in his eyes. A frightening brilliance gleamed in them. "You have no idea the problems your meddling caused me. I risked everything for this moment. I have years invested and everything I own—and in one thoughtless act, you burned up everything I've worked for."

His arm tightened around me, pulling me closer. A quick jerk could snap my back. Heat radiated from his skin.

"Not everything," I reminded him. "The missing papers are some-where. And you want me to find them."

His grip eased, the fire retreating. "Yes," he said slowly. "The papers." His true desire. He released me and stepped away. "Banques convinced me you might be useful. And I am a forgiving and fair man. You know that, right?"

I nodded, feeling like I was trying to outrun an angry bear and with every step it was gaining ground.

He smiled. "Good." He reached out and ran a knuckle along my jaw. "Besides, you were only an underling following orders. And now you follow mine."

Garvin had told him I'd once been a thief. A good one. Which probably explained why the queen had sent me to retrieve Beaufort. Montegue said they had combed the entire estate, including several floors of archives in Raehouse, still certain the documents had to be somewhere. The attack on Tor's Watch had been a surprise—no more than a moment's notice as tarps were thrown free from wagons at the front gates and weapons were fired. But it was their first time shooting the oversized launchers, and their aim was off. Instead of taking down the wall, it took down the center tower of the main house. Screaming could be heard from within. Ballengers and employees alike were running for their lives.

I tried to block the thought, to feel nothing as he described it to me, but screams I hadn't even heard carved holes through me. I imagined the panic. Vairlyn shouting orders, trying to rush everyone to safety. Searching for her children. *Samuel.* Was that how he died?

"Are you listening to me?" Montegue asked sharply.

"Of course," I answered, shoving the growing fear far away. Montegue wasn't an inexperienced monarch being led along by a power-hungry general. He was a cold-blooded plotter—*the architect.* He didn't stumble upon an opportunity—he created it. How long had he been planning this? It made me think of the Komizar, who had built his army for years to create an unstoppable force. He'd also had an insatiable desire for more. Just how much more did this king want?

Montegue went on, telling me it wasn't likely that the Ballengers had time to gather anything before they fled, much less a thick stack of parchments, and yet the coveted documents appeared to have vanished.

I wrinkled my brow, trying to appear appropriately perplexed. I worked for him now, and I wasn't as far in the inner circle as I thought. In fact I was still scrambling on the edge, trying to keep one foot in.

"Find them," he said. It wasn't a request. It was an order from king to thief. What if I did find them? What would I do?

Destroy them. I heard the urgency in Phineas's last words again. The fear. The regret. Great gods, what had he done? *The magic of the stars.* What did that even mean?

Imagine the possibilities.

I was sure the king and Banques already had.

I spent the next two hours searching every corner of Cave's End, running my fingers along bookcases and desks, looking for hidden doors and secret nooks. I managed to find a few panels that led to hidden empty spaces. That was all. Divot Head served as my escort, and his dull lifeless eyes watched every move I made. It was obvious that all the rooms had already been searched. Bedding in the chambers was stripped and strewn. Wardrobe doors left open and emptied of contents—most of it littering the floors. The king's logic was sound. I knew if the family was racing to get people into the vault, there was no time to gather food, much less Phineas's papers. Gunner probably didn't even know for sure that they were of any value. The king had said Phineas wrote them in the language of the Ancients from which he had procured most of his knowledge of the elements, and it was a language only known to a few. He had promised to transcribe them and send them to the king soon, but then I had intervened.

We came to one room that was neat and orderly. "The lieutenant's quarters," Divot Head explained. "He has duties here and at the arena."

"Do I search?"

Divot Head shrugged. "Already searched."

I did a cursory search anyway. The only unusual thing I found was a woman's chemise under the bed. Apparently this lieutenant had done some entertaining here. Other than that, the room was sparse. Whoever this lieutenant was, he wasn't settling in for a long stay. I couldn't blame him. The overwhelming gloom of abandonment hung in the air like a heavy cloud ready to burst with despair. Who could live among this desolation for any length of time?

We finally returned to Raehouse empty-handed. By then the king was gone, along with the children, to the arena. Banques stood over a table with Paxton and Truko, studying maps and ledgers and discussing goods that would bring the arena more profit. Why did they need money so badly? They controlled everything now. What else could they want?

When Banques's tone turned sharp, I noticed Truko's fist curl behind his back. He was used to being the one giving orders, not taking them. We were all learning new tricks. *Jump? Certainly. How high, Your Majesty?*

"Nothing to report from the search," Divot Head announced succinctly, then left.

They all turned away from the table to look at me, and Banques sighed. "I hope I didn't make a terrible mistake convincing the king you might be of some worth."

Terrible mistake. The words. His voice. It whittled through my bones. *Devereux Banques.*

"Who are you?" I asked. "Who are you really?"

He smiled, reached for a map, and began rolling it up. "I knew it was only a matter of time before you made the connection. But now that you're on our side, it doesn't really matter anymore. You're not that much different than me, I suppose, switching sides."

Goose bumps rose on my arms. "Who are you?" I repeated.

He slipped the map into a leather cylinder and set it with a stack of others. "I'm afraid that, thanks to my treasonous older brother, I had to abandon one of my names six years ago. After he sullied it, all that name did was close doors for me." He grabbed another map and began rolling it. "I was once a rising star in the Morrighan military. Did you know?"

"No," I answered quietly.

"I was headed for great things and a distinguished career, but that ended when my brother betrayed the king. No one trusted me after that. I was a pariah, and my future was destroyed. I was practically run out of Morrighan. Luckily, the new young King of Eislandia took me on as his kingdom magistrate."

I stared at him as he spoke, his image transforming. I saw him with more weight, more height, more years. Lines around his eyes. I saw his coal-black hair lighten to white. But the voice was the same. *Brother.*

"Devereux Banques Illarion," he confessed. "But I actually prefer the name Banques. My mother's ancestral line was much stronger. Regardless, it all worked out in the end. Now I'm leading a far more powerful army than I ever would have commanded in Morrighan. Wait until they see who I've become." He smiled, the thought warming him as if he had already imagined the revelation many times.

He told me that his brother had come to him two years ago, still on the run and in search of refuge and funds—along with an interesting proposition. Unfortunately, the king had no funds to offer—but he knew who did—the Ballengers—and the timing was perfect. It couldn't have worked out better. With a well-rehearsed story, it didn't take long to get

Beaufort and his crew entrenched in the Ballengers' good graces. A slate of well-timed attacks on trading caravans also helped motivate the Ballengers into action so they wouldn't drag their feet.

I remembered how he had choked me the first time we met. *So you're the one who—*

Now I know what his unfinished thought was—*the one who captured my brother and hauled him off for execution.* "And how do you feel about me arresting your brother and turning him over to the queen?"

He laughed. "That part actually amused me."

"You never had plans to rescue him?"

"Oh, we will eventually."

"He could have been executed already."

He shook his head, a confident smirk pulling at the corners of his mouth that was so like Beaufort's it was chilling. "No. My brother's as slippery as they come—and with an unmatched golden tongue. He'll tell the queen something that will stay her hand. A little sweating will do him good. After he's squirmed for a bit and paid his penance for robbing a young captain of his career, his brother might just bail him out."

"You aren't afraid he'll expose you and the king?"

"He won't, not if he wants his stake in this."

"And what would that be?"

Banques smiled. "In good time, soldier. In good time." He turned to Paxton. "Take her to search the main house. With all the rubble, we could have missed something."

My chest was hollow as we headed to the main house. I was a fish that had been lured and hooked over and over again. *The magistrate of Eislandia was Beaufort's brother.* No wonder when Jase's father inquired about Beaufort's past, the magistrate said he had no information on him. He didn't want Karsen Ballenger to turn him away.

The deceptions deepened at every turn. I wasn't even sure *whom* I was dealing with anymore. Even the most cunning quarterlord, at day's end, was still only a quarterlord with the singular goal of chugging an ale and adding a few coins to his purse. Their secrets were few, and those few I uncovered easily. I understood them and what the consequences of defying them were. But here . . .

This was not my world.

I brushed a damp strand of hair from my forehead. Nothing and no one was who they seemed to be. Even the crafty Beaufort hadn't foreseen that he might suffer at his own brother's bitter hand.

I didn't think I could be thrown any more off-kilter or kicked any lower—but then we reached the main house. I wasn't sure what I had expected. Destruction? Tumbled walls?

But whatever I had imagined, it hadn't prepared me. Paxton and I didn't speak as he escorted me in through an opening in a wall created by the blast. I heard the lonely trickle of water as we stepped into a hallway near the front foyer, but other than that, the house was unnaturally silent. Open books fluttered in the wind. The sky shone above us through a vicious gash in the roof. Water dripped from it like tears, soaking whatever lay below. The distinctive flowered washbasin from Priya's third-floor chamber lay shattered in several pieces on the first-floor landing. The staircase was mostly intact except for a few crushed rails, and a tapestry still hung from a wall, untouched, while just across from it the enormous tower spindle from the roof lay atop a heap of stone, like the severed horn of a fallen beast.

I walked up the stairs, Paxton lagging somewhere far behind me. Every new broken thing carved away another piece of me, all the pieces in me that had come to care about Tor's Watch as much as Jase did. But I wasn't supposed to care. I couldn't let Paxton know that every new piece of carnage gutted me. I stopped and stared at a white shirt hanging from a splintered rafter. The tattered fabric waved quietly in the breeze like a Ballenger flag of surrender.

At the second-floor landing, a pile of rubble was tangled with what might have once been a bed. Whose bed? Vairlyn's? Gunner's? Feathers swirled down the hallway like ghostly birds, sprung loose from quilts and pillows. And then I came across a lone shoe—the slipper I had borrowed from Jalaine. I stared at it. The emptiness closed in. It pressed on my chest as if I lay beneath the tons of rubble. A house that had been full of family was broken, scattered, destroyed. I reached for a wall, using it to steady myself. One misdirected blast had done all this.

I continued toward Jase's room. That wing was still intact, though the force of the blast had sent rubble and splintered wood flying down hallways. I pushed open his chamber door, and a different kind of destruction greeted me. Bedding was knifed, drapes torn away, bookcases overturned. This wasn't caused by a blast but by an invader. Every book that Jase had spent a lifetime transcribing had been stomped beneath careless feet.

Jase had been so full of expectation and plans. And now this—

I stared at the utter chaos of the room, spinning his too-large signet ring on my thumb. I had made a promise to him. It all seemed like folly now. Was my hubris greater than the king's? What if I couldn't keep my vow? *What if I couldn't even save Lydia and Nash?* Panic rose in me. I gasped for breath, then turned and fled the room. I ran down the hallway, then up the stairs, heading for the solarium, where I had last seen Jalaine— somewhere she had escaped to that was far from everything else, a place where she could shut out the world.

Paxton called after me, ordering me to stop. I heard his footsteps pounding after mine. He was right on my heels as I burst through the double doors of the solarium, but in an instant my panic flared to blind rage, and I leapt upon him, slamming him against the wall. In the same motion, I whisked the stolen scalpel from my boot and pressed it to the tender skin of his neck where a vein pulsed wildly.

"Put it down now," he ordered, but his eyes were sharp with fear. He licked his lips. "You won't kill me. You can't. Think about the children. You know the rules."

"*The rules?*" I yelled, unafraid of anyone hearing me from the rooftop room. "*The rules?*" The scalpel trembled in my hand.

"He'll do it. One nick on me, and he'll kill them. You don't know what he's capable of."

"Shut up!" I screamed. "Shut up, you miserable piece of horseshit! All that matters is what *I'm* capable of!" The scalpel shook in my hand. Tears streamed down my cheeks. I had never felt so out of control. The room pulsed with white-hot light. I hated that he was right. The cost of killing him was too great, and I knew I couldn't do it. But the hunger to kill him was still crushing me, and I pressed the scalpel a little harder. A bright red line of blood glistened on his neck. "He was your kin," I sobbed, "and you hunted him down like an animal!"

Paxton leaned his head back against the wall, trying to pull away from the blade. His fear only made me want to kill him more, and the burning hunger inside me surged brighter. I watched tiny droplets of blood spring up along the line I had cut, wetting the blade.

"He's alive, Kazi," he whispered. "Jase is alive."

My loathing for him sprang into something wild and feral. "You lying coward. You'd say anything to save your worthless skin."

"Please." He swallowed carefully. "I was going to tell you when I was sure it was safe. When I was sure I could really trust you. It's true. I swear. He *was* alive, at least. He was hanging on by a thread when I took him to Caemus at the settlement. They're hiding him in the root cellar. He and Jurga were cutting out the arrows when I left."

Caemus? *Paxton knows Caemus? And Jurga? He knows about the root cellar?* I stared at him in disbelief. It was impossible. How could he know these things? I eased back with the scalpel. "What about Jase's hand? The ring?"

"I took the ring from his finger before I left him with Caemus. I had to produce a body—or part of one, one way or another, or they never would've stopped hunting for him. It was the hand of a soldier that I killed. Not Jase's."

My head swam.

I couldn't think.

Alive? Jase was alive?

And Paxton had saved him? I lowered the scalpel. It made no sense. I searched Paxton's face, thinking it was another cruel trick, but his eyes remained steady, looking back into mine.

Truth.

Truth.

I doubled over, unable to breathe, like I was still pinned to the bottom of the deepest darkest sea, but I could see light shining on its surface and I was trying to reach it. My knees buckled, and Paxton grabbed me as I fell to the ground. Rasping noises jumped from my chest, and I shook as I tried to inhale.

Paxton knelt and held me. The room rocked. He brushed the hair from my face with his fingers. "Breathe, Kazi, take your time. I know it's hard. Breathe."

I coughed. I choked. A hoarse breath finally filled my lungs.

He tilted my chin upward, alarm in his eyes. "When I saw you fighting to save his life, I thought—" He winced. "But I wasn't sure. You really do care for him."

I didn't answer. He had already read it in my face.

"I'm sorry I couldn't tell you sooner," he said, and then added more warily, "But I have to warn you, he was badly injured—very badly. And he only had Caemus and Jurga for healers. You need to know, he could be dead by now." He eased his grip on me. "I haven't been able to go back. It's too dangerous. I might lead someone straight to him. I don't know if—"

"He's alive," I gasped. "If anyone can hang on by a thread, it's Jase. Caemus and Jurga, they'll make sure—" A storm of emotion gripped my throat again, forcing me to slow and take several deep breaths, and then I squared my shoulders, trying to trick my body and mind into some measure of control. "Did Jase say anything when you left him?"

"He wasn't conscious. He was barely breathing." He grimaced. "There were five arrows, Kazi. One was in his chest. It didn't sound good."

"But he was alive?" I said, needing him to confirm it again.

He nodded uncertainly and answered, "When I left him."

Paxton was tender, sympathetic, saying he was sorry again for not telling me, but his primary concern had been Jase and the children, and he wasn't certain if he could trust me. He hadn't been able to trust anyone in a long while, and even though he saw me fighting to save Jase, I had, after all, whisked the *Patrei* away against his will. My actions had left him confused. He pulled a kerchief from his pocket and handed it to me. If I hadn't been sobbing, I would have laughed. It was so like Paxton to have a neat folded kerchief. I took it from him, wiping my nose and eyes, but then sense flooded back in and I shoved him away.

"But you're working for them. *Why?*"

His neck lengthened like an arrogant rooster. "I'm not. Not any more than you are."

"You're running the arena. How can I believe anything you—"

"Who do you think got the medicine to you when you were locked up? And the extra food?"

My next accusation vanished. That was *him*? I remembered the fear I sensed on the other side of my cell door when the medicine was dropped. I looked at him again—really looked. I wasn't the only one who had lost weight. His cheekbones were sharper, and unkempt edges had appeared in the previously polished Paxton. He had a stubble of beard, as if he had ceased to care about fresh shaves and impeccable grooming. The signs of desperation were all over him, but I still couldn't shake my misgivings about him. Paxton had harbored only animosity toward the Ballengers and Jase in particular.

"Why?" I asked simply. "What game are you playing?"

"If I'm not on the inside playing the traitorous Ballenger who has a history of selling out his kin, I'm on the outside, and that means I'm dead like those you saw hanging from the tembris—and so are a lot of other people. I wouldn't be of use to anyone, including you. I don't have the luxury of being a self-righteous loyalist. I'll play the traitor as long as I have to. I'm guessing I'm playing the same game as you are."

"I mean, *why*? I know why I care. Why do *you* care?"

His brows pinched with annoyance, and in that moment, he reminded me of Jase, that same Ballenger impatience sweeping across his face. My stomach twisted in half.

"A thousand reasons," he answered. "Is it really so hard to figure out? I know Jase and I have had our outs over the years—our grains run in different directions—but I'm a Ballenger too, just as much as any of them. He and his family can't steal that from me. All that history? That's *my* history too. I have a stake in this. Most important, some of the family I may not care a horse's ass for, but Lydia and

Nash, they're only children. They shouldn't be used as pawns or as shields."

A noble cause for the unscrupulous Paxton? But if protection ran hot in the Ballenger blood, maybe it ran in his too.

Then he told me everything—at least everything he knew. And it only got worse.

*They thought themselves
only a step lower than the Gods,
proud in their power over heaven and earth.
They grew strong in their knowledge
but weak in their wisdom,
craving more and still more power,
crushing the defenseless.*

—Morrighan Book of Holy Text, Vol. IV

CHAPTER TWENTY-THREE

JASE

WE HAD TO APPROACH FROM A NORTHERN ROUTE IN CASE WE encountered anyone. The extra time it ate up crawled under my skin like vermin. I felt like a miserable summer dog covered with fleas, but keeping our disguises believable required that everything add up. Kbaaki would never approach from the south. Coming at this time of year at all was suspect, but we already had an excuse in place for that.

We created our own trails through the Moro mountains, passing through a forest where, in the past, we were more likely to run into one of the mythical beasts of Ballenger lore than another human. But this wasn't the past. Wren and Synové hadn't known any more than Caemus, but they confirmed his observation—an army had moved in, and they swarmed everywhere—searching for Ballengers, no doubt. The peace and certainty of an empty forest were gone. I was on alert, listening for every sound.

"What makes you think we'll find any of your family outside of that hole in your mountain? Caemus said no one's seen them, and word is they're all trapped in there."

Wren, unfortunately, was no longer broodingly silent. She and Synové had wanted to ride into Hell's Mouth demanding answers as representatives of the queen. I told her all we'd end up with was two more prisoners to worry about. If Paxton had run the Ballengers underground, had commandeered the town and arena, and had taken Kazi as a prisoner, he wouldn't hesitate to do the same to them. But as Kbaaki traders, we'd get some answers at the arena, and then more information from my family. Once we knew exactly what and whom we were dealing with, we'd make our moves. Still, Wren had poked and prodded me ever since we left, trying to unravel my plan. I stopped Mije. The itching, the worry, the fear was finally getting the best of me.

"What do you want me to do? *Nothing?*" I shouted. I heard the strain in my voice, the lack of control, and I hated it.

"Whoa, slow down, boy," Synové ordered. "We're on the same side, remember?"

I swallowed. Same side. Sometimes it didn't feel like it.

Wren raised an unaffected brow. "This is what I do, *Patrei*. I work out the kinks in plans, and yours has them all over the place."

"There's something he's not telling us," Synové said. "I can see it in his eyes."

The only kink I had was the one in my neck from Synové always trying to interpret what I was thinking, and from Wren, who kept asking questions I had no answers for.

"There's nothing in my eyes but trail dust."

"Give it up, *Patrei*," Wren demanded. "Come clean with us."

"You just have to trust me," I answered. There were some things we didn't share outside of the family—ever.

Wren rolled her eyes. "Trust you?"

But she knew she had to. I knew this mountain. I knew trails she could never find. I knew my family. And most of all, I knew where one of those powerful weapons was hidden. Paxton and Truko had declared a war, and I was going to give it to them—once I got Kazi back. Everything hinged on that first. What about Rybart? Caemus hadn't mentioned him. Maybe he was cut out of Paxton and Truko's plans. I might have to make a side deal with him and enlist his help.

"Remember," Synové chirped, "we're only pretending to be your trusting, loyal wives."

"And that's only *if* we encounter anyone in these forsaken woods," Wren added. "In the meantime, we're Rahtan looking for a fellow soldier."

I shot her a skeptical glance. I knew Kazi was far more than just a fellow soldier to them. They were twisted almost as tight as I was. Not to mention, they were—

I shook my head. *My wives.* They were dressed as Kbaaki too, their faces painted like mine. Synové wore a jeweled earring in her brow too. There was no more jewelry at the settlement, so Wren had pulled her fur hat low, forcing her dark curls over her brows. It made her piercing eyes peeking from beneath them appear even more ominous.

I sighed. I had Kbaaki wives looking over my shoulder.

There were so many things I didn't want to think about. That we were sneaking into my *own* territory. That Samuel might be hurt—or worse if the letter was true. That Beaufort had played the Ballengers for complete and utter fools. That Paxton had taken over everything. That I hadn't killed him one of the many times I'd had the chance.

Most of all, I didn't want to think about Synové's dream. Kazi chained and bloody, lying on a dark prison floor. *Still as a statue,* she had said. I had grabbed her arms and shouted, *But was she alive, Synové?* Her tears had stopped, but her eyelashes were still clumped together in wet spikes, her eyes swollen and red. Her mouth fell open. *I don't know,* she had whispered. *She was soaked in blood. She wasn't moving. I don't know if she was alive.* And then she began crying again. Caemus had shot me a wary glance, as if Synové confirmed his suspicions, and I stormed out of the shed. Wren had found me leaning against a wall trying to breathe. I was still bare chested, and she laid a cloak over my shoulders and whispered, *Kazi said sometimes dreams are only dreams, the same as any other. That's all it was. We have to believe that.*

Only a dream, I told myself. That's all it was. An ugly dream that I couldn't shake.

I watched the sky grow darker as we crossed a ridge. Once we were on the north face of the mountains, the wind became fierce, whipping at my cloak and hat. In minutes the sky filled with rolling black clouds. "*Dammit,*" I said under my breath, looking at the heavens. Were the gods against me? No doubt Wren would toss this up as one of the kinks in my plan. I could taste the storm in the air. Salt, metal, and pine, the taste of mountain being swept into the sky. A heavy storm was coming, the kind that sent animals running into their caves and dens, the kind of storm that brought inches, maybe even feet of snow—not the dust we'd been getting. We'd have to make camp early. I knew of a sizable ruin less than a mile away that would shelter both us and the horses.

By the time we reached the ruin, tucked in a dark part of the forest, the snow had already begun swirling in biting gusts, the air so cold the coin-sized snowflakes clung to our furs whole and bright, refusing to melt. Synové and Wren both looked like they were wearing sharp, glittering crowns.

I got a fire going quickly, and while Wren unwrapped food and cut a fat loaf of bread that Jurga had sent with us, I mentally recalculated our path. If too much snow fell, some narrow trails would be impassable and other routes would make our trek even longer. I pulled the saddle from Mije, angry, twisting carelessly to set it down, and a sharp pain stabbed at my side. I doubled over and dropped the saddle, forcing back the groan in my throat. I didn't want Wren and Synové to think I was a liability. On the outside the wounds were healing, but inside, some parts were still torn and raw.

It didn't escape Wren's notice. "Those were some pretty spectacular wounds you got, *Patrei*. No one ever taught you to roll and duck?"

My stupidity burned in me. I should have pulled back as soon as I saw the tumbled spires. I should have retreated into the forest with Kazi and assessed the threat. But it had been so still, so quiet. So empty. No lights shone from any of the remaining towers. It all looked so desolate and I was drawn into its black void. Instead of turning away from the threat, I had raced right into it, determined to save my home, risking something I loved even more—Kazi. I would never forgive myself if—

I straightened, defying the pull in my gut. "My wounds aren't so spectacular. And you could call me Jase."

They looked at each other as if weighing the thought, then laughed.

"So, *Patrei*," Synové said as she laid out our cloaks around the fire, "you and Kazi ever get a chance to open that gift I gave you?" She plopped down on the soft fur, her long copper braid gleaming in the firelight, and smiled, waiting for a full accounting.

"Yes, we did," I answered. "Thank you."

She and Wren frowned.

"*And?*" Synové prompted.

I knew what she wanted to hear, and maybe she deserved to hear it. The words hovered on my tongue but then I couldn't speak. Everything froze inside of me, and all I could see was Kazi.

She was blushing, and her cheeks were like a hot smoky sunset. I had never seen her squirm like that. She had stared for the longest time at Synové's gift resting in her palm.

The package had practically unraveled in my hands. Maybe I had helped it along. I wasn't sure, but I was curious, something inside of me eager.

What is this, Kazi?

Our words sounded in my head, clear as the moment we said them.

A feastcake, she had answered.

And then she lifted the cake, curious too, and there, tucked beneath the waxed cloth, was a long red ribbon. I lifted it, and it caught in the breeze, the red satin waving between us. *What is this for?*

Kazi shook her head. *I'm afraid Synové got carried away. These are for—*

She took a deep breath, her lips rolling tight over her teeth. *Never mind.*

I looked at her lowered lashes, maybe some part of me knowing already, a strange anticipation growing in me. *Tell me,* I said. *I want to know.*

Her mouth pulled, uncomfortable, and I wanted to kiss away her worry. *A feastcake and red ribbon,* she said, *are part of a Vendan ceremony.*

I had relived that moment again and again. When I was barely alive in the root cellar, I was certain that memory was all that kept me anchored to this world—"*Patrei?*"

"Jase!"

I looked up. Both of their gazes were fixed on me like I had grown horns.

"What's the matter with you?" Wren snapped.

"It's not important," Synové said, furrows lining her forehead. "You can tell us when you're ready. We don't—"

"Tell me about your gift," I said. Synové's dream was suddenly urgent in my head again. "I *need* to know. The gift your queen has, the one you have, the one that—"

Wren lifted both of her hands in denial when I looked at her. "Not me," she said. "I don't have anything."

Synové puffed a loose strand of hair from her face. "Everyone has something," she countered and sat back on her heels, eager to talk about it. She told me the gift was a kind of knowing. "Almost like another kind of language, the queen says, one that's buried deep inside us, but we don't always understand it. It's another sense that needs to be nurtured. It's what helped the Ancients survive after the devastation. The queen says when they had nothing else, they had to return to the language of knowing to survive."

She said it manifested itself in different ways for different people. The queen sometimes saw visions, sometimes heard a soft voice, and sometimes it was only a warning beat crouching low in her gut. Synové's own gift leaned more toward dreams, but she had a hard time discerning which ones actually meant something. "I'm still trying to figure it all out. The queen tells me to be patient, to nurture my gift, but sometimes it scares me."

"It always scares you," Wren added.

"What about Death?" I asked. "Do you see him?"

She and Wren looked at each other, some sober thought passing between them. They knew about Kazi. "No," Synové answered quietly. "I don't. Not the way Kazi does." She shivered. "And I think what Kazi has is more of a curse than a gift."

Wren frowned. "Maybe. Maybe not."

Synové hugged her arms. "I'm surprised she told you. She doesn't like to talk about it, even with us."

I nodded. "She told me that when Fertig's crew attacked us and he was choking her, she saw Death standing over his shoulder, pointing at her."

"Death was not in my dream, if that's what you're wondering," Synové said, her fingers nervously twisting the end of her braid. "That much I know for sure."

"But if you're looking for certainty, *Patrei*," Wren added, "you're not going to get it from the gift anyway."

And that was exactly what I wanted. Certainty. My blood raced with the hunger of it, and it burned hotter with every mile we traveled. It wasn't fleas under my skin now but sparks, countless days of healing and waiting and uncertainty building up that I couldn't stand anymore. I wanted all things hard and sharp and solid and sure. I wanted stone, and steel, and sword. I wanted the razor edge of a knife slicing a throat, and hot blood dripping over my hand. Paxton's blood. And then Truko's, and anyone else who had betrayed us. I wanted the certainty of Kazi back in my arms. And anyone who had tried to take that certainty away from me would suffer before they died. I wanted my family safe and whole and ready to avenge it all. I wanted Gunner, Priya, Mason, and Titus taking charge in my absence, already making a plan.

I looked into the fire, my anger rising, and caught Wren watching me. Her eyes glowed with the flames as she shook her head. "No one wants to be on the wrong side of what's burning inside you, *Patrei*. *That* is certainty I'd be willing to bet on."

"Me too," Synové added.

Neither one offered me assurances that Kazi was fine, or even that she was alive. They knew the uncertainties of life. Kazi had told me that their parents had been brutally murdered. They knew that people we loved died, and like Caemus had said, no amount of wanting or anger or bargaining with the gods could change that, or bring them back.

And yet, I still bargained with the gods every mile we traveled.

Please don't take her away from me. I will do anything.

Anything.

Wren handed me a thick trencher of bread with smoked rabbit and sliced apples piled on top. As we ate, we washed it down with weak Vendan ale that we passed around in a skin between us. Synové snapped her fingers at me if I sipped too long. She had talked almost nonstop, somehow still skillfully downing her trencher and meat as she happily told us about draining antelope blood into skins. She glowed with satisfaction as she recounted Griz's outrage over dispatching Bahr before he was delivered to the queen. "Technically, I didn't dispatch him. Everyone saw it was the racaa's doing," she reasoned, licking the glistening rabbit fat from her fingers. "Racaa don't digest bones, did you know?"

"No, I didn't know," I answered and handed the skin of ale to Wren.

"They vomit them up like an owl. I'm sure one day I'll find Bahr's pile of bones in the Cam Lanteux, woven together in a nice little ball with his undies. A perfect end for—"

Wren put her hand out, and Synové was instantly silent. Her dark curls bobbed as she turned her head, listening for something. Between the wind whistling outside and the nickers of the horses, I hadn't heard anything, but now hairs rose on the back of my neck. A vibration. Pounding. Something was close.

I set my half-finished trencher on my cloak and stood as I drew my sword from my scabbard. The quiet whine of steel on steel pierced the air as horses galloped into the foyer of the ruin. Three men rode in first and then, just on their heels, three more. We had visitors. My first thought was that we were outnumbered, and my second was, would any of them recognize me? Would the disguise work? They pulled back when they saw me ready with my sword, Synové with an arrow nocked and aimed, and Wren with a *ziethe* gripped in each hand.

"Whoa, friends. We're just riding in from the storm. It caught us by surprise," one man called. I didn't recognize him, but I heard the Shiramar drawl, which meant he was likely one of Truko's men. I resisted the impulse to pounce on him and demand information. I knew how to get it, but the numbers weren't in our favor. He rode closer. "Mind if we share this shelter? That's all we want. I'm Langston," he added, patting his chest, as if knowing his name would ease our minds.

I exchanged a glance with Wren and Synové, then nodded to him. The only answer had to be yes. Wren and Synové sat back down on their fur cloaks, and we stored our weapons but kept them near. People with nothing to hide would always share a safe haven in a storm—especially Kbaaki.

"Welcomes, friends," I said, laying on my thick accent. "Warm yourselves."

Langston swung down from his horse. The others followed his lead, stomping their boots and shaking off layers of snow from their cloaks, beards, and hats, and pulling away scarves. Two men, apparently lower ranking, were left to tend the horses, removing saddles and shaking out blankets while the rest came over to warm themselves by our fire. As far as I could tell, I didn't know any of them. It could be they were traders from Shiramar, except that no trader would be on these remote trails unless they were lost. My gut told me they were also Truko's men, part of the army that had taken over Hell's Mouth.

"Kbaaki, huh?" Langston said, raising bushy brows still dusted with snow. He pulled off his gloves, stuffing them in his vest. "A little late in the season to be so far from home, isn't it?"

The practiced ruse was ready on my tongue. "The king's daughter ez sick. His siarrah says only smoke of spirit wood will cleanse the demons from her. He offered us a full chest of gheirey for spirit wood, so here we are."

Langston nodded, knowing a full chest of gheirey was a fortune and worth a trip in winter. He made quick introductions of his three companions who had joined us around the fire. "Cain, Ferrett, and Utreck," he said. Cain, who stood just on the other side of me, was tall and muscular, and I assessed that he was the greatest threat. His eyes scanned our belongings as if taking inventory—from the furs spread around the fire, to our weapons set nearby, to our packs piled in the corner. It was not simple curiosity. They were the eyes of a scout, searching for signs.

"Going to the arena for the wood?" he asked.

I nodded. "Faster than the forest." The nearest forest of spirit wood was sixty miles south, and chopping the rubbery wood was no easy task, not to mention messy. Buying it at the arena from a dealer was logical, since someone was sick and we were in a hurry, but I still wanted to turn the questions back to him as quickly as I could. "And why are you out in this fury?"

"A different kind of reward," Langston answered, but he didn't elaborate on what kind.

"On patrol," Utreck offered. "Looking for—"

"Game." Langston cut him off, but the answer was already spilled. Scouts didn't "patrol" for game. They were hunting down people. He eyed Wren and Synové, who still hadn't spoken. Their efforts at Kbaaki accents had failed, so it was agreed they would remain silent if we encountered anyone. "These are?"

"My wives," I answered. "Ghenta and Eloh. I'm Vrud." Wren and Synové nodded to him. His gaze lingered on them a bit longer than I liked. Was he suspicious, or did he have other things on his mind?

Ferrett, a short hefty man, sidled close to Wren and smiled. He was missing a front tooth, and the rest were crooked and looked like they were about to go missing too. Wren shot him a warning glare, *Stay away.*

"You too good for a friendly hello?" he sneered.

"They only speak Kbaaki," I said.

Langston looked down at my sheathed sword lying on the furs. "Since when do Kbaaki carry long swords?" The weapons were a problem. At the settlement we gathered together what we could. Caemus gave us axes, and the rest of Synové's and Wren's weapons were doled out between us. I got Synové's sword. Kbaaki usually carried a long machete-type saber.

"It was a gift from the king. I'm not sure I like it but didn't want to insult him."

"You'll get used to it," Cain said. "A little heavier than those machetes of yours, but the weight can be an advantage once you get the hang of it."

I nodded as if I appreciated his insight. And then the other two men, done with their work, joined us. One was introduced as Arman, but the other I already knew—it was Hagur from the livestock auction—the one who had cheated us. I wasn't sure if he would recognize me, but I wasn't going to make it easy. I looked down so he wouldn't see my eyes. He'd seen his imminent death in them once—before I gave him a second chance—and that was something he wasn't likely to forget. The sparks simmering beneath my skin grew hotter. How many Ballenger employees had abandoned the family and were working for Paxton now?

Cain spotted the half-eaten trencher I had hastily set down when they rode in. His eyes darted to me. I knew what he was thinking before he said it. I thought it myself when Jurga packed the thick loaf, thinking it would be long eaten before we encountered anyone.

Cain said the word that was already clanging in my head. "Bread?"

Feet shifted. Silence deepened. The crackle of the fire disappeared.

I kept my gaze down. "It was a gift," I explained. "From a traveler we passed."

Langston scrutinized me more closely. "You seem to be one lucky man, Vrud. Two wives, gifts from kings, and way out here, fresh-baked bread?" His hand went to his hunting knife.

Wren sighed dramatically, drawing his attention away from me, flinging her role away like an old soup bone. She spoke in flawless Landese. "You got a problem with one little loaf of bread, Langston?"

They all stared at her. The ruse was already up, but now Wren had given me a one-second lead, and one second meant everything.

I dove for my sword, rolling over the furs, lobbing it upward, and sending the loose scabbard flying into Ferrett's chest.

Wren shoved the rattled Ferrett into Utreck, and Synové kicked Langston in the back, sending him stumbling over the fire, and as he fell, Wren planted her *ziethe* into his gut. The others were all drawing weapons now.

Cain was on top of me in seconds, pouncing like a ravenous wolf, catching me before I could stand, pressing with all his weight as he tried to stab his dagger into my neck. My arms shook, struggling to hold him back, my head close to the fire. I saw the hunger in his eyes. Hunters, they were all hunters. And then a knife struck his cheek.

Synové had dived for her weapons belt and was sending a barrage of throwing knives through the air. Cain fell back, howling like a mad dog, blood gushing from his mouth, and I turned his dagger on him, shoving it into his chest. In almost the same moment, Hagur charged past me after Synové. I was still on the ground but lunged for my sword and swung it, slicing into his lower leg. He screamed and crashed to the ground, but on his heels Ferrett hurtled toward me with his ax raised over his head. I rolled, trying to avoid him, but then with the precision of a hawk swooping in on its kill, Wren whirled and sliced his head from his shoulders.

Arman fell last, an earsplitting scream seeming to propel him as he rushed forward, swinging a mace over his head. Cain's dagger flew from my hand and lodged in his skull, sending his mace crashing against a wall.

Down. They were all down.

"Everyone okay?" I asked, limping toward the still body of Utreck to make sure he was dead. I had seen Synové wrestling with him, but there was no blood—then I saw the side of his skull was caved in, maybe from the heel of Synové's boot.

Synové leaned forward, her hands on her knees, catching her breath. "Fine," she answered.

Wren looked at her cloak and growled. Ferret's head had fallen onto it, leaving a pool of blood. She pulled on the cloak, sending the head rolling off into the wall where his body already lay. She scowled at her stained cloak.

I looked around at the bloody carnage. All of them dead—except Hagur.

I stared at him, remembering him begging for a second chance on the steps of the temple. His fingers had been laced together and his expression was molded to look like one of the stautes of forlorn saints that were within. And I had given that second chance to him. He lay on the floor now, his lower leg angled to the side. Except for a small piece of flesh, it was severed at the calf. His eyes were wild as they met mine, still uncertain who I was. His breaths were shallow, panting, like a small puppy. His head wobbled.

"Hello, Hagur," I said. He blanched, his already pale face turning the sickly color of a grub. He knew for sure who I was now. I pulled a belt from Cain to use as a tourniquet as I walked toward him. His elbows pushed against the floor, trying to scoot away from me, but he couldn't even move inches.

Once, I thought, *just as the gods forgave us once.* That is all.

"You're dead," he rasped.

"The gods have brought me back to life," I answered. "But no more second chances for you."

His face glistened with oily perspiration. He was dying. I knelt beside him and worked quickly, wrapping the belt around his stump. He screamed as I tightened it. He wasn't going to bleed out until I got answers.

Once the blood flow was stopped, I asked my first and most important question, "Where is Kazi?"

"I don't know any—"

"The Vendan soldier who was here!" I grabbed his vest and yanked him forward. "Where is she?"

He screamed in pain. His eyes rolled in his head. "I swear—" he gasped. "I've been on the mountain. On patrol. I haven't seen her. But Banques—he has prisoners. Some of them he's already hanged—"

"Hanged?" Wren yelled. "Hanged who?" Her normally cool temperament cracked with desperation.

"Loyalists," Hagur gasped.

"Where are they? Where is he holding them?" I demanded.

"Some in town. Some at the arena. Some at—"

He hadn't had time to explain more when Synové demanded a different answer. "Who is Banques?"

"The general," he whispered, his voice barely audible. "Second in command."

A general? Every answer he gave us only created more questions. "Who is first in command?" I asked. I knew there was precious little time left for answers. He was barely conscious. "Paxton? Truko?"

"He's smarter than you think. He won't ever—"

His eyes closed and his head rolled to the side, and I slapped his face, trying to wake him. "Who? Tell me, you bastard!"

I grabbed his vest again, lifting him forward, ready to shake him awake, but Wren stopped me, pushing him back to the floor. "Don't waste your energy, *Patrei*. He's dead."

I stared at him, my fists still curled in his clothing, not willing to let go of this two-time traitor. I was ready to cut him open and dig out the answers with my fingers. *Where is she?*

"Leave it, *Patrei*," Wren said softly, pulling my hands loose from Hagur's vest. "Let's go catch ourselves a live one. One who can talk."

CHAPTER TWENTY-FOUR

KAZI

Paxton's secrets came out over the course of the day, only when we could manage safe moments to talk alone. It began in the solarium, where we tossed rubble and overturned furniture as we talked, so it would appear we were searching the house—and not conspiring—in case anyone listened from below. Most of the windows of the solarium were still intact, but cold wind whistled through a broken one, keeping the air crisp. Our movement helped keep the frost from our bones.

The bush I had seen Jalaine meticulously clipping in the corner was now dead, its leaves brown and curled. We only had a little time to talk before the king would return to Tor's Watch and we would return to the inn with him. I tried to absorb everything Paxton told me, even as I studied him, trying to understand who *he* was.

He told me that contrary to the official report issued by Banques, Rybart hadn't led any attacks on Hell's Mouth. He was just a convenient scapegoat, and once he and his men were dead, they couldn't defend their names or intentions. The depth and breadth of Montegue's conniving made me marvel. He was shrewd, patient, smart. He knew how to deceive and play people. He understood misdirection as well as I did.

It was the king who had murdered Rybart—or at least one of his guards did by his order—because the king never got his hands dirty. It could have just as easily been Paxton or Truko, but Rybart had made the mistake of standing to leave first. That was his downfall—his utter disgust with the king.

Paxton explained how they had all been called to the king's chambers. None of them liked being summoned, Truko least of all, but Montegue was staying at the Ballenger Inn in unusually luxurious quarters that they knew were well beyond his means. That alone had piqued their interest. They joked about it as they walked there, wondering if he would stiff the Ballengers or pay his debt by washing dishes. Once they were seated in the posh parlor of his suite, the king said he had a generous proposal for them all. He was taking over Hell's Mouth and Tor's Watch, and he was willing to cut them in on a percentage of arena profits in return for managing it. The king knew little about the trade business, and he needed their expertise to keep the revenue flowing. He told them he had the army and weapons to carry out his plan, and it was about time that the Ballengers were ousted.

Paxton remembered exchanging a snide glance with Rybart and Truko. He said they were probably all thinking the same thing—the king was insane. Paxton had stifled a laugh and was thankful now for that small bit of wisdom. Rybart stood to leave first, saying, "Not interested." He didn't try to hide his cynicism or offer the king even minimal respect. Though they all wanted a greater piece of the arena trade, they knew better than to try to steal it from the Ballengers, and the bumbling king was the last one they wanted to partner with.

"Bumbling," Paxton repeated, his gaze briefly unfocused, like he was reliving the moment his eyes had been opened to the king's true nature. "None of us could have been more wrong about him. Our biggest mistake was underestimating him." He said he was on the verge of standing to say the same as Rybart when, the next thing he knew, blood was spraying across his lap and face, and the end of a sword was jutting from Rybart's chest. The guard behind him pulled it free, and Rybart crumpled awkwardly back into his seat. Dead. And the king continued the meeting with barely a blink.

"What about you two?" Montegue had asked. "Interested?"

Yes was obviously the only answer—at least temporarily—or so Paxton thought. But again, he had underestimated Montegue. The army, for one thing. Before the meeting was over, they were already marching into town, and their numbers and weapons were formidable. The king had also known exactly how to sow doubt, turning one comrade against another, already bribing Paxton's own men to turn each other in for disloyalty. Everyone now was on the king's side, at least by appearances. Those who thought they could conspire with a colleague against the king found themselves being turned in and hanged. He'd been infiltrating Hell's Mouth for months with his own men. Plants. It made everyone tight-lipped and afraid to talk with anyone.

"I only have two in my crew that I still have regular communication with and I'm certain I can trust—Binter and Cheu. Other than that, I'm cut off from everyone. I think I can trust Truko, but we don't talk much. I think he's afraid too, but I can't be sure. His *straza* have definitely turned. The king has infiltrated or subverted nearly everyone and everything. Whether they like him or not, they're afraid to step out of line because they don't know who is waiting to stab them in the back."

"How does he get these backstabbers' loyalty?"

"Greed and fear. He's made extravagant promises, and more frightening threats—and he has the power to back up those threats."

Paxton berated himself for not figuring it out. He had become suspicious when he was suddenly selling large quantities of ore from his mine to supposedly second-party dealers—which turned out to be fake. He traced the purchases back to the Ballengers. He knew Jase was up to something, but he wasn't sure what. When the king began placing large orders for pig iron, he didn't connect the two. "He claimed he was forging some new plows and farm equipment for his three farms—but I knew he had already sold two of them off. It was a very hushed transaction. No one was supposed to know about the land sales, but one of his foremen came to me asking for work. I thought his purchase of iron for more plows was just more of his spectacular mismanagement, and I was happy to sell him iron he'd never be able to use. I just didn't put two and two together. I didn't think he was capable of anything like this."

"Selling off his holdings was how he paid for the mercenaries?"

"That was only a down payment. He has another payment that's due soon."

"So that's why he needs the revenues from the arena so badly."

"That's right. A massive arsenal of weapons is only as good as the army that carries it."

I shook my head. I still didn't understand how it could be *massive*. "Jase told me about the supplies he had ordered. There was only enough for a small war at best, and most of those were used up with experimentation."

"You really think Beaufort would be honest about anything, including supplies? They weren't using up the supplies with experiments. They were stockpiling them and shipping them out. How, I don't know. Or to where. They keep that a closely guarded secret—"

I gasped. *The olives! The casks!*

They weren't the nonsensical words of a dying man. I remembered when Phineas had said them, blood sputtering from his lips. That was how they had accumulated such a huge arsenal. For months they had smuggled the explosives back out of Cave's End in empty casks that once held wine or olives.

"They're in olive and wine casks," I said. "Phineas told me."

"Casks?" he breathed out with wonder. He told me there were a hundred and four warehouses behind the arena and it was a daunting task to search them without arousing suspicion. He'd only been able to search maybe a dozen so far, but he had been searching for crates.

"Seventy-two," I said. "Is there a warehouse with that number?" I told him about the paper I had nicked from the king.

He nodded. "Back near the paddocks. I'll check it next."

He went on, telling me about the ballistae they had created. "They're even more deadly than the launchers. One shot was all it took to take the temple down. They're forging more of those now."

"But sooner or later they'll run out of ammunition."

"They claim they've only used a fraction of what they have and soon they'll have more."

"How is that possible? We destroyed the plans."

"They have the perfected product in their possession, and they know all the ingredients. It won't take the chemists he's hired long to replicate the formula. It's imminent."

I remembered Beaufort's last words to me. *It will never be over. Not now. A door has been unlocked.*

But somehow we had to close that door again. The king already had Hell's Mouth under his thumb. The only reason he would need more—

Paxton voiced my thoughts before I could finish them.

"He hasn't said it outright, but his sights are set on other kingdoms. He wants their wealth to be his." He had overheard Montegue and Banques talking about what was essentially blackmail—fees for crossing rights in the Cam Lanteux within two hundred miles from Eislandia's borders. Fees for a lot of things the other kingdoms would have to pay, or else.

The *else* was going to happen whether they complied or not. Phineas had offered him the universe, and I had seen the fire in Montegue's eyes. He would settle for nothing less.

"And maybe even more than their wealth," Paxton continued, "he wants power and respect. He won't hesitate to use any kingdom who defies him as an example to the others."

"Like he did with Rybart to make you and Truko jump."

He sighed. "Yes, just like that."

"King's back! Heading out!" a voice bellowed from below. They banged something against a metal pipe in case we didn't hear. No one kept the king waiting.

On our return to the inn, I rode next to Montegue and Nash at first, but upon hearing I had turned up nothing in my search, the king quickly resumed an animated conversation with Banques. Paxton's grim warning had come to pass.

The chemists had done it. The formula had been re-created. Production would resume as soon as more supplies arrived. By year's end, the king hoped to double his already formidable arsenal. The air was suddenly colder. Thinner. More dangerous.

I looked at Lydia, who rode with Banques, and gave her a bare nod. Assurance. *Bide your time. This nightmare will soon be over.* Even though it was becoming worse by the minute. She looked away, but I saw the veiled fear in her eyes.

Neither Montegue nor Banques cared when I fell back with Paxton. I had a plan brewing in my head. It was as perilous as cuddling with a viper. It screamed of failure, but I'd had it since I visited the cemetery this morning. It had seemed impossible then. To accomplish it, at the very least, I needed an ally.

And now I had Paxton.

Was he really an ally? The recurring worry thrummed in my head. He was a man Jase had loathed and a man I didn't truly know. But as I had learned so recently, people could be many things they didn't seem to be. Even Jase had turned out to be someone far different from whom I had imagined. Should I take a chance on another Ballenger? Or did Paxton have other motives than what he had told me?

Most people did. Our wants were rarely all wrapped up in one neat package. Even mine weren't. I knew I had to get a better sense of Paxton first, before I brought him into my confidence. Was a short ride back to the inn enough time to build trust? It had to be. I had an overwhelming sense of time slipping away. At every turn, the game changed, the people changed, the stakes changed. *His sights are set on other kingdoms.* I feared time was running out for everyone, but especially Lydia and Nash. Until they were safe, I could do nothing to help anyone.

I glanced sideways at Paxton. I had never brought anyone else into my plans before. It created a whole new kind of fear inside me.

We let the distance between us and our entourage grow longer, and with the wind in our faces, it became safe to talk. The arrogant tilt of his chin, the flip tone in his voice, it was all still classic Paxton. But beneath the façade, another side emerged, a side much more serious and reflective that he had worked to keep hidden. When I steered our conversation into the personal, I watched him hesitate, squirm. He shook his head when he admitted that he was ashamed of what his drunken great-grandfather had done, ashamed of the scheming of his own father and how he had colluded with other leagues to get Tor's Watch back, but he was just as angry that his cousins, the Ballengers, could never forgive the trespass of an ancestor and visited retribution upon all the spawn who came thereafter. His mother had worked to teach him the family history, saying it was his too and he should hold his head high.

"So that's where the arrogant tilt of your chin comes from?" I chided.

His eyes narrowed, and he grinned. "Something like that."

"What about your run-ins with Jase? They're legendary."

A single brow arched. "Are they?" He huffed out a pleased breath. "I was hot-tempered back then—but so was he. And maybe sometimes I took it too far." A frown pulled at the corner of his mouth. "I threw him down a well once," he admitted. "He was sixteen. I was eighteen. I told him to cool off. I thought it was an amusing metaphor he would appreciate. I also thought someone would come for him, but he nearly died. He was stuck down there for two days." Paxton shrugged. "He'd done as bad to me. But I did regret that stunt. I think it pretty much killed my chances with Priya."

"Priya?" I said in disbelief. "How could you think you ever had any kind of chance with her at all?"

Perhaps I was too blunt. His temples tinged with color, and he shrugged. "Long-held infatuations are resistant to logic, I suppose. I'd had a crush on her ever since I was a gawky, tongue-tied thirteen-year-old and she was a mature, sophisticated fifteen-year-old beauty. We had finally met formally, at a funeral. It seems that's the only way us Ballengers ever get together. While she was grace and stars and glitter, and smelled like fresh summer blooms, I was a stumbling oaf, and that's being generous. I tripped over every word I said. I even accidentally spit on her. It was a disaster. Our paths crossed in town from time to time after that, but she always made an obvious point not to look my way. I imagined that one day maybe she would appreciate my finer qualities. Truth is, I still get a little tongue-tied when I'm around her. Funerals and such. They're not really conducive to good conversation."

"You're still infatuated with her?" Again, maybe too much disbelief was evident in my tone, and he adamantly shook his head to dismiss the notion.

"No. Of course not. We're not children anymore. But the king was making me nervous. For a while he latched on to the idea of sparing Priya's life and taking her as his wife—marrying old with new—appeasing everyone. Two kinds of royalty, he called it. A crazy idea, but it greatly appealed to him until recently. Now I think he may have moved on and set his sights elsewhere." His gaze rested on me.

"Because he knows Jase wanted me," I said.

"But couldn't have you."

I understood. "He wants to best the *Patrei* in everything."

"Something like that."

When we arrived at the inn, the king had already gone inside with the children, and as we dismounted, Banques told Paxton to escort me to my room. "You're having dinner with the king tonight," he said to me. "You'll find some appropriate clothing in your room. I'll send my lieutenant to retrieve you. Be ready."

Retrieve. Like I was a piece of baggage. Maybe that was exactly how Banques viewed me—baggage he'd like to be rid of, especially if the king got too close to me. Banques was possessive of his attentions.

The appropriate clothing turned out to be an elegant evening dress that raised both Paxton's and my brows. We talked as I washed up and changed, not knowing when we would get a chance to talk privately again. We both agreed that until Lydia and Nash were out of the king's and Banques's hands, we were helpless to stop their grander schemes. I laid out my plan to him. He balked.

"No. No, no, no," he said, shaking his head. "It won't work. They're only small children. They would panic."

"They're stronger than you think. They can do this—as long as you can."

He bit his lip, thinking it over. He had no better plan, and he knew it was better to stay ahead of the danger instead of reacting to it. We had to do something. Soon. He sighed, conceding, but still hesitant. "I have my two men that I trust with my life—and with Lydia's and Nash's. All right. Tomorrow." He rubbed his neck, still trying to get his mind around it. "You're sure?"

I nodded. "It was Jase who kept me alive, Paxton. When I thought it was impossible to go on, I heard him telling me to keep going. *You can do it*, he said. *Just a little farther.* That's what we have now. Just a little farther to go. This will work. And once they're free, so are we."

A small moan rumbled in his chest. "All right. I'll take care of it on my end one way or another. In the meantime, work on your limp." And with those few words, I watched the shifty side of Paxton emerge again, coming out of hiding, and I welcomed it. I didn't need the fearful Paxton—I needed the unscrupulous one—the one willing to throw his cousin down a well to teach him a lesson.

CHAPTER TWENTY-FIVE

JASE

CAEMUS HAD NEVER SAID ANYTHING ABOUT A GENERAL. Soldiers, yes, but a general meant something more. It meant something larger and more organized than a league leader seizing power and throwing a few weapons into willing hands. I had already added up how many soldiers Paxton, Truko, and maybe Rybart could pull together by pooling their resources. Maybe a mismatched lot of two hundred at the most.

But a general meant some sort of formal army. I turned it over in my head when I wasn't thinking about people hanging from trees. Just what had Beaufort been planning? And who was in charge now that Beaufort was no longer a partner in this scheme?

The storm had stopped, but the snow it left was still high enough on the ground to make the narrow pass I had planned to take impossible to navigate—which also made it one of those kinks Wren had warned me about. We had to circle around and take a more time-consuming route on a southern face where the snow was only a few inches deep.

Synové cursed and pointed to Mije's rump. "We missed some blood there."

I looked behind me and saw the telltale spots, dark and crusty on his black coat. "Whoa, *gutra hezo*," I said and swung down from the saddle. We had cleaned the blood from our faces, furs, and weapons—it was important that we not be implicated in the deaths of six men should they be found, nor did we want to attract the attention of other predators on the mountain, like the packs of wolves that ranged here in winter. I glanced up at the sky. Or a hungry racaa who had perhaps acquired a taste for human flesh after Synové's stunt with Bahr. I poured water into my hand and rubbed it into Mije's coat.

"*Gutra hezo?*" Wren said.

"Mije's used to hearing it from Kazi. I thought—" I didn't finish. I didn't know what I thought except that I wanted to hear Kazi's voice, even if it was me saying her words. I wanted to repeat and remember every word that had ever passed between us, to keep it all alive.

"You spoil that horse as much as Kazi did," Synové chirped. She used the opportunity to tell me about the day Kaden, the Keep of Venda and one-time Assassin, gave Kazi the horse. She had been eyeing Mije in the paddocks for weeks. Synové, Wren, and Kazi were all thirteen years old and had been approved to advance on to Rahtan training, and that meant they would each be given their own horse to keep, care for, and train with.

"All Rahtan horses run on the hot side, but Mije was more of everything. Kazi ached with wanting that horse, but Kaden had already told her no. He said Mije was strong willed, and too much horse for Kazi."

Synové said Kazi didn't let up, though, and one day she jumped into the paddock with Mije. He was a young horse and full of snarl and spit, but that was what Kazi loved about him. He stamped and tried to scare her off, and she stamped right back at him. It was a stunning standoff, with Kaden yelling at her to get out of the ring, but then she called to the horse and held out her hand to him.

"That crazy wild beast came straight to her, nuzzled her palm, and the rest is history," Wren said. "The Keep couldn't deny Kazi, and the horse became hers that very day."

"She bribed Mije," I said.

Their heads both spun toward me. "What?" they said at the same time.

"She'd secretly been sneaking him dried berries from the kitchen pantry for almost two weeks. That's why he came to her. He was expecting a treat." Kazi had told me the whole story, pleased with the shocked expression on the Keep's face.

"I'll be damned," Synové said, smiling at this revelation, apparently pleased that Kazi had left nothing to chance. "Seems you two told each other everything." She looked slyly at me, her eyes narrowing. "What about me and Mason? Did you tell her about us?"

Wren rolled her eyes. "Not much to tell there."

I nodded. "Kazi was surprised."

Wren's attention whipped to Synové. "What about you and Mason?"

Synové laughed and told Wren there was more to the two of them than she had let on. "We might have stolen a kiss once or twice." This time it was Synové who rolled her eyes, implying that it was more than a kiss.

It ignited a small squabble between the two of them, Wren telling her it was dangerous to get involved with the enemy. "Look at the trouble it got Kazi into—" She caught herself and looked at me.

"Am I still the enemy?" I asked.

"You're a pain in the ass is what you are, but not the enemy—for now."

Strangely, coming from Wren, it almost sounded like a compliment.

Synové scoffed at her. "Are you saying you aren't eager to see Samuel again?"

Wren glared. "No. I am not eager. Nothing happened with Samuel and me."

"But you wanted it to." She tapped her chin. "Or maybe it was Aram? I still can't tell those two puppies apart."

Wren hissed out a frustrated breath and rode a pace ahead, finished with the conversation. "Blazing saints," she mumbled as she rode forward. "I need Kazi here."

Synové continued to chatter about Mason, imagining he would be very happy to see her in spite of their caustic parting and the threats they had hurled at each other, but all I could think of was Samuel.

My little brother, I had always teased. He was a half inch taller than me. I hadn't told either of them about the note saying he was dead. I had discounted it, convincing myself it couldn't be true, but now, after seeing the tumbled walls at Tor's Watch, knowing an army had taken over Hell's Mouth, knowing my family had run for their lives and were hiding in the vault—it didn't seem impossible now.

My throat swelled, thinking of him dead, and a choked sound slipped out. I coughed to mask it. Wren looked back at me, suspicious. She never missed anything—maybe that was why she was angry she hadn't caught on to Synové and Mason.

"How did Mason really get that scar on his neck?" Synové asked. Silence never lasted long around her.

"He didn't tell you?"

"A drunk barber, he claimed." She sighed. "Mason and I didn't talk much—at least not the way you and Kazi did. It was more of a physical thing with us."

I remembered Mason confessing his attraction to Synové, but I was certain it was more than just superficial attraction. I remembered his voice, his eyes darting nervously to the side when he said *she makes me laugh*. It was a hard admission for him, caring about someone like that.

"If it was only a physical thing between you two, then why do you care how he got it?"

"A girl can be curious, can't she?"

Synové might be my temporary wife, but Mason was my brother. I didn't give away his secrets. "You'll have to ask him yourself."

She grumbled under her breath, mostly in Vendan, but the last word she said sounded a lot like *toad*.

Maybe she knew that when and if she met up with Mason again, he wasn't likely to speak to her at all. Maybe it wasn't just physical like she claimed. Maybe she knew him better than she let on. One thing about Mason, he had a long memory. Even if they didn't talk a lot, Synové had figured out that much. He had lost both of his parents to betrayal. Synové was dead to Mason.

Wren walked on one side of me, her shoulder casually brushing mine, and Synové, good loving wife that she was, held my hand.

We drew stares. Not because I was Kbaaki walking with my two wives, but because we were here at all. Home was a long way north for us, and winter had descended. Our excuse for being this far south had to be told over and over, first at the stables where we were required to leave our horses. It was a rule the Ballengers had initiated years ago. We'd decided that it made for a better buying and trade experience, instead of having the narrow avenues of the arena clogged with horses, mules, and wagons. We had runners who would transport merchandise to the stables for customers. I regretted that rule right now. It made a quick getaway more difficult.

I knew it wasn't just being here out of season that drew stares—part of it was that Kbaaki were always slightly intimidating. They were quiet, watchful sorts, which was what made them such good hunters. But their quiet ways and stares unnerved some people. They were a large people too, not Griz large, but tall and broad-shouldered—even the women. Synové was a large girl, almost as tall as me, and easily passed as Kbaaki. Wren was smaller, but her intimidating stare more than made up for her size. Mostly, though, I think people always thought there was something slightly unearthly about Kbaaki and their mysterious knowledge of potions and poisons.

"Keep your eyes straight ahead, husband," Wren warned.

Synové squeezed my hand. "Remember, we're just a family in search of spirit wood."

My eyes had been sweeping every corner of the arena. It was hard not to. Impossible maybe. I was looking at the changes before we ever got inside the arena. Soldiers were positioned on the bridge over the entrance—launchers slung over their shoulders. My launchers. The ones I had paid for—dearly. More soldiers were stationed on the floor where we shopped, but they were only armed with halberds or swords. I searched the faces but hadn't recognized anyone yet. Where did they all come from? And where were the Ballenger employees? Dead?

I had no doubt that more soldiers spied us from positions in the eight towers that looked over the arena floor. What had become of Garvin? Was he dead? Forced to work for them? Or maybe he had escaped. He was good at slipping away unnoticed. Somewhere up there, Paxton and Truko might even be eyeing me right now—maybe from the Ballenger apartments while they drank Ballenger wine and ate our food.

And somewhere in this arena maybe they were holding Kazi.

Knowing her ability to disappear, she had to be somewhere very secure. Or she was hurt. Or—

I couldn't think of any more possibilities. "Over there," I said, tilting my head at a man standing near one of the tower entrances. "Him." I finally saw an employee I recognized—Sheridan. A squarely built man with bushy red brows to match his beard. He hadn't worked for us for long. Titus had hired him, and I had only spoken briefly to him once. He was one of a dozen floor security, tasked with defusing squabbles before they could escalate. But they were also there to direct customers to the merchandise. The arena was large and like a city in itself, not to mention the rows of warehouses and paddocks that sprawled behind it.

"He's a big one. You sure?" Wren asked.

"Looks like he could be loud too," Synové added.

I was sure. He was either caught up in the takeover and forced to work the arena or he had willingly joined their ranks, and I was about to either make his day much better—or much worse.

"*Sa dre foraza?* Eh, eh—" I called to him, pretending I was struggling with the language. "Spe reet wud. We are looking for—"

"Spirit wood? You might be able to find that in warehouse eighteen. Late in the season to be carrying it, but they're a specialty vendor who has a bit of everything. Through that tunnel. Just look for the numbers on the—"

I shook my head apologetically. "Your numbers. I do not—read."

He tried to explain and even wrote the number in air, but I only creased my face with more confusion. He finally gave up and waved us forward. "This way. I'll show you."

The thing about spending half of your time in the arena as you were growing up was that you knew places, all the hidden places no one else knew—and didn't want to know. Places every Ballenger parent had forbidden their children from going but we did anyway. It was a rite of passage, older cousins leading the younger down dangerous paths to frighten them. Most important, I knew places a security team couldn't see from the towers—the only blind spots we had.

I walked next to Sheridan, heading for the short tunnel that led to the warehouses behind the arena. Wren and Synové followed close behind us. With their bulky fur cloaks, they provided a convenient shield. As we approached the tunnel, I saw that it was clear.

"The arena," I said as we entered the tunnel, "eez different since I was here last."

"New management," he explained.

"No more Ballensher?"

"No." He laughed. "They're long gone."

"They sell?"

"Run out of town. Bad management."

He went on to disparage the Ballengers and then admitted they were holed up in that mountain of theirs, probably dead by now. He only hired on because he knew they were going to be replaced.

"How? You have seer?" I asked.

He laughed again. Apparently I was quite amusing. "No," he answered. "Inside connections."

Sheridan was a plant? Someone to help in the takeover?

He didn't see it coming. One second he was walking straight ahead, and the next my weight was shoving him sideways into the black shadows of an abandoned stairwell. Wren and Synové jumped in front of me, throwing open a door. My arm was crooked around his neck, but he was fighting back. Until I held a knife to his chest.

"Quiet," I ordered as I dragged him deeper into the hidden bowels of the arena, stepping over tumbled stones and passing through dusty webs. Synové lit a candle as Wren relieved him of his weapons—a knife and a club—then ran ahead opening one door and then another, sometimes having to force it with her shoulder.

"A dead end," she said when a landing ended in a pile of rubble.

"No, back this way," I said. With little light, it was hard to see, but a small walkway to the side of the stairs led to a jagged hole in the wall and another set of stairs. We finally emerged into what my siblings and I called the cemetery—a vast underground world filled with the Ancients' metal carriages. The air was heavy, filled with a peculiar dusty scent that was almost sweet. I tried not to think too much about what it was. Poor ventilation in this nearly sealed tomb was what helped keep the carriages— and other things—from crumbling into dust.

Synové groaned when she set her flickering candle on the runner of one of the carriages and it illuminated the Ancient still sitting inside. He wasn't the only one. There were hundreds of petrified remains, Ancients trapped in the sealed tomb when their world came crashing to an end. Sheridan began to struggle under my grip, no longer caring about the knife at his chest, and I shoved him away. He stumbled back against one of the tall carriages, and the impact made the rusted carcass shift and settle.

"You can scream all you want to down here, Sheridan," I said. "No one will hear you."

This time I would get my answers—no matter how long it took— and there was no worry that anyone would interrupt us.

He looked around, taking in the vast cavern, the single candle illuminating just a small portion of it. Hundreds of carriages and just as many bones glowed in the dim circle of light. Ancient people were slung over open doors or hanging out windows, many still bearing their discolored brittle skins and horror-stricken expressions. He looked back at me and then studied Wren and Synové. Their drawn weapons shimmered with the flickering golden light. He wasn't laughing anymore.

"How do you know me?" he asked.

"You used to work for me," I answered. I pulled my hat off. Raked back my hair.

With my inked face, he still didn't recognize me. "Jase Ballensher," I said with the accent.

He cursed.

"Hmm," Wren agreed. "You never know when a little loyalty might come in handy, do you?"

"I'm going to make this simple for you, Sheridan," I said. "I ask questions. You answer them. And every time you lie to me, my friend here is going to cut something of yours off. And trust me, I'll know if you're lying."

Wren spun her *ziethe*.

"Where's the Vendan soldier?" I asked.

His hands curled into fists at his sides. "That girl? They're holding her in town."

Holding her. A brief moment of relief filled my lungs. That meant she was alive.

"Who's holding her?" I asked. "Banques? The general? Paxton? Who's in command?"

"In command of what?"

"The town, the arena. Everything."

"The king," he said uncertainly, as if he didn't understand the question.

"What king? Which kingdom?"

His face screwed into a question mark. "The King of Eislandia, you fool! Montegue!"

The words couldn't quite sink in.

"Montegue invaded the town? You're trying to tell me that bumbling fool is running everything here?"

"That's exactly what I'm telling you. It's within his rights. His kingdom, his town. His Vendan soldier to take into custody for attacking a squad and killing four of them." He paused, a grin lighting his eyes, and added, "His Vendan soldier to do with however he *pleases*."

I jerked forward, ready to twist his head off, but Wren held me back. "Don't bite, *Patrei*. He's just baiting you." I knew that. He wanted me to jump him. Did he think he'd wrestle away one of my weapons in the scuffle?

"What about Zane?" I asked.

"What about him?"

Blessed gods, I prayed Gunner had killed Zane before all this went down. That he wasn't loose and—

"Is he alive?" I asked.

Sheridan smiled. "He's had a promotion since he worked for you. He's a lieutenant in the king's army now. Probably in charge of that Vendan soldier you're so concerned about."

Wren's grip on my arm tightened.

Sheridan used that moment to lunge, not for me, but to the side, aiming for the candle on the runner only a few feet away. He dove, his hand knocking it over, and then the light was gone. Complete blackness engulfed us. There was shuffling, then the sound of pounding footsteps and, over it all, shouts. Ours.

The candle!

Find it!

Where is he?

None of us dared swing our weapons because we couldn't see one another. Synové's flint box sparked again and again, until she was finally able to catch the corner of her fur cloak and a small flame glowed bright enough from it for us to locate the candle and relight it.

I heard more scuffling, grunts, and panting from somewhere deep within the cavern, far beyond our circle of light. Carriages wheezed and collapsed as he stumbled into them in the dark.

"Come out, Sheridan!" I yelled. "There's nowhere to go."

He didn't answer.

Wren cursed. "We'll never find him in there."

I stared into the dusty blackness. "We don't have to," I answered.

We left, wedging every door shut behind us, though between the smothering darkness and the maze of crumbling carriages, he would never find the doors anyway. Sheridan had sealed his own fate. In a matter of days, if not hours, his horror-stricken face would join the army of those already down here.

Errdwor is their leader. He tells me his name and pounds his chest. He shakes with rage. He is older than me. Bigger than me. Stronger than me. He says I must obey. That I must open our gate. But he is not angrier than me. He was one of those who killed my grandfather.

—Greyson Ballenger, 15

CHAPTER TWENTY-SIX

KAZI

TOMORROW. I JUST HAD TO MAKE IT THROUGH ONE MORE DAY.
Once Lydia and Nash were safe, there would be no holding back. No
biding my time. Munitions would be found and destroyed. Kings and
generals would die. The papers the queen ordered me to find would be
confiscated from Gunner, who certainly had them stashed somewhere.
And I would be with Jase again. I would take care of him. Nurse him
back to health in the root cellar until he could manage to ride again, no
matter how long it took. Whatever it took. And then we would rebuild
Tor's Watch together. A dream that I thought was stolen began to bloom
in me again, unfurling like spring in the middle of winter.

I finished lacing my dress, taking a good long look at myself in the
mirror, and frowned. It wasn't a dress for a quiet dinner or an interroga-
tion. It was more of a party dress for a grand occasion and it was far too
revealing, but whatever was in store for tonight, I had to play along.
Distract and deflect. It was another kind of juggling, and for one night I
could do it. I had to secure the king's trust in a greater way so he would

drop his guard. *Feed his fantasies. Let his ego be your accomplice. He's only a mark, like any other*, I told myself.

But he wasn't like any other. I knew that. Even bloated merchants had rules they had to follow, people they had to answer to. The king answered to no one, and the only rules he followed were the ones he had made and could change on a whim.

I pulled on my bodice, trying to stretch it upward. I felt like Wren trying to make sense of an impractical piece of clothing. It was—

Stay. Don't move.

I spun. The room was quiet, unnaturally still, yet the air prickled. I felt the ghosts hovering, watching. Their cold feet paced, nervous. One of them slid a cool fingertip along my jaw. *Shhh, Kazi, don't—*

A firm knock on my door had me turning again. The chill vanished. Had Paxton forgotten something? Or maybe my escort had arrived early. The fact that I still required an escort at all showed I hadn't earned their trust yet, even if I was officially now in the king's employ. I had to chisel away their remaining doubts by tomorrow. If Paxton could do his job, I could do mine.

"Coming," I called.

I turned the bedside lantern to low and grabbed my cloak, eager to get this evening behind me, eager for tomorrow to begin. But when I opened the door, the face that greeted me made no sense. Shadows swam in my vision. For a moment I was nowhere in time, floating, lost. My blood drained and my breath disappeared. I couldn't move, every muscle suddenly useless. Liquid. Then terror shot through me, and on its heels, a hot rush of awareness returned. I slammed the door shut, but before I could latch it, he burst in, a fit of strength and rage, the door flying open, striking me and sending me stumbling back.

He pounced, pinning me against the wall, one hand a vise on my wrists, the other on my throat, not leaving any space between us for leverage, as if he had practiced this move for months. His skin burned against mine. "Surprise," he whispered.

My throat closed, air struggling to find a way in. "I'm your escort for tonight," he said. "A lieutenant in the king's army now. How's that for sweet justice?"

His voice was a thousand spiders crawling over my skin. My shoulders trembled against my will. It was only the two of us, and there was nowhere to go. *You're not powerless anymore, Kazi. Fight back.* Instinct and reason battled inside me. Natiya's constant words in training knocked inside my head. *Know your weaknesses, but play to your strengths.*

He was taller, stronger, heavier, a terrible weight pressing against me, but the greatest weakness I had were the king's rules. *If you ever so much as bruise . . .*

"I almost lost a finger because of *you*," he hissed. "Maybe I should take one of yours now as payment. Or maybe I should take something else?" He pushed harder, his full weight crushing me against the wall. "Your dead lover nearly killed me. I wish he could see this now."

Zane wasn't as afraid of me as I thought he would be. He was loose, hungry, emboldened, because now he had the strength of the king behind him. Because I was trapped, just like my mother had been.

Almost trapped.

As Natiya had ordered, I knew my strengths.

I had practiced too. In my mind.

A hundred times. A thousand times. All the ways.

Spit.

A twist of a wrist.

The jerk of an elbow jamming into a nose.

A knee in a groin.

Knuckles in the throat.

A strong kick to the kneecap.

A house of cards fluttering to the ground.

I didn't need a knife. Or a scalpel.

I knew all the ways.

And then as he lay writhing on the floor, a final crushing heel to the temple.

It was amazing how vulnerable the human body was.

He would be disabled, if not dead.

And very bruised.

If I killed him now, it would jeopardize everything. The king was expecting Zane to deliver me to his side, not to find him dead on the floor of my room. Besides breaking the rules, it would make all trust vanish. Killing him would unravel our plan and make this chance of saving Lydia and Nash disappear. It might even mean their deaths. Paxton was already busy setting our plan in motion. We were too close now. Tomorrow was too close.

"The king is expecting me," I said.

"Don't worry. I'm taking you to him—but I'm early. You didn't notice? There's a lot that can happen in twenty minutes. Don't you want to know what happened to your mother? Go ahead. Ask me." The faint lantern light glowed in his dark eyes, his taunt bringing him pleasure. *Where is the brat?* The room whirled. My skin burned. *Think, Kazi. Steady. Find your escape.*

"Banques," I choked out.

"What?"

I forced in a ragged breath. I had something more deadly than a fist to his throat. Something that would both frighten and finish him. He was already a dead man. He just didn't know it yet.

"You won't be doing anything once I tell Banques about you."

"Tell him what?"

"That you betrayed him. That you caved under questioning and gave up his name to Jase. *Devereux.* You told Jase he was the one who gave you the money for the labor hunters. How do you think that will sit with the general? Think you'll still be his lieutenant? No, you'll be swinging from a rope faster than you can wet your pants."

Instant panic shone in his eyes. He knew the general was fond of hanging, and his confession giving Banques over to Jase was easily a hanging offense.

"I only gave up his first name," he reasoned. "Not the rest. Your lover was about to cut me into pieces."

"You think that will matter to Banques?"

"I could just kill you now," he said, his hand tightening on my throat.

"And how would you explain that to the king who has added me to his payroll? I'm an employee now, just like you—and one he is far more fond of, in case you hadn't noticed."

His chest heaved and his eyes shrunk to tiny glass beads as he searched for a way out of this conundrum. His words tripped out ahead of his thoughts. "If you—if I'm dead, you'll never find your mother."

I flinched, feeling like I had been struck, my skin stinging. "My mother is dead," I replied.

"No, she isn't. And I know where she is. It's not far from here."

"You're lying. I know—"

"She's alive. I'll take you to her as soon as I can. But you keep your mouth shut about me to Banques. Understand? Or you'll never find out where she is."

His words were flat, dull, dead inside me. He was only searching for a way out of this. A way to keep me quiet. She wasn't alive. But what if—

Only this morning, I had thought Jase was dead too.

What if.

I didn't believe it, but I agreed to his terms. Having something deadly to hold over Zane's head could be useful if events spun out of control—an unwilling ally at best. I made a bargain with this devil, the very man who had ripped out my soul and now bribed me with the false hope of returning it.

I agreed because right now tomorrow mattered more than eleven years of wanting. But after tomorrow, I would still know where to find him. After tomorrow, everything would change. But he didn't know that. Yet.

Walking down a hallway with a monster I had feared for more than half of my life was the longest walk I had ever taken. It was endless and I was an empty shell by the time we reached the dining room. My resolve floated somewhere outside of me, like a ghost I couldn't see.

Head up, Kazi.

You can do this.

Feet forward. We're almost there.

Almost.

Jase.

He was alive.

That was all I needed to remember.

And that tomorrow was almost here.

CHAPTER TWENTY-SEVEN

JASE

IF I'D THOUGHT THE ARENA WAS BAD, THE TOWN WAS WORSE. Maybe it was desperation that made me think things would go in my favor just for once. Or that the gods would intercede. Surely all my vows and prayers had to count for something.

But not today.

Hell's Mouth was always gray in winter. The frost on the tembris dulled their leaves, as it did the skies, but this gray reached deeper, like a leech had sucked away the town's lifeblood. It was cold in a way I had never seen before, even the faces that passed me. None had life in them. Though the air was frigid, my temples blazed. I wanted to run, hunt down the king and kill him. Why hadn't someone already done it? Where were my magistrates? Wren jerked me closer to her side, sensing a madness overtaking me.

"Careful, husband," Synové warned. "We knew it would be bad." But I heard the catch in her voice. It was overwhelming her too. The brokenness wasn't just in the buildings or the cobbled streets—it permeated the air—and soldiers posted at every avenue and every roof-top kept hopelessness pinned in place.

Kazi was alive. Here. Somewhere. Some part of me had thought we would walk down the main street and I would spot her coming from the other direction and I'd sweep her into one of the many hidden passages I knew here.

Wren sucked in a breath. She saw the temple before I did. Even from the far end of the street and our small sliver of view, I saw the piles of rubble.

Caemus had told me, but telling didn't prepare me. The shining façade that had once greeted visitors was gone. The altar was still oddly erect, frozen out in the open, like a deer caught unaware in a blind, too afraid to move. Every vow I had ever made began in the temple—

Except for one. One vow began in the wilderness with Kazi.

I swallowed.

Montegue was responsible for all this? I still didn't believe it. He had no army and no money for one. He barely had an interest in ruling.

What about his tax money you keep? Could he be angry about that?

Kazi's doubts circled in my head. When we sent the tax money, we always gave him a full accounting of where the one percent we kept was spent. Montegue had never responded or objected. I'd assumed that was because our accounting showed that the one percent didn't begin to cover the costs of magistrates, repairs, cisterns, schools, the two infirmaries, and more. The list went on and on.

What if he deliberately chose a site that was in clear view of your memorial to aggravate you?

Montegue baiting us? I had thought that was impossible too because the king knew nothing about us or the memorial—but Zane did. And now I knew that Zane worked for the king. Anyone who lived in Hell's Mouth for any length of time knew of our yearly family pilgrimage to the site to repair the simple memorial and offer prayers of thanks for Aaron Ballenger and his sacrifice. If the settlement location was deliberately chosen to rouse our anger, that would mean our recent trouble wasn't a power struggle spurred on by my father's death, as we had believed, but a plan that had been in the making for a very long time—before my father died.

I spotted Aleski, our post messenger, walking toward us, his white-blond hair wild and loose beneath his hat, his lips chapped and cracked from the cold. He pushed a barrow of supplies. He had family in town, but he was rarely here, usually on the trail. Aleski had worked for us for years. He and Titus had once been very close, but even after they parted ways, they remained friends. I had a split second to decide—let him pass, or question him. He would not betray Titus or the rest of the family. I was certain.

"Meester," I called, lifting my hand in a stopping motion. We ambled toward him, and he lowered the barrow handles. When we were close, I whispered his name. His eyes widened and then filled with tears. "*Patrei?*" He swayed slightly, like he was ready to collapse.

"Pull it together, Aleski. We're Kbaaki. You're giving us directions. Point toward the mercantile."

He nodded and lifted his hand, pointing, but tears spilled down his cheeks. "They watch everything."

"I know. They're watching us now," I answered. Soldiers on the opposite corner had turned their attention toward us.

He wiped his nose. "We thought you were dead. That soldier who took you away said you'd been hanged. She said—"

"That soldier? You mean Kazi? Where is she?"

"She works for the king now, for the whole rotten bunch of them."

"No, she doesn't, Aleski. Trust me, she's his prisoner. If she said anything—"

"Hurry it along, boys," Wren whispered. "They're watching and coming this way any second."

"Is it true?" I asked. "Montegue is behind all this?"

He nodded. "Him and that general. We've tried to fight them." His voice was strained and full of apology.

"Aleski, I know. Their weapons are too powerful—"

"They're strolling this way," Synové warned in a singsong tone.

"Tonight, once it's dark, come to the south livery," I said. "We'll talk more there."

But Aleski continued on. His words ran together, desperate and crackling with hatred. "They hang loyalists from the tembris as a lesson." He rattled off names, Drake, Chelline the dressmaker, and more. I knew them all, and it took every bit of strength I had to keep the smile on my face as he spoke. "They confiscated my horse," he went on. "They're taking them from anyone who once worked for the Ballengers that they think might be a loyalist. I have family here in town, my mother and sister—I can't—"

Every time Aleski's voice cracked, my frozen smile did too, but my father's words seeped between Aleski's desperate ones. *When you have no strength left, you have to choice but to reach deep and find more, and then share it. It is the* Patrei's *job to lead.*

I grabbed his shoulders. "What is the rule, Aleski?" I whispered. "Catch them off guard. You know that. Take them by surprise. And that's what we're going to do. Why isn't the town decorated for Winter Festival? It's less than two weeks away. Do it. Today. Tell everyone to do it. Plan a celebration. Make these bastards think they've won and you're going about your business. Don't tell anyone I'm alive—not just yet—but tell them to be ready. The Ballengers are taking this town back."

"What's going on over there?" one of the soldiers called.

I patted Aleski's back as if thanking him and returned my hands to my sides.

Spirit wood. That was what was going on.

Aleski was already moving down the street with his barrow, carrying my message to the people of Hell's Mouth, and the soldiers explained to three out-of-place Kbaaki that spirit wood could only be had at the arena. "But they close early in winter. You'll have to go tomorrow." Vrud, Ghenta, and Eloh thanked them in their broken tongues, then asked about lodging.

There was none. The Ballenger Inn had been taken over by the king and his officers, and the other two inns were full. Staying at the stables with our horses was our only option.

I felt their eyes on my back as we walked away.

I felt the eyes watching me from the rooftops, wondering.

Is this big brute going to be trouble?

Yes. I was going to be trouble. In due time. They would be sorry they had ever laid eyes on this brutish Kbaaki. But for now, they would only see me head straight for the livery as we said we would, their concerns relieved.

What is the rule? Catch them unaware.

Aleski was going to tell me everything he knew to help me do just that.

Greyson will not speak to us. He lies in his bed, his eyes frozen on the ceiling. His hands are always fists. Miandre is gone. They have taken her. And we don't know how to get her back.

—**Theo, 13**

CHAPTER TWENTY-EIGHT

KAZI

I BURST INTO THE ROOM, STUMBLING PAST ZANE TO PUT DISTANCE between us. I was propelled like I was racing down a Vendan alleyway, searching for a shadow, needing a dark stairwell to hide behind, a place to disappear.

Montegue noticed. Sudden moves by me were still suspect. Whatever he was saying to the circle of young women surrounding him, he cut off mid-sentence and stared at me. I nodded, acknowledging his gaze, then stepped more confidently into the middle of the room, trying to erase my shaky entrance. His attention returned to his admirers, who hung on his every word.

We were in the expansive parlor of the Ballenger Inn. The iron chandeliers overhead glowed with flickering lights, and the conversation of dozens of the king's many cohorts buzzed through the room. Judging from Banques's rigid order, I was expecting a small, interrogation-filled dinner with the king, but this looked more like a party. A celebration? For what?

Truko was passing by, a tankard of ale in each hand, and I stopped him. "What's going on?" I asked.

"You didn't notice? The town began decorating today for Winter Festival. General Banques is pleased and thought a celebration was in order." Truko himself had a pleased expression. Maybe it was the bottomless pitchers of ale that lit his face with a smile, or maybe he was fully in partnership with the new leadership now, all those arena profits too tempting. Paxton said he thought he could trust him, but I wasn't so sure. Jase had told me he was the greediest of the league leaders, that he would steal the socks off a baby if there was profit in it. He continued on his way, saying someone was waiting for their tankard, and the celebration closed in tighter around me, the room growing increasingly hot.

The townspeople were decorating for a festival. Gaiety on the streets of Hell's Mouth? It was a well-aimed punch in my stomach.

They're forgetting the Patrei. *Moving forward.*

Was the king right? Was I the one who had misjudged the murmuring crowd? Resentment shot through me. Of course the general was pleased. But if loyalists backed off and moved forward, what would that mean for Lydia and Nash? For the rest of the Ballengers still trapped in the mountain? Tomorrow seemed a lifetime away. Where was Paxton? I strained to find him in the mass of bodies.

I moved farther into the room. A long table arranged down the center was already overflowing with food and decorated with gay ribbons and garlands. Tall brass candelabras twinkled with candles. More tables around the room were set in a similar manner to accommodate all the guests. For someone worried about finances, Montegue seemed to be spending coin freely. I finally spotted Paxton over in the corner speaking with Garvin. He eyed me briefly, then looked away, as if he feared detection, and I looked away too. I was always afraid I was being watched, if not by Montegue, then by someone who had his ear.

Oleez filled steins with ale and goblets with wine, and Dinah delivered them to guests. I spotted the women from the dinner party several nights ago, now dressed in even more extravagant gowns—and there were others too. The king's admirers appeared to be growing in pace with his growing domination. But I knew at least two—Oleez and Paxton—were not among them. Maybe there were more who pasted on smiling, obedient expressions for fear of their lives. I scanned the crowded room and wondered who any of them might really be—allies, enemies, or maybe undecided. Were they frightened and just trying to survive? Were they hanging garlands on their homes too? Were they forgetting the *Patrei*? *Of course they are, Kazi. You called him a convicted criminal who was served justice. You said he was dead and told them to move on.* Did Paxton loathe playing the traitor as much as I did?

I spotted the seer I had met at the Ballenger party. She sat in a corner, alone, a small goblet of drink her only company. Her hood was still pulled over her head as if she expected to leave any moment, or maybe it was just that she wanted to remain unnoticed, a dark shadow in the corner. Was she the one who had warned the king about a bitter season coming? I knew her gift was genuine. Jase had told me about her as we burrowed beneath a blanket on a cold plain.

The seer warned me about you. She said you were coming to cut out my heart.

She spoke true. It didn't hurt too much, now, did it?

It hurt plenty. But I don't want it back. It's yours to keep—forever.

I had unbuttoned his shirt and kissed his chest then, like I was kissing a wound, his skin hot against my lips, while my hands explored other places. *Forever,* I had whispered. *I'm holding you to that,* Patrei.

Forever. We had tossed the word around easily. We owned the world. For those few weeks, the word seemed fashioned just for us. We were headed back to establish a new kingdom. To establish a new family.

He wasn't conscious. He was barely breathing. He could be dead by now.

And then there were other words that I crushed beneath my feet, refusing to hear. Once Paxton told me Jase was alive, I couldn't accept anything else. *Five arrows, Kazi. One was in his chest. It didn't sound good.*

I looked back at the seer. Did she work for the king now? Surely a seer couldn't switch sides—she only knew what she knew. But did I dare go near her? Would she see my secrets as she had before? Or would she have news of Jase?

I crossed the room before I could think about it any more. *Maggielle*, Jase had called her. I knelt before her, looking up into the shadows of her hood, my heart bunched into knots, hoping she could offer me something. *News.*

"Is there something I can get for you, Maggielle? Another drink perhaps?"

Blue ice glowed beneath her wrinkled lids, and wild spirals of black and silver hair circled her face.

She shook her head. "There is nothing I can do for you. I see no face or name, but I do see betrayal. You will be caught up in its snare." Her head turned like she was trying to see deeper into my thoughts. "Guard your tongue. Guard your trust even more."

But instead of guarding my tongue, desperation took hold of it. "*Jase.* What do you see of him?"

"The *Patrei*," she said slowly, letting each syllable roll through her graveled throat. The grim sound made my stomach twist. Her lids lowered so only a sliver of blue showed beneath them, but in that fleeting moment, I saw time, stars, and galaxies pass through them. She looked up abruptly, her eyes skimming the room. She grabbed her goblet in her crooked fingers and took a shaky sip. "It is time for you to go. Hurry. I see nothing else."

Nothing? No, she had seen something, but she didn't want to tell me. Because she didn't trust me, or because it might destroy me? I stood and stumbled away, forgetting to even thank her, unsure why she had dismissed me so abruptly. She was worried about betrayal? Nearly everyone in this room had betrayed me already. And earning my trust was already a rare feat.

Dinah was suddenly at my elbow. "The king said to bring you this." She held out a large goblet of deep red wine, the surface shivering.

I took it from her shaking hand. "What's wrong, Dinah? Are you cold?"

"No, ma'am," she said quickly and hurried away. Nervous. Perhaps afraid of spilling a glass and incurring the wrath of—nearly anyone. Or afraid because she, too, didn't know whom to trust.

The evening proceeded, it seemed endlessly. Was there really so much for these constantly evolving circles of people to laugh and chat about? Without Wren and Synové here to help me navigate a party, I was lost and drifting. I wondered what they were doing now, how they were, and what mission the queen had sent them on. Paxton was an ally, but he was no Wren and Synové. I didn't know if he even had any fighting skills or only relied on his *straza* to get him out of tight spots. But he had been able to whisk Jase away without detection, and I prayed that feat was all devious craft and no luck.

I moved around the room, trying to look like I fit in—like I was truly, in name and heart, now a converted and loyal employee of the king. Chatting happily with potential Ballenger traitors was not easy, so I imagined I was in the *jehendra*, smiling, strolling, juggling, while I eyed a fat, juicy pigeon to slip beneath my coat. But instead of stealing food, I tried to procure information, because after tomorrow my hands would no longer be tied and I would have a new mission—find where Banques and the king had the ammunition stored, and then somehow destroy it— without destroying the entire town.

A dinner bell was finally rung, and guests were shown to their seats.

I noticed that Montegue was seated at the end of the table with Banques, Paxton, Truko, and Garvin, and they were already in deep conversation about something. I was led to the other end of the table and startled when I saw that Zane was seated across from me. My stomach crawled up my throat. It was going to be a very long evening. I kept my eyes down, trying to remember that tomorrow all this would be over—if Paxton did his job as planned. I stared at the dishes servers laid before me and nudged the contents with my fork, but I couldn't eat them. My appetite was gone. I focused instead on silverware, and a napkin I continually adjusted in my lap. Montegue was absorbed in food and conversation so I at least didn't have to perform for him. Everyone ate, minutes passed, my food grew cold. I eyed the silver knife next to my plate shimmering beneath the candlelight, begging to be used. *Die tomorrow, Kazi, for everyone's sake, die tomorrow. Not today.* But averting my eyes from the knife couldn't block out the sounds, and I still heard Zane speaking to guests around us as if everything in the world was right for him. His words wrapped around me like a sickening shroud. I sank into a black world, a world where a stick was too far out of my reach.

Come out, girl!

He spoke of other things, but all I heard were words that refused to die.

You'll bring a nice profit.

Where is she?

Where is the brat?

My eyes shot up, and then I couldn't take them away. They were frozen on his face the way they had been that long-ago night, and it felt like the room held only Zane and me. Only us, connected by my mother and five terrifying minutes. I found myself crawling out of a dark prison inch by inch. I looked at the mole on his wrist, his bloodless skin, his stringy hair and black eyes. He felt my glower and turned. I dipped my knife into the cold crockery dish, spun it cleverly around so butter curled upward in ruffled circles like meat being shaved from a hock. Zane's next words hung in the air, unsaid, his black eyes shifting from me to the knife and back again. I slathered the curled butter onto a thick slice of bread, then dipped the knife back into the crock for more, spinning it again, imagining it boring into Zane, curling flesh, cutting away a piece of him at a time.

"Very clever how you do that," the woman seated next to Zane said.

I slathered another curl of butter on my bread, then dipped the knife in for more.

"You like butter, do you?" another guest noted.

"No," I answered, "in fact, I detest butter. I only like the way the knife feels cutting through it. So smooth and easy."

Zane's eyes froze with fear. Maybe not because he thought I would stab him, but that at any moment I might burst out and tell everyone about him, that I would steal his life from him the way he stole mine. My mind was what he feared, and the dark plans it might be fashioning. My mind was something he couldn't control. Not even with the promise of seeing my mother again. *She is gone, Kazi. Gone.*

But I heard her voice. Fresh. New. There. *My* chiadrah. *Eat, my darling. You must eat.*

I couldn't let it go. Hope. It rose up from some hidden place inside me.

Damn him to the hottest corner of hell for doing this to me again.

I released the knife, letting it clatter loudly against the crockery, and ate my cold dinner. Food should never be wasted.

Dinah nudged me. "The king is asking you a question," she whispered.

I looked up. The king and everyone at the other end of the table was staring at me.

"Is there a problem?" Montegue asked.

I wiped my mouth with my napkin and set it aside. "No, Your Majesty. Just hungry and absorbed with the food." I apologized and asked him to repeat his question.

"I understand that you tell riddles. Will you entertain everyone and tell us one now?"

Riddles? My temples burned, wondering how he knew. I had never told riddles to anyone but Jase and—

Garvin must have seen the confusion on my face. "Mustafier," he spoke up. "A merchant who sells trinkets on the arena floor. He sings your praises."

Mustafier. I didn't know his name, but I did remember him. The logophile who gave me the vine ring as payment. Still, I wondered at the king's motives. Entertain everyone? I doubted that. There was nothing he loved more than hearing his own voice. Maybe his point was that he knew things about me, things I didn't even realize he knew. He had ears and eyes everywhere.

I stood and thought for a minute. The room remained quiet, waiting.

"All right," I said. "Here you go." I told several short riddles, easy ones about trees, eggs, and noses. After each one, muttering circled the table as guests discussed possible answers, but the king was always the first to answer.

"Surely you have something harder for me to guess?" Montegue said after the fourth one.

Many. But sometimes the point of a riddle wasn't its difficulty but the depth of its distraction. "Let me think for a moment," I answered, but I already knew one that would offer sufficient distraction. "Listen carefully," I said. "I won't repeat myself." He nodded in reply, and I began.

"I sleep in a cave, dark and small,

Rarely do you see me at all.

But an angry word can lure me out,

Slashing and roaring, and tearing about.

Sometimes I sneak slow, my prey in sight,

I'm deceptive, stalking, with lethal bite.

My mighty stabs, my stinging whip,

Catch my enemy in their brutal grip.

But sweet delights draw me out in haste,

Luring me, naked, with seductive taste.

Honey, wine, cakes so sweet,

Sugared cookies, fruited meat,

But desire's tug can seduce me too,

I'm always searching for a kiss that's true."

This time there were no mutterings. Several mouths hung open. They were either stumped or words like *naked*, *seduce*, and *kiss* had sent their minds skittering in breathless directions. I noted the bare hint of a swallow in Montegue's throat. His eyes sank deep into mine. He knew the answer.

"A rather lofty riddle for such a simple piece of flesh," he finally said.

"Simple? On the contrary, Your Majesty. The tongue outlives the body. It can topple kingdoms—and create them. It can lead armies and destroy them. Its power is not in its size or beauty, but its cleverness and enduring strength."

"How can something be powerful if it's easily seduced?"

I shrugged. "Maybe that's the curse of our humanity. We all need sustenance of some kind, don't we?"

"A true kiss?" Garvin called out, laughing. "Do you really believe in such a thing?"

Yes, you backstabbing asshole, though I would never expect you to experience anything true.

But I tilted my head thoughtfully and answered, "It's only a simple riddle, Garvin. Meant for entertainment. Take from it what you will. But just because you've never experienced anything true doesn't mean it couldn't exist. You've never washed behind your ears either. It doesn't mean that, by some miracle, it couldn't one day happen."

Everyone laughed. Montegue only offered a small distracted smile. His mind was elsewhere.

Dessert tables were filled, and guests once again meandered in circles, chatting and laughing. I was ready to poke my eyes out with the glut and pretense. All I wanted to do was excuse myself and return to my room, but then Oleez swooped in at my elbow, pretending to refill my already full glass. She smiled as she whispered, "I understand I should speak to you."

My heart kicked against my ribs. *He did it.* Paxton had convinced the king. He said he would pass the word to me through Oleez. I had seen him and the king leaning close during dinner, deep in conversation, Montegue absently rubbing his cheek in thought.

"Yes," I answered quietly, looking around to make sure we were a safe distance from any prying ears. There was no time for more than the barest details, so I kept my instructions short. "Tomorrow morning you will be sick. Vomiting. Unable to accompany the children where we are going. You'll suggest to the king they'll be fine on their own with one of the guards watching over them. You must be convincing. Once we're gone, you'll leave the inn and go into hiding. It won't be safe here for you anymore. Do you have someone you trust who will hide you?"

She nodded.

"Good. Then you must disappear completely. And tell no one."

Her eyelids creased with fear. "I'll be safe, but what about the children?"

"Keep smiling, Oleez. You never know who is watching," I warned, then laughed, trying to undo any damage her stricken expression may have done. "I will do my very best to keep them safe, but it won't be easy or without danger."

"They're already in danger. He hates Ballengers," she whispered through a smile. "All of them. I see him stare at the children sometimes. His expression frightens me. Every day I worry that he will—"

She stepped away, the carafe she held sloshing with her quick movement.

"I need you in my study." I whirled to face the king. "There's something we need to discuss. *Now*." He walked away without looking back, knowing I would follow.

Had Paxton's suggestion backfired?

Something had gone wrong.

CHAPTER TWENTY-NINE

JASE

"DON'T," SYNOVÉ WHISPERED. "DON'T EVEN THINK ABOUT IT."

She'd caught me staring at the Ballenger Inn. From the side of the livery, I had a view of one lit window. Something was going on there tonight. A party of some sort. And I knew in my gut, Kazi was there. *She's working for the king now.* I knew that wasn't possible, but something was keeping her there. What was it? Blackmail? What could Montegue be holding over her head?

"It's hard not to think about it," I answered. Hard didn't begin to describe it. My insides churned as I tried to come up with a way to get in the inn, some way to get her out, and my eyes ached with staring at that window hoping for one small glimpse of her. She was so close, but I couldn't get to her. I had already run through a hundred possibilities, but what excuse would a Kbaaki trader give to the guards posted at every entrance? A fake party invitation? Force my way in? Did she even know I was alive?

Synové leaned against the stable wall beside me, the night so black I could barely see that she was there at all. She sighed. "I know what it's like not to be able to get to someone and help them. When Kazi went missing that first day, I wanted into Tor's Watch so bad I was ready to kill all those wretched watchdogs of yours and your guards too. I could have, you know? All of them."

Synové ran hot and cold on confidence. Right now she ran hot. "Maybe," I answered. "My guards are pretty good shots."

"Pretty good?" She snorted. "That's about as impressive as a half-finished bridge across a river."

"Then what stopped you?"

"Wren. She talked me out of it. It wasn't part of the plan. She knew it was just my emotion all charged up. We work well together that way. Balance, Kazi calls it. We keep each other's heads straight."

"Is that what you're doing now? Trying to keep my head straight?"

"She's all the family I've got, *Patrei*. Her and Wren. I'm not going to lose her because you want to kill a bunch of dogs."

I squeezed my eyes shut, grateful she couldn't see me in the dark. *I'm not going to lose her either.*

I pushed off from the livery wall. *Forget the party invitation.* I needed some power, and I knew where to get it. "Aleski's not going to show. Let's get out of here." Our next stop was to retrieve my lone hidden weapon and a bag of ammunition. There was no sense in waiting, but Synové put an arm out to stop me.

"Pack up now? We need rest, *Patrei*, and Wren is rustling up some food for us, not to mention traveling at night would draw attention."

"We can eat on the road. And I know back roads—"

"The *streets*. First we have to get through these damn streets that have eyes on every corner. What are you going to say when they ask you where you're going at this hour? You can't—"

The livery door flew open, golden light spilling across the alley. It was Wren. Her expression made both Synové and me draw our weapons.

"We have a problem," she confirmed.

I stepped forward and looked through the doorway. Aleski stood behind her—and he had brought company.

"I'm sorry, *Patrei*," Aleski said. "I had no choice. I had to tell them."

CHAPTER THIRTY

KAZI

WAS IT URGENCY OR ANGER I HEARD IN HIS VOICE? I MENTALLY prepared my answer for him, but as soon as he shut the chamber door, he turned and said something entirely different from what I was expecting. "You lied to me this evening."

I was at a loss, and my mind raced trying to think what misstep I had made. Nearly everything about me was a lie. "I don't know what—"

"You claimed you were absorbed with your food, but it was Zane you were absorbed with. You loathe him. Why?"

Zane. My skin crawled at just the mention of his name.

I shook my head and turned away, but in two steps, the king was next to me, his hand gripping my arm, but not in a threatening way. "Tell me," he said quietly.

I couldn't reveal the depth of my revulsion for Zane or the reasons why I hated him. Jase was the first and only person I had ever shared every ugly detail with, and even that had been painful. I had also made a bargain with Zane. A futile, empty bargain of silence, but that slim sliver of hope—I couldn't let it go. "I have nothing personal against him," I answered.

"It's the Previzi, then? I witnessed your tirade against them at the arena—just before you slugged the *Patrei*. Why do you hate them?"

"Do I need a reason? Their activities are illegal."

"And yet you were once an accomplished thief."

"A thief who remembers starving on the streets of Venda. The Previzi never treated people like me kindly, or even with the slightest bit of compassion." These words I didn't have to invent. Every one was true. "We were beneath them," I said. *Vermin, crapcakes, nothing.* "They paraded their fancy goods past us, then sold them all to the Komizar and rich merchants. They only offered the rest of us their moldy bags of grain crawling with weevils—if that. More often, we were showered with their disdain. Their haughty sneers will always be burned in my memory."

He studied me. "Hunger is what drove you to become a thief?"

I shrugged. "Starvation can be quite motivating."

His stare dissected me, the sly king who calculated every move. But a flutter and a fraction of a second revealed dusky eyes that were hungry. He held back, wary. He did not come by trust easily, and I was glad. I didn't want that moment to come too soon. Tomorrow. At just the right moment. "I understand the sting of disdain," he finally said, "but that was a long time ago and Zane is useful to me. He's a comforting, familiar face at the arena. Merchants know him. I'd like you to bury your past grudges."

I noted his use of the word *like*, instead of simply ordering me to bury my grudge. *Patience, Kazi. He's circling, swimming closer.* I paused as if I was weighing his request. "If he's useful to you, of course. I will do my best to bury the past."

"Besides," he added, "you're not beneath the Previzi anymore. You work for the king. Soon to be the most powerful king on the continent. Remember that."

"Yes, Your Majesty."

His eyes rested lazily on my face. "In private, you may call me Montegue."

Closer. But it wasn't the kind of closer I was ready for just yet.

"You wished to speak about something?" I prompted, hoping to move on.

"Banques informed me you did a thorough job searching today. He was pleased with your work."

"Really? He seemed disappointed when I spoke with him."

"The general is not one to lavish praise freely. But he told me you uncovered a few hidden spaces we didn't know about."

"Nevertheless, I found nothing."

"But at dinner this evening Paxton told me you had a *moment*, as he called it, in the main house. He said you hesitated as if you sensed something. Does this mean you have the gift?"

I frowned even as a smile lit within my chest. *Well done, Paxton.* I played down the abilities that Paxton had seeded, but the king responded exactly the way we wanted him to, like he was reading lines from a play that we had written.

"No," I answered, "nothing like the queen, if that's what you're thinking. But sometimes . . . I don't know. I do get a feeling."

"Paxton thinks we should return there tomorrow and do another search of the main house. I agree."

I sighed as if unconvinced. Like everything else, it had to be his idea. "As you wish. I'm grateful to be in your employ and at your service, but I can't promise anything. There was a wing, though, that I had a nagging sense about. I don't know what it means, but I would like to try again."

"It's settled, then. We go back tomorrow." He paused and looked down at my foot. "I noticed you've had a limp this evening. Paxton said you injured it today?"

"My leg?" I said, looking down like I hadn't noticed. "Oh, it's nothing. I caught my foot beneath a fallen timber today and twisted my ankle a bit. That's all. I'm sure it will be fine by morning."

"We'll make a stop at Gods Pavilion on the way. You can soak it there."

I knew he'd want to stop there anyway—Paxton said he almost always did on his way to Tor's Watch—but my limp assured it. I feigned surprise. "Thank you. That would be helpful—and very kind of you, Your Maj—*Montegue*."

I was about to excuse myself, thinking our business was finished, when there was a tap on the door. Dinah opened it gingerly, then entered with a tray holding two glasses and a small crystal carafe of dark amber liqueur. Though he wasn't stumbling, the king was already well liquored up from a long night of celebrating. One more glass, and I was sure he would be tripping over his feet, and I was certain the second glass was for me.

Montegue released my arm and waved Dinah to a low table in front of a lush overstuffed couch with wooden legs that looked like claws. She set the tray down, then glanced at me, almost impatiently, maybe as a warning. Perhaps she thought I couldn't handle the king—or the strong drink. Montegue dismissed her, but she looked over her shoulder as she exited the room, her chestnut curls peeking from her cap. I nodded to reassure her, but her eyes lingered on Montegue.

"Anything else, Your Majesty? Attend to the fire in the hearth, perhaps? I can stay and—"

"No. I'll tend to it. You're dismissed." She closed the door reluctantly behind her.

The room was chilly, but the king digging logs out from the pile and getting his hands dirty? His expertise was in keeping his hands clean. He was anxious for her to leave.

"I can do it," I offered and knelt on the thick rug before the hearth to pull kindling from the leather sling beside it. I stirred the hot embers with a poker and set the dry sticks on top. The small flames licked upward.

The clink of glasses sounded behind me. I glanced over my shoulder. Montegue was staring at me, a drink in hand. A second filled glass sat on the table waiting for me. I turned back to the hearth and grabbed a log.

There was a long silence, and he finally said, "So, none of your kisses with the *Patrei* were true?" My spine stiffened. I thought this conversation would happen in the morning. Not now. He should be with his guests, but I suppose the king did what he wanted when he wanted.

"I already told you. Anything you saw was only—"

"Yes, I know, part of your job. But you said it was a pleasant way to pass the time."

I shrugged indifferently. "I suppose his kisses were passable, but nothing about them was lasting or really mattered. I've already forgotten them, to be honest."

Forgotten. A word he valued when it came to Jase.

"Tell me more . . . What was the *Patrei* like?"

It was always on his mind. He still battled Jase's ghost. Killing him wasn't enough. His obsession with the *Patrei* made me understand more than ever why Paxton had to produce a body. Even if I had to endure the horror of a dismembered hand wearing Jase's gold ring a hundred more times, I was grateful for Paxton's clever deception. It was all that kept Jase safe and gave him time to recover. I poked the coals, and sparks flew upward. Could I lie convincingly in detail to Montegue about Jase? Could I say he was a greedy, arrogant coward when I knew

Jase was the exact opposite of all those things? Simply saying I hated him was one thing, but having to go into the details of who Jase had been was another.

"You knew him longer than I did," I answered. "You probably knew him far better."

"But I was never a guest in his home. I never ate a meal with him, never punched him, held a knife to his throat, or arrested him and dragged him across the continent. You spent many *intimate* moments with him."

I heard his emphasis on *intimate*, and the question the single word held. Was there more than a kiss between us?

"Yet, in spite of the time spent with him, I failed in my ultimate goal—and the conceited ass reminded me of that fact every day. You, on the other hand, killed him. You beat him at his own game, and managed to do it without even getting your hands dirty. I'm the one who should be asking you questions. You achieved your goal, while I did not. And for a Rahtan, that is not an easy admission."

I heard the wheeze of the couch as he settled into it. I stood and he motioned for me to join him. I sat on the opposite end. It didn't take much to distract him from his original question. It always came back to the fantasy, the world a mark builds, the sense and value they make of their lives, the story they've invented that must be fed: *You are shrewder, wiser, more worthy.*

Let the illusion bloom.

That was my job.

As I sat down, I had to toss only one small morsel to him, a simple query for him to tell me everything. *How long have you been planning this?* Because if I knew anything after engaging hundreds of merchants in the *jehendra*, it was that everyone had a story that they burned to tell, the true story they believed no one else could ever get right, the injustices they endured, the unserved accolades they deserved. As a thief on the streets, I had become proficient at listening to them, nodding, agreeing, prodding them along, watching marks lose sight of this world as they drifted into another. And with every word I listened to, I gained their confidence. At last, someone who understood them.

Montegue's focus shifted from me to the fire, the fantasy alive in his gaze. He was pleased that I had asked, and leaned back, propping his feet up on the low table in front us and lifted the small glass of amber liqueur to his lips. He gulped it back and poured another.

The story unraveled seamlessly, as if he had told it in the darkest corner of his mind a hundred times, which I was sure he probably had. It was a story that held equal parts of bitterness and pride. That was what he wanted me to hear, the triumph of his cunning and patience, but there was another part to his story I knew he didn't mean to reveal to me. His crippling need. It churned inside of him.

Disdain. Now I knew why he said he understood it. The word was a choking vine winding though him. I listened, nodding, even as I chilled at the depth of his jealousies. Their roots twisted deeper than I expected.

The plan had been forming in his head since he was twelve years old, and was revised as time passed. It became an obsession for him. *For eleven years.*

"You were practically a child," I said, trying not to sound too shocked.

"Successful plans take time," he answered. "Of course I couldn't proceed with any plan while my father was king, but I always knew that one day Tor's Watch, the arena, all of it—would be mine, but I couldn't do anything about it until my father was dead."

"Did you kill—"

"My father? No. That was just more good luck. It was how I knew the gods didn't want me to wait any longer. They wanted me to have all this, and then when I met Beaufort, I knew the gods wanted me to have even more."

The gods favored Montegue? How lucky for him. I wasn't sure if even he believed it himself, but he had to paint the picture of his rightness, the sheer holiness of his plan. If he said it enough times, it would become true.

"You already ruled over Eislandia, and you had the fortress in Parsuss. Wasn't that enough?"

He chuckled. "*Fortress* is a generous word for a drafty, crumbling twelve-room citadel. You've never been to Parsuss, have you?"

"No."

He said that his father split his time between three farms the Montegues had owned for generations, the one in Parsuss and two in the highlands not far from Hell's Mouth that raised sheep and grew summer crops. The three together barely kept food on the table and paid the few laborers they employed. The meager taxes his father collected paid his small stable of officials who kept the kingdom running, the coffers always bleeding into red. I asked about his mother, and he said he had never known her—she died when he was a baby. It was always just him and his father, and the few laborers who came and went. It was a lonely life.

"And then, when I was twelve, I visited the Ballenger arena with my father. It was much smaller back then, mostly farmers, but it still looked enormous to me. I was a wide-eyed rube." His nostrils flared as if his own naïveté repulsed him. He took another drink. Had he parodied himself? The green rube who played the bumbling king? "I'd never seen so many traders and so much merchandise in one place. Every corner was filled with noise and food, and possibility. It crackled through the air as alive as a whip. I was transfixed. The world was at everyone's fingertips—except, that is, for the king and his son.

"Karsen Ballenger was giving my father a tour. I trailed behind, along with half the Ballenger brood. Jase was maybe seven or eight at the time, a runny-nosed little brat who didn't even know how much he had. Karsen was orating on and on about the Ballenger history, trying to convince my father that they were the first family of Eislandia, here long before the Montegues. My father asked to see this vault with all the history written in it, and you know what Karsen said to my father?"

Montegue paused, his lip twisted at the memory. "*No. He told him no.* He said it was only for family. He told the ruling monarch of Eislandia *no*, without so much as an apology or blink."

He repeated the word *no* quietly, but I still heard all the anger it held. "And then you know what my father did?"

I knew I didn't need to reply. This was a story he had lived over and over again. The answer was ready on his tongue waiting to be spit out. "Nothing," he finally said. "My father did absolutely *nothing*. He bought the seed and stock we had come for and we left, two cows trailing behind us. I burned with shame the whole way home, and I decided on that ride back that I would not be a farmer like my father. I would not blister my hands on a hoe or break my back behind a plow, and most of all, I would not suffer the disrespect of underlings.

"By the time we got home, my shame bubbled over, and I screamed at him and called him a stupid farmer. And you know what he did?"

I shook my head.

"What he always did. Nothing." He winced and swigged back the last of his liqueur, then grabbed the carafe and poured himself more. "I decided that day I wasn't going to be the man my father was, the man who was the sniveling butt of all the kingdom's jokes, the king no one listened to. Do you have any idea how hard it was to hear subjects say they had to check with the *Patrei* first when I gave them orders? My own magistrates in Hell's Mouth deferred to Karsen Ballenger, and then to Jase. I will not be a nothing ruler."

"Farming is an honorable profession. The Ballengers have farms."

"The Ballengers *had* farms," he corrected. "The Ballengers had everything, but now it's mine, as it should have been all along. A mistake was made three generations ago. The border should have included the arena and Tor's Watch. Then maybe my father would have been a proper king I could have been proud of. Now *I* will be that king. The greatest ruler the world has ever known. When I have a son, he will be proud of his father, and I will get respect the Montegues always deserved—from *all* the kingdoms."

My breath pooled in my chest. The way he said *all*, the way his jaw clenched, the way the haze from a night of drinking vanished and his eyes turned to hard glass—it reminded me of someone else.

I recalled standing on the edge of Blackstone Square, hidden in the shadows listening to the Komizar speak as he rallied forces for his growing army. *All of them*, he had shouted. His voice was strong and seemed to reach to the mountains. *All the kingdoms will bend a knee to Venda—or be slaughtered.* I was ten and immune to swaggering talk by then—except from the Komizar. His words always contained a chilling promise in them, unlike anyone else's. Some had thought he was a god. I had thought him a demon. I remembered slipping deeper into the shadows as if he might spot me from afar, as if he had some special power, and maybe even now I still wondered if he did.

All. That's what I heard in Montegue's voice now.

His hunger ran deep. Eleven years deep. So deep he was willing to use children as a shield and hang innocent people from trees to ensure obedience. Willing to pay labor hunters to steal away his own citizens. Willing to murder the rightful ruler of Hell's Mouth and confiscate his holdings. How many things was he willing to do that I didn't even know about yet?

Imagine the possibilities.

I was afraid to.

His feet dropped from the table to the floor, and he rose abruptly. "It's getting late," he said. "You should turn in. We'll be leaving early."

I was caught off guard by his sudden dismissal and was surprised by how deliberately he stood, no sway or stumble to his stance. He didn't seem drunk at all. "Of course, Your Maj—"

And then he took hold of my wrist and slowly pulled me close, firm and sure.

"Do you want to kiss me? Compare a *Patrei* to a king? See if it could be more than passable?" he asked.

I gaped at him, searching for an answer. I had thought his mind would be more consumed with the missing papers and my supposed premonition than on the small matter of a kiss, but after hearing how long he'd been planning this invasion, I guessed that maybe there was no such thing as a small matter when it came to the Ballengers, especially the *Patrei*. I weighed my answer carefully, knowing a *no* could send him into a sullen rage, but a too-eager *yes* could spike his suspicions and make him think I was using him the way I had used Jase. And he very much wanted me to judge him differently than I had Jase because he was a king and was different, better, smarter. He had to best the *Patrei* I had rejected, the *Patrei* who had wanted me. My pause made his fingers tighten on my wrist.

I blinked, as if embarrassed. "I admit, I am curious."

"Of course you are."

His other hand slipped behind my back, and he pulled me closer, lowering his face to mine, but before our lips met, I twisted free and stepped back.

"Curious," I said firmly, "but cautious." I wrung my hands and tripped over my words. "I will not deny there's a strong attraction, but—" I shook my head. "I'm not sure exactly what I'm trying to say. But I've seen the women circling around you. I don't want to be one of them. I don't want—" I gasped and looked at him as if horrified. "It's not that I—What I'm trying to say is I'm certain your kisses are more than passable, and I admit I've wondered about them, but I want more than—" I sucked in a long, shaky breath. "I need to stop. I'm afraid nothing is coming out quite the way I intended. May I sleep on this?"

He regarded me for a long while, his black eyes fixed on mine. "You want something more than what you had with the *Patrei*. Something true."

I blinked, certain he could hear my heart pounding wildly. "Is that foolish of me?"

Of course it wasn't. Because he was more worthy. More beautiful. More of everything. My words made complete sense.

A faint smile lit his eyes. "Go. Get a good night's sleep. We'll continue this conversation in the morning."

And with that, he dismissed me to return to my room. Without an escort.

Because a soldier in his employ confessed her strong attraction to him. She wanted more than what she had with the *Patrei*, and with all her fumbling, he imagined that she even blushed when she said it. She was certainly someone trustworthy enough to walk to her room alone. She would be back. She wanted him, after all. As she should.

CHAPTER THIRTY-ONE

JASE

W<small>E HUDDLED IN A CORNER OF THE STABLE JUST OUTSIDE</small> M<small>IJE'S</small>
stall, keeping our voices low so the sleeping stable boy in the livery office
wouldn't waken. I couldn't stay angry at Aleski, especially after the bone-
crunching embrace I received from his older sister, Imara. She had all
the brawn that Aleski did not. His lean physique served him well as a
post messenger, and her tall, muscular stature served her equally well as
a farrier.

"You took a chance coming here," I said.

"Not me," Imara answered, patting her bag of tools beside her. "No
one thinks twice about seeing me walk into a livery."

Wren was busy admiring the gifts Imara had snuck in her bag—two
dozen tiny but very sharp, well-weighted throwing knives that could be
easily concealed.

Aleski said they hadn't arrived together but converged after first
stopping at a local pub.

"They still allow us to drink," Lothar fumed. "They want us to spend
money."

"I think the ruse of the festival is already working," Aleski said. "More citizens were out tonight." He thought that seeing the cheerful garlands and the citizens relaxing made the guards' tight grip ease too. He saw two of them joking on a corner with the cooper, which they had never done before.

"There was even a party going on tonight," Imara added. "I hope the whole bloody lot drink themselves into oblivion."

My mind went back to the party. Was she there, or did they keep her locked up when they didn't need her? What was Montegue's hold on her? The questions ate away at me like buzzards picking my bones.

For the first time, we heard the full course of events that led to the takeover, not overheard pieces of the story shared by Caemus, or grudging bits shared by traitors.

They told us it began with a two-week bombardment of raids on caravans and fires that besieged the town. Every day a new place was hit. Gunner was torn in every direction, and it kept every Ballenger employee scrambling. The town had ceased to sleep. Mason had added patrols in town and on incoming roads. Gunner and Titus had just as many watching the arena and caravans. Then for several days everything went calm. They thought it was over.

"And then the king's army rolled in with weapons," Lothar said. "There was complete chaos. Building after building was reduced to rubble. No one knew what was happening." Lothar said when the dust settled, Banques claimed they had confiscated the weapons from a Ballenger warehouse—an enormous stockpile the family had gained through illegal means. Banques also claimed that the Ballengers had been blackmailing businesses for more protection money to finance their unlawful activities instead of keeping the town safe from Rybart's league—who he claimed had engineered the attacks.

"We knew none of it was true, and not a single family or business backed up his wild claim, but what we believed didn't matter. He had all the power and used it to quash any dissent. He—"

"Who *is* this Banques?" I asked. "Where did he come from?"

"He's first in command after the king," Imara answered. "He's a general, and it seems he has the training to go with it. He's commanding a formidable army, but a few who have been to Parsuss are certain he was the king's local magistrate before all this happened."

The magistrate in Parsuss? The one who had written us saying he had never heard anything about "this Beaufort fellow" when my father had inquired about him? They'd been thick as thieves all along. It all started to fall into place. The king had used us to finance his weapons, working in lockstep with Beaufort. He used us in even a worse way than Beaufort had. And then he enlisted Paxton and Truko to keep the arena running—the sweetest deal ever proposed to them. Aleski spit when he mentioned Paxton's name. Somehow his complicity was worse than Truko's.

"A day after he roared into town, the king announced that Rybart was killed during the takeover." Lothar recounted. "Then he ordered his captured crew to be hanged. They all denied it with their last breaths. The next day in the forest, they caught Drake in one of their snares like he was nothing but an animal, and a few days later, they hanged him from—" Lothar shook his head, unable to continue.

My temper had steadily risen with every word. "The king's an invader and murderer. Why hasn't someone just taken him down?" I hissed, trying to keep my voice low. "There's plenty of skilled archers in town—those who crewed our skywalks! Surely someone's had an opportunity for a shot at him. Doesn't he ever walk the streets? Ride his horse?"

Imara, Aleski, and Lothar all looked at me blankly.

"You don't know?" Imara finally asked, so quietly I thought she had lost her voice.

A cold sweat sprang to my face. "Know *what?*"

She looked at Aleski, and he answered. "He has Lydia and Nash. Everyone would love to see him dead, but they're afraid to make a move. He claims he's protecting them, but we know why he really has them. For his own protection. His implied threat is obvious."

I didn't realize I had stood until I suddenly had five sets of hands digging into my arms and chest, holding me against the stable wall. *He has my baby brother and sister? Using them for protection? That's what is keeping Kazi there. That's why she won't leave.*

Wren's hands pressed against my chest. "Don't go getting crazy on us now, *Patrei.*"

I shook my head, indicating it was safe to let me go. I had no intention of getting crazy. My only intention was getting revenge.

We began formulating plans for our own army. Weapons. That was all I could think of now, and what I would do to get them.

CHAPTER THIRTY-TWO

KAZI

CLOUDS OF SWIRLING PINK STEAM HOVERED ABOVE THE SPRING
in the pavilion. They were the breaths of the gods, according to legend,
and the mineral-rich hot spring was their gift to mortals.

Just beyond the rails of the pavilion, there were more breaths—those
of the dead. I felt them stepping closer, their sighs whispering through
the pines. Gods, ghosts, and maybe angels, they all watched. Waiting.

On the ride here, my mind was consumed with every detail, including backup plans in case something changed, something as unpredictable as rain or snow, but the sun had at last peeked out from behind gray
clouds, adding some cheer to the day. I took it as an omen. If the king
could take his father's untimely death as an omen from the gods, I could
take the appearance of intermittent sunshine as a sure nod from them.

I had awoken before dawn, my pulse skittering like a snared bird,
but when I caught sight of the graveyard, a strange calm descended. It
felt familiar. I remembered: The wild anxiety was always followed by
calm. It didn't matter if it was a square of cheese, or a starving tiger, or

two small children. My mind shifted as we drew near, focusing not on everything that could go wrong but on everything I had to do right. Once step at a time. You can't panic when you're walking a tightrope over a pit of vipers.

I stood at the pavilion rail, waiting for Montegue.

Several yards away, I heard him dismissing Banques, Paxton, and Truko to go on to Tor's Watch, saying we would catch up with them soon—it was only a short way up the hill from the graveyard. I had walked the distance with Jase on my first day here. Montegue's tone was impatient. I was sure Banques was not happy being displaced by me, even temporarily, but he didn't argue. Paxton had planted a bug in his ear too, one that made him eager to continue on to review more arena records. The king's safety was never part of the discussion. He would be fine. Squads of soldiers still blocked each end of the road that was adjacent to the graveyard. No one could get in, and a small contingent within the graveyard was there to provide additional protection. One soldier—Broken Nose—was assigned to supervise the children, and three more who weren't familiar to me were posted around the pavilion to protect the king.

As Paxton rode away, I noted that he was particularly well-groomed today, the sides of his head freshly shaved and his russet ponytail gleaming in a neat line down his back. Maybe he at least wanted to look presentable hanging from a tembris if he was caught.

When Montegue turned back toward the pavilion, he patted his vest as he approached. It was an unconscious habit of his. Anyone who carried treasure on them—whether it was keys, a gold signet ring, a purse of coin, or for Montegue, a tiny vial that contained the promise of unlimited power—checked their treasure often. Who wouldn't? His hand returned to his side. His treasure was still there. Safe.

I remembered how Griz had mocked him. How I had mocked him.

But he was more cunning than all of us. That was what made me nervous, staying ahead of what smoldered inside of him—what he managed to keep so well hidden. He was only twenty-three, but he seemed like an old man too, filled with three lifetimes of ambition and cynicism. *Someone like Phineas only comes along once every few generations.*

And maybe someone like Montegue too.

Lydia and Nash were already off playing among the tombstones. Once within the safe protection of the graveyard, with its sheer mountain wall and forest cover on one side and heavily armed squads on the other, Montegue couldn't be rid of the children fast enough, though they were on especially good behavior today. They'd been coached by Paxton and Oleez this morning. They were to cause their guard no reason to drag them back to the pavilion before the appointed time. Play quietly in the graveyard, recite the history of Fujiko twice, and then it would be time to return.

Montegue's pace was deliberate and eager. It seemed it didn't matter if it was possessing the magic of the stars, controlling a continent, a kingdom, or a true kiss from a lowly thief that his adversary had desired, they were all balms that could heal the slivers festering beneath his skin and each had the power to finally make him whole, make the world fall into balance, make his story true.

He walked up the steps and stopped in front of me. His need was visible. I saw it in his hooded eyelids as he imagined what could be. I listened. Pretended I heard his heartbeat. For these few seconds, he was fragile, human. Hungry. I couldn't see him as a monster. I had to see him as a man. A man was beatable.

"So now that you've slept on it, are you still wondering?" he asked.

I had hoped it would take him longer to get to the subject that burned him.

"Yes. I—"

"You don't have to wonder, you know?"

A few more minutes. That's all I needed until—

He pulled me into his arms and kissed me.

My pulse rushed and my mind raced, trying to take command of the situation again, trying to—

But now I was immersed in it. I sensed that every move of his was planned, perfected, timed. He had wanted to catch me off guard. Surprise and show me. His kiss was gentle at first, his lips barely grazing mine. He whispered my name against them, *Kazimyrah*, but then his lips pressed harder and his tongue was in my mouth. His grip grew stronger, like iron, and I remembered his warning: *I'm stronger and could overtake you easily.* He pulled me closer as if proving it, every part of him pressed against me, his breaths growing heavier, and I feared this was no longer an orchestrated kiss, but one that was quickly veering out of control. Where were they? Why did we choose Fujiko? We should have chosen a shorter history. But I met his kisses with eagerness of my own. My hands slid upward along his sides until I was gently cupping his face, every move designed to convey I was entranced. *Where were they?*

"Well?" he whispered against my lips.

I answered by pressing my mouth to his. *Yes, a king is a step up from a Patrei.*

"Excuse me?"

I gasped and pulled away, and we both turned. Lydia stood on the first step of the pavilion, Nash just behind her.

"What are you doing here?" Montegue bellowed. "Go play!" He glared at Broken Nose, who stood just behind them.

"But I have to *go*," Lydia said woefully.

"Go?" he replied, not understanding at first, and then it hit him. "You mean?" He growled with exasperation. "Then find a tree and pee! You're not a baby!"

"I'm afraid to go by myself," she whined. "I heard howling."

"Take her into the woods!" Montegue said to Broken Nose.

Lydia's lip trembled. She didn't move.

"I have to go too," Nash added, his voice filled with as much woe.

I sighed and put my hand on Montegue's arm. "She's of an age and more shy about that kind of thing. Maybe she'd be more comfortable with me. Let me go with them both to take care of their business, and then I'll get them settled over by the wash searching for eyestones. That should keep them occupied for a good long while so we can have some—*time*—without interruption."

He sucked in a frustrated breath between clenched teeth. "Hurry," he ordered. And then to Broken Nose, "Once she has them settled, *do not* bring them back until you hear me call. Do you understand?"

Broken Nose nodded, betraying no emotion, but I guessed that he seethed with resentment for being saddled with this job. I was grateful it wasn't No Neck watching them today. He would have been more difficult.

We quickly left to take care of the urgent matter. Broken Nose grumbled once we were out of earshot of the king, insulted that he'd been charged with playing nursemaid. "I'd have drowned them both like feral kittens a long time ago if I had my way." There was no jest in his tone, and if the king or Banques gave the nod, I knew he would gladly do it. Lydia and Nash didn't flinch at his remark, and I wondered at the horrors they had endured every day as prisoners of the king, because though he tried to paint it differently, there was no question—they were his prisoners.

Jase would be enraged but proud too at how they had held up under this strain, showing more strength than many adults could muster. Jase would—

My chest tightened. I had already decided not to tell them they would be seeing him soon. I didn't know what kind of shape he would be in, or if he even—

He could be dead by now.

I wished Paxton had been less honest with me.

We walked briskly to a copse of shrubs about halfway into the grave-yard. Broken Nose waited on the other side to give Lydia privacy, but he kept an eye on me. Every minute counted so Lydia and Nash finished their business quickly.

As we continued on toward the dry creek bed, I asked him to slow his steps for the sake of the children. "Do you have a name?" I asked. "So I don't have to keep calling you Guard?"

He brushed away the question, saying a name wasn't important, but with a little more prodding, he finally admitted his name was Lucius.

"How did you break your nose, Lucius?"

"The butt of a halberd," he answered, then smiled. "But the fellow who swung it fared far worse."

"Good to know." *Lucius.* A helpful detail. The wash came into view, but then I stopped short, putting my hand out to stop the children too, as if I was afraid.

"Wait," I whispered. "What is *that*?" I pointed into the shadows at the Ballenger tomb. The door was partway open. "Grave robbers?" I said. "Should we go get someone?"

Broken Nose scowled at me with offense. "What do you think I'm here for? I'm not just here to play nursemaid to them." He pulled his sword free and walked cautiously toward the tomb. I ordered the children to stay put and followed close behind. When we were a few yards away, he called toward the dark entrance. "Come out!"

No one appeared, and he edged closer, craning his neck to see what threat might be inside, forgetting about the one right behind him.

I had never killed anyone this way before. Whenever I had plunged a knife or sword between someone's ribs, it had been in combat—noisy, messy, desperate, and fast. This was slow. Stalking. Waiting for the perfect moment. I didn't like it, and yet I welcomed it. I had never killed someone for a better reason.

Every step was calm. Except for the steady *whoosh* of my heart in my ears.

"Do you see anything?" I whispered.

"Nah," he answered, as if disappointed, and stepped inside. "Nothing."

At least the children wouldn't see it happen.

One step. Two. He turned. And I plunged the scalpel into his throat and slashed.

Swift, silent, exact. As precise as juggling an orange.

And more permanent than the butt of a halberd.

He couldn't call out, couldn't lift his sword. I took it from his hand before he fell to his knees with a *thunk*, facedown on the floor. I wasn't sure he even knew it was me, but I did know he wouldn't be drowning anything again—children or feral kittens. I pulled his cloak away before it could be soaked with his blood and set it on the center internment stone along with his long sword, dagger, and push knife, then went to the door and waved the children forward.

"Don't look," I said, when they reached the tomb. "He's dead and can't hurt you." And then everything went from slow to rushed. There were fifty crypt spaces in the tomb, each marble front approximately a two-foot square. More than half of them were already occupied, Ballenger names engraved on the outer marble faces.

I knelt down so I was eye level with Lydia and Nash and hurried to tell them everything they needed to know. "By this time tomorrow, you'll be safe with friends, but the next several hours will take tremendous courage, the kind the *Patrei* has—the kind you have too. Do you understand?"

Lydia nodded, her jaw set hard.

Nash's chin dimpled, trying to keep tears back.

"I can't stay here with you. I have to lead them away. But no matter what you hear, no matter who calls to you or threatens you or threatens me, you will *not* answer. You will even hear me calling for you, but I'm only pretending to not know where you are. You must remain completely silent, even if I scream. It's all part of the plan." I squeezed both of their hands. "And it will fail if you call out—remember, we are not just saving ourselves, we're working to save all of Hell's Mouth—so you mustn't cry, whimper, or even whisper to each other. It will be dark, and it will be cold, but once it is night, someone will come for you and take you away to where you'll be safe. And you'll ride your own horses. No more riding with the king. You'll like that, won't you?"

"Yes," they both answered quietly.

And then I told them where I was going to hide them. "But Sylvey's body isn't there. It never was. It's just an empty chamber." *But no one else will know that.*

"Where's Sylvey?" Nash asked. He never knew her. She died when he was just an infant, but he knew of her. Ballengers never forgot their history—or their family.

"She's buried in the Moro mountains."

Tears puddled in Lydia's eyes, worried for a sister she had no memory of. "Will the gods be angry that she's gone?"

"No," I said, pulling her and Nash into my arms. An ache clutched my throat. "The gods know where she is. It's a beautiful place where she was meant to rest. The gods are pleased." I had never been so grateful for a broken law in my life. Thank the gods Jase had stolen her body. Even if they went so far as to search the tomb, no one would ever break into a crypt they believed was occupied with a sanctified body.

I pushed them both away so I could look into their eyes. "And now you must tell me one last thing. It's very important. Do you know if there's another entrance to the vault?"

They looked at each other and then back at me. "We aren't supposed to tell. We didn't even tell the king. Only family is allowed to know."

"But I *am* family. I'm your sister now. Jase would want you to tell me. Please."

"You're our sister?" Nash said.

"You're never going away again?" Lydia added. "Because family doesn't go away."

"Never," I answered, guilt stabbing me, because I knew sometimes family did go away even if they didn't want to.

Nash looked at the dead guard in the corner to make sure he wasn't listening. "It's by the waterfall," he whispered.

"There's a cave. Left, left, right, left. I memorized that," Lydia said proudly. "Once inside, those are the tunnels you take."

"And there's bats. Lots and lots of bats in the first big cave," Nash added.

"Which waterfall? Where?" I asked. There had to be a hundred waterfalls in the mountains behind Tor's Watch.

They both looked at each other, unsure. "It's a long ways up the mountain. I think," Lydia answered. They began reciting the few hazy details they remembered. A long, skinny meadow. A toppled tree with roots that rose higher than a house. A giant blue rock that looked like a bear standing on its hind legs. That was all they could remember, and I prayed it was enough.

I went to Sylvey's crypt at the end of the middle row and unscrewed the rosette fasteners, then carefully removed the marble front and set it aside. Next I removed the inner shutter and looked into the long dark space, hoping there was no trace of a body ever being in there. It was clean, and there was plenty of room for two small children. I laid out the guard's cloak inside and lifted them both up onto it, then wrapped it around them to keep them warm.

"Remember," I whispered, "once it is night, someone will come for you. Until then, not a peep."

They both nodded. I started to bend down to replace the shutter and marble front, but Nash reached out and grabbed my arm. "*Vatrésta*," he said.

"No, Nash," I corrected. "*Vatrésta* is for a final good-bye. We will see each other again. *Chemarr* is for a short farewell."

"*Chemarr*," they both said back to me, and then I sealed them in the crypt. I pressed my fingers to my lips and then to the face of marble that had Sylvey's name engraved on it. *Chemarr. Watch over them.*

Relief and fear flooded my chest at the same time as I pressed my back to the tomb door, wedging my feet against the ground while I shoved it closed one grunt and push at a time, sealing them inside.

CHAPTER THIRTY-THREE

KAZI

"THERE!" I SAID, SMILING AS I DASHED UP THE PAVILION STEPS. I let true victory shine in my eyes—the hardest step was behind me—though the king would interpret my triumph differently. "All done. They're happily searching for eyestones." I shed my cloak and weapon belt, laying them over the railing beside Montegue's.

He was already sitting on the first step, soaking his feet. "What took you so long? I was about to send a guard to get you."

"I wanted to give them some extra incentive and found this." I pulled a large, colorful eyestone from my pocket that was about the size of my little finger—just the right size—and held it up. "I told them whoever found the most stones would get this one as a prize. They're searching in earnest now. They'll be occupied for a good long while."

He smiled. "Well played, soldier." He motioned to the step next to him. "Come soak your foot."

I sat on the lone bench in the pavilion, which was across from him, stalling for time as I slowly took off my first boot. I had to draw this out for at least another half hour.

"The town looked festive this morning, didn't it?" I said, a topic I knew he would like, proof he was winning them over.

"Yes," he agreed. "They're finally coming around. Moving on. I knew they would. I ordered the hanging bodies removed from the tembris. It seemed like the right response. They will see me as a fair ruler willing to meet them more than halfway."

The right response? Cutting down innocent rotting bodies? Such a kindness. I checked the revulsion rolling up my throat. "A wise move," I agreed and pulled off my sock, tucked it in my boot, and began unlacing the other. "And it will certainly help elevate the festive mood."

He talked about other changes that he and Banques had in the works, assigning new magistrates nominated by the townspeople for the districts, rebuilding the livery that had been burned down, and breaking ground on a new temple that would be bigger and better than the last one. "And soon I won't need to travel with the children at all."

I pulled off my boot and set it beside the other. "What will become of them?" I asked cautiously, biting back my next words. *Would you kill them?* But he managed to anticipate my thoughts anyway.

"I would not kill them, if that's what you're wondering. I'm not a monster."

"I know that," I answered quickly, trying to soothe his injury. "I was thinking of Banques. I heard him call them a necessary evil."

"We have to do what is best for the kingdom. We'll send them away where they can forget about being Ballengers. They'll have a nice fresh start."

A fresh start? Or would they simply be prisoners somewhere else? He spun everything into a golden solution that eliminated his culpability. I twisted the sock I had just pulled off around my fingers. Even though I knew that now he would never get his hands on them again, his words still plagued me—the things he planned that I hadn't even begun to grasp. "Send away? Where?"

"Zane knows places. He—"

"*Zane?*" I blurted out before I could stop myself.

"I told you—you have to bury your grudges with him. Zane is useful to me, and as a former Previzi driver, he knows of places not that far from here that will take them in for us."

He was going to give them to Zane.

Zane.

"Places? More than one?" I asked. "You plan to separate them?"

"Yes, we decided it would be easier for them to make a clean break from their past that way."

And ensure that they forget. I knew what it was like to be isolated. Alone. No one to tell you stories. Memories drifted away. I was Nash's age when I lost my mother, and Lydia was only a year older. *Yes, Montegue, send them away and eliminate two young Ballengers who might grow up and challenge you one day. Break them, destroy them, but at the same time, keep them close just in case you need to bring them back again to serve some scheming purpose of yours. You are a brilliant monster.*

I struggled to keep my mind fixed on the endgame. A game that had new rules that I had made—not him. *He won't be able to do any of these things, Kazi. Stay focused on each step. You're almost there.*

"What about the Ballengers?" I asked. "What if they come out? They'll want their kin back."

"There's been no signs of life. They're probably all dead. And if they aren't, they soon will be. If you don't find the papers soon, we'll begin blasting. I can't wait much longer. I'll have to take my chances that the papers won't be destroyed in the process."

"Blast through a mountain of solid granite? Do you know how long that will take?"

"Or the blasting might drive them out."

Of course. He didn't really believe they were dead.

"Paxton drew us maps," he said. "He used to be a Ballenger, before his line of the family was thrown out on their ear. His great-grandfather told him about the layout of the vault. We've estimated that the shortest route to the grand hall should only take three or four days of blasting."

Grand hall? There was no grand hall. The vault was not an underground palace! The rooms were roughly all the same size, one room connected to another, connected to another, plain and functional. Paxton was lying to them, and he had even drawn maps! Maybe that was the bug he planted in Banques's ear—maps that would take them in all the wrong directions. I was beginning to love that man and every devious bone in his body.

I rolled up my trousers and went to join Montegue, but before I could step into the pink waters, he reached out, lightly brushing the bruise on my ankle with his thumb. "Tender?" he asked softly. Proving, courting, pretending he cared. *I am not a monster.* No doubt preparing to show me in greater depth just how kind he could be.

I winced. "A little." The stain produced by an overnight poultice of fruit skins and flower petals made for a colorful and very painful-looking bruise. "But the soak should help. Thank you for being so thoughtful."

"I want you healed and strong," he said, his hand lingering on my ankle then sliding up my calf. "That's what's important. I noticed your limp was worse this morning."

"It's only stiff after a night of rest. I need to work it out. This will help." The hot water might also make the stain disappear. A miraculous healing. I was sure even Montegue wouldn't buy that. But he wasn't likely to ever look at my ankle again after this moment. Soon, he wouldn't care about my ankle at all.

I sat on the top step beside him, and he closed his eyes and breathed in the steam surrounding us—the strength of the gods. The veins in his neck were raised, and I wasn't sure if it was from exhilaration or strain. I let out a pleased moan as if I was already feeling the curative action of the water. Twenty more minutes. And somewhere in that twenty, I had to kiss him one more time. Hold him.

"Did he make you promises?" he suddenly asked.

Promises? Surprise thumped in my chest. I couldn't stay ahead of his thoughts. I didn't have to ask who *he* was.

I shrugged, molding indifference across my lips. "If he did, I can't remember."

Montegue grabbed my upper arm, making me look at him. "Remember."

I nodded. "Yes."

Truth. Jase promised me a lifetime with him. He promised a mountain full of trees and a family that would grow to love me again. He promised we would write our own story.

And I made promises too.

I stared at Montegue, letting his eyes look into my soul, command it, own it, get lost in it. Drown in the fantasy.

"On our return trip, he promised that I would grow to love him one day," I said.

"And?" His eyes sank deeper into mine.

"He seemed so sure about everything. It made me wonder. Could I possibly grow to love a man I hated? I had been wrong about so many things. I had made so many mistakes."

"But?"

An orange in the air.

"But some things are true. You feel them in your gut and can't force them. You can't—"

Another orange.

I reached out, my hands holding either side of his face. "Some things—"

He leaned forward and his mouth met mine, then he pushed me back so we lay on the floor of the pavilion. His kisses were heated, hungry. True. His fingers just as zealous, fumbling with my shirt.

My hands slid beneath his vest, across his chest, searching, hungry too. His weight pressed down on me, pinning me beneath him.

"Montegue," I whispered. "The guards."

"They aren't watching."

"They are," I said. "They shouldn't see the king like this. Maybe we should go on to Tor's Watch. The office. It's private." I pushed against him.

He looked at me, his pupils shrinking to pinpoints, knowing I was right. The most powerful king on the continent, of course, should not be rutting like a buck in a forest.

He rolled off me and yelled to the back of one of the guards who dutifully pretended he didn't know what was going on in the pavilion, "Get the children! We're leaving."

The guard left, and Montegue hurried to put on his boots. I did the same. He didn't notice that my bruise had vanished. A piece of the fantasy filled his eyes instead—delivered by a thief.

By the time we were booted and belted and our cloaks were in place to leave, the guard came running back without the children. "They're gone," he said, his face ashen. "I can't find them."

"What?" I snapped, whipping around to fully face him. "Where—"

Montegue cut me off. "How can they be gone? Where's the guard who was watching them?"

"I can't find him either."

I stormed down the steps. "What do you mean? How—"

"They have to be here," Montegue said, looking out at the graveyard. "They must be hiding. Playing one of their games."

"Lydia!" I called. "Nash! It's time to go!"

The graveyard remained still. The guards, Montegue, and I all spread out, calling their names. Montegue's voice grew angrier and louder the farther we went into the graveyard with no response.

"They were all at the wash when I left them," I said, my tone sufficiently worried. "They have to still be there."

But when the wash came into view, it was empty. I turned and faced Montegue, shoving him with my hands. "What did he do with them? Do you even know that guard?" I yelled. "Where is he?"

Montegue whirled and headed back for the pavilion, taking two of the guards with him. "Keep looking here!" he ordered over his shoulder, his cloak waving behind him. "We'll check with the squads on the road. Maybe they tumbled down the embankment."

Once he was gone, I told the remaining guard to search all the bushes near the base of the bluff. "I'll go check the stand of sycamore at the far end."

We parted ways, but before I reached the sycamore, I stooped at the base of a tall old spruce with thick, gnarled roots at its base, and pulled away the mounds of needles I had piled between them to hide the dead guard's weapons. I replaced my dull sword and dagger with his very sharp ones, and added his short but deadly push knife to my belt.

"Lydia!"

"Nash!"

The calling continued in the distance.

And then it became oddly silent.

I headed back toward the pavilion, prepared to ask for news and suggest we search Tor's Watch next, but then I saw Montegue walking toward me. Slowly. Deliberately. Behind him was a squad of soldiers, and one of them held a launcher.

And walking just a step behind him was Dinah.

Blood drained to my feet. Nothing about this was right, but I kept walking forward, playing it out. Montegue's face was hard, his chin lifted as he looked down at me. Really seeing me.

"Where are they?" he asked flatly.

Dinah shook her finger at me as the pitch in her voice rose higher with every word. "Her! It was her! She did it! Oleez told me! She said the children weren't coming back. That we had to leave. But I had nothing to do with it! Nothing! I came as soon as I knew! I'm loyal to His Majesty. I'm—"

"Shut up!" Montegue ordered. But she didn't shut up, and his hand swept backward, hitting her face and knocking her to the ground.

I stared at her, horrified. Dinah betrayed us? *Stupid girl. What have you done?* Oleez had been certain she could trust her and needed to bring her with when she escaped. Did Dinah think this would gain her favor with the king, or was she just hysterical with fear? She lay there whimpering, and Montegue turned back to me.

His jaw was rigid. All the passion that had consumed him just minutes ago was now channeled in a new direction. His attention dropped to my feet. "I see your limp is gone."

I nodded. "A miraculous healing."

His cheek twitched. "We can still work this out," he said, making a poor effort to soften his voice. He had no intention of working it out. I saw the inner workings of his mind—he was an architect working on a new plan. "You were frightened for the children," he continued. "I can understand that. I—"

"Really, Montegue? You would forgive me? How lucky I am. Because of course, you are not a monster, as you have told me so many times."

His stance shifted at my sarcasm.

"How brave will you be now without children to shield you?" I asked. "Will you still ride freely among your adoring subjects?" I laughed just to rub it in, because I knew how much he hated disdain, and I wanted him to feel this moment all the way to his marrow.

He was immovable, a stone standing in front of me. "Where are they?" he repeated.

"Out of your clutches and far away by now," I replied. "They have a good hour lead and a skilled soldier helping them. Lucius is quite remarkable."

"Lucius?"

One of the guards behind him answered, "The soldier who was assigned to them."

"He was in on it too," I said. "See? I know your own soldiers better than you do. How many of those standing behind you right now are really on our side? How many of them might be aiming an arrow at your back even as I speak?"

Blink last. He knew the game too, and he resisted the urge to turn around, but I saw the flutter of his lashes and the doubt that swept through his eyes. He glanced at the dull, useless weapons at my side, already planning a new strategy.

As he eyed me, I eyed other things. In a split second I judged the positions of the soldiers behind him, two with arrows nocked, four with swords drawn, and four with halberds poised to charge. I eyed the soldier who aimed a launcher at me. He couldn't fire it. He was in too close of range, and the blast would surely injure or kill the king as well. I noted the clouds passing overhead, and the shifting light and shadows, and when the sun might be in the soldiers' eyes. I tried to remember how many steps to the wash behind me, and what trees, tombs, and gravestones stood in the path for cover, and then I tried to remember the steepness of the embankment along the road, and where the soldiers stationed below were positioned, and then the distance to the deep canyon just beyond it. *Pivot. A new plan.* It all flashed through my mind in a few short seconds. I had to decide whether it was viable, but it was obvious the odds were not in my favor. Not remotely. Not this time.

Montegue smiled as if he knew what I was thinking and stepped closer. "There's nowhere for you to go. Put your weapons down, and we'll talk."

A grin lit his handsome face, and his voice was warm. But I saw the flush at his temples, the tension in his shoulders, the rage that seethed in him. I would be thrown into a cell and left there to rot until he had wrung every bit of information out of me that he could. That was not an option either. I would never reveal where Lydia and Nash were.

His eyes drilled into me, judging the timing of his moves too. And then he lunged. Because he was stronger and could overtake me easily. Because he had the gods on his side.

But this time I didn't have a pickle fork clutched in my hand. Beneath my cloak, I gripped something else in my fist.

CHAPTER THIRTY-FOUR

KAZI

MY ARM SHOT OUT, SLASHING UPWARD, THE RAZOR-SHARP PUSH knife catching him in his chest and jaw. He fell back, screaming, clutching his face as blood spurted between his fingers. In the flash of chaos as soldiers leapt to help the king, I turned and ran for the wash.

"Fire!" he screamed. "Fire!"

I heard scrambling and shouts behind me.

"Get out of the way! Out of the way!" someone yelled.

Arrows whirred past. I heard the *thunk! chink! whoosh!* as they hit tree and stone, and purred past my ears.

I was about to jump into the wash, when the force of an explosion ripped through the air. I was thrown from my feet and sent rolling down the dry creek bed. Dirt and rocks sprayed all around me. Splinters of stone pierced my skin. Dust choked the air, and my ears rang with pain. I rolled to my feet and kept moving. I couldn't see through the cloud of dust, but I knew the direction I needed to go.

Rocks crunched beneath my boots as I ran, the air still thick with dust, but once I was past the cloud, another volley of arrows screamed past me. I varied my steps like an unpredictable rabbit, then ran up the opposite side, out of the wash, and down an incline, finally out of their line of sight, but I was running so fast I couldn't stop when I hit the embankment, and for a few seconds I was airborne, hoping I wouldn't hit the tree straight in my path. I reached out, grabbing a branch that flung me in a new direction, narrowly missing a trunk, but then I hit the ground hard, tumbling out of control, the thick bed of slippery needles giving me nothing to grab hold of, rushing me downhill like a raging waterfall. I flailed, trying to find something to hold on to, and finally dug in my heel as I grabbed a sapling. My grip ripped its branches clean as it slowed my slide, and I came to a stop just before I reached the road below.

The cover of the trees had at least hidden my descent from the soldiers stationed on the road, but the soldiers above me were still in pursuit. Their arrows were blocked by the trees between us, but not for long. I had no choice but to make a run for the canyon that lay past the road. Screams and orders echoed all around me—including the voice of the king—and the soldiers below turned, weapons raised, looking into the trees for the source of the commotion. I threw a pinecone past them, hoping to divert their attention, if only for a second—that was all I needed—and I ran.

"There!"

"Stop her!"

The road exploded beneath me, and I was in a free fall again, tumbling down the steep canyon embankment, but this time it was not trees in my path but rocks. I was pummeled, every bone banged and crushed, bouncing over rocky ground like an out-of-control rag doll, unable to stop, the ground punching me again, and again, until I finally fell over a ridge and landed on the stony shelf below. Everything went from loud and explosive to still. The sky swirled above me in shadowy reds. I felt wetness and warmth. Blood. It ran into my eyes, blinding me. I winced, lifting a shaky hand to swipe it away, and my breath caught. My shoulder. This time it was pain that blinded me.

Frustrated shouts rolled through the stony canyon again.

"Where is she?"

"Where did she go?"

I was temporarily hidden from view by the tall ridge.

More shouts, and then Montegue, his voice blaring over the others.

"Get down there!"

"Find her!"

And then a desperate "Out of my way! I'll stop her!"

Did he plan to send a wall of fire blazing down the canyon to burn me to a crisp? His heart's true desire.

But then I heard a scream. A loud, glorious scream that bounced off the stony canyon. It was the sound of thwarted dreams. The sound of fury and betrayal.

The king's scream.

I teetered on the edge of consciousness, but I smiled.

He had found the gift I left for him, the very colorful eyestone I had tucked in his vest pocket. The eyestone that was about the same size as a magical vial.

My other hand painfully slid inch by inch across the stone to my side, feeling my pocket to see if it still held the king's treasure. It was there.

Out of his hands. And I would make sure he never got it back.

None of this was supposed to happen until later, not until we were on the way to Tor's Watch to continue our search. I would slip silently into the shadows, then lead them on a wild chase far away from the grave-yard. The next morning Paxton would meet me. Dinah changed that.

I knew I had to run. I had to go. But I couldn't move. I had come down the steep canyon face the fast and hard way. Far above me, I heard them calling for ropes. It wouldn't be long before his soldiers followed the slower way. I had to keep moving and lead them away from the grave-yard and Lydia and Nash. But everything hurt so badly. My shoulder, my head, my hip.

When I tried to move, the world went white with pain again. I gasped for air.

I braced myself, digging my nails into my palms as I reached up and felt a knobby bump on my left shoulder where there shouldn't be one. It was dislocated. I heard bits of rubble tumbling down the canyon face. They were coming. "You can do this, Kazi," I whispered to myself. "You have to." I had watched Natiya once, after she had fallen from a horse—

I pressed my right hand over my mouth, not allowing myself to scream, and turned my other palm upward. Slowly, I slid my injured arm over my head. *Relax, let the muscles do the work.* But between the pain and knowing soldiers were already scaling down the canyon, it was impos-sible to relax. I shook with pain. My good hand moved from my mouth to the hand that was now over my head, and I gently tugged on my wrist. *You can do this.* I tugged harder, the stony ledge spinning. I was afraid I might pass out. A mewl escaped from my lips, light vibrating behind my eyes, and then there was a soft pop.

My held breath escaped in a hot, miserable gasp.

It was back in.

The sky still bobbed above me. I took a deep breath, and then another, letting my lungs fill and my senses return, but there wasn't time for more. I struggled to my feet, using only my right arm for leverage. I held my left arm snug against my ribs and stayed close to the ledge wall so I wouldn't be seen from above, then looked out at the canyon for an escape.

The floor of the canyon was only about another twenty feet down. I planned my path. Once I was out in the open, I would have to move fast—if I could. My whole left side had taken the brunt of the fall. My leg ached too. I studied the shadows. It was closing in on noon, and there were few of them. But there were enough—trees, boulders, the wild growth of shrubs. I saw the line I would follow.

I pulled the vial from my pocket and stared at it. I had only seconds to decide. *It imprints on whatever it touches.* After all these months next to the king's heart, could it serve anyone else's desire but his? Could it serve mine? Temptation, reason, and fleeting seconds battled within me. But I didn't know how to use the magic or even know if I could, and there was a good chance I would be recaptured. I couldn't let it fall back into his hands. I surveyed the ledge wall and spotted a tiny crevice at the bottom. I tucked the vial inside, and a small lizard scurried out.

And then I ran.

I was spotted almost immediately.

More screams echoed from above. *"Fire! Fire!"*

He would never let me go, not just because of what I had stolen from him, but also because of what I had never truly given him.

"You are nothing!" he screamed. "Nothing without me! Do you hear me? Nothing!"

I had almost reached the shadow I was aiming for when the canyon thundered with another bone-rattling explosion, a tree splintered into a thousand pieces, and I was thrown to the canyon floor.

CHAPTER THIRTY-FIVE

JASE

"Did you hear that?" Wren asked.

I had just finished doling out coins for the stable master when the faint noise rumbled.

"Thunder," the stable master called after us as we walked out the door.

When we reached the yard where Synové was waiting with the horses, she looked up at the sky and asked, "What was that?" Her brow was riddled with suspicion.

"Not thunder," I answered. There was a crack to it—a hard, snapping sound I recognized. A launcher. But it was somewhere in the distance, not here in town. Soldiers practicing? Or were they destroying more of my home, trying to wipe out all evidence of the Ballengers?

As we rode our horses to the west artery out of town, we could see there was some sort of commotion going on. Soldiers were running with weapons drawn, bursting into businesses on the boardwalks, searching for something. Down the smaller avenues, I could see them doing the same with homes. When we reached the end of the artery, it was blocked. There was a throng of people pressing toward the guards, wanting answers. I got off my horse, keeping my hat low and my head down, and pushed my way through the crowd to where the soldiers stood behind a blockade.

"Wez do not live here," I explained. "Wez need to go."

"Nobody's leaving. Town's shut down. Come back in a few hours. The roads should be open by then."

"But—"

"Move along!" he ordered, pressing his halberd to my chest.

I carefully backed away.

We tried to get out through the other arteries, but they were all blocked too. There was a tight net around the town. Synové asked a shopkeeper what the soldiers were searching for. She wouldn't answer, especially to strangers like us. Everyone in town had grown accustomed to being very tight-lipped, but then we heard a soldier pounding on a door, and when the elderly man who lived there opened it, the soldier had to repeat himself twice so the aged man could hear. They were searching for an older woman with gray hair.

"Have you seen her? She's missing."

The old man shook his head, but they searched his house anyway.

What had she done to make them shut down the entire town? Whatever it was, I hoped it cost them plenty, and I applauded her bravery. We checked back in a few hours later. The roads were still closed. Even I could see, there was no getting through. Whoever this woman was, she was trapped and would be found—unless she had escaped already. I prayed for the latter.

I wasn't the only one furious with our plight. There was grumbling among the townsfolk who had business at the arena, but they knew better than to grumble too much. Instead they went about decorating the town, like docile pets, but I knew what it really meant. They had heard the promise from Aleski. By the end of the day, every storefront had garlands woven of herbs, hay, or greenery. It was time to celebrate the birth of the gods—and, soon, the bloody departure of the king.

We took our horses back to the livery and used the time to study the town. Just as Imara had told us, there were twelve rooftop guards armed with launchers at the center plaza. Another two on skywalks. And one on a recently erected platform that was used for announcements—and hangings. There were no hanging bodies now, but empty nooses still dangled from the tembris. Altogether in the plaza alone, there were fifteen guards with launchers who could see every move we made. Along each avenue there were another two to three on skywalks, and at every entrance into town, another three or four.

"By my count, we've got sixty-four of those badass bruisers up there," Wren said. I wasn't sure if she was talking about the soldiers or the launchers, but either way, my count was the same. On the streets there were about the same amount of troops, though they were harder to count because they were always moving. The ground troops were armed with only the usual types of weapons, perhaps in case any crazed townsperson got ideas about commandeering one of those launchers—which was probably on the mind of every single person in the city.

Aleski had estimated about a hundred and thirty soldiers were on duty at all times. There were more posted at the arena and Tor's Watch, plus a special detail assigned just to the king and his officers. Lothar estimated the entire forces were somewhere between four and five hundred. The Ballengers had about half that many with employees alone, and a town of thousands that would fight on our side. The king's army could easily be taken down—if not for the weapons. They trumped any power I could muster. The king held the winning cards.

And Lydia and Nash.

Aleski said Oleez was looking after them, and now of course, Kazi was too. My mother was probably wild with worry, but Lydia and Nash knew what to do. They had been schooled. Wait it out. Play along the way Miandre did. Help will come. But they were so young—younger than she had been. And more innocent. My fingers curled into a fist.

Know your enemies as well as you know your allies. Know them better. Make their business yours.

But I hadn't known the king was an enemy. Neither had my father. And now it seemed that was exactly how he planned it. Neither of us ever suspected he was working with Beaufort. Our eyes and suspicions were always on hungry league leaders and new players who wanted to make a name for themselves—like the ones who had murdered Mason's parents. Them, we paid attention to. We made their business ours.

The king was only a farmer to us, and not even a good one. We had no reason to suspect him. We might as well have been told that horses could fly, and that was what he was counting on. *For how long?* Beaufort had been with us for a year, so he had to be scheming long before that.

I could count on one hand the number of times Montegue and I had met face-to-face. He rarely came to Hell's Mouth and then only stayed for a handful of days, and now I wondered if that was by design too. Could he only keep up the charade for so long?

The first time we ever met was when we were children and my father gave his father a brief tour of the arena. I couldn't remember much about that encounter except that Montegue was a few years older than me and gawky, all elbows and angles and constantly tripping over his own feet. His hair was a mess too. Always in his eyes. Everything about him was disheveled. I'm not sure we even spoke.

Maybe that encounter had cemented my image of him. But for the most part, I had forgotten he even existed until years later, when his father died and he was crowned the new king. It wasn't until a year after that he finally showed up in Hell's Mouth.

By then we were the same height.

"So you finally found your way up here," my father had said. "I wasn't sure you'd ever come, but then your father rarely did either."

Montegue had mumbled a few words about harvests, then mentioned the collected taxes being short.

"I'm afraid that's all you're getting, boy," my father answered. "It takes a lot to run a city. If you need more, you're going to have to work for it like everyone else."

Boy. Montegue didn't flinch but I remember his eyes shifted to me. I thought he wasn't quite sure who I was. "Jase Ballenger," I said.

"I know who you are. We met nine years ago."

His response had surprised me. I wondered about it at the time. I had changed dramatically since I was a seven-year-old—by over a hundred pounds, two feet, and a lot more muscle. Had he asked someone who I was? But that would mean he was watching me from afar.

I should have paid attention to that detail, but he smiled and shrugged, forgetting about the taxes, and said he needed to be on his way. The fields wouldn't plant themselves.

The next time I saw him was in Parsuss. I'd gone with Mason and Titus to talk to the new Valsprey handler in the kingdom message office—to work out a side deal with him. Commerce was growing at the arena, and we needed faster communications with merchants in other kingdoms. Montegue had just been leaving an inn, a spot of spilled gravy staining his tunic, when our paths crossed. He had asked how things fared in Hell's Mouth, motioning his hand in entirely the wrong direction.

"North," I said. "Hell's Mouth is *north*."

"Which is that way," Mason added, pointing.

Montegue chuckled. "Easy mistake." And then he asked about taxes again.

"They're not due until the end of the year," I answered. "You do know when that is, don't you?"

"Send them along early, will you? Funds are short."

We left without saying good-bye. And we didn't send the taxes early.

I only saw him periodically after that, mostly just in the last year or so. He seemed to come to the arena every few months, chasing after some new losing venture. He never mentioned taxes again. His mind was on his new endeavors. And now I knew those endeavors didn't include farming.

Wren grabbed my arm. The ground vibrated, and we both froze.

"Out of the way!" a soldier yelled as he turned the curve and galloped toward us. "Out of the way!"

A carriage came rumbling just behind him, and Wren and I jumped to the side. Soldiers on horses pounded along beside it. I fought for a glimpse inside, but it went by too fast. It stopped in front of the Ballenger Inn. There were urgent shouts, commotion, orders to open the door, but I could only see a huddle of cloaks and hoods rush into the inn.

Once all the soldiers were gone and the carriage was standing empty, I went and peeked inside. The seat was covered with blood.

For two more days, the town remained shut down without explanation, and I was torn between wanting to leave and wanting to stay. I didn't know who the blood belonged to, but during those two days, I never saw a single glimpse of Kazi, or Nash, or Lydia. Or the king.

When the roads finally opened again, I knew I had to go. It was the hardest thing I ever had to do—to leave them behind when I knew they were here. But this was not something I could do alone. I needed help. I needed the family.

Before I left, I pulled the red ribbon from my saddlebag and tied it to a garland wrapped around a post outside the Ballenger Inn.

"Hey, what are you doing there?" a soldier called, waving me away.

"For yours festival, no? Showing support of town? Shall I takes down?"

"No," he answered. "That's fine. You can leave it."

I finished tying it off and left. If Kazi saw it, she would know I was alive, and I was here, and help was coming.

Do not pass a rose without stopping to smell it.

    It is a gift that may not always be there.

I think that is what my mother had said about roses.

All these years later, it comes to me, as I sharpen our spears.

I have not seen a rose since the day she said it. I cannot even remember what they look like anymore.

I'm not sure why she thought a rose was important.

                                     —Miandre, 16

CHAPTER THIRTY-SIX

KAZI

SCAT! VERMIN!

Maybe that was what I was now. All I had ever been. An animal.

For hours, I leapt. I ran. I backtracked. I circled. I scuttled beneath bushes, and thorny branches scraped at my skin. My bones throbbed and my breaths were ragged, but like a hunted animal, the urgency of the moment was paramount, and my racing heart masked the pain. At least for now.

You are nothing!

Or maybe I was less than vermin. A shadow.

That was what I needed to be. Something they couldn't catch.

They were in fast pursuit, which both terrified and comforted me. *Yes, follow me. Come away from the graveyard.*

At one point I was surrounded, trapped, and hiding in a shadow. They didn't know I was there. For long minutes I didn't move. My throat ached with dryness, but I didn't swallow. And as the sun moved, I willed the shadow into place.

They crawled over the mountain, circling, searching. I heard their calls and taunts. And then one voice rose above the others. Zane's. He had joined the hunt. *Come out, girl!* I pressed myself tighter against the mountain, becoming part of the stony wall. I felt his hot breath on my skin again, his hands on my throat. I felt his hunger invade every part of me, and I trembled beneath my cloak. What would get me first? The plummeting temperatures, the wrath of the king, or maybe a Candok bear who wanted his shallow cave back?

But not Zane. Anything but Zane.

I held my hands up to my face, trying to breathe warmth into them. *One more night, Kazi. Make it one more night.*

Their voices faded. They were moving on. Zane was moving on with them. *He can't hurt you anymore.* My head knew that. My pounding chest didn't. And now he had a greater incentive to kill me. I was no longer working for the king, and I knew his dangerous secret.

I reached up, sliding my fingers into another sharp crack.

You need a backup plan!

But they didn't play by the rules!

And neither will your enemy!

I remembered watching smugly as Kaden chewed out an opposing team that Wren, Synové, and I had beaten in a training exercise. Cheating had been our backup plan. We went outside the stated boundaries. Whatever it took to win. Kaden understood that.

I didn't feel so smug now.

I'd had two backup plans for today, but neither had included a traitor, and both had included a horse. Not to mention I had made the dire mistake of tucking my gloves in my saddlebag. I thought I would be going back for them.

My fingertips bled as I scrambled up the steep face of the mountain, roots and rocks scraping my freezing skin raw. Dusk was closing in, the sun already gone behind the mountains, and temperatures were rapidly dropping. The wind cut through me like icy knives.

I told myself the pain, the pain everywhere, from my shoulder to my head to my leg, was good, like hunger in a belly. It would make me more determined, sharp. I told myself a lot of lies to keep me going. Because every step I took made Lydia and Nash safer.

It had always been part of our plan to lead soldiers in the opposite direction, far away from the graveyard so Binter and Cheu could arrive after dark to quietly retrieve the children from the tomb and take them to the settlement. Paxton would circle back late that night to make sure they were gone. That part of the plan was still intact. I'd had soldiers hunting me all day long, spotting me and then losing me again. They were like wolves salivating with my scent, the graveyard long forgotten.

Bleeding fingers meant nothing. Cracked ribs and a swollen shoulder meant nothing. Leading the soldiers away meant everything.

At least now I was in the mountains behind Tor's Watch, far from the graveyard. When I got to the top of the ridge, I began searching for someplace to hide for the night—a deep cave where I could light a fire—but there was none. I wouldn't make it through the night without some sort of protection. I hollowed out a place between the roots of a tree, wrapped myself tightly in my cloak, then pulled the rotting mulch of the forest floor on top of me for insulation. My bones creaked. They ached like a crumbling house settling into the earth. I felt things squirm beneath my clothes and crawl over my scalp. I prayed none of them were poisonous.

My eyes were already heavy, closing.

Sleep, my chiadrah. *Sleep.*

I felt my mother's hand, cold on my cheek. Heard the rustle of a leafy blanket covering me.

"Am I dying?" I asked.

No, my beloved. Not yet. Not today.

———⊰⊱———

In the morning when I woke, I couldn't move. It was as if every bone in me had been sewn to the earth. They refused to be punished any more. I lay there wondering if this was how I would die, that a soldier would find me and all I could do was watch as he plunged a spear into my chest.

But it was morning. The first rays of dawn shimmered through the trees. *Morning.* The thought sent a different kind of heat streaming through me—Lydia and Nash were safe.

By now they were with Jase. It didn't matter if they were all stuffed down in a dark root cellar. They were together, and out of the king's clutches. That was all that mattered.

Paxton had assured me that Binter and Cheu, who were his *straza*, had done far harder things than whisking away children in the middle of the night. And they were both partial to Lydia and Nash, and more stubborn than winter frost. They would do this as long as we did our part.

We had done our part. I felt a weight lifting, a silver stitch pulling tight.

Today my goal would change. Keep moving. Stay alive. Truly evade the soldiers. And find the other entrance to the Ballenger vault. His family needed to know Jase was alive—and that they had a weapon hidden right beneath their noses.

I rubbed my muscles with my good arm, forcing warmth back into them, and finally struggled to my feet.

There! Something over there is moving!

I ran. As much as I could run.

The king would not give up until he had me—and his magic—back in his grip.

⸻◦◦◦⸻

I had made it to the far side of Tor's Watch when I heard a noise. I hid behind a tree. Horses. A jingle. Creaking. I silently slid to the ground, then peeked past the forest at the road that Jase and I had once ridden down together. It was the back road that connected Tor's Watch to the arena.

The noise grew louder and then, between the trees, a wagon came into view. It was piled high with hay—and Zane was driving it. I sank closer to the ground. Jase had told me he was the one who had made all the supply deliveries to Cave's End for Beaufort and his crew. But he was an esteemed lieutenant of the king's army now, and still making deliveries to Tor's Watch? Deliveries of hay for horses? Zane and the wagon disappeared through the trees, but then four heavily armed soldiers came into view riding right behind him. He had an escort? Or did they just happen to be riding in the same direction?

A jay screeched over my head, and the soldiers' heads turned. I pressed my chin into the dirt. Blood pounded in my ears. The jay continued to squawk like it was trying to point me out. *Shut up, you stupid bird! Shut up!* It seemed like the soldiers were looking straight at me, but then their eyes scanned the treetops and they moved on—and I ran.

⸻◦◦◦⸻

I shivered on the floor of the rocky alcove, pulling my cloak tighter. I had heated stones at dusk, but they had long since cooled, and it was too dangerous to light another fire. I had covered so little distance today, and here I was, my third night on the run. I tried not to be disheartened, but

I wasn't sure I could make it through one more night. I rewrapped my fingers with my chemise I had torn into strips.

The hidden vault entrance couldn't be far from Tor's Watch, but with soldiers thick around me, I had to go many directions I didn't want to go.

I managed to make it to the place where Paxton and I had planned to meet up, but there was no sign that he had been there. It didn't surprise me. He was dealing with an unexpected scenario too. As soon as he had heard the loud booms of the launcher, he would have known something had gone wrong, that the plan had changed, but I worried he had suffered a worse fate than me. He was the one who had suggested taking me to Tor's Watch. He mentioned my injured ankle and my premonition. And the next morning, once Binter and Cheu were discovered missing, the king would know he was part of the setup. If Paxton hadn't slipped away by then, he would have no chance. Had he been able to get away? Or was he dead? Already hanging from the tembris?

I rubbed my eyes, trying to block out the image.

The wind howled outside, scooping its freezing fingers into the cave.

Imagine the possibilities, controlling the wind, the seasons.

The cold.

What if the stardust had been near his heart for so long, it knew his desires even from afar? What if—My mind was spinning in directions it shouldn't.

I curled into a ball and prayed morning would come soon. Tomorrow I would find the hidden door. I would find the family. I would put an end to this hellish nightmare.

I closed my eyes and searched for dreams that would warm me. Dreams that would get me through the night.

Jase's back looms in my vision. His hair ruffles in the breeze. We are just beginning our journey. I stare at him as he rummages through my saddlebag.

"Hey, what are you doing over there, Patrei? Stealing something? Do I need to arrest you?"

"I hope so," he answers eagerly. He turns. Synové's gift is in his hand.

I shoot him a disapproving frown. "It's only the first day," I say. "She said to wait until mid-journey."

"But I'm curious now . . . aren't you?"

He pouts in that maddening way that makes my stomach squeeze. That makes me want to kiss the pout right off his face.

"Yes," I answer. "I'm curious."

The package unravels in our hands as if it wants to be found out. Look inside, it seems to whisper.

We are easily seduced. Its magic lures us, and we are its willing victims.

And then I look up and all I can see are Jase's deep brown eyes and the question in them.

I rolled over, pulling my cloak tighter around me.

That's all I wanted to see, Jase's eyes and the magic they held—a different kind of magic—as I drifted deeper into sleep.

———✦———

They'll listen, Kazi, and they will love you. It will all work out. I promise.

Love is not something you can force, Jase. It will happen or it won't.

It will.

He was so certain, but he understood families better than I did.

One thing I did know was I loved Lydia and Nash more than I loved my own life, and knowing they were safe made it possible for me to do everything I could now to save Hell's Mouth. But there was more than Hell's Mouth that needed saving.

Montegue's sights were set on everything. He wanted it all.

The papers, Kazi. Get the documents. I had orders from my queen. Papers didn't just disappear. Someone had taken them, and I had to get to them before Montegue did.

The remaining spires of Tor's Watch were hidden from view now, but earlier I had used them to help me navigate my path. They were my initial marker. I remembered where the spiraling ribbon of bats in the sky had been in relation to them. Thank the gods the sun was shining today, because once surrounded by tall trees that all looked alike, it was easy to get turned around in the forest.

I stepped lightly as I went, always watchful, but the silence was hopeful. The soldiers were concentrating their efforts elsewhere—at least for now. *A skinny meadow, a toppled tree, a large blue bear rock, a waterfall, and a cave with bats. Lots of bats.*

If I could find even one of those, I was certain I could find the others, and then I stopped, taking in my surroundings again. I looked behind me and forward again. I was walking in what could be a long, skinny meadow—or what might be a green meadow in spring. Now with winter, it was just a brown leaf-littered indentation surrounded by trees.

My pace picked up, and I turned, searching in all directions for anything else, and then, in the distance, just past the meadow, I spotted a rock. An enormous rock, the color of a cornflower, that looked like a standing bear.

I ran, and somewhere in the distance, I thought I heard the roar of a waterfall—or maybe that was just the roar of blood in my ears. I was almost there. I knew it.

But then, out of nowhere it seemed, several yards ahead of me, someone was standing in my path, a spear poised over one shoulder and a knife in the other.

I froze, staring at the painted face that was striped to blend into the forest. Rags were wrapped around his head, camouflaged with leaves and small branches. His clothes were the same. Whoever it was, he looked like he was part of the forest come alive. And then I noticed it was a her. The person in front of me had a full chest and the curves of a woman.

And then another one stepped out not far from her, and I whirled at the sound of a third one behind me, all dressed the same.

And then it finally sank in who they were.

CHAPTER THIRTY-SEVEN

JASE

"WHAT ARE WE GOING TO DO WITH THE HORSES ONCE WE REACH the cave?" Synové asked.

"There's room," I answered. "They can go in too, at least a good part of the way."

"So does this make us family?" Wren asked. "Because I don't need any more family."

"It makes us something," I said. "You can decide."

"Family, as I see it," Synové answered. "This is a pretty big secret. The *hidden entrance,*" she said with hushed drama. "We either have to be family or you have to kill us. Isn't that how these kinds of secrets work?"

Wren took out her *ziethe* and spun it. "There's alternatives."

"Family," I confirmed. Wren's alternative wasn't appealing. But the truth was, they were Kazi's family, and that made them mine too. And they were laying their lives on the line for her—that made them an even deeper kind of family.

Wren stopped her horse and put a finger to her lips.

We all stopped and listened. Footsteps. Scrambling footsteps. And grunts. We signaled one another, and I quietly slipped from Mije. Synové nocked an arrow.

There had been a lot of soldiers combing the mountain, I assumed in search of the gray-haired woman. We had encountered one group, but once they questioned us, they let us continue on our way, convinced we were only hapless Kbaaki trying to return home. But these footsteps sounded different. Someone alone. And in a hurry.

Maybe the woman who had escaped? If she was in trouble with the king, it meant she was probably a loyalist. We could help her. We got a late start leaving town, but we would make it to the vault before nightfall if we didn't encounter any problems. She could come with us.

The rustling footsteps grew louder. It helped mask my own footsteps. I held my finger to my mouth, signaling Wren and Synové to remain quiet as I crept close to the ridge. The noise was just below me. I looked down the small embankment to another path that paralleled ours.

Someone was scrambling up the slope. My head pounded as I tried to decide between staying concealed or leaping over the embankment.

I leapt.

CHAPTER THIRTY-EIGHT

KAZI

"WELL, WELL, LOOK WHO WE HAVE HERE," PRIYA CROWED. HER knife was still unsheathed.

They circled around me, and I turned, trying to keep an eye on all of them.

"I'm on the run from the king," I explained. "I've been searching for you. The family. I want to help—"

"Sure you do," Gunner said, smiling. The kind of smile that was deadly.

"It's not what you think. I'm not—"

In an instant the smile was gone and his face gusted with rage. "My brother is dead! That's what I think! You murdered him, and now you're as good as murdering the town!"

"I didn't kill Jase! He's alive! I swear!"

Gunner nodded, and suddenly Mason's arm crooked around my neck, choking me, jerking me backward while he pressed the tip of a knife to my side.

Priya grabbed the front of my cloak, her hand trembling. "You hanged him! You hanged my brother! I heard it out of your own mouth!"

"You were there?"

Her eyes glowed with hatred. "We snuck down for medicine, and I heard every word. Now that you're on the outs with the king, you think your lies will get you anywhere with us?" She spit in my face, then shoved me harder into Mason, letting go of my cloak.

"He's alive, Priya! I promise! I had to say those things. The king forced me! He's a madman. But Jase is safe. Paxton took him to—"

"Paxton!" Mason tightened his grip on my neck. "You better shut up while you're ahead."

Gunner chuckled and stepped closer, his amusement more frightening than his rage. "You're worth a lot of money now, you know? We heard the news today. Seems you betray everyone in your path. The king and Banques have a noose set aside just for you, and there's a hefty bounty on your head to make sure your neck fills it. Money isn't of much use to us, though." He ripped my cloak off and then took my belts and dagger. "These are the kind of things we need now." He felt my pockets. "You have any medicine on you?" He grunted when he found they were empty.

"No. I—Please, listen to me. Jase is at the settlement. So are—"

"If Jase were alive, he would be here!" Priya yelled.

Gunner's hand shot up, gripping my face. "You picked the wrong family to betray, soldier." He looked at Mason over my shoulder. "We have what we want. Kill her."

"Wait! Please! I love Jase! I—"

"Shut up!" Priya ordered, but her eyes stared into mine, sharp and alert like she saw the raw truth there. *I love Jase.* It couldn't be faked. She had to see it.

Mason's arm pinched tighter around my neck.

"What are you waiting for?" Gunner said to him. "Do it."

"A body right here might not be a good idea," Mason answered. "And maybe we should—"

Gunner rolled his head in disgust. "Oh, for the love of gods. Here—" He reached out and grabbed my hair, pulling me away from Mason, then twisted me around and jammed my arm up behind my back—my bad arm. I gasped with pain, and white light shot behind my eyes. "There's a better way," Gunner said. "The slower way she deserves. We'll let her hang the way she hanged Jase."

He began dragging me back through the woods, then down a slope, until we hit level ground again and a thick bed of leaves swished beneath our feet. I pleaded with him as I stumbled, telling him I was on the run because of Lydia and Nash, that I had hidden them in the Ballenger tomb, but it only enraged him more. My words meant nothing. I was the enemy. There wasn't a single thing I could say that would make him think otherwise. We reached a clearing, and he let go of me. They all stared at me, and I wondered what was going to happen next.

"Enjoy your journey straight to hell," Gunner said, and gave me a hard shove. I stumbled back but then everything seemed to explode around me. Leaves flew through my vision, and my body sprang upward, ropes pinning me awkwardly. I couldn't understand what was happening and then I finally realized I was caught in a snare. I hung there, my body twisted, and I tried to untangle my limbs. Tried to find a way out. Panic rose in me. "No, no, no." Not now. Not when I was this close.

Priya watched me struggling, her eyes cold slits. "They'll be by before too long. A whole squad of them patrols this way every day. I'll help them out." And then she screamed, a loud, desperate scream that vibrated through the trees. A signal to the soldiers. Someone had been caught.

They all turned and ran, disappearing into the forest like they had never been there.

"Priya!" I called. "There's a weapon! Jase hid a weapon . . . in the greenhouse."

But they were gone.

I frantically tried to reach the top of the snare, but my weight made it impossible to open.

I heard shouts. Soldiers getting closer.

And in seconds, they were there.

CHAPTER THIRTY-NINE

JASE

I LANDED ON TOP OF HIM AND THEN WE WERE BOTH ROLLING, slugging, and wrestling for control over each other.

"Dammit!" he yelled. "Get off me, you stupid Kbaaki!"

Almost as fast as I had leapt, I heard Wren cursing and Synové ordering me back. "I have him! Back off!" She was ready to shoot an arrow between his weasel eyes.

And then I pinned him, my knee on his chest, my hands wrapped around his throat.

"Stop!" he rasped, pulling at my fingers.

"I should have done this a long time ago."

His eyes widened, not because I was choking him but because he recognized my voice.

He stared at me like I was the mythical beast of the Moro mountains. "Jase? You stupid bastard! Let me go!"

"Get some answers first," Wren said. "Then kill him."

But before I could ask him anything, he started giving me answers to questions I hadn't even asked.

"It was me, you idiot! I was the one who took you to the settlement! I'm the one who took your ring!"

My grip on him loosened. I didn't know who took me to the settlement, but I was certain it wasn't him. He was up to something. "What game are you playing now, Paxton?"

I let him push me off. He rolled away, crouched on his knees, and grabbed his bleeding mouth. "Devil's hell! That's the second time you've done this to me! If I lose this tooth—" I saw his tongue fishing around in his mouth. He spit out blood.

"You think I care about your teeth? All I care about—"

His head turned sharply, his eyes blazing like a demon. "Shut up! Do you hear me? Shut up and listen! I don't have time to explain! Kazi's here, somewhere on this blasted mountain, running like me! Trying to get to the vault. But she's hurt, and I don't know how bad. Things went wrong. We stole Lydia and Nash!"

In this steep terrain, two riders were too much for one horse, so I walked next to Paxton, leading Mije behind us while he told me everything he knew. He dabbed his split lip from time to time with one of those ridiculous monogrammed handkerchiefs of his. For the first hour I couldn't shake my distrust of him. It was ingrained in me. But I forced myself to listen. He knew secrets no one else knew—things Kazi had told him about us. She had told him about Sylvey's empty crypt. She trusted him, so I tried to trust him too, but it didn't come easy. He told me he was strong-armed by the king to work the arena, but he didn't do it just to save his own skin. He confirmed that the king was behind the attacks and invasion. Paxton wanted to find a way to break his stranglehold on the town—working from the inside instead of the outside.

Why? I thought. *Why did he want to help us?*

"Isn't the arena what you've always wanted?" I asked, still skeptical.

He looked sideways at me, his eyes angry slits again. "The arena? Sure, I wanted it. But not so much that I would steal it from my—" He stopped short, avoiding the word. The word didn't fit between us. *Family.* We might be blood cousins, but we were more like comfortable adversaries. I had grown used to him as an annoying thorn in my side.

"You don't know anything about me, Jase," he continued. "There's lots of things I want. Right now I just want to make sure Kazi's safe and get those power-hungry devils out of Hell's Mouth. The rest I'll figure out later." *Protect.* Sometimes I forgot he was a Ballenger too.

It seemed impossible that we had a mutual goal now.

He told me he used my ring to fake my death. That was why they stopped looking for me. "Kazi took it hard, but it was the only way I could get them to call off the search. And to be honest, I wasn't sure if I could trust her. She turned on me one day and held a blade to my throat, sobbing that I had hunted you down like an animal. I'm pretty sure she intended to kill me. When I confessed that you were alive, she collapsed in my arms. That's when I knew for sure, that nothing between you two had been a farce."

His voice changed when he talked about her. He liked her, respected her maybe. It was a side to him I had never seen. "She told me you were what had kept her going when she wanted to give up. Something about promises you had made to each other and hearing your voice telling her to keep going—just a little farther. And that's what she did."

I swallowed. Cleared my throat. I remembered shouting those words out in anger and desperation as I held her chin up and we floated wildly down the river. I had shouted them to an enemy because my survival had been completely entwined with hers by a chain. Now I couldn't survive without her for a different reason.

As Paxton and I climbed the mountain on foot, Wren and Synové spread out, trying to cover as much ground as we could, Synové riding ten lengths to one side, Wren ten on the other when the terrain allowed it, all of us looking for any signs that Kazi had passed this way.

Paxton said both he and Kazi knew there was another entrance to the vault but didn't know exactly where it was. All Paxton's grandfather had passed on was that it was in a cave, which left a lot of mountain to cover. Kazi was going to question the children for more specifics before she left them in the tomb, but he didn't know what she had found out.

I wasn't sure how much they remembered anyway. My mother and I took them there about a year ago. Nash had been fascinated with the bats. He would remember that much, I was sure. And I remembered Lydia reciting, *left, left, right, left*, determined not to forget the paths in the caves.

"You're sure Lydia and Nash made it to the settlement?" I asked.

Paxton nodded. "The tomb was empty. I went back late that same night to be sure. Binter and Cheu took them. They left a mark so I would know it was them."

His *straza*. I remembered them well. They didn't just have brawn. They were sharp and crafty and as nasty as scorpions. Not much could stop them. Tiago had once said we should try to hire them. But they were loyal too. Paxton had chosen well.

He told me that Oleez had been in on it too and had gone into hiding. I realized then that it was her that the soldiers had been searching for. Dinah, a girl who had worked in our kitchen, had betrayed them. That was how things spun out of control.

"You said Kazi was hurt. How?"

"Not hurt bad enough that she couldn't run, but she was blasted off the road above the canyon. She fell a long way. For a while she was leaving a trail of blood."

"Blasted?"

"They tried to stop her with a launcher."

Those were the sounds we heard three days ago. Montegue was hunting down Kazi with weapons we had created.

Paxton said it wasn't until the next morning that they caught on to his involvement and he had to run. He tried to leave hints that he was headed back to Ráj Nivad. "There's a price on her head. Probably mine now too. Montegue will do anything to get her back. Besides stealing Nash and Lydia, she stole something else of his—"

"Found something over here!" Wren called, waving us over.

Tracks. Muddy boot prints on a slab of rock. They were Kazi's, I had no doubt. Wren and Synové agreed.

We increased our pace, but saw nothing else for another hour, until we were almost there, and then on the ground, almost covered in a litter of leaves, I spotted a torn piece of fabric. "Over here!" I called. I picked it up and rubbed the fabric between my fingers. It was thin and stained with blood. Synové took it from me and examined it. She smiled. "Her chemise," she said. "She's using it for a bandage of some sort. She made it this far."

Then she made it all the way. The entrance was just a little farther ahead. I bent over, my hands on my knees. I closed my eyes, sucking in deep breaths. Everything inside me had squeezed tight.

"Keep going, *Patrei*?" Wren asked.

I nodded, not trusting myself to speak. How many weeks had I been waiting for this moment, afraid it would never come? All the days in the root cellar, the wondering that drove me mad, the fear that I would never get the chance to hold her in my arms again, or tell her how much I loved her. Tell her how sorry I was that I hadn't been careful, that when I saw the fallen spire, I ran toward my family instead of thinking of the family at my side.

I blew out a cleansing breath. The waiting was over, but before I could straighten or even open my eyes, Paxton nudged my arm. "We have visitors."

—=◦◦◦◦=—

Our path was blocked ahead.

"Those some of the mountain creatures you told us about?" Synové asked. "They don't look too friendly. Do I start shooting?"

But two of them already had arrows drawn, and Synové had a good ten steps to reach her bow and quiver on her horse. The advantage was theirs.

I counted four, but they blended into the forest, covered with dirt and leaves and fauna so it was hard to tell how many more might be surrounding us. But the stance of one of them caught my attention. It was familiar. The way his legs were planted, the chin tilted, obstinate. *Gunner?*

"Gunner!" I called. He shook his head, bewildered.

He stared at me for a long while and finally answered, *"Jase?"*

"Yes! It's me!" I threw off my fur hat so he could see my hair, and ran toward him and the others.

They called my name over and over again, and then when I reached them, their hands were touching my face as if making sure it was really me. Priya, Mason, Titus, Aram, all of them hugged me, and then I was back to Gunner again.

"You're supposed to be dead," he said, his voice filled with confusion. His gaze shifted to Wren and Synové, who were walking up behind me with the horses. They had pulled their fur hats free too. Paxton walked with them. Mason, Priya, and Aram lifted their bows again. The joy drained from their faces. "What are you doing with *them*?" Gunner asked.

"Put your weapons down. They're helping me. Where's Kazi? Is she inside?" I asked.

"Them? Helping you? What's the matter with you, Jase?" Gunner said, his question thick with suspicion. "Where have you been?"

"Where's Kazi?" I asked again.

"Gone. We don't have to worry about her anymore."

"What do you mean *gone*? Was she here?"

"She was, but we got rid of her. I threw her into one of their snares, and a patrol grabbed her. I was going to kill her immediately, but this way is actually better. Let her body rot up on the tembris like all the others."

I stared at him, not believing what he had just told me. I grabbed fistfuls of his shirt. "Tell me you're lying, brother. Tell me you're lying before I kill you!"

"Did you forget what she did to us? How she used us? She deserves what she got! How could you not know that?"

"How long ago?" I asked, desperately praying there was still time to go after her.

"Hours. This morning. She's in a cell by now. Or maybe hanging already if we're lucky."

I shook my head. "No. *No!* She came here for help! Did you listen to her?"

"Why would I listen to anything she said? That's what started all this! Listening to her lies! *You* listening to her lies! She's been helping the king, for gods' sakes! She earned her fate. What's the matter with you?"

"Did you even give her a chance? She came to you! To the family! Did she tell you I was alive?"

"Yes, but—"

"That she was forced to say those things about me? That Lydia and Nash were safe?"

He didn't answer, but his eyes were hard beads staring into mine. She had told him.

"You're a fool, Gunner! A stubborn fool who never listens! Who doesn't think before he acts! And this time you've gone too far!"

He jammed his hands against my chest, pushing me away. "What's happened to you? Working with them and defending her against the family? I don't even know who you are!"

I slammed him up against a tree, my hand around his throat, feeling like I could snap his neck with one squeeze. "I am the *Patrei*! And you will help me get her back or—"

"Or what, Jase? What are you going to do? I am your brother!"

My chest heaved. "And Kazi is my *wife*!"

CHAPTER FORTY

KAZI

FAMILY LISTENS. THEY WILL LOVE YOU.

They will listen.

They will listen.

I had been staring at the fire for so long, I hardly knew the rest of the room existed.

It was lit with only a small fire in the hearth that was quickly dwindling down to coals. A chain around my neck was attached to the center pillar. I sat in a chair, one of the few pieces of furniture in the room. Against the wall was a bed covered with a rough-spun blanket, and a small pine chest sat beside it. They had dragged me up several flights of stairs. With open rafters above me, I decided it was an attic room, maybe a servant's quarters. A small window high on the wall where the pitched roof met was black with night now. Besides the chain around my neck, my hands were tied to the arms, and my ankles to the legs of the chair. I was not going anywhere.

Banques had told me to wait for the king, like I had a choice. "He wants to have a little talk with you."

He laughed as he yanked the chain, then left.

The room closed in. Shadows danced on the walls. The inn was deathly quiet. Not even timbers or floors creaked. The fire didn't crackle. There was only the glowing burn.

I heard the slow tick of a clock in my head. Time running out. No more second chances. I pulled at the ropes on my wrists and ankles. They only cut deeper into my skin.

There is always a way out, Kazi. Blink last. Die tomorrow. I twisted and pulled at the ropes again, but they didn't give, just as they hadn't every time I tested them.

Enjoy your journey straight to hell.

Everything sank inside of me, dry and dead. Hell. It had finally caught up with me.

We all have fantasies. Even Jase and I had them. Fantasies we fed. *It will all work out.*

But sometimes it didn't.

Sometimes life and fantasies and family all went completely wrong.

Finally, I heard something.

Footsteps. Faint. Even. Steady.

Montegue was coming.

CHAPTER FORTY-ONE

JASE

MY WIFE.

I had promised Kazi we would tell them together when they were all gathered round. At the dinner table, I suggested. I had imagined what it would be like. Everyone full of expectation, knowing something was brewing. The table would be full with all our favorite foods, braised rabbit with fool's sauce, fish stew, and sage cakes, and there would be toasts. Multiple toasts circling the table twice. Hugs. Happiness. Teasing. Laughter. We would tell them *together*. That was how she wanted it. How I wanted it.

Instead I had screamed the announcement without her. There was no happiness in it. It was a murderous declaration. How many promises to her had I broken? It was probably a small thing to worry about now, but it burned through me like acid. It was just one more thing that had spiraled out of control.

We headed toward the waterfall. I had been ready to jump on my horse and race down the mountain after Kazi, but Wren, Synové, and

Paxton had held me back. "We need a plan. A good one to fix this botched mess," Wren growled, glaring at Gunner. Paxton said it would be a few days at least before she was hanged—as if that was good news that would comfort me. The king would interrogate her first, and knowing Kazi, she would hold out. Only when he was sure he could get nothing useful from her would he hang her. Banques would announce it first too. He always wanted an audience, witnesses to justice, he called it. But his true purpose was a message: *Defy us, and this will be your fate too.*

My stomach turned inside out as I asked the question I wasn't sure I wanted an answer to. "What will he do to her in those few days?"

"I don't know," he answered, but I heard the worry in his voice.

I walked briskly ahead, leading Mije beside me.

Priya caught up with me, grabbing my arm, trying to explain. Mason stood behind her. "Good people do bad things, Jase. They make mistakes."

I wrenched free from her grasp, not slowing my pace. "Don't defend him!"

"Jase." She stepped in front of me to stop me. Her eyes glistened. "We helped turn her over."

I stared at both of them, the betrayal stabbing deeper. "Then you're both dead to me too. You let hatred rule your head."

I stepped around her.

"What do you think you're doing right now, Jase?" she called after me.

I kept walking.

As we approached the falls, Gunner doubled his pace to intercept me. "Where do you think you're going?"

"The vault. We came here for help. I will get it from someone I trust."

"*They* are not family," he said, shaking his finger at Wren, Synové, and Paxton. "You cannot show them—"

"I am the *Patrei*, and I say they are. Step aside." My hand went to the dagger at my side.

"Gunner," Mason whispered, trying to get him to back down, maybe nervous about what I might do. He had good reason to be nervous.

Gunner didn't move, but his voice lowered. "What did you mean when you said she was your wife?"

"Just like it sounds. We're married. We married on the first day of our trip back here."

"A Vendan marriage?"

Wren stepped forward defensively. She and Synové were barely controlling their rage. "You have a problem with a Vendan marriage, beetle brain?"

He didn't answer, meeting her angry glare with his own, but he stepped aside, and we continued walking to the vault, disappearing behind a stand of trees, disappearing behind a waterfall, disappearing into the darkness of caves.

A torch flickered in my hand.

Left. Left. Right.

Our horses were stabled in the last cave, a smaller one than the greenhouse but with a roof hole large enough to let in some light, and there was water.

Left.

We hiked up the last incline. It was nearly impossible to see the door. It was covered with the same kind of algae that covered the cave walls.

Aram squeezed past me with a rock in his hands. He pounded on the cave wall. A code.

We heard the low, grating turn of a wheel, and the door pushed open.

Hawthorne, one of our tower guards, stood behind it. He startled when he saw me and raised his sword. With my heavy fur cloak and stained face, I was a tall, hulking menace he didn't recognize.

Aram put his hand out to reassure him. "It's Jase," he said.

"*Patrei?*" he whispered.

I clapped his shoulder as I went past him. Everyone followed behind me.

The first room, a wide hall just outside the bunk room, was lined with workers, guards, groundskeepers, stable hands, and children, some curled in balls sleeping, others tucked next to each other for warmth, their faces gaunt, weary—Omar, Tamryn, Kwan, and Emma. There was a rumble of whispers as I walked in. *Patrei.* Two children took one look at me, Wren, and Synové, and ran. One of our oldest employees, Judith, a caretaker at Riverbend, sat against the wall, her usually perfect braided hair now wild around her face. Her pink-rimmed eyes were watery, and she lifted her hand toward me. I knelt and embraced her. She clung to me and cried into my shoulder. "You're here, *Patrei.* You're here. Good boy, Latham. Take care of things now." Latham was my grandfather's name. He died before I was born.

"I'm here," I whispered back to her, as if that would make everything all right. But it wouldn't. I was only a man and barely that, struggling myself. She had three lifetimes of experience over me, but I knew to her the whispered name *Patrei* was more than a single man. It was a history, generations of promise, determination: *We will survive this. We will make it through as we always have.*

But determination was not what I saw. Instead I saw weariness and despair. These were the ones who had made it into the vault. Who hadn't?

I moved on to the bunk room. It had been cleared of the old bunk frames. In fact all of the broken girders and dust were gone. It wasn't a historical relic anymore but an active shelter. More who had escaped the blast and invasion lay on blankets, pallets, cloaks, piles of straw, anything to keep them off the cold floor.

Eyes opened. Heads turned as I passed. Freya, Tomás. A few were injured. Dressler, Mishra, Chane. Their heads were wrapped with rags, or their arms were in slings. A murmur rose. Fear. A few rushed from the room.

"It's me," I said. "Jase. And these are my friends. It's all right."

Wren, Synové, and Paxton all held their hands up, indicating they weren't going for their weapons.

The murmur grew to loud chatter rolling through the room. Several stood, stunned, and then Helen and Silas stepped forward to embrace me as I passed. They touched my face and looked at the ring in my brow. Then a large man leaning heavily on a cane stepped forward. It was Tiago. His previously round face now had hollows beneath his cheekbones. I looked down at his leg. "Damned blast," he explained. "Flying debris severed half my calf." He shrugged. "But I still have all my toes." He threw his arms around me. His leg may have been weak, but his grip was still fierce.

"A hundred and thirty-four," Titus said. "That's what left in here now. But there were more. Twenty have died so far."

So far.

The study was more of the same, but in the sickroom were the more seriously injured. I went to each of their pallets. A few of them moaned, but most didn't know I was there at all. I didn't even recognize them at first but Aunt Dolise and Uncle Cazwin were among them. Titus said they rarely came to and then shook his head as if he didn't hold much hope for their recovery. Synové stooped to pull a blanket over one of our archers, who lay on the floor, half covered, his skin sallow and his lips cracked.

The storeroom was next. The shelves were mostly stocked with overflow from other storerooms on the grounds, crates of candles, lantern oil, a few blankets, dates. So many dates. My mother had always stocked too many. They had been my father's favorite. But most of it was just a dusty collection of items that had accumulated over time, not edible, and useless for daily survival.

A few basic food supplies were kept there as a matter of tradition, mostly sacks of grains, and crocks of honey and salt that were rotated in and out every few months. In my entire life, they had never been put to active use in the vault. We had a long-standing joke in the family that when some food tasted off, it must have been made with supplies from the vault. The shelves were mostly empty now.

By the time we passed through the storeroom and into the kitchen, those inside had heard the claim that I was alive and had begun to stand. The murmuring voices of dozens became louder. Patrei? *The* Patrei *is here?* But in the sea of faces, the first one I spotted was Samuel.

I crossed the room to him, maybe I ran, but I was holding him, squeezing him so tight he whispered, "Jase, I can't breathe."

I released my grip and held his face in my hands instead. "You're *alive.* I got a message. I thought it was from Jalaine. I—"

At her mention, his expression changed.

"Jalaine," I said, my eyes quickly scouring the room, my pulse speeding. "Where is she?"

His lips pressed together, and he shook his head. "She didn't make it. Jalaine is dead."

I blinked, the room going in and out of focus. My insides were suddenly weightless. And then my mind jumped to the only other face I hadn't yet seen. "Mother?"

Priya had come up behind me. "Mother's fine, Jase. We'll take you to her."

But first they sat me down at a table in the kitchen and told me about Jalaine and how she had died.

CHAPTER FORTY-TWO

KAZI

A RIBBON.

I concentrated on that now, trying to stop the mad fear beating in my chest.

When they dragged me into the inn today, a red ribbon flashed past my vision. I realized now it was probably only one of the many festival decorations, but in the flash of that terrifying moment as I was pulled through the inn doors like a piece of live game, I had imagined the ribbon to be something else, tied there just for me. I allowed myself to slip back into that world, a world where there were breezes, promises, tomorrows, and Jase.

Cool air streamed over my cheeks.

Jase's hair rippled in the wind.

What is this, Kazi? he asked, looking at the feastcake and ribbon in my hands.

They're part of a Vendan ceremony.

What kind of ceremony?

Wedding. A wedding ceremony, I answered. *Vendan ceremonies are simple. These, a moon, and witnesses are the only requirements. I guess Synové thought she had it all figured out.* My cheeks warmed and I began to rewrap the package.

Jase put his hand out to stop me. *Is it such a bad idea?*

We stared at each other and I saw the inevitable in his eyes. What we both already knew in our hearts. *No*, I answered.

Our lips met, and he whispered words between them: *Show me, Kazi. Show me what to do. I want you to be my wife.*

With Mije and Tigone looking on as our witnesses, I took his hand and wrapped the ribbon around his wrist and he did the same with mine. We tied it off together. *And now vows should be spoken*, I told him.

What kind of vows?

Whatever is in your heart, Jase. That is all that matters. Tell me what is in your heart.

He took my free hand, held it to his lips, then nodded.

Kazi of Brightmist—

His voice caught, his emotion as near to the surface as mine. Then he began again, but he took his time, as if searching for the perfect words.

Kazi of Brightmist . . . you are the love I didn't know I needed.

I could still hear the soft flapping of the ribbon in the wind as we lifted our hands to the sky. *Bound by earth, bound by the heavens*, I said once we finished our vows, and Jase repeated the words.

There was no moon. Our witnesses were horses. We didn't follow the rules, but we never had. It didn't make our vows any less true, or make us any less married.

We had stared at each other for a long while afterward, almost in disbelief. We were wife and husband. I broke off a piece of the feastcake and placed it in his mouth, and he did the same for me. *It is done*, I told him, then added, *almost.* He skimmed his thumb along my lower lip, wiping away a crumb, and then we walked together into the ruin, the ribbon fluttering behind us.

Bound by earth. Bound by the heavens.

Wife and husband.

Montegue could never take that away.

His footsteps grew louder then stopped just outside the door.

He was here.

CHAPTER FORTY-THREE

JASE

SAMUEL TOLD PART OF THE STORY. TITUS WEIGHED IN. MASON added a few words. Gunner remained silent.

With me gone, Gunner had put Jalaine back on at the arena office. They all thought it the wise thing to do. She ran the office better than anyone. That day she had run an errand, and Samuel guessed that when she returned to the office she found him and the men who guarded the door on the floor, blood running from their heads. Samuel had drifted in and out of consciousness. He saw strange men rummaging through drawers and closets, trying to find the day's revenues. He figured that Jalaine had walked in, spotted the intruders, and then saw him lifeless on the floor, and had run.

"By then the whole arena had been overrun," Titus said. He and Gunner were trapped in the apartment when it happened, with unknown attackers banging on the barred door to get in. They had both looked out the apartment window trying to figure out who the attack was coming from. They saw Jalaine run to the tower above the office where the

Valsprey lofts were kept. She disappeared inside and then she was at the terrace wall releasing one of the birds, but arrows began flying through the air. One of them brought the Valsprey down.

Was this the bird that had somehow managed to reach Kazi and me? Why else would Jalaine release the bird unless she was sending a message?

"The next thing we saw was—" Titus paused. His lips rolled over his teeth. "We saw Jalaine fall from the top of the tower. They threw her over the side." His hands pulled into fists on the table, but his eyes were empty, like every bit of emotion had already been drained from him. He said the banging on the door stopped, and he and Gunner managed to make it to the office to get Samuel, but they couldn't recover Jalaine's body from the arena floor. They lived and hid in the forest for a week before they were able to reach the vault. They didn't even know who the attack came from for another week after that.

Mason leaned forward, his head in his hands. "We still don't know how Rybart was able to launch such a large assault. For weeks he was everywhere."

"And the weapons?" Titus added. "The king says we were stockpiling them, but we know that's not true. All we can figure is that when Zane was making deliveries, he stole the plans and cut a deal with Rybart."

"It wasn't Rybart attacking the town," I said. "It was the king. Beaufort was working with him from the very beginning. He's the one behind all this, he and his magistrate, who is now his general. Zane was the go-between."

"What?"

"From the beginning?"

"The king?"

Disbelieving mumbles circled the table.

Paxton nodded to confirm what I said. "Rybart and his crew were victims in this too."

The mumbles quieted and glares were aimed at Paxton, his first words met with hatred. They still weren't ready to believe anything he said, even the truth, and I wondered if some of them might fly across the table and throttle him. They had seen him standing with the king, and I realized Kazi held the same reviled place in their hearts.

I came here for help and found the opposite. I discovered a vault full of disheartened survivors. I discovered my sister was dead. Discovered that Kazi had been thrown to the wolves by my own family. That my wife was going to be hanged. *I promise you, Kazi. They will listen. They will love you.* The kitchen was suddenly suffocating. I couldn't breathe. More broken promises surfaced. *You'll be fine in the morning, Sylvey. I promise. Close your eyes and sleep.* I stood abruptly, the chair flying backward, and I turned and walked out. Back through the storeroom, the study, the catacomb of rooms. A rumble of footsteps followed after me. *Where are you going, Jase? What are you doing? Talk to us.*

I reached the main entrance tunnel and crossed to the greenhouse door, spun the wheel, and opened it. I needed to make sure it was still there, like my last hope hadn't disappeared too.

"Jase!" Priya called. I glanced over my shoulder. They were all following me, maybe afraid I would do something crazy. I had just learned my sister was murdered and my wife had been turned over to a fiend. Doing something crazy seemed like the sane thing to do.

I passed mounds of fresh dirt. This was where they were burying the dead. Spades were still stuck in the soil, ready, like they were waiting for more.

A goat skipped away. Where it had come from, I had no idea, but it hadn't fallen in. I looked up at the hole high in the cave roof. Foliage surrounded it like a lush green collar, and water dripped from the vines. Usually it had a calming effect, but with fresh graves dug below, there wasn't too much that was calming about the greenhouse now.

I crossed the cave, no, I stomped like my steps would bend the world to my will, that it would somehow stop the madness. I climbed the uneven side of the cave, finding footholds in the rock, then reached behind a stony ridge, yanking the bag of ammunition out first and then the launcher.

I turned and held it up. "Did she tell you about this too?"

Priya's face pinched with shame. She nodded. "I heard her as we ran away. She said you had hidden a weapon in the greenhouse. I looked for it when we came back but couldn't find it. I thought it was only more lies."

"Even after—" My throat felt like it was swelling shut. "Even after you betrayed her, she tried to help you. And she would have told you exactly where it was, if you had given her the chance."

"We didn't know, Jase," Mason said.

I looked at the launcher in my hand. *This.* This was all I had to try to save her—one launcher against their hundreds. I dropped it to the ground and stepped closer to the huddle staring at me.

"She laid her life on the line to save me!" I said, pounding my chest. "She laid her life on the line to save Lydia and Nash! She never showed any fear, but you know what she was afraid of? You! All of you! Do you have any idea how much courage it took for her to return here with me? She heard all those things you said to her. What you were going to do to her. I told her that you would understand. You would listen. That you would love her again. Because that's what families do." I felt myself cracking into a thousand pieces. "I guess that makes me a liar, doesn't it?"

Priya shook her head, her eyes glistening, and she reached out and pulled me to her, held me, and I broke down in her arms. A big hulking Kbaaki, sobbing on her shoulder. They all gathered round, holding me, holding one another, Samuel, Aram, Titus, Mason, and Priya. Everyone but Gunner.

He turned and walked out the greenhouse door.

We untangled ourselves. Wren, Synové, and Paxton stood off to the side, their eyes wide, as if afraid to be drawn into a circle of fury and tears that made no sense, not even to me. Was it possible to love and hate someone at the same time? It was habit for me, habit to turn to family, but maybe it was time to break that habit.

And then another voice: "Jase."

We all turned toward it.

Samuel stepped forward. "Mother, you're supposed to be lying down," he scolded.

"It's true," she said, staring at me. "You're alive."

I stared back, not sure what to think.

She put her hand on her swollen belly. "Your father's last gift to me." She shook her head. "I know, it's not a good time for another baby."

A baby? No, it wasn't a good time. It was a very bad time. "But you said that about all of us, didn't you?" I answered. "We came at the worst possible time? It all worked out, though."

She nodded. "And it will work out again."

I went to her, and this time she was the one crying on my shoulder, my mother who never shed tears. And then she made me repeat that Lydia and Nash were safe. "Yes, they're safe. Paxton's *straza* took them to the Vendan settlement." I told her they'd be well cared for but would have to stay there until this was all over. "It's the safest place for them to be." I explained that they would be hidden in the root cellar just as I was, and that it was Paxton who had taken me there after I was injured in an attack.

She looked at Paxton and then, without hesitation, she went and embraced him, murmuring her thanks. He awkwardly returned her hug, looking over her shoulder at me uncertainly.

I nodded.

He patted her back.

She turned to face me again, wiping her eyes. "Even in the hardest of times, our family grows in unexpected ways," she said. "Now, what's this about you being married?"

CHAPTER FORTY-FOUR

KAZI

THE DOOR CREAKED OPEN. SLOW. EVERYTHING WAS SLOW, AS IF he was savoring the moment, watching me at his mercy now. My back was to the door, and I couldn't turn, but every deliberate step shivered through me. Heel to toe. Owning the room. And me. Then silence, bone-numbing silence as he paused. I felt his eyes on my head, my neck, my back. Would I feel a blade there next?

"Hello, soldier."

My cheeks swelled with nausea.

He walked to the hearth, his back to me, and knelt, throwing kindling on the fire, and then another log. The flames blazed upward and brightened the room. "Cold?" he asked.

The room was suddenly stifling. Hot. But not from the fire. Sweat trickled down my back.

"Nothing to say?" he whispered. "And you had so much to say just the other day."

He stood and turned, staring at me, and I saw his face for the first time.

His beautiful face he had loved so much.

A jagged, stitched gash ran from his chin all the way up to the corner of his eye.

It was still puffed and red and angry.

"What do you think?" he asked. "There's more of your handiwork beneath my shirt. Would you like to see it?"

I shook my head.

His eyes were blacker than I had ever seen them. They sank into mine like claws. "You could have had everything," he whispered. "You could have sat at my side and shared all the riches of victory." He bent over, his hands pressing my wrists harder into the arm of the chair, his face close to mine. "Now you are going to die with nothing. You'll be nothing . . . but maybe I could still forgive you?"

"Really, Montegue? Are we going to play this game?"

His breath was fire against my face, a dragon sniffing his prey. "But you play the game so well."

He knelt in front of me, and his hand slid around my ankle and slowly traveled up the inside of my leg.

I bit my lip to keep it from trembling. "I don't have it," I gasped when he reached my thigh.

It didn't stop him. He smiled, and the scar pulled at the corner of his mouth. "And I should believe you?"

"Why didn't you have Banques search me?"

"And deprive myself of this pleasure?"

"It's because you don't trust him."

"Look at what temptation did to you." His hand continued to roam.

"I tossed it away!"

He laughed. "I'm not a fool, Kazimyrah, and neither are you. A thief would never throw away such a valuable treasure. Where is it?"

"It's gone, Montegue. You'll *never* get it."

He stood, his composure cracking.

"So you hid it. *Where?*"

I remained silent. He paced the room, tightening and flexing his fingers, then stopped in front of me again.

"They found you up on the mountain. Where were you going? Meeting up with more loyalists?"

I replied again with silence.

"Where are the children?" he asked, perhaps hoping to frighten me more. He knew I cared about them more than his precious dust. When I didn't respond, he added, "We're searching, and we *will* find them. It would be best to tell me now so something unfortunate doesn't happen. They did love me, you know."

Revulsion rose in the back of my throat. "They hated you. I hate you. You're nothing but a ruthless, ambitious monster."

He grabbed my face. His fingers dug in, his eyes wide and fierce. "You wanted me!"

"The only thing I wanted from you was for you to die. That gash on your face? That was only due to my bad aim. That slash was meant for your throat."

He yanked the chain around my neck upward, the metal digging into my skin. His gaze was frozen, his hand trembling, and I was sure he was about to kill me. He wanted me to be afraid, and I was, but I also wanted to crush his fantasy first, the way he had crushed mine. There were things I still wanted to say, things that would make him suffer far more than the scar across his face.

"I planned to kill you from the moment I learned that it was you who ambushed my husband."

His hold on the chain loosened. "*Your what?*"

"The *Patrei* was my husband. We were married."

His mouth hung open. "I don't believe you."

"You live in a fantasy world, Montegue. You can believe whatever you want. But I loved Jase, and he loved me. That's why I desperately fought for his life." I leaned forward and smiled. "And his kisses? They made yours laughable."

He let go of the chain and stumbled away like he had been stabbed.

"You will never be loved the way he is loved," I continued. "Not by me or anyone. Jase is more of a man and leader than you could ever hope to be."

He whipped around to face me, his jaw rigid. "Yet he is dead, and I am here ruling everything. In the end, *I* am the leader of it all, and that proves who is the greater man." His hand swiped through the air. "I am done with you. I have other ways to make you talk. Banques!"

The door opened almost immediately, his lackey always at attention. He instructed Banques to *take care of me* and procure the information he needed. "But don't damage her face. It wouldn't look good for a public hanging. We're a civilized reign, after all. Let's keep this dignified and quick. The town is busy decorating for the festival, because *I* am a great leader. I wouldn't want to put an unnecessary damper on their spirits."

He started to walk toward the door.

"You're a coward, Montegue!" I yelled, catching his gaze. "A weak-kneed coward! A nothing king, and that's all you'll ever be! A nothing king who never gets his own hands dirty!"

He stopped, his chest expanding with a deep breath. The *shing* of his sword sliced the air as he drew it. It shook in his tight grip as he stared at me. This was it. This was the moment, and maybe I wanted it to be. I would rather die than be made to talk. But then he slowly slid his sword back into his scabbard as if he had thought of something.

"Don't touch her," he said to Banques. "I'll be back."

His gaze returned to me. "And, soldier, trust me, my hands will be dirty on this one."

CHAPTER FORTY-FIVE

JASE

WE SAT ON A LONG BENCH AT ONE OF THE TABLES IN THE EMPTY kitchen. Dinner was past, and we ate what was left of a big pot of venison soup. My mother insisted. Wren, Synové, Paxton, and I agreed we would make our plans as we ate, but then Mason came and sat down opposite me, then Titus and Samuel, until the whole family, even Gunner, was crowded around the table. Aram brought over a chair cushioned with pillows made from empty grain sacks stuffed with leaves for my mother. He whispered to me that her pregnancy hadn't been easy. There had been bleeding, and Rhea had ordered her to stay off her feet. It was too soon for the baby to come.

There was awkward silence as we ate. The clink of spoons against metal bowls was the only sound.

"How many archers do we have?" I finally asked. Left. That was what I meant. How many had survived the attack.

"One," Priya answered. "You may have seen him in the sickroom."

One? We'd had sixteen archers stationed at Tor's Watch. At any one time, we had as many as eight posted.

Priya told us about the pandemonium that struck the day the army blasted down the center tower of the main house and then the fortress wall. The posted archers had fought valiantly, and more came to fight beside them, but they had no chance against the powerful launchers. Their fight did buy time for those inside the gates, though. Mother had been in the garden, and had run to each of the houses, ordering everyone into the vault. Aunt Dolise had been in the kitchen and swept pantry staples and medicines into a bag. She and Uncle Cazwin were the last ones running for the vault when they were hit by rubble from another blast. Aram, Priya, and Drake dragged them and the supplies the rest of the way into the tunnel and then the door was sealed. They didn't know where Trey and Bradach were. Our cousins had been in town visiting friends when the attack began. There had been no sign of them since, and Priya assumed they were being hidden. At least she hoped that was what had become of them.

As we spoke, vault refugees filtered into the room—Tiago, Hawthorne, Judith, and more—perhaps curious about their returned Kbaaki *Patrei*, or eager to hear news from the outside, or maybe searching for hope. They settled in quietly, sitting on tables and chairs or leaning against walls.

My family took turns telling me details, but Gunner was noticeably silent. When there was a lull, Mason leaned forward and asked, "How? After everything she did to us, how did you end up with her?" His dark eyes skimmed Wren, Synové, and Paxton. *And them.* But he didn't say it aloud.

Synové heard it just the same. Her spoon slipped from her hand and rattled against her bowl.

I told them everything, starting at the beginning with Beaufort and what I had learned on our long trek to Marabella. I spared no gruesome detail, especially the ultimate fate Beaufort and his crew planned for us, the details they took pleasure in torturing me with, including what they intended to do with Priya, Jalaine, and Mother once they had killed the rest of us. They needed to hear it too, to know the ugly specifics so they would fully grasp just what we had escaped. Beaufort had played the ultimate game of bait and switch on us, keeping our eye on one prize, while he prepared another one for us.

"There never was a cure," my mother said quietly. I heard shame in her voice, like some part of her had known all along that it was too good to be true.

I shook my head. "No. The only thing awaiting us was another Ballenger massacre," I said, then looked at Gunner and added, "If not for Kazi." I knew he felt my gaze, even if he wouldn't meet it.

"Once we made it to Marabella, Kazi spoke to the queen not just on my behalf, but on all of our behalves. She told her how Beaufort had first wheedled his way into our lives with his promise of a fever cure. She told the queen about Tor's Watch's place in history and our long stewardship of Hell's Mouth. She told her how we had all pitched in and rebuilt the settlement at our own cost. The queen was very grateful—and curious about our world. She wanted to hear more, so I told her. When I was finished, she and the King of Dalbreck made a proposal to me, an important proposal, and I accepted it." I looked around the table and the room, making sure they were all listening.

"The Queen of Venda and the King of Dalbreck conferred, and they agreed that Hell's Mouth should be returned to us. They also agreed we should be a recognized kingdom of the Alliance. The first kingdom," I said.

"Because of Kazi," Wren added.

"That's just one of the many reasons Jase *ended up with her,*" Synové said, her tone bitter as she looked pointedly at Mason.

There was stunned silence.

And then some tears and disbelief.

"A kingdom?"

"The first kingdom?"

I heard Kazi's name on their lips as they sent up prayers.

"A blessing from the gods . . ."

"The girl Kazi, watch over her."

"Keep her safe."

"There's more you should know," Paxton interjected. It was the first time he had spoken up, but his cocky edge had returned, his hand chopping the air to make his point, his annoying habit of the past that always made me want to punch him. It didn't anymore. He had some stored-up anger too. There was noticeable bristling on the other side of the table as he spoke. He was only being tolerated because of me, and the fact that my mother had publicly embraced him.

He told them things he hadn't even told me yet. "She killed four men trying to save Jase from an ambush. I saw it happening as I raced to get there. It was the most horrible, frightening, and awe-inspiring thing I've ever seen, and any one of us can only pray that someday someone will love us as much as Kazi loved Jase to sacrifice everything, including her life. She stayed behind to fight more soldiers off after she sent his horse into the forest to give him time to get away from them. That's when she was stabbed and captured. And then by sheer fortitude, because they were barely feeding her, she recovered, with the burning goal of saving Lydia and Nash next. And she did. She—"

"How?" Priya asked, her eyes drilling into Paxton. "Drake died trying to rescue them. We were afraid to try again, not until we had more help. We sent a messenger to Cortenai, the nearest kingdom, but there's been no word. We're not sure if the messenger even made it past the patrols. How could Kazi do this? She's not a magician. *How?*"

Paxton froze, his mouth hanging open as he stared back at Priya. He was oddly speechless.

"Before she was a soldier," I intervened, "Kazi was an experienced thief. It's what she's good at. She stole Lydia and Nash from beneath the king's nose and hid them."

"*A thief?*" several said at the same time.

"Hid them *where?*" Priya asked cautiously.

"She hid them in Sylvey's empty crypt."

Horrified expressions circled the table.

"But . . ." my mother said, "the crypt isn't empty."

"Yes, I'm afraid it is, Mother," I replied. And then I told them what I had done. What Kazi had known. What she had done to save them.

"You desecrated Sylvey's tomb?" Titus asked.

"Yes," I answered.

There was another long uncomfortable silence, maybe as they tried to reconcile the lie I had perpetrated for all these years—*the crime*—with the fact it had saved Lydia and Nash. Maybe trying to absorb that Kazi had another life as a thief that they had known nothing about, or that she had murdered the guard, who now lay rotting in the sanctified Ballenger tomb. Or maybe that Sylvey was buried in an unhallowed grave high on the mountain. It was a lot to take in at once.

"A thief," Mason said, still mulling it over. He knew she had been an orphan on her own since she was six, but I hadn't told him how she had survived. I could see it all adding up in his eyes now.

My mother combed her fingers through her hair, her eyes squeezed shut. I knew the truth about Sylvey was an enormous blow to her. It wasn't just that I had committed a serious crime, or that her daughter's body was not resting in peace where she and my father had laid it, but that I had kept this lie a secret from them all for so long. She finally opened her eyes, folded her hands in front of her on the table, and lifted her chin. "What's done is done," she said. "When this is all over, we'll have a quiet ceremony at Breda's Tears with a priest to consecrate Sylvey's final resting place. This news will go no farther than this vault." She looked around the room, steel in her eyes, as if she dared anyone to challenge her decision.

My mother, always moving forward. That's what mattered. This led us back to her original question that brought us to the kitchen table. She wanted to know about my marriage.

I told her the same thing I had told Gunner, that we married weeks ago on our way back home. She asked for the details of the marriage. There weren't many to tell, only a few about a ribbon, vows, and feast-cake.

"And it was only the two of you," she said.

I nodded.

"They had horses for witnesses," Samuel mused, the barest hint of a roll in his eyes.

"Mije and Tigone," Wren clarified, her eyes pinning Samuel to his seat, and then flashing a glare at the still-silent Gunner. "Horses that are smarter and more loyal than most people I know."

"And there was no priest," my mother added, mostly to herself.

I saw the glances around the table. No witnesses. No priest.

"But there was feastcake," Synové said enthusiastically. "And nothing says married like a polished-off feastcake."

She smacked her lips and smiled at Mason. He looked away.

My mother pressed her palms together in front of her. "But vows were spoken?"

"Yes," I answered.

She leaned back and nodded. "Very well, then. I not only have a new daughter, but one who has sacrificed everything to save our family. We must find a way to get my daughter and your wife back."

The room remained silent. Instead of a rallying cry, I only heard hushed despair. They had already tried and failed with Lydia and Nash.

I stood. "We're not defeated unless we give up. We are going to be a kingdom—*and* we're going to rescue my wife because she has risked everything for us and time is running out for her."

"I can still lift a sword," Tiago called from the back of the room.

"So can I!" from Judith and others.

"We can storm the inn!" from someone else.

"An ambush!"

"We'll break her out!"

"Poison their water!"

"Blast our way in with your weapon!"

The room came alive with ideas, but few inside these walls had seen the town and what we were up against. A charging brigade of cooks and caretakers, and even a fierce but injured *straza*, was no match for heavily armed soldiers posted on every rooftop. Not to mention there were all the townspeople, whom we couldn't put at risk. We had to find a way to get to Kazi without killing citizens in the process. And getting her killed too. Blasting our way in would likely do just that.

Synové and Wren glanced at me, hearing the futility of the suggestions.

Gunner stood up. "We could make a trade." The room quieted.

"Trade *what*?" Priya asked. "A bag of sour grain?"

"Me," he answered. "As far as they know, I'm the *Patrei*. I'm sure they'd like to get their hands on me. They want to kill all the Ballengers. Why not give them the top one?"

I stared at him. We all knew it wouldn't work. He probably did too. I had already wrestled with the thought myself. I shook my head. "If they were people of their word, maybe, but they're not. With the gross imbalance of power, the logistics of a trade are impossible. They would take you and keep Kazi too. A noble gesture, though." I heard the bitterness in my voice. I would not show him gratitude when he had brought this about. Now that he knew we were going to be a kingdom he was sorry? I couldn't forgive him for what he had done.

More ideas continued to be thrown out, none of them viable. It was getting late, time running out, and my gut churned as I ruled out each one. I felt desperation taking hold inside me. We needed to find a solution *now*. I needed to think and rethink. I had to retrace every step. Think of every possibility. *Don't go doing something crazy*, Caemus had warned me, but maybe that was exactly what I needed to do, something that no one would expect. I told everyone to go turn in, we'd talk more in the morning. But I had no intention of sleeping—not until I figured out a way to get Kazi back.

I stared at the shimmering red votive. The alcove at the end of the entrance tunnel had been made into a prayer niche. When Wren and Synové started to follow me here, I told them I needed some time alone to think. They went off with Paxton into their own corner to do some thinking.

My initial idea of using my weapon to get more weapons was fine for fighting an army but only begged for disaster when it came to rescuing Kazi. I couldn't shoot any guards holding her without killing her too. I couldn't blast my way in without endangering her, and we had no way of knowing exactly where they held her. Paxton said it could be anywhere in the inn, from cellar to attic, or even at the arena. We would only know exactly where she was when they marched her out on the skywalk to be hanged. I considered the idea of a trade again. Me. Yes, they would keep us both, but at least I would be with her. But what if they held me somewhere else, and I wasn't with her at all?

I had knelt when I reached the niche. I had planned to pray when I got there, but every prayer had already been wrung from me. I sat back on my heels and stared at the prayer candle, thinking of all the vows I had made, the priest marking my forehead with ashes. Sanctifying—

There was no priest?

I knew that would disturb my mother. The Ballengers had traditions. Births, deaths, weddings. Priests were part of them all.

I had warned Kazi this would happen. She had been sitting on my stomach eating berries, occasionally slipping one into my mouth, her finger lingering, tracing my lips.

You know, I had told her, *my mother will expect us to marry again in the temple.*

She had popped another berry in my mouth and frowned. *Why? A Vendan wedding isn't good enough for you Ballengers?*

I had pulled her toward me, and the berries in her hand spilled to the ground. *What's wrong with getting married again? I would marry you a hundred times over.*

She kissed me, berry juice still on her lips. *Only a hundred?* she asked.

A thousand times.

She pulled away, her brow raised, and she looked down at me, her interest suddenly roused. *Would there be feastcake each time?*

Mountains of it, I promised.

She laughed and swooped down to nibble my ear. *Then I suppose we shall marry in the temple.*

But the temple was no longer there.

"A thousand times over, Kazi," I whispered. "I would marry you more than a thousand times."

The scuffle of footsteps jarred me from a windswept wilderness back into the musty dark tunnel. It was Gunner.

I stood.

His eyes were red. He shook his head but was silent, like words were dammed up inside him.

"Go on," I said. "Say what you have to say and leave me alone."

He swallowed. "I'm sorry, Jase. I'm sorry." His voice was barely a whisper.

"Gunner—"

He stepped forward, his arms reaching out, and he clutched me. My shirt pulled as he grabbed fistfuls of cloth in his fingers. I reluctantly lifted my arms and held him as he cried. My oldest and toughest brother sobbed in my arms, and I didn't know what world I was in anymore.

His chest shuddered as he tried to explain and then he pulled away, shaking his head again as if ashamed, but now the words poured out like he couldn't stop them. He said I was right, that he didn't listen, but he thought I was dead, and he was so angry and tired and busy. These past weeks had been hard—every day someone dying, digging graves in the greenhouse, hunting, just trying to keep everyone fed, sneaking down to town for more medicine, almost getting caught, not knowing how they would ever get Lydia and Nash back.

"And Jalaine—" He choked on her name. "If I hadn't put her back on at the arena. If I—" He slid against the wall to the floor, clutching his skull, sobbing again. "I can't get the image out of my head, watching her fall."

I closed my eyes, trying to shut out the horror of the image. Gunner's sobs tore through me like they were my own. I joined him on the floor and he told me when Kazi appeared, he blocked out everything she said. He didn't want to listen. He only wanted revenge. "I was wrong, Jase. And I know ten of me isn't worth one of her, but I would trade my life for hers if I could."

"I know," I answered. "I'm sorry too, brother." He wasn't the only one carrying a load of guilt, or the only one who had made mistakes. Priya was right. I had let hatred rule my head. Gunner judged too quickly. So had I.

He wiped his face and looked at me. His eyes were wide and he looked slightly demented. "I have an idea," he said. "It probably won't work. It's crazy, but what else do we have?"

Crazy? We had nothing else.

"It involves pulleys. They're still there."

I knew exactly what he was suggesting.

"But we have no rope."

His face lit up. "Wrong. We have enough rope to tie up all of Hell's Mouth twice. Overstock in the storeroom."

I leaned back against the wall beside him, my mind spinning. It was crazy.

Catch them off guard. Take them by surprise, Aleski.

It might work.

That was what we would do.

Shifty, a thief, a trick of the eyes.

I knew the answer to Kazi's riddle.

And mine.

We thought they were gone. We thought it was safe. But more scavengers always come. Miandre went to the forest for herbs and they took her. They won't give her back. Now, she shouts at the gate with them. Calls us names. She is one of them now. But she is not. I have seen her look back over her shoulder at me. I see her eyes. She wonders when we will come for her. Soon, I want to tell her. The next time they come we will be hiding in the forest. Waiting. The others say it is impossible. The scavengers are bigger than us and too many. I tell them, there is always a way to make the impossible, possible. We will find that way. I pray that I am right.

—Greyson, 17

CHAPTER FORTY-SIX

KAZI

BANQUES WAITED IN THE ROOM, STARING AT THE FIRE, A PUZZLED expression on his face. "Even I don't know what he's up to, but I'm certain it's not something you'll enjoy. I'll give you a bit of advice. Tell him what he wants to know now. You will eventually. Save yourself the agony."

"Let me go, Banques. You're facing a more certain fate than I am. He'll eventually kill you. He doesn't even trust you. He'll turn on you— it's just a matter of time." My voice sounded calm, but I was anything but that inside. My mind skipped from one thought to another, desperately seeking a way, one last way out, even pleading and begging, though I knew that was futile. Maybe that was what happened when you were about to die. You stopped thinking rationally and your mind scraped, clawed, and scratched for any last grain of sand that could keep you from falling over a cliff.

Banques turned to me and laughed. "Montegue needs me more than I need him. Do you have any idea how much power I have? More than

I ever dreamed of. When I was a captain in Morrighan, I had dreams of commanding my own outpost one day. Colonel—that was the whole of my aspirations. Now I'm a general, and I command *the* most powerful army on the continent. And they only number five hundred troops so far. That's what's astounding. And soon we'll be adding to our stockpile of power. It's a beautiful thing."

Beautiful? What kind of madman describes weapons as beautiful?

He continued on, absorbed in his machinations. "We're devising a ballista now that could strike targets miles away. Every kingdom will be—" He smiled and shrugged. "Let's just say, we will be the center of everyone's universe now. Nothing could make me give up that kind of power, especially not for someone like you. I have dreams Montegue hasn't even thought of yet. He is the perfect partner in this venture."

Distant barking erupted, yelping, as if hyenas had found a rabbit and were tearing it apart. Banques turned toward the door. The barking grew louder and was accompanied by footsteps. Banques shook his head.

My back was still to the door, but I heard it bang open, and the room was instantly filled with wild snarling and barking. Montegue stomped forward and spun my chair to face it all.

A handler held the leashes of two straining dogs. Not just any dogs. *Ashti.*

Sour saliva bloomed in my mouth.

Montegue untied my arms and legs, but my neck was still chained to the center pillar. "Stand up," he ordered.

I did, and he pulled the chair away.

"Look how eager they are," he boasted, as if he controlled them. "They're drooling over you already." He leaned close and whispered. "Is this getting my hands dirty enough for you? Whatever Banques had planned for you, I promise it would have been nothing compared to this. I'm told there is no death that is quite like it. Very slow. Very painful.

Some liken it to being burned alive—but gradually. It can take several days."

I remembered the few hours of pain I had endured when I was bitten by them in the Ballenger tunnel. It was unbearable. Jase told me the agony of such a death could last as long as a week.

"I hid your vial behind the bench in the pavilion," I confessed. "I was going to go back for it but then I didn't get the chance."

"Good," Montegue said, nodding. "That's a start. We'll check it out right away. "

He walked over to the handler and took the leashes from him. "If you're finally telling the truth, you'll get the antidote."

And then he let the dogs loose.

CHAPTER FORTY-SEVEN

JASE

Judith used a heavy wooden spoon to lift a steaming cloak from a large pot of boiling dye. "What do you think, *Patrei*? Black as midnight, as you ordered."

"It's perfect, Judith."

She moved on to the next cloak. She had come alive since yesterday, her hair back in its neat braids, a renewed purpose showing in her face as she studied the bubbling water. In fact, the whole vault had come alive. They had all been up since long before dawn. Sleep could wait for another day. Gunner and I hadn't slept at all. Once we decided on our course of action, we went rummaging through the vault for supplies and then decided who would do what.

Everyone had a job. Even the children. They were busy weaving leaves and moss into caps that Tiago and Hawthorne were stitching together. My mother, Rhea, Wren, and Samuel were measuring out lengths of rope. Gunner was right. We had almost as many shelves full of rope as we had dates.

Aram and Titus had left for town while it was still dark. They needed to be there by first bell when Banques made announcements. I prayed there would be none today. Every trip up and down the mountain was a risk, but Titus and Aram knew the mountain like the back of their hands. They would also try to seek out Aleski and Imara. Aleski needed to spread the word that everyone was to show up for Kazi's hanging. We needed a full plaza. We were also going to need more horses, and if anyone could manage to "borrow" a few without it being noticed, it was Imara.

"Like this," I instructed Mason, showing him how to load the launcher. He was the one who would have to fire it. I would be busy with other duties. "You can get four shots out of every load of ammo, but you should only need one." I tried to recall every instruction Bahr had given me. It had been a long time since I had fired it.

"Keep it snug against your shoulder," I told him. "The mount will absorb most of the shock, but there will still be a strong kickback. Keep a wide stance to your feet." He aimed it, imagining a target on the far wall of the greenhouse. Unfortunately, he couldn't actually test it, especially not inside the cave. Even outside, the sound could travel for miles and draw attention, and with clear skies, it couldn't be mistaken for thunder. We removed the ammo and continued his practice. "Eye your target the same way you would if you were shooting an arrow, then keep it steady while you pull the lever back, nice and smooth."

"Maybe I'm the one who should be shooting that thing," Synové said, then shrugged. "That is, *if* you need someone with good aim."

"My aim is good," Mason replied between gritted teeth.

Synové grunted in return.

She already knew what her job was. A fiery arrow. Maybe several of them. Blasting a hole in a wall didn't require precision. Igniting the contents did.

Priya stomped across the greenhouse toward me. "We're all going to die, you know?"

"You didn't think so when we were twelve."

"I do now. He can't tie a proper knot to save his life," she grumbled, jerking her head toward Paxton, who trailed a few paces behind her.

"That's what you're for. To teach him."

"I think I have it now," Paxton said apologetically. He stuttered over a few more words and finally said, "I'm sorry."

Priya blew out a long puff of air and rolled her eyes.

"Maybe we will all die," I answered. "But if we die, we die fighting."

"Don't go reciting history on me," she answered. "Who are you? Greyson Ballenger?"

"I need his eyes on this, Priya. Please."

She looked at me, her frustration draining, her expression filling with worry instead. It was crazy. I knew I was asking a lot. She closed her eyes and nodded as if fortifying herself, then turned to Paxton. "Let's go, genius," she said to him, and they returned to their knot practice.

We're all going to die.

Maybe for the first time, I really understood all the generations of history I had studied and transcribed, and Greyson Ballenger's desperation when he shoved sticks into the hands of his newly adopted family.

Maybe I finally understood that history wasn't just written on walls and in books but made in a thousand daily decisions, and some of them went wrong, some went right, and some decisions just had to be made because time was running out. Waiting for someone else to write your history was no way to live. Sometimes it was only a certain way to die.

I walked across the greenhouse and stopped to look at one of the finished cloaks, black on the outside and a forest of color on the inside. A perfect lie.

Here you go, Patrei. *Listen up.*

I saw Kazi looking sideways at me. Her grin. Her pursed lips. The line of concentration between her brows. Her voice. It was all clear in my head.

> *I have two arms but not a bone,*
> *I can't be hurt with knife or stone.*
> *I have a head but lack a face,*
> *I don't need eyes to match your pace.*
> *I'm shifty, a thief, a trick of the eyes,*
> *My robes are made of mystery and lies.*
> *I am short, I am thin, I am monstrous and tall,*
> *But when midnight comes, I am nothing at all.*

A shadow.

A trick of the eyes.

And that's what I would become.

What we would all become.

CHAPTER FORTY-EIGHT

KAZI

MONTEGUE SAT ON THE EDGE OF THE BED LOOKING DOWN at me.

"It wasn't there," he whispered.

It had been a few hours. I was already weak and shivering with fever. They had moved me to the bed, but my neck was still chained. They didn't bother with tying my hands and feet. His healer was busy wrapping my wounds. There was one bite on my forearm, another on my thigh, the pain already unbearable. Banques, Zane, and Garvin stood near the door. They had just returned from the pavilion.

Every word I said was an effort, strained and shaky. "It's dark," I gasped. "I promise you it's there. Unless one of them took it."

Montegue brushed a strand of hair from my cheek and shook his head. "No one took it. Maybe when I return in a few hours, your tongue will become a little looser."

I pulled at the shackle around my neck, my fingers desperately feeling the lock. Even if I had something to pick it with, my fingers shook uncontrollably, and then the cramping started. Every few minutes, a violent spasm doubled me over. The room spun, blurred, the floor bobbed. *Your tongue will become looser.*

It was my greatest fear. What if it did become looser? What if, as I lost a grip on reality, I said things? What if I answered his questions? Told him where Lydia and Nash were? Or where the other vault entrance was? What if I told him Jase was alive?

Practice, Kazi, practice what you will say, no matter how bad the pain becomes.

Hours passed. Days. Weeks. Forever. I screamed for them to come back.

My skin flamed. Burned.

My eyes were coals. My lips melted against my teeth.

Fire seared my throat.

The iron ring around my neck was molten.

I don't where they are! I don't know where—

I don't know! I don't—

I . . . I . . .

I . . .

And then I broke.

I told them everything they wanted to know.

Every practiced word.

The arena.

The stables.

The temple.

Darkcottage.

Cave's End.

I sent them chasing everywhere.

Until the words were gone, and there was only pain.

———◦◦◦◦———

Zane was suddenly there. My mother was running for the stick in the corner. *Where is she? Where is the brat?* The seconds, the years, they swirled in a fog. Zane's face pressed close to mine. *No one will believe you now. You would say anything to save your skin. Keep your mouth shut, or I will kill your mother. It will be your fault if she dies. You can still save her.* I blinked and he was gone. Gone. I wasn't sure if he had ever been there at all.

———◦◦◦◦———

Zane, coming back again, and again, his lips touching my ear, whispering my worst nightmares.

———◦◦◦◦———

Please. Come back.

Please. Let me die.

But they wouldn't come back. And they wouldn't let me die.

———◦◦◦◦———

The blanket was wet beneath me, soaked with my sweat. Cold liquid touched my lips. I felt my tongue again.

The pain rolled back. The fire in my throat cooled.

I heard voices. Faces loomed in front of me, but my eyes wouldn't focus. A hand gently curled around mine. "It's Jase. Can you hear me, Kazi? I'm here."

"Jase?"

"Yes, it's me. You're going to be all right, but I need your help. Lydia and Nash are dead. But if I hurry, I can still save them with the stardust. Where is it, Kazi? Tell me. Hurry."

"No, they can't be dead. They can't—"

"It will be all right." His lips met mine, his tongue exploring my mouth, his hand caressing my cheek. "Just tell me, my love, tell me where it is."

How does Jase know about the dust? How could he—

Maybe she doesn't know?

She knows. Never trust anything a thief tells you, not even when they're delirious.

Garvin's voice.

The cool liquid spread from my lips to my fingertips. The room stopped spinning.

And then I saw the face looming above mine.

It was Montegue.

The voices were nightmares now. I couldn't trust any of them. They pounded in my head.

It's Jase. Lydia and Nash are dead. Tell me where it is.

No one will believe you. You can still save her . . .

Keep your mouth shut or I will kill her.

Tell me where it is.

Something cold trickled down my throat. The pain receded again, and I saw Montegue standing at the end of my bed. He ordered everyone out of the room.

"It's only been two days since you were bitten," he said. "You have days of this agony to go." He held up the glass I had sipped from. "The healer gave you a painkiller. It will only be an hour or so before it wears off and the pain returns."

He pulled the chair up to the bed and sat down beside me. He took my hand in his. "The antidote would end your suffering for good. Maybe we can—"

"I will never tell you anything, Montegue."

"You will. Trust me, you will."

And so it went every day. Or maybe it was every few hours. I wasn't sure. I lost track of light coming through the attic window. Blinding light was always behind my eyes until cold numbing liquid was poured down my throat because they wanted to give me another chance. An hour or two of lucidity and questioning followed, and then I was plunged back into my fiery hell.

More cool liquid.

More questions.

But even my moments of lucidity were growing blurry. Every time they brought me back from the brink, I was weaker. All I wanted to do was sleep, fade away in these brief moments of calm. Dream. Hold on to something good. But even sleep was withheld from me. Sometimes Montegue, Banques, and Zane would sit around the room and talk kingdom business, waiting for the medicine to take effect and for my shaking to stop. It was as if they were keeping a friendly vigil at a deathbed.

More chairs were brought in. Sometimes they argued, stealing my peace in these brief pain-free minutes.

They're grumbling for payment.

They'll get it.

Taste this.

Delicious. Pass the decanter.

Two more loads. That's all.

Why isn't it done already?

I can only move one load a day without rousing notice.

Finish it. It's not safe where it is. Too many come and go at the arena.

And they found a squad of murdered scouts in a ruin yesterday. It was a bloody mess. There are still loyalists out there.

You hear that? We need to get it below ground. Do it tomorrow.

More wine, Your Majesty?

Include spy as a charge. That will validate our attack when it comes.

Someone throw water in her face. I want her looking at me when I ask questions.

⸻ ⬦ ⸻

The healer's hand shook as she poured more of her medicine into a glass. Another convulsion twisted my body. She leaned close and I heard a faraway voice. Hers? *I'm sorry. I have no antidote. I never did. But I do have other poison I could give you. It would finish this for you. They would never know. Nod if you want me to give it to you.*

⸻ ⬦ ⸻

Death paced the room, watching me. Impatient.

He walked to the end of my bed and stared, his bony fingers curling around the bedpost, his stare cutting through me, as if he knew what I was thinking. *Blink last. Make it one more day.*

My shoulders shivered with his chill. I had always thought those were my words, but they were *his*. They had been his all along. I remembered the fear that gripped me that long-ago night. His whisper. His challenge for to me to stay alive.

I felt his fear now. Or maybe it was his anger.

Make it one more day.

CHAPTER FORTY-NINE

JASE

THE MOON WAS A SHARP SCYTHE IN THE SKY, SMOKY ORANGE against a backdrop of stars. A reaping moon. Not enough light to expose us. We were shadows, trees, an army of specters that were there, but not there at all.

We assembled at the base of Kalliope, the largest tembris just past the outskirts of town. Her arms reached far into the other tembris. Next came Eudora, then Acantha, and Gaia. The sisters, we called them.

Synové's blunt whirred upward through the night, then fell back to the ground, circling one of the lowest branches. We used the string attached to it, to hoist up a heavier knotted rope into the towering tembris. Six of us would be going up.

Five days we had been waiting. The announcement only came yesterday. I had paced the vault like a madman, wondering what they were waiting for. What was taking them so long? It was insane to be eager for her hanging—but I wasn't going to let her hang.

We would be in position when the sun rose.

Soldiers stationed on roofs would be looking down for trouble when they should be looking up.

CHAPTER FIFTY

KAZI

TONIGHT I WOKE. OR MAYBE IT WAS A DREAM. BUT MY EYES seemed to open. The room was as black as the deepest, darkest hole in the world, and I was falling into it, a hole that had no bottom, but through the attic window, a light shone, the brightest light I had ever seen.

Hold on to me, Kazi. Let me show you the stars.

I watched a sparkling galaxy pass by the small window. From the lowest star on the horizon to the highest one in the heavens. Some were horses racing across the sky. *Don't look down. Keep your eyes on the stars. That one there is Thieves' Gold. And over there is Eagle's Nest.* I watched them glitter, listening to Jase whisper the stories of the universe.

Hold on to me, Kazi. I've got you. I won't let go.

"I know, Jase," I answered. "I know."

She's still shaking.

Give her more.

I'm not sure it will help.

She has to walk out there on her own.

A hand roughly patted my face.

Wake up, soldier. On your feet.

More liquid was pressed to my lips. I gagged.

Drink it.

I don't think she can hear you.

She's half dead already. She's not going to make it to the gallows.

The crowds are waiting. She has to make it.

More cold liquid. More coughing, choking, but the shaking stops. Blurry shapes become people. The same people.

"This is your last chance to save yourself, soldier. Give them over to us. The Ballengers have only betrayed you. We know there's another entrance. That's where you were going when you were caught. Tell us where it is."

"The temple. The stables. The arena. The—"

Montegue grabbed my arms and shook me. "Why? What makes this worth your life?"

"A vow. Jase."

"Jase is dead."

"Only to you," I said.

"Her mind is gone!" Banques snapped. "Let's get on with this."

———◦◦◦◦———

A door slammed shut. I was in some kind of cart. The wood planks beneath my hands were damp. No matter how hard I tried to focus, I felt myself slipping, losing my hold on the world.

You are going to die with nothing. Be nothing.

Montegue was mistaken.

Maybe sometimes life and fantasies and family did all go completely wrong. But I had loved and been loved deeply and completely, not once but twice in my life. I would not trade that for all the riches that Montegue had to offer.

CHAPTER FIFTY-ONE

JASE

I TUGGED ON MY GLOVES AND SQUEEZED MY FINGERS. THEY needed to be warm, ready.

We had been waiting all night for dawn to come.

Besides my own, I had replayed everyone's role in my head at least a dozen times, though it was too late to change anything now.

It would begin with Mason, Synové, and the icehouse that was three avenues away from the plaza, behind the cooperage. The roar of the crowd would be their signal.

Most of the icehouse was belowground. That's where the munitions would be. All Mason had to do was blow the roof off of it. Synové would follow with a volley of fire arrows.

And that would lead to my turn.

The crowds were already thick, nearly all of them in gray and black cloaks. Soldiers with shields arrived, lining the stairs to the platform. Zane arrived. Garvin arrived. Garvin with the eyes of a hawk. But like the soldiers on the roofs, he would be looking down.

I had never seen Banques. I kept looking to Paxton to see if he had arrived. That would mean the execution was imminent. Paxton shook his head. Not yet.

I couldn't see Priya, Wren, or Titus. They had taken positions in other trees that gave them clear shots of plaza rooftops. I could barely see Gunner or Paxton, who stood on the same limb as me, their dark cloaks turned inside out with the dawn, now part of the shifting tembris canopy.

My chest pounded with the waiting, and then Paxton nudged me. *There.*

A man had emerged from a carriage. He wore a black uniform, and a wide gold braid swept across his chest. He walked briskly up the stairs, his cape rippling behind him. His thick black hair was slicked back and glimmered almost as much as his gold chest braid. A magistrate turned general. He was younger than I expected.

He took a place on the platform. There was still no sign of Kazi or Montegue. Were they both still in the carriage? Paxton held his hand out in a calming sign. Wait.

Banques addressed the crowd and began reading the crimes against Kazi. Theft. Attempted regicide. Spy for the Kingdom of Venda. "And maybe worst of all, an attack on innocent children. Lydia and Nash Ballenger are recovering from the assault, thanks to the king's quick action to protect them." A murmur ran through the crowd, and Banques nodded approval. There was still no sign of Kazi. Where was she? Why were they waiting to bring her out? I looked at Paxton. He shook his head. This was not normal. "For her crimes against Eislandia she is sentenced to hang by the neck until dead before these witnesses today. Let it be known to all the kingdoms that Eislandia will not tolerate interference by foreign nations, nor attacks on its citizens. The king is committed to protecting his subjects by any and all means."

He lifted a hand to the guards still standing by the carriage. They opened the door, and the king stepped out. Montegue. A hush ran through the crowd. Even from high in the tembris I could see the long slash across his face. The evidence of attempted regicide. But what I noticed more than his scar was another kind of transformation, all the way down to the way he walked. He was taller, stronger—even his shoulders seemed wider. His chest puffed out with power. This was not the incompetent farmer I had known. He ascended the stairs with confidence, looking older than he had just a few months ago. He raised his hand to the waiting crowd, and there was a shower of cheers. He paused midway on the stairs and seemed to take it in, his head turning as he skimmed the crowd. For a spare minute, he was wide out in the open, an easy shot for Synové, maybe even for Priya, but we still didn't know where Kazi was. I swallowed the burning temptation to sweep down and kill him now.

He stepped up beside Banques, guards with shields taking positions all around them. Sweat trickled down the side of my face. *Just bring her out. I need to see her.*

Gunner reached out and put a hand on my arm. I nodded. I was all right.

Montegue repeated some of the charges and piled on more, not giving any more details than Banques had, but then added, "The prisoner was given the opportunity to confess her treachery and receive the king's mercy, but she refused, and for that this soldier and spy has sealed her fate." He signaled guards standing by an enclosed cart. "Bring the prisoner forward. Let her meet justice."

They opened the small door, and one soldier crawled halfway inside. It looked like he was struggling. Was Kazi resisting? And then he pulled her out. I got my first glimpse of my wife in weeks, and I knew immediately something was wrong.

She stumbled forward, and the guard caught her arm to keep her from falling.

Her hands weren't tied. A Rahtan soldier being led to execution without being bound?

Guards on either side of her helped her up the steps. From my vantage point, I couldn't see her face well, but she didn't appear to be injured, though she was thin. Her cheekbones were more prominent. Had they been starving her? I looked at Paxton and Gunner. They nodded, ready.

Montegue stepped close to Kazi, whispering something, and then he lifted her face roughly. I couldn't tell if her lips were moving or not, but Montegue jerked away angrily and ordered the two guards to take her across the skywalk to where the noose waited.

One of the guards centered her on the platform while the other reached over the rail and pulled a guideline to draw the noose near. It was time.

"Hang!" A voice called from the crowd, which served to make everyone in the plaza cheer in chorus. "Hang!" It echoed through the plaza and beyond—to at least three streets away, where Mason and Synové waited.

I readied myself, my boot firmly in the loop of the rope.

A blast sounded. There was no mistaking it was a launcher.

The king and Banques ducked low, soldiers covering them with their shields, while the soldiers on rooftops edged closer with their launchers raised, searching the streets. Soldiers on the streets turned, looking in all directions, and then right on the heels of the blast, before they could regroup or make sense of what was happening, an ear-shattering explosion shook the ground. Buildings rattled, and an enormous black plume spiraled into the sky just past the plaza. Debris rained down. There were screams and pandemonium. Citizens ran, and soldiers sprinted everywhere. An attack seemed imminent, and Kazi was temporarily forgotten.

And that was when I jumped.

CHAPTER FIFTY-TWO

KAZI

THE WORLD FLOATED IN A BLUR AROUND ME, BUT I HEARD THE
sounds, the creak of the cart door opening, the order of the guard for
me to come forward, the *thunk* as I stumbled against the floor, and then
hands clamped around my arms. *Twist, lift, kick.* My mind was willing,
but my arms and legs wouldn't listen.

And then I heard Montegue's voice again, felt his warmth as he
pressed close to me. "Did you hear that? The crowd? They love me. I am
not a nothing king. I am a great one."

My lips moved, but I wasn't sure if I said the words aloud. *Fool. You're
a fool, Montegue. Truly great leaders don't have to chase love. It finds them.*

He clutched my face in one hand, his fingers digging in, and jerked
my head up so I had to look at him. His dark eyes swam in and out of
view. His lips were a blurred, angry smear in front of me.

"I lied to you," he whispered. "I did kill my father. And it was the
most satisfying thing I have ever done—until now. Watching you hang
today will eclipse that."

He had heard my words. I had managed that much. It was perhaps my last small victory. I smiled.

He pushed me away, and I felt myself being guided forward once again.

"Stand here," a guard whispered. Stand. The medicine was wearing off. I already felt the fiery pain crawling up my scalp, my knees burning, crumbling, and then a sound split the world in half. My head tilted back and I saw a winged shadow swoop down from above, and I guessed that Death's angel had finally come to get me.

Make it one more day, Kazi.

I tried to resist, but I was too weak and his grip was too strong.

CHAPTER FIFTY-THREE

JASE

THE WHIR OF THE ROPE IN THE PULLEY BUZZED IN MY EARS. MY cloak, my hair, everything flew upward as I flew down. The skywalk shook when I landed, and Kazi fell into my arms. "Hold on to me, Kazi! Put your foot in the loop."

But she didn't. Her legs didn't move, and her arms hung limp at her sides. I wrapped my arms around her waist, squeezing her to me, and sent a piercing whistle through my teeth—the signal that I had her and to bring me up. I wasn't there more than three seconds, a shadow, a trick of the eyes, and then we were flying upward again, and halfway up, the ballast that Gunner and Paxton had shoved from the tembris passed by us—three bound soldiers' bodies that more than countered our weight.

"Take her!" I said when we reached the top, and Paxton and Gunner hoisted Kazi over onto the limb, then pulled me over too. "They must have drugged her so she wouldn't struggle," I said. "I'll have to carry her."

The tembris limbs were wide enough for us to run mostly unseen from below, but with Kazi in my arms, I couldn't jump the gaps and had to carefully navigate them instead. It slowed us all down, sometimes having to hand her over between Gunner, Titus, and myself to cross safely from one limb to the next. Order was already returning below, and a carefully orchestrated theater of citizens directed by Aleski shifted, moved, and absorbed Mason, Synové, Aram, Samuel, and Hawthorne so they would become lost in the crowds. Appropriate horrified screams were offered up for soldiers who had fallen from rooftops, so the king and Banques would know that the citizens were taken as much by surprise as they were. By now the dead ballast we had thrown over was leading some eyes up into the canopy.

"Kazi," I whispered as we ran. "Kazi!" Her lids were heavy trying to focus on me. I pressed my lips to her cheek. Her skin was burning up. And then she began shaking. What was wrong? This wasn't just a drug to sedate her.

Up ahead, we met up with Priya, Wren, and Titus. "How many did you shoot down?" Gunner asked.

"Three."

"Three."

"Four. But one of them fell without his launcher, the devil."

And then panic flooded Wren's face when she spotted me just behind Gunner and Paxton. She leapt between limbs until she was at my side. "What's wrong?" she asked, her fingers searching for wounds. "*Kazi*," she hissed. Kazi's head barely turned.

"I don't know," I answered, "but we have to keep going. We need to get to the horses before they do."

I held Kazi tight in my arms as they lowered us to the base of Kalliope. Imara was waiting with the horses. One had been meant for Kazi, but now she would have to ride with me. Titus and Aram had staked out a ruin for us to hide in until nightfall.

I laid Kazi on the ground to do a more careful search for wounds.

"You don't have time!" Imara warned.

But Wren and I pulled away her shirt, and that's when I saw it—fine, spidering lines crawling up her chest like lace. Poison?

Then I felt the fullness of a bandage beneath her trouser leg. I cut open the fabric and found the first wound. Wren found the other on her arm. Bites. Dog bites. Disbelief flooded through me.

"She's been bitten by ashti," I said.

Everyone had circled around us and was looking down at her.

"She won't make it through the night at the ruin," Gunner said.

Priya groaned. "She's going to need the antidote. Fast."

"Half their army is already chasing us down," Titus said. "If we don't hide out in the ruin until nightfall—" He left the sentence hanging, then cursed.

The only antidote I knew of was in the healer's bag—in the vault—halfway up the mountain. We'd have to make a run for it in broad daylight.

A decision didn't have to be made. I began gathering Kazi up in my arms, and Gunner began giving orders. Priya and Paxton would ride forward, he and Wren behind, with me and Kazi in the middle, since it would be hard for me to fend off attacks with her in my arms. Titus would go to the ruin to wait for Mason, Synové, and the others, and tell them what had happened. They would head back after nightfall as planned. He asked Imara to return to town and spread the rumor that riders had been seen on the opposite side of town, heading in the other direction, then he altered our planned route. It would mean crossing two roads, but it would shave an hour off our ride.

Mije stamped as if he knew his mistress was in distress.

Paxton held Kazi in his arms as I climbed up in Mije's saddle, and once he had lifted her up to me and everyone had mounted, I yelled, "*Baricha!*" and Mije flew like a winged demon, kicking up the soft dirt in his wake.

───※───

Under the best of conditions, it was a three-hour ride from town to the hidden entrance. In some places, a horse couldn't go any faster than someone on foot. Every time we had to slow, my breath backed up in my chest. How long ago had she been bitten? I had never known anyone who had actually died from an ashti bite before. But my father had. When I was eight and he was teaching me commands and a healthy respect for the dogs, he told me that a friend of his had died from a bite. They were snowed in at a station high above the lumber camp and couldn't make it down the mountain for the antidote. *It's not something you ever want to see, boy. I wish I could erase it from my memory.* His friend died after six days.

This was no accident. Montegue had done this to her. Why? If he had already sentenced her to hang, why would he do this too?

Because she knew where Lydia and Nash were. She knew where the entrance was.

She had information that could destroy my family, and she wouldn't give it up to him.

Because she had betrayed him and he wanted her to suffer. I kept the anger at a distance for now. I knew it would consume me. For now Kazi was all that mattered. But I knew the rage would come, and then even the gods couldn't keep me from Montegue.

I pressed my hand to Kazi's mouth, forcing back her groans.

I'm sorry, Kazi. I'm sorry. Just a few more minutes.

We hid in the trees and undergrowth as a platoon passed on the road that led from the arena. About half of them were on foot, the other half on horses. Two wagons loaded with hay traveled in the middle of the caravan.

"*Shhh*, my love," I whispered softly into her ear, trying to soothe her. "*Shhh*."

At the same time, I stroked Mije's neck, willing him not to stamp or whicker. Sound from him might be mistaken for one of their horses, but we couldn't take a chance.

When they passed out of sight around the bend, we slowly and quietly crossed the road, not wanting even the barest vibration to alert them, and once back in the cover of the forest on the other side, we flew into a gallop.

We made it across the second road that led up to the back side of Tor's Watch without encountering anyone, but now we were traveling along a narrow ridge single file, and our progress was painstakingly slow. Kazi shook, another spasm squeezing the life from her, her jaw and fists clenching, her moans growing louder, and then she went limp and quiet, which frightened me even more. I checked her pulse. It was faint, like her body was giving out.

"Stay with me, Kazi," I said to her over and over again. "Stay with me. We're almost there." But we weren't.

Priya was leading and called back, "How is she?"

"Not good."

Most of the time we didn't talk for fear of alerting a patrol, but on this sheer, rocky side of the mountain, there was no one near to hear.

I talked to Kazi, unsure if she could hear anything, but hoping it would keep her from slipping away from me. "Besides eating a mountain of feastcake, we're going to have to dance that jig I taught you. In front of everyone. That means we'll need to practice. Maybe we'll teach Wren and Synové too. They're here with me, Kazi. They're here for you. We're all here for you. Stay with us." I pressed my lips to her temple. "Stay."

"Or we can dance to this one." I began humming "Wolf Moon." I knew it was a tune she liked. "It doesn't have to be a jig. Anything you want, Ambassador Brightmist. Including that apartment on the upper level. I'll make sure it's always stocked with bowls of oranges."

Summer and winter. Anything.

⸺◦◦◦⸺

The narrow ridge finally opened up onto a forest-filled plateau, and I told Kazi, "Hold on, Ambassador. We're going to fly again. We're almost there."

And we almost were.

We rode through a clearing, the falls only minutes away, and I thanked the gods for our clear passage, but I thanked them too soon.

"Behind us!" Gunner yelled. I glanced over my shoulder. Out of nowhere, a patrol appeared, galloping on horses and gaining ground fast, with archers leading the way. Soon we'd be in range.

Wren and Gunner came up on either side of me. "Nine of them," Gunner called.

"Ten," Wren corrected. I couldn't do any fighting with Kazi in my arms, and there was no way the remaining four could take on ten.

Paxton fell back with us. "Ride ahead," he yelled to me. "We'll be your cover. With us behind you, they won't see you veer into the woods. Priya and I will go one direction, and Wren and Gunner the other to lead them away. We'll keep them on our tail."

I couldn't argue. I was of no use to them, and time was running out for Kazi, but I knew they were risking everything.

"Go!" Priya ordered. "Now!"

I rode ahead, holding Kazi tight in my arm, and yelled to Mije, "*Baricha!*" to push him faster, a command that had saved me once. I prayed it would save Kazi now.

We disappeared into the cover of the forest in one direction, while my family disappeared in the other.

I rode Mije into the cave as far as I could, and now I ran.

"Stay with me, Kazi!" It was no longer a plea, but a command. "Stay with me! Do you hear me, dammit? Don't leave me!"

There were no more spasms. No more groans. The last time I'd felt for her pulse, I couldn't find it.

My lungs burned. My arms ached. The torch in my hand shook wildly, scraping walls, sparks showering.

I threw the torch to the ground, then laid Kazi near the door. I grabbed a rock from the cave floor and banged on the wall, forgetting the code.

I gathered Kazi back into my arms.

"Open it!" I screamed, kicking the door. "Open the door! Now!"

It was an eternity before I heard the low growl of a wheel and the door finally opened.

CHAPTER FIFTY-FOUR

JASE

I burst in, Kazi limp in my arms, and I called for the healer, rushing through one room to the next. Everyone pointed in different directions, uncertain where she was.

"That way."

"She's in the sickroom."

"Over there?"

"Maybe in the kitchen."

"Let me carry her for you."

"No!" I stumbled into the kitchen. Everyone had stood by now, already hearing the commotion as I ran through the vault, and when they spotted Kazi in my arms, the center table was swept clean. I laid Kazi across it, and my mother and the healer rushed over.

"She's been bitten by ashti! She needs the antidote! Do you have it?"

"Someone get my bag from the sickroom!" Rhea ordered, then pushed me away to examine Kazi. She shook her head as she looked at the wounds and discoloring on Kazi's arms, legs, and chest, then felt her wrist for a pulse. "Her heart is racing like a rabbit's. How long ago did this happen?"

"I don't know. Maybe days ago."

She looked at my mother. I recognized that look. It was the same one she had given my mother when my father was on his deathbed.

"No!" I said. "She'll make it!"

"No one said she wouldn't," Rhea replied. "We'll do what we can. Now let me work."

The antidote had to be coaxed down Kazi's throat, drop by drop. Some spilled out from the corner of her mouth and had to be spooned back in. Long minutes passed just trying to get the three thimblefuls of medicine into her. Rhea gently rubbed Kazi's throat, trying to encourage her muscles to swallow. She was dehydrated too, and water was given in the same manner, one slow drop at a time.

"Give us a little privacy now," Rhea said to everyone in the room. "I need to clean the wounds."

Everyone left but me and my mother. My mother brought warm water from the hearth, and she and Rhea began carefully washing and searching Kazi's whole body for bites, even the bottoms of her feet. But the one thing we noticed right away were the bruises everywhere. Her whole left side was a dozen shades of blue and purple. Paxton had told me she'd fallen down a rocky canyon wall and then had been on the run for days before she was recaptured. After cleaning the wounds on her arm and thigh, Rhea said, "They're deep, but they won't need stitching. And this one here . . ." She pressed on the one-inch scar on Kazi's abdomen. "This is from something else. A knife, I suspect." She shook her head as she covered her back up. "What this girl has been through."

"Let's move her to my pallet. It's more private there. She can rest," my mother suggested, then looked at me. I saw the terror in her eyes, the questions she had just had time to consider. I had come back alone.

"I don't know where the others are," I said. "We had to split up. They'll be here, though." It was all I could give her for now. I scooped Kazi into my arms and carried her to the small room off the kitchen.

We'll do what we can. How long ago did this happen?

I lay on the pallet beside her. Holding her. Keeping her warm. Talking to her. Doing everything I could to keep her in this world.

I stared at her face. Her lashes. Ran my thumb over a bruise on her cheek.

I kissed her lips. "Wake up, Ambassador Brightmist. We still have work to do."

She didn't stir.

Four hours. Six hours. Eight hours passed. The vault was stifling with the tension of waiting. Waiting for Kazi to wake. Waiting for the others to return. There was no word from anyone. What had become of Priya, Paxton, Wren, and Gunner? Four against ten. For all the time Priya spent alone in an office with numbers, she could be fierce, but I wasn't sure how adept Paxton was at anything, though long ago he had flipped me into a well without much effort. I never thought I would find that comforting.

Finally, just after dark, there was banging on the cave wall. We all ran to the door. It was Wren and Gunner. They were both covered with blood.

"Not ours," Wren said as she marched in. "Where's Kazi?"

Gunner was right behind her, holding his arm. "Mostly not ours," he added. He had a gash on his upper arm.

I took Wren to see Kazi and explained what the healer had said. Wren knelt beside her and rested her head on Kazi's chest. *"Tantay mior, ra mézhan,"* she said softly.

I knew one of the words.

Kazi had taught me the Vendan words for wife and husband. *Shana* and *tazerem*.

She taught me the other words for family too.

Ra mézhan. My sister.

Gunner and Wren had washed up and changed at Judith's urging. The blood frightened the children and probably everyone else too. Wren's hair dripped, and her face was nearly scrubbed clean of the Kbaaki stain, but some of the blue dye still circled her eye. Jurga had said the dye wouldn't last more than a couple of weeks, especially if we washed. They sat at the kitchen table now, eating soup and telling the rest of us seated around them what had happened, while Rhea demanded that Gunner hold still so she could properly clean and stitch his arm.

"We split up as planned," Gunner said. Five had come after them, and they assumed the other five went after Priya and Paxton. They managed to stay ahead of the soldiers for a few miles. Gunner knew the forest better than they did and finally reached a rock formation he had been heading for.

"We circled around and ambushed them from behind," Wren said.

Gunner winced as Rhea scrubbed his wound. "She took down four. I took one."

"Four?" Tiago asked.

"Imara gave us some fine throwing knives," Wren explained. "And I put them to good use."

My mother came back from checking on Kazi. "But no sign of Priya or Paxton?"

"Priya knows the forest as well as I do," Gunner answered. "They'll be fine." But his reply was too fast, like the worry was forefront in his mind too.

We all knew it was about more than just knowing the forest. It was the odds too—and who was fighting them. Gunner had Wren on his side. Priya had Paxton.

I went back to check on Kazi and get a few more drops of water into her. I talked to her, told her the riddle she had asked me to repeat so often, and then told her Wren was here, "In case you didn't hear her come in." I brushed the hair from her face. "*Hamir, ra shana.* Please."

As I laid her back on her pallet, there was loud banging on the cave wall. In code.

My mother and I got to the door first. I spun the wheel and threw it open.

It was Paxton, and he was alone.

My mother sucked in a broken breath.

"Where's Priya?" I asked.

"She's coming. Unsaddling the horses. She lost the bet."

"*Bet?*" I said.

"Who would take down the first soldier."

"You had time for bets?" my mother snapped.

He walked past us and into the kitchen, collapsing into a chair. His face was streaked with dirt, and his whole left side was soaked with blood. "Just a flesh wound," he said. "I think."

"He was showing off," Priya interjected, coming in just behind him. "Tried to take on two at the same time."

We all stared at her. Her hair was wild and tangled around her shoulders, her face as grimy and blood-spattered as Paxton's. She shrugged. "Okay, so he's lousy at knots, but he knows his way around a sword. Up on the table, genius. You're going to need sewing up. Where's Rhea?"

Rhea appeared in the doorway. First she sighed and then she cursed. She was weary of patching people back together.

◦◦◦

Late in the night, the next crew rolled in. I thought it would be the last, but it was only Titus, Samuel, Aram, and Hawthorne—along with some unexpected extras—Aleski, Imara, and their mother, Beata. Aleski had been spotted by soldiers grabbing a launcher so they all had to run. Mason and Synové were notably absent from the group. Titus said they had never shown up at the ruin. He suggested that maybe they had a hard time getting out of town. *Or they've been caught.* He didn't say it but I knew we all thought it. My mother held her swollen belly. In one day, how many sons and daughters would she have to fear for?

I led her to a chair. "Sit," I said. "Please. You can hear everything from there."

They dumped their haul onto the table, and we looked it over. As Priya, Titus, and Wren had been shooting soldiers from roofs, the rest had been waiting below to gather up the launchers that had fallen with them. They had managed to hide eight launchers beneath their cloaks. But five of them had no ammo.

"Jackasses," Hawthorne hissed.

My small bag of ammo would be stretched thin.

But at least Rhea didn't have anyone to stitch this time. At least not until Mason and Synové showed up. If they showed up.

And finally, late the next morning, they did.

Like everyone else, as soon as they came in, they asked about Kazi. Synové dropped a bag she was carrying and ran to her. Mason dropped his launcher and followed.

Gunner walked over to the bag Synové dropped and looked inside.

His brows shot up. "Ammo," he said. "A lot of it. It looks like at least twenty loads."

When Mason and Synové returned, the questions started.

"Where have you been?" Priya demanded first.

Mason glanced at Synové, then back at Priya. "We had to lie low for a while."

"We found a ruin to hunker down in. There were soldiers everywhere, you know? Luckily it was nice and cozy while we waited them out."

Nice and cozy? I eyed Mason. "What about the loads? Where'd you get them?"

Mason rubbed his head. "She had this crazy idea that we could get some out of the icehouse before we blew it up. She wouldn't let up."

Synové's brows pulled down defensively. "When opportunity knocks, you don't go punching it in the face."

They told us that they had been hiding in position for hours waiting for the hanging to begin. They could hear the crowds gathering a few streets away, but everything where they were was quiet as a graveyard. The soldier guarding the icehouse from the roof with a launcher ambled over to the other side, they guessed so he could catch a glimpse of the hanging.

"And those soldiers on the ground around the icehouse?" Synové said. "Pffft! All they had were a few measly swords and halberds."

Mason's mouth pulled in a smirk. "Turns out her aim with knives is as good as it is with arrows."

Wren's hands slapped the table. "Imara's knives!"

"Yes!" Synové answered, and the two began excitedly chattering about their qualities, forgetting about the rest of us. They drew Imara into their conversation.

Mason looked at me, bits of straw stuck in the thick ropes of his hair—maybe from lying low in the ruin. "I know it wasn't in the plan, but—"

"When opportunity knocks, you get nice and cozy with it, right?"

Mason grimaced. "It's not what you think—"

"Come on, brother," I said and put my hand on his shoulder. "Sit down. What you did was smart. Well, I assume most if it was, anyway. We need every—"

"*Patrei?*" It was Judith. She stood in the doorway. "It's Kazi. She's stirring. Talking in her sleep. I think she's coming to."

It didn't matter that Judith had only come for me. Everyone followed me through the door.

CHAPTER FIFTY-FIVE

KAZI

I COULD FEEL MY FINGERS AGAIN. MY TOES. AND THEY DIDN'T
burn. Was I dead, or had they given me more medicine for the pain?
What did Montegue want to know now? I opened my eyes. I was in a
tiny dark room I didn't recognize. There were no windows. Had I been
thrown into another cell? My head still swam, ached, but I felt my strength
returning, my muscles becoming my own again. *Dear gods, no. Did I
confess something? Did they give me the antidote because I gave them information?* I blinked, trying to flush the haze from my eyes. And then I heard
footsteps. A rush of them. They were coming back. I closed my eyes,
trying to think what to do.

One of them stepped closer and hovered over me. I felt his warmth
as he leaned close.

"Kazi, can you hear me? It's Jase. I'm here. Everything's going to be
all right."

Montegue's face loomed behind my eyes. His tricks. His manipu-
lations.

You're going to be all right, but I need your help. Lydia and Nash are dead.

Hope and terror knifed through me. My fingers curled around something cold and hard at my side. But the voice. It was—

I opened my eyes, and a frightening face loomed close to mine. The blurred glitter of a jewel was shining in his brow, and a menacing tattoo swirled over his face.

My knee jutted upward. If I was going to die, I was going to die fighting with whatever strength I had left. I heard a groan, an *oomph* as I pushed him to the floor and held the spoon in my hand to his throat. He writhed in pain beneath me.

"Kazi."

I blinked again.

The eyes. Brown, the color of warm earth.

His voice.

"Kazi, it's Jase," he said again, the pained grimace finally fading from his face.

"You going to kill the *Patrei* with a spoon?" I turned my head. It was Wren, her hands planted on her hips. "Not that I don't think you could."

The room was crowded with people. Synové, Vairlyn, Titus, Priya, and more. Staring at me.

I looked back at the man beneath me.

Jase.

Stay with me, Kazi.

It hadn't been a dream.

The spoon tumbled from my hand, and I fell down onto his chest, holding him, my face pressed into his neck. His arms circled around me, holding me as tight as I held him.

I heard sobs. But they weren't mine or Jase's.

It felt like I said his name a hundred times.

"Enough already," Synové sniffled after a minute had passed. "We want some of that too."

I got to my feet, and Wren and Synové swooped in, giving me long, smothering hugs. I looked at the stain on Synové's face that matched Jase's. "I'll explain later," she promised.

The weight that had hung inside of me for days lightened when I spotted Paxton. *He made it.* He stepped forward, his face puckered, and threw an arm around me, his other arm in a sling. "They're safe," he whispered in my ear, his voice breaking, and quickly stepped away. And then I faced Jase's family, crowded in the doorway. I froze. I wasn't sure what to do. I didn't see Gunner among them, but the last time I had seen Priya and Mason, they were throwing me into a snare and leaving me behind to be captured.

Jase must have seen something in my eyes. He asked everyone to leave. "Give us a few minutes," he said. Maybe he knew how I had ended up in the king's custody. Maybe the way I'd attacked him just now had given him a small glimpse of what I'd been through. Thank the gods it was only a spoon in my hand.

The door shut on the room that was little more than a closet. It was dark except for a small candle burning in the corner. I was still unsteady on my feet, and Jase helped me sit back on the pallet.

"We're in the vault?" I asked.

He nodded.

I reached up and touched his stained face and the ring in his brow.

"A disguise," he explained, then told me what had happened to him since the ambush, from his days recovering in the root cellar, to searching the town for news of me, to swooping down from the tembris to steal me away. Death's angel, it was him.

I shared details of the past weeks with him too, from my first days as a prisoner in a dark cell. But mostly I concentrated on how brave Lydia and Nash had been, and how much they believed in him.

"The crypt? They weren't afraid?"

"Not as much as they were afraid of Montegue. They knew what he was using them for. I'm sorry if hiding them in the crypt exposed your secret. It was the only way, Jase, the only way I could steal them and be sure Montegue wouldn't find them. Does your family know?"

He nodded. "I'm afraid they know everything. Including—"

"*Us?* You told them about us?"

"I blurted it out as I was choking Gunner. I know it wasn't the way we planned."

While choking his brother? Hardly. I sighed and rubbed my temple. My head still ached. "I suppose nothing's gone quite the way we planned." I lifted his hand to my lips and kissed his knuckles. I smiled against them. "But I guess that's how good thieves keep all their fingers. They slip into the cracks. They find shadows. They make a new plan when the last one utterly fails."

He stared at me like he was still absorbing everything, just as I was. How close we had both come to never seeing each other again. "Right now my only plan is to kiss my wife. And I am fairly certain not even the gods can derail that." He leaned forward, and his hand slipped behind my head.

There was a sharp rap at the door, and a voice called through it. "Supper, *Patrei*? Should I bring some bowls?"

Maybe the gods couldn't stop it, but soup and a waiting family could.

"We should join everyone," I said.

"Are you sure? If you don't want to go out there, I understand. I know what happened, Kazi. You don't have to—"

"I have to face them sooner or later."

Jase had his arm around me as he escorted me out. I was still shaky. On top of being poisoned, I hadn't eaten in days, at least not that I could remember. When we walked into the kitchen, the room grew quiet and heads turned. Some set their spoons aside. A few stood as if uncertain what to do. The room was full, not just with Jase's family, but with others who had taken refuge in the vault too, employees I recognized from the houses and tunnel. It was more overwhelming than I expected. I wasn't playing a role anymore, or here among them under a pretense. I felt naked. I didn't know who to be.

"Keep eating," Jase told them, guiding me toward a table. A man stepped in front of us, one of the stable hands. He knelt on one knee and kissed my hand, but then seemed too flustered to say anything and scurried away. Another took his place, a woman who placed a rough woven amulet in my hand. "Hear you got that devil in the chops nice and good." She vigorously nodded her approval before someone else stepped forward.

"You saved the *Patrei* and the little ones. We are in your debt." Similar sentiments rose from the others who moved into our path. Jase nodded and thanked each one. I was too stunned to say anything. I was Ten, the girl who stayed in the shadows. It felt dangerous to be openly acknowledged this way. Before we reached our seats, Vairlyn stood and intercepted us. She pulled me into her arms. Her grip was fierce, and I noted the bulge in her belly for the first time. A baby? Jase forgot to tell me that part of the story.

She pulled back and cupped my face in her hands, her sapphire eyes glistening. "My daughter."

The word snatched away my thoughts and I couldn't speak.

Vairlyn seemed to understand. "I was not always a Ballenger," she whispered. "Trust me, it will get easier."

The healer embraced me next, but not before she wagged her finger at me. "No more dogs for you, understand? Twice is my limit."

I nodded. "My limit too," I answered. "Thank you."

Jase pulled out a chair for me at last and I sat. Wren and Synové seemed to be studying me. Was it worry, or were they as uncomfortable as I was, and waiting to follow my lead? The last time we had all been gathered around a table with the Ballengers, we had slipped birchwings into their food to knock them out.

I stared at the bowl of soup set at my place. Did revenge lurk there? But they had saved my life. All of them. Jase had told me so. It was still sinking in. I would take a chance on the soup. I didn't see Gunner in the room, but Priya and Mason sat at the end of the table. I couldn't bring my eyes to meet theirs. The soup was my savior. Soup I knew what to do with, and luckily it didn't send sideways glances at me. I was suddenly ravenous. I tried not to eat too quickly, and Rhea cautioned me to take it slowly. I sipped the broth a slow spoonful at a time. There was a long, difficult silence, everyone absorbed with their dinner, but then suddenly conversation erupted in a rush.

"Venison and wild leek soup. It's pretty much all we eat these days," Titus said.

"Breakfast, lunch, and dinner," Aram added.

"Gods' glory, what I wouldn't give for one small potato," Priya moaned.

"If only the forest had potatoes—and maybe some parsnips too," Samuel agreed.

"We bake flatbread every few days," Vairlyn reminded them. "And have you forgotten about the dates? We have a lot of those."

Mason sighed. "No one can forget about the dates."

"I like them," Synové said.

Mason ignored her.

Judith banged her spoon against the large pot on the hearth like it was a bell. "That all you got to talk about? Soup?"

Silence returned to the kitchen. The heavy undercurrent that had been circling below the surface was now thick between us. Priya stood, hesitating, her chin tucked and her lashes lowered, then finally she lifted her eyes to meet mine. "The truth is some of us don't know what to say. Thank you is not enough. Apologies are not enough. Until the day I die, I will live with the shame of what I did to you. When you told me that you loved Jase—" Her voice wobbled and she closed her eyes. She nodded as if she was trying to encourage herself to keep going, then opened her eyes and continued. "When you said you loved him, I knew. *I knew* you were telling the truth. I should have at least listened, but I didn't want to hear it. I wanted to watch you suffer, the way we had, like that would somehow solve everything. I was wrong."

I didn't want hear her apologies or her thanks. I just wanted her to stop. "If I thought someone had killed Jase, I would do the same," I said.

She shook her head. "No. You wouldn't, and you didn't. I know the whole story. When Paxton told you Jase was dead, you could have killed the king and run, but you stayed. Because of Lydia and Nash. Because you had made a vow to Jase to protect his family. Saving them was more important to you than the momentary satisfaction of revenge. When I helped throw you into that net, that's all I wanted, revenge, not the truth you were trying to share with us."

Mason's head hung low, staring down at his soup. He nodded. "Me too," he said. He exhaled a long, slow breath and looked up at me. "I'm sorry, Kazi. I know it's not enough, but I'm sorry. I just lost one sister because of all this madness, and now I nearly lost another by my own hand. A sister who is a true Ballenger."

I wanted to melt beneath the table. Was this what families did? Bared their souls in front of an entire room of people? Their confessions left me raw. These were the kind of conversations I didn't know how to have. I had only just learned to share everything with Jase, and now I had to do it with all of them?

Jase's hand slid to my thigh beneath the table and gave me a reassuring squeeze.

"When you discovered your mistake, you risked everything to right it," I replied. "I suppose that's all any of us can ever do. Try to make it right."

I stared at Mason, and then Priya, the last few days of terror and pain still too fresh in my mind. They had risked their lives to save me. I was grateful. But I was angry too. I was too many things I still didn't understand, and it seemed everyone was waiting for me to say something that would solve everything. *Tell me, tell me, tell me now.* Montegue's demands still circled in my head, his taunts, his hands searching me, the heavy weight of a chain around my neck. I had only just woken from my nightmares. I searched for some way to turn the conversation. Pivot. My specialty, but it eluded me. A breath trembled through my chest.

Paxton suddenly raised his finger, poking it into the air in his annoying classic way. "So, Jase, what is this about you having three wives? Tell us about that."

All the attention turned away from me and toward Jase, and air swept back into my lungs.

A new conversation caught fire around the table, and Paxton shot me a sly wink.

It was what I needed, a moment to gather myself, to breathe, to remember who I was, and what I still needed to do.

I walked down the vault tunnel that led to the entrance. When I had asked where Gunner was, Jase said he'd taken his dinner to the niche by the door. Gunner thought I might be more comfortable if he wasn't there. I couldn't disagree, but I needed to talk to him.

He sat against the massive door that closed us off from Tor's Watch and watched me as I walked toward him. A deep scarlet votive flickered in his lap, and his mouth hung half open. If I hadn't known better, I would have thought he was drunk. When I stopped in front of him, he set the votive aside and stood. His eyes narrowed. "You going to kill me?" he asked.

"Funny, that's exactly what Jase asked me when I told him I needed to talk to you alone."

"Jase nearly did kill me when he found out what I'd done." He cleared his throat, then eyed me squarely. "I wouldn't blame you if you did."

"Believe me, I've thought about killing you many times, Gunner, but not for the reason you think."

"I suppose any reason would be good enough."

"But it is a reason you need to hear. Of all the things you ever did to me, the worst happened months ago. There are some things in my life I haven't gotten over. Things I may never get over. For a Rahtan who has worked hard to become strong and smart and overcome everything through intense training, that weakness eats at me. You knew that weakness."

I took a step closer to him. "You could have shot me with an arrow. You could have done a hundred things, but instead you dangled Zane in front of me, knowing what he had done. In an instant, you brought back the horror of a night to a small child. That's what I became. A terrified child looking for her mother. For that, I should kill you. I was six years old, Gunner. *Six.*"

"I didn't—"

"Don't. Don't tell me you didn't know. You were as precise as a surgeon cutting out a heart. You knew exactly what you were doing to me."

He grimaced and nodded.

"And then you let him loose to terrorize me more. You didn't care—"

"I didn't let him loose. That part was an accident. In the chaos of that night, he escaped. We were all rushing to follow you, and he wasn't locked up securely. He broke out of the warehouse and disappeared. I'm not saying that as an excuse—I know there's nothing I can say or do to earn your forgiveness—"

"You're wrong. There is one thing. I will try my best to find a way to put this behind us, to forgive you and move forward, for Jase's sake, if you give me a truthful answer to *one* question."

"I'll tell you the truth about anything, whether you forgive me or not."

"The papers. The ones that were in Phineas's quarters. Where are they?"

"Papers? There were no papers."

Gunner explained how they went through the ashes of the workshop, hoping to recover something, and then went on to the scholars' quarters and found nothing.

"Who helped you search?"

"Priya, Titus, and Samuel . . ." He rubbed the back of his neck. "Tiago, Mason. I think that was it."

"Could one of them—"

"No. Nobody took anything."

Someone did. Papers didn't walk off on their own, and I knew I had seen a stack of them the night we took Phineas. The king had known they existed too. "All right," I said. "But you won't mind if I check with the others."

"Check," he answered.

We looked at each other, and I guessed the same question lurked in both of us: Could we really move forward?

And maybe the same answer: We were family now. What choice did we have?

We walked back to the kitchen together.

We are forty-four now. Our family continues to grow.
Yesterday we added three more children. We found them
scrounging through the ruins. They were afraid but Greyson
offered them food, just as Aaron Ballenger had to me
when he found me wandering alone.

I am not that frightened girl anymore. I have changed. So
has Greyson.

I see him looking at me differently now. I look at him differently too, and I wonder about all the feelings inside me
that I don't understand.

I have so many questions and no one to ask.

Everyone older than me is gone.

—**Miandre, 22**

CHAPTER FIFTY-SIX

JASE

IT WAS BEGINNING TO LOOK LIKE THE FORMIDABLE ARSENAL WE
had always envisioned. More than enough to protect caravans from raiders. Nine launchers were laid out on the table, and beside them were a
stack of loads. Twenty-eight, which translated into a hundred and twelve
shots. That was a lot of damage and firepower.

But it wasn't enough.

Paxton had tempered our elation quickly. "The king has a warehouse
of munitions—thousands of loads—plus two hundred more launchers and
enough soldiers to carry every one of them. The only reason he's been
guarding the town with a handful is because he can. He made a show
when he roared in that first day, blowing up everything, and it worked.
Everyone has a healthy respect for his power now."

"You mean a healthy fear." I stared at our stack of ammunition. My
fingers tightened around the back of the chair. "We'll get more, then," I
said. "Enough to make our own show. Where does he keep it?"

That was the question Paxton had been trying to answer since all this began. The king and Banques kept it a closely guarded secret. It was somewhere at the arena, he knew that much. Kazi had told Paxton to check warehouse seventy-two—the number that was on the piece of paper she had stolen from the king, but Paxton never got the chance to go there.

"Seventy-two is near the end of the third row. We could approach at night from behind through the pastureland," Priya suggested.

"Getting to it is one thing," I countered. "Hauling out thousands of pounds of munitions is another. I've been to the arena, and it's crawling with guards, and our towers are manned with more of them. They can see everything."

"Then we don't haul it out," Aram said. "We just commandeer the warehouse and claim it as our own. We have enough arms to defend it. If it's out of their hands, their power is gone."

"Until they blow you to kingdom come, the same way we did with the icehouse," Mason said. "They still have enough loaded launchers to do that."

"Or we could blow up the munitions ourselves," I suggested. "It would be an even fight then."

"Even? He has five hundred trained soldiers," Paxton said.

"Mercenaries," I corrected. "Their loyalty only goes as far as a full bag of coins. On our side we have citizens prepared to take back their home."

"We could do it," Judith said. Tiago and a few others echoed her enthusiasm.

I watched Aram and Titus scan the room, sizing up our motley group in the vault. Several, like Tiago, were injured. Paxton still had an arm in a sling so he wouldn't tear loose the stitches in his side. Their spirits might be willing, but their ability to fight was in question.

"There's more in town who would gladly fight with us," Aleski said as if he'd read my thoughts.

"Hundreds more," Imara confirmed. "It won't take long to get them organized. Every one of them is hiding some sort of weapon, whether it's a sword, club, or hoe. We can—"

"Jase?"

I turned and saw Gunner walking toward me carrying Kazi. She was limp in his arms. I ran and took her from him. "What did you do?"

"Nothing, I swear. We were walking in the tunnel and her eyes rolled back and I caught her before she fell."

The healer rushed over and felt Kazi's head, and then her wrist.

"What's wrong?" I asked, trying to make sure she was breathing.

"Shhh, *Patrei*. Her pulse is steady. It's only exhaustion and a full stomach that have overtaken her. Whatever she has been through in these last few days, you can be certain sleep was not part of it. The agony of the ashti is consuming. She needs rest. That is all."

There will be times you won't sleep, Jase.

Times you won't eat.

Times you wish the world would stop for just one day.

This was one of those times.

I had stared at the ceiling for most of the night, except for when I was staring at Kazi. She slept soundly, her face serene. *She needs rest. That is all.* What had she been through these past days? As tired as I was, the question kept me awake. I knew she had only told me a small part of what she had endured. When I asked about Zane, she shook her head, and I saw fear return to her eyes. He still had a hold on her past, but now he knew it and had reopened the wound to his advantage. She said he threatened her with lies about her mother.

When I asked about Montegue she told me he was a power-obsessed monster, then added, *But other than power, he was mostly obsessed with you, Jase. He remembered every detail of your first meeting when you were both children.* I guessed we had that in common now, but I was obsessed with him in an entirely different way, and I was more interested in our final meeting, one I hoped to arrange soon. She told me how he had taunted her, and put a chain around her neck like she was an animal. Some things she couldn't even say. *Later,* she said. *I promise.* But I saw the pain in her eyes. I wanted to kill him. That's all I wanted to do. But I had a lot of other things I had to do too. Like keep everyone in here alive.

You'll be torn a hundred ways . . . Remember that you have a family, a history, and a town to protect. It is both your legacy and your duty. If the job of Patrei were easy, I would have given it to someone else.

I rolled over and looked at her again. Right now the only job I wanted was to be Kazi's husband. A good one. A husband who only made the right decisions. I never had a chance to ask my father about being a good husband. At his deathbed vigil, it was the last thing on my mind. Now some of the questions I had asked seemed far less important. There was still time to ask my mother, though, and I would. They'd had a good marriage. They had never hid their affections for each other from their children. More than once we had caught them on the stairs, in the kitchen, or in the gardens, in a passionate embrace. Priya would roll her eyes and ask, *When will they get over it?* Maybe that was one of his secrets. Through all the hardships, the losses, the setbacks, he courted her until the day he died.

And now he had a baby coming that he would never see. It would be up to the rest of us to pass along his memory to our new brother or sister.

My mother had insisted on bunking in the study with Priya, so Kazi and I had the snug little room to ourselves. I warned everyone not to come banging on the door, not even with offers of food. We would come out when Kazi woke and not before. While she slept I had scrubbed my face clean, the rag turning the water in the bucket to a dark murky blue, and then I carefully removed the ring from my brow to return to Jurga. I didn't want Kazi to wake to a face she wasn't familiar with again. I slid my arm over her middle, tugging her a little closer, my lids finally heavy. Her body was warm against mine, and I fell into a deep sleep. I didn't know how long I had slept when I felt a weight on my chest.

"*Kisav ve, ra tazerem.*" Kiss me, my husband.

Warm fingers raked through my hair. A knuckle brushed my cheekbone.

I opened my eyes. Kazi looked down at me, the candle barely illuminating her face.

"You're awake," I whispered. "You should be sleeping."

"I've slept for hours. So have you. I don't want to sleep anymore." A worried crease pulled between her brows. "I want to know that this isn't a dream. I want to know that this is real."

She brought her face close to mine, our lips barely meeting.

"It's real," I whispered. I felt something wet fall on my cheek. I reached up and brushed my thumb beneath her eye. "Kazi, it's all right. I promise it's real."

I rolled to the side so that now she was lying beneath me. "You're here in the vault, with me, in my arms. We're together, and we will stay together, no matter what."

Her eyes glistened in the candlelight, fixed on mine as if she were afraid to look away.

"Kiss me, Jase. Hold me. Whisper to me. Touch me."

She tugged part of my shirt free from my trousers, and I sat back, my knees straddling her hips. I pulled my shirt over my head. Her shirt came next. I kissed her. I held her. I whispered to her. I touched her.

I understood her fear.

We held on to each other like it was the first time.

My lips grazed her skin, tracing her shoulders, the hollow of her neck, the small dip between her ribs, savoring every part of her, the warmth of her touch, her whispers, and the shiver of her breaths. And then my lips traveled up again to meet hers. I pulled her close, my breath shuddering in my chest, the scent of her skin reaching deep inside me, her breaths beating at my temple, and then, when my lips trembled against hers, she pulled me impossibly closer and whispered against them, "I love you, Jase Ballenger, and I will for all of my days."

———⸎———

We lay next to each other, our energy spent. Her head nestled in the crook of my shoulder, and her fingers skimmed circles on my chest. We didn't talk about the last few days, but recounted our days in the wilderness when we first met instead. I sensed she needed memories that would fill her up instead of drain her. Maybe I did too. A reminder of what I was fighting for, a normalcy I hadn't felt since a skeleton bird fell from the sky. We talked. We disagreed. We remembered. We laughed. It was the first time I had laughed since we'd been separated.

And then, after a long silence, she said, "I failed miserably last night, didn't I? I don't know how to be a daughter or a sister in a family like yours, Jase. I never know what to say or do."

"No one expects you to be anyone but who you are, and right now everyone thinks you're a hero. I'd run with that if I were you."

She sighed. "It was awkward around the table. You're all a finely tuned machine, and I'm the oddly shaped cog that doesn't fit."

"You think we're all alike? I'm as different from Gunner as he is from Priya as she is from Mason. We're a family, that's all, Kazi, one that has grown together. You may not see all the seams or gaps, but they're there, just like with you, Wren, and Synové. There are just more of us. It tends to camouflage a lot."

"But you have all that history together."

"That doesn't erase who we are individually, or how you fit in. A family's not a puzzle with a set number of pieces. It's more like a well— the fuller, the better."

"Unless someone steals a bucket or two. You told them, didn't you?"

That she was a thief.

How she knew I didn't know, but Kazi could interpret even the smallest glance.

I sighed. "I wasn't keeping it from you, Kazi. I swear. There's just been so much going on that—"

"I know, Jase. I know. We still have a lot to catch up on."

"They hardly flinched when I told them."

I winced. *Hardly flinched* was not the most bolstering of word choices. "I haven't told them you're ambassador yet. There's still that?"

A smirk pulled at the corner of her mouth. "Thank goodness for small surprises."

———

It was later than I thought when we finally emerged from our small enclave. With no windows in the vault, it was hard to tell day from night, which was why everyone spent at least part of the day in the greenhouse. The small circle of cave-top light infused some sense of order and sanity into the days.

Kazi sat with Wren and Synové in a corner of the kitchen in deep conversation, eating a late breakfast, which was, no surprise, venison and leek soup. The gamey smell clung to the air, the walls, to everyone's clothing. We sweated venison and leek soup.

Mason had sent me a quiet signal as soon as I emerged with Kazi. We needed to talk. Privately. I joined him, Priya, and Gunner in the storeroom.

Priya lifted up a burlap sack. It sagged at the bottom with only a few handfuls of grain. "This is all that's left."

Worse, the three of them had gone out to hunt this morning, and they had to quickly retreat back behind the falls—the mountain was crawling with soldiers.

"If the patrols don't back off soon, next up is the goat. It only produces a few cups of milk a day, but it's something for the children," Mason said.

Gunner shook his head. "The soldiers won't back off. Between me and Wren, and Paxton and Priya, we left a whole squad of them dead not far from here. Not to mention our little heist of Kazi yesterday. They're like packs of rabid wolves out there, and they're after our hides."

It was Montegue who was driving them, the lead rabid wolf, who was probably frothing at the mouth by now. Did he know it was me? I didn't think so. In my few seconds on the skywalk, he was huddled beneath a shield, his courage on display before the entire town. He was beating his chest now to make up for it.

"Don't butcher the goat. Not yet," I said. "We'll go out when—"

Suddenly the shelves in the storeroom vibrated.

The ground shook.

The walls shivered.

Dust fell from the ceilings.

I heard some shouts.

Children screamed.

"*What's going on?*" Gunner wondered aloud.

We went into the kitchen. Most everyone had jumped to their feet, looking around. Others came in too. Titus, Aleski, my mother, and

Samuel. The shaking seemed to have quieted as fast as it had descended, but then the ground quaked again.

"Devil's hell," Paxton said. "He's blasting."

"He told me he would," Kazi added. "He's blasting through the mountain to get to us." She said only the valuable papers he wanted from inside the vault had kept him from blasting in the first place.

"Papers?" my mother questioned. "What kind of papers?"

"Ones that contained another fomula that Phineas had created. If anyone here has them, now would be a good time to hand them over."

There was a stir of talk, confusion, but no one knew anything about any papers, and in these close quarters, it would have been impossible to conceal much of anything.

Another rumble shook the ground.

Paxton hissed. "It's not papers he wants anymore. He just wants us dead."

"We have to get everyone out of here," Gunner said.

"Out where?" Mason asked, throwing up his hands. "Out the back entrance onto the mountain where all the soldiers are patrolling?"

"That's exactly what that lowlife wants," Synové growled.

"No," I said. "Everyone stays put for now." I knew with so many injured and weak, we wouldn't have a chance. My mother was moving slow, and Tiago could never navigate a steep mountain with his injured leg, much less run if he needed to. They'd be picked off like lambs, not to mention those in the sickroom like Aunt Dolise who couldn't move at all. We couldn't just leave them behind. "We still have a huge mountain of solid granite around us," I said, trying to reassure them. But the truth was, I didn't know if time was running out. Food definitely was. The choice was being taken from us. We had nine launchers. Nine of us could make a run for the arena. At least one of us would make it. Without ammo, the king was powerless. "We have to get to the arena and destroy the munitions. Today."

"Today."

"I'll go!"

"Yes, let's make this an even fight."

Everyone murmured agreement.

Except for Kazi.

"No," she said. She stood and rubbed her head like she was trying to remember something.

"What is it?" I asked.

She took a few steps, still thinking, and finally shook her head. "The munitions aren't at the arena anymore. They moved them to Tor's Watch."

"What are you talking about?" Questions erupted around the room. Even Paxton questioned her. This was news to him.

"Underground," she added. "They're somewhere underground. Here."

We reconvened in the study—behind closed doors.

While she was on the run, Kazi had seen Zane making an oddly timed delivery on the road behind Tor's Watch—with an armed escort. She hadn't had time to wonder about it because she was running for her life. But after she had been captured, while she was half delirious with the poison and pain, she overheard the king tell Zane to finish moving the last two loads from the arena. That it was too dangerous to keep something there.

I remembered the armed caravan we encountered on the road escorting two wagons piled with hay. Now it all made sense.

Unfortunately, this changed everything.

Blowing up warehouse seventy-two behind the arena in the light of day was risky—maybe even a suicide mission that could reduce all the warehouses to rubble. But blowing up the entire store of munitions beneath Tor's Watch might accomplish exactly what the king was trying to do, but faster—destroy the vault. And finding the ammo was another trick. There were large cellars under every house and outbuilding on the property. There was more storage beneath the stables. And we had an icehouse too that was mostly underground, not to mention Greyson Tunnel itself and the tunnels that branched off of it, like the one that led to the vault. We no longer had one place to search but many.

Paxton leaned forward and blew a puff of air through his hand. "With something worth guarding, they aren't going to have just a small contingent of soldiers posted at Tor's Watch anymore. They'll be everywhere."

"We can't all waltz in and search the grounds in the light of day anyway," Gunner said.

"Or wait for night and use torches," Aram added.

A louder boom sounded through the room. Dust sprinkled down onto the table between us. Waiting for night wasn't an option at this point.

"*Dammit!*" Priya pinched the bridge of her nose, then madly swiped away the dust.

Kazi cleared her throat. "There is someone who could waltz through Tor's Watch in the light of day."

I looked across the table at her. She had been silent until now, conspicuously quiet, almost as if composing a riddle. Now I knew the riddle she was trying to unravel.

"No," I said.

"But—"

"No!" I said more firmly. "Rhea would never allow it either. You just—"

Kazi stood. "Listen here, *Patrei*. I'm part of this family now, and I say yes."

Brows rose around the table.

Synové grimaced. "She's got you there, *Patrei*."

"She's Rahtan too, don't forget that," Wren added.

"Not to mention," Kazi continued, "I'm the ambassador around these parts, and ambassadors trump *Patreis*." She put her hands on her hips. "There! I guess everyone knows everything now."

CHAPTER FIFTY-SEVEN

KAZI

JASE STOOD AT THE END OF THE TUNNEL, HIS HAND RUNNING over the smooth metal of the vault door, as if searching for a flaw. It was the first time I had noticed how perfect it was. Still shiny, not even a scratch, and it was centuries old. His hand ran along the seam next, where the frame was embedded in the granite mountain, like he was a tailor checking for the craftsmanship of a coat—a very old coat. His fingers lingered. I saw the weight on his shoulders. Protect. It was in his blood.

The ground shook again. I imagined Montegue up on the mountain setting off the charges himself. He had been robbed of the pleasure of watching me hang.

"We have to go, Jase," I said. Though Tor's Watch was just on the other side of that door, the route we would have to take would be much longer.

He raked his hair back and turned, his eyes meeting mine. He nodded. I knew what he was thinking. *It would have to hold. The Ancients had built it to hold.* But was an old vault door any match for the magic of the stars and the wrath of a king? Jase had warned that, depending on where the explosives were stored, blowing them up could mean leveling all of Tor's Watch. *There might be nothing left.*

Nothing. A dynasty. A legacy. The silence was numbing. *What other choice do we have?* Vairlyn finally said. Dust was falling, the pantry was bare, and the king was pounding his way closer. The family agreed, disagreed, went in circles, searched for quick solutions because the persistent rumbling around us was proof that time was running out. The final hard decision was left to the *Patrei*, a tremendous burden to bear, but his expression remained steady. He said that there was no other choice. Ridding the king of his arsenal was our only chance.

"Bring the horses in from the outer cave," Jase said to Titus. "It won't be safe for them out there."

Titus balked. "Horses in here?"

"Make room," Jase answered calmly.

Next he quashed a second bid by Paxton to go along. Paxton was already pulling at his sling to take it off. "No," Jase said. "I'll need you later, cousin. Not on this run."

His answer was firm, but the way Jase said *cousin*, it sounded important and brought Paxton closer into the fold. Paxton nodded.

I might juggle oranges, but Jase juggled just as much in his head. People, horses, vault doors, a complicated family, me. No wonder his father had named him *Patrei*. But now I knew that title wasn't a magical cure for worry. Jase seemed to hide it away where no one could see, a skilled sleight of hand, but I saw it in the tuck of his chin, his sideways glance. He was my husband, and his secrets were mine. He pushed himself to make everyone else stronger. He was willing to sacrifice his home and centuries of history to protect what mattered. *Sometimes it takes just one person who won't let evil win.* The queen had been talking about Greyson Ballenger, but today, my husband was that person.

He bent over and pulled a pack over his shoulder with one hand and grabbed his launcher with the other. I wouldn't be waltzing into Tor's Watch alone—Jase had made that clear from the start. I might be good at finding things, but it would take all of us to blow those things up. *Rahtan, Ten, Shadowmaker, no title you hold is going to make me change my mind on this one*, he had growled to me under his breath as we got our gear together. *And only today does an ambassador trump a* Patrei, he added, and then kissed me, long and hard. *We'll see about that, pretty boy*, I whispered back to him. He tried to act amused. The worry was building.

We picked up our gear and headed for the back entrance door. We sounded like an army as we marched down the tunnel. We had a team of eight. Wren and Synové were the first to volunteer. Imara, Mason, Priya, and Samuel were also going—armed with launchers. The four remaining launchers would be left behind and used by Titus, Gunner, Aram, and Aleski to guard the main vault entrance, if the moment came to open it.

As we traversed through the caves to the falls, Priya fell into step beside me. She wanted to tutor me on the layout of every room in Tor's Watch, but then she caught herself. "But . . . you probably already know them all, don't you?"

There was no point in trying to hide the obvious anymore. "Yes, I do. Every nook and room, including your office and what hangs on your walls. It was my job, Priya."

Her mouth hung open for only a second and then she nodded. "Well, I guess that's a lucky thing for all of us, then, isn't it?"

I couldn't deny it, even if it made her uncomfortable. Very lucky.

Becoming part of a family would be perhaps one of the hardest things I had ever done.

We never emerged from behind the falls into the forest because just behind them there was another path—an isolated one—that led back over the mountain toward Cave's End. It was a strenuous climb that sometimes required helping one another up sheer faces of rock, and handing up packs and weapons before we climbed onto a ledge ourselves. Our path kept us invisible from patrolling soldiers, though we all still wore the camouflaged cloaks they had made to rescue me.

Wren was armed with her *ziethes*, and Synové carried her bow and a full quiver of arrows on her back. They also had Imara's knives that they spoke quite fondly of, like they were furry pets. *Ra mézhans*. My sisters. It felt good to be walking beside them again. Jase's Kbaaki wives. The whole ordeal was almost worth it, just to hear the crazy stories they told, though I knew Synové added a good bit of embellishment.

When we reached some level ground, I noticed Synové eyeing Mason walking just ahead.

I remembered the nasty threats that had been hurled at her and Wren. "The family is treating you both well?" I asked.

"Well enough," Wren answered. "Vairlyn is kind."

"What about Samuel? I was surprised that Jase chose him to go along, considering his hand."

Wren shrugged. "Samuel's light on his feet. He knows how to be quiet and take orders, a much underappreciated quality. And his hand is strong enough. Those launchers aren't exactly precision weapons. Plus he's gotten pretty good with his other hand."

"Hmm," Synové said, licking her tongue over her lips. "Pretty good at *what?*"

Wren moaned. "Don't start," she warned.

"What about you and Mason?" I asked. "What's going on there? I hear you two spent the night alone in a ruin."

Synové shook her head as if surprised. "Listen to you!" she answered.

"Asking all kinds of intimate questions! Is this what your husband did to you?"

I smiled. "Maybe so. I've gotten better at sharing and talking."

She sighed. "I don't know. As one of his other wives, I found his talking to be a bit boring. All he ever wanted to talk about was *you*."

"True," Wren agreed.

I looked directly at Synové. "You're avoiding my question," I said. "Well?"

She didn't have a quick comeback. Her mischievous smile disappeared. "It's over," she finally answered. "Mason's civil enough. He dutifully watched my back. But he's about as forgiving as a drunk soldier's tongue. You'd think my lies were a true stab in his gut. Now he has all the passion of day-old bread. We're done. Finished. Glad to be rid of him. He wasn't a good dancer anyway." She shrugged like it didn't matter. Maybe it didn't. Many had fallen by the wayside with Synové. Like Eben and several before him. She moved on. But as we walked, I noticed anytime Mason spoke, her attention perked up, and then she grew quiet.

The blasts were louder from out here. Occasional bits of rock rained down. We speculated that the king was blasting from a spot above the vault not far from Greyson Tunnel.

"Here, give me your hand," Jase said. He reached down from a high ledge, helping each of us up. "Keep your voices down. It's only another ten minutes from here," he warned. We emerged on a flatter plateau, with plenty of forest and greenery. "Stay right behind me," Jase advised everyone, pointing to the center of the plateau, "or you'll end up back in the greenhouse. It's a long fall."

From here Jase never let go of my hand, and I didn't want him to. *We're together, and we will stay together, no matter what.*

My heart hammered in my chest. The last time I had approached Tor's Watch with Jase—

"Hold up," I said to the others, and I pulled Jase behind a tree. "I know this is not the right time, but—"

"What is it?"

"I love you, Jase. No matter what happens up ahead. I want those to be the last words you hear from me. I love you."

He touched my cheek. "Hey, we're going to grow old together. Remember?"

I nodded.

"And my mother lit a candle for you this morning. That makes you the patron thief of Tor's Watch now. Which almost makes you a saint."

"I've been called a lot of things but never that."

He grimaced. "Yes, you're right. It's a stretch."

I punched him in his shoulder, and he pulled me into his arms. "I love you, Kazi of Brightmist, and I promise you, these will not be my last words. Or yours." He pressed his lips to mine, warm and full and true.

"Oh, green toads, stop, you two!" Synové hissed. "The world is about to end. There's no time for this."

She was right. There was never time for last words.

We lay flat on a ridge that overlooked almost all of Tor's Watch. From here we could see Cave's End, the main house, Raehouse, the workyard that led to Greyson Tunnel, the gardens. It was nearly a perfect bird's-eye view. The three other houses were mostly hidden behind the granite overhang of Cave's End. I could only see one small corner of Darkcottage. From below, I never guessed this ridge existed. It just looked like a sheer, foreboding granite backdrop to the entire fortress.

We could also see the front gates from here. Paxton was right. Now that they had something worth guarding, the soldiers stationed here had tripled. Where was their treasure hidden? I studied the grounds, looking at where soldiers were posted.

"I counted twenty walking the walls," Jase whispered. "Fourteen on the ground, that I can see." He smiled. His family knew of this ridge—a potential weak spot in their security. They always had an archer posted on an interior wall above the workyard just for the purpose of watching this part of the mountain. Banques had no one posted on the interior wall. Only the outer walls were secured.

"Oh, such easy shots," Synové moaned. The guards' backs were mostly to us, because they were looking out past the walls for potential intruders, not ones who were practically inside already.

"Steady, girl," Wren whispered back. "Toppling guards will only bring the whole hive down upon us."

The plan was to search Greyson Tunnel first. I had managed to slip through it undetected more than once before, and it was the obvious choice for storage. Its back entrance, where the poisonous dogs had once been posted, lay just below us—fifty feet down sheer, sloping rock. *Slide on your stomachs*, Jase had instructed us. *Don't make noise when you land.* He made it sound easy. I remembered my bouncing cascade down the canyon face. I had made a lot of noise.

"Ready?" Jase whispered.

I nodded. Priya went first to show us. Apparently the Ballenger brood had done this before. "But I didn't have breasts then," Priya complained, nervous about going down too. The folded curve of the mountain covered most of her descent from guards on the walls. Mason, Imara, and Samuel followed, always waiting for Jase's signal to be sure the guards' heads were turned away.

But as I watched the pacing guards, something else caught my eye beyond the walls. Through the trees, a quick shimmer of light. A sword? And then I noticed movement. In the forest past the back gates were more soldiers. A lot of them. Once I knew they were there, it became clear. They were guarding the road. Why not the front road leading into the fortress?

I looked back at Tor's Watch, studying it more closely. In the gardens just in front of Darkcottage were four soldiers, not idly going from one place to another, but stationed. I looked at the distribution of other guards. The workyard only had one, the front gates only two, and yet Cave's End had four on its short stretch of fortress wall, two in the shadows of the foyer, and more stationed just beyond on the road. I suddenly pictured Montegue patting his vest, his interior pocket close to his heart where his treasure was stored. It made sense. A small, safe interior pocket.

CHAPTER FIFTY-EIGHT

JASE

ANOTHER BLAST SHOOK THE AIR.

I forced myself to keep my focus where it needed to be and not worry about what was happening in the vault.

"Kazi, your turn," I whispered. And when I was sure all the guards were looking the other way, I said, "Go."

She slid down the cold rock, her hands spread to slow her descent the way I showed her. I knew she had only recently fallen down a face of rock, and her body still had all the bruises to show for it, but she was calm and skilled and slid to the ground as smoothly as a leaf. Once she made it to the bottom, I followed. We all barely fit in the small crevice of space outside the guards' view. I planned to make a quick dash to open the tunnel gate and wave them through—hopefully before one of the guards turned and saw us. "No," Kazi whispered, "We don't need to search Greyson Tunnel. The munitions are here."

Kazi eyed the shadows of the interior wall, the trees, the roof of the cave, charting her way across the grounds before she ever moved. Once she left, she varied her steps and pace, a shifting shadow in the landscape. When she made it to the other side, I followed in her steps. We told the others to wait until we signaled them from the other side.

We slipped into a terrace room that still bore the evidence of a messy search. Cushions tossed, tables overturned. From there we watched the two guards who stood in front of one precise section of stone wall—the section that had a door that blended in with all the other stone. It was the hidden doorway I had been so fascinated with when I was a child. Zane must have told them about it, otherwise they never would have known. The guards held launchers cocked and ready to shoot, with their backs tight against the stone, staunch in their duty. There was no slipping around them.

"How can you be sure it's in there?" I whispered to Kazi.

"It's in the heart of Tor's Watch," she answered confidently. "Away from all the exterior walls, easy to guard, deep underground, impossible to shoot like an icehouse, and it was already empty, waiting to be filled. Like a little pocket in a vest."

I studied the guards. How would we get past them? Whatever we did, it couldn't be loud so it would alert other guards. The fact that their launchers were cocked was disturbing. Even a fall could set them off, and a struggle certainly would.

Kazi stepped away from the tiny slit in the drape we peeked through and looked around the room. She stopped in front of a tapestry on the wall and eyed it. "I have an idea," she said as she shed her cloak. She pulled the tapestry down and wrapped the colorful silk around her waist.

"What are—"

But she was already moving on to another item, some plan already concocted in her head. She grabbed a crimson runner from a table and began tying up her hair as she told me her plan. "Color is the best of distractions," she said as she scooped up three silver goblets, "or anything shiny. It tends to make almost anyone senseless, much like a fish, at least for a few seconds."

I began to object, but she stopped me cold, pressing her hands to my chest. "Jase, this is the waltzing in the light of day that we talked about. Trust me." Every muscle in my neck pinched, but I nodded, knowing she wouldn't back down, and with steady blasting continuing to echo around us, it was no time for arguing.

She stumbled into the foyer, laughing, carrying two goblets in one hand and pretending to sip from the one in her other hand. She acted startled when the guards raised their launchers at her and then she began laughing uncontrollably. "I'm in the wrong place, aren't I?" she whispered, like they all shared a secret.

I stared, barely able to breathe. The guards' launchers remained aimed at her as she smiled, entertained, and risked everything to save people she barely knew.

One of the guards cursed, uncertain what to do. She clearly had no weapons on her.

"Have you seen Zane anywhere?" she asked. Kazi knew that name would get their attention—the lieutenant. And he did have quarters here and probably a reputation to go with them, if her discovery of a chemise in his room meant anything.

The guards rolled their eyes, exchanging a knowing glance. "He told me to meet him here," she giggled, "and I'm afraid I got a little bit ahead of him." She lifted the goblet as evidence. "Want some?"

They stepped away from the door, walking closer toward her. My pulse raced. Their launchers were still cocked.

"How did you get in here?" one of them growled. "Did—"

Kazi stumbled, a silver goblet slipping artfully from her grasp and into the air but she managed to catch it just as gracefully. Their eyes were fixed on her now. "That was lucky, wasn't it?" she said. She pretended to down the rest of her empty goblet. "I'm actually not bad at this. Zane always loves it. Want to see?"

"No. Come along now. You need to—" One of them uncocked his launcher and rested it against a pillar and marched toward her.

But then she began tossing the goblets in the air, spinning them in a higher and higher arc as she stepped backward—and they stepped closer. Their eyes followed the spinning silver. It was convenient, I thought, that they were the same height. It would make it easier. *A little farther now.* She threw the goblets a little higher, and one of the guards actually let out an astonished huff of air. They were far from the door now, the one soldier dangling his launcher from his lowered hand, like he had forgotten it was there.

Far enough. I nodded to her.

Kazi let all the goblets fall back into her hands. "There you are, Zane! Finally!" she said, looking past their shoulders at me. They both turned, but as they did, I swung and my sword swept over their throats. Kazi grabbed the dangling launcher from the one soldier's hand as they both fell with dull thuds to the floor.

We dragged their bodies into the terrace room and gave the others the signal to start coming over when it was clear. Imara came first. I told her to stand watch while we checked the cellar. "Tell the others to wait for us when they get here."

I cautiously cracked open the tunnel door that led to Darkcottage. No soldiers occupied it, and we crept silently to the other end. Three casks were stacked near the passage door, as if set aside for some purpose. Maybe more supplies readied to be shipped to town to replace the supplies we had blown up? Or maybe they were for blasting into the vault.

I paused, staring at one of the casks.

"Forget it, *Patrei*," Kazi whispered. "I know it's tempting, but we don't need anything to slow us down. You try running with that, and we'll all be dead."

Tell me about the stars, Nisa asks.

She does not mean the ones in the sky,

But the ones that fell.

Aaron Ballenger said only two came from the heavens.

The rest were flung by the anger of men.

How is that possible?

I do not remember the stars falling anyway.

I only remember the storms that followed.

The smoke in the air.

The shaking ground.

The burning skies.

The billowing mountains,

The churning seas.

The cries of people—and the screams of those who preyed
upon them.

Instead I tell Nisa the story that was told to me.

> *Once upon a time, long long ago,*
>
> *Before monsters roamed the earth,*
>
> *All the stars hung quietly in the sky,*
>
> *And great cities made of wonder and light,*
>
> *Reached up to the heavens to meet them,*

But then a star was flung to earth by the gods,

To destroy the wicked—

We hear the scavengers howl at the end of the tunnel.

They rattle the bars of the gate.

We will kill you, they call. They roar like animals.

Let's go back inside the vault, I say.

I will tell you the rest of the story there.

—Miandre, 18

CHAPTER FIFTY-NINE

KAZI

I FELT THIS SAME TREPIDATION THE FIRST TIME I WALKED DOWN this tunnel and didn't know what I would find at the other end. I pressed my ear to the passage door, listening for the smallest sound. There was none, and I eased it open.

The cellar was lit with a single lantern hanging from the wall. I stepped out of the hidden passage and looked at the top of the cellar stairs. The door was closed. I signaled Jase out, then stepped farther into the cellar. The first time I had been here, I had searched this room in complete darkness. I didn't realize how large it was, or how high the ceilings were—and now all of it was filled with row after row of casks that reached to the rafters, and they still reeked of vinegar and wine.

It's a beautiful thing. Imagine the possibilities.

This was what we came for, what we hoped to find, but the reality still stunned us both into silence. What Jase was thinking I wasn't sure. Maybe he saw all the months that Beaufort had strung him along, all the false hope he had nursed for a fever cure, the king knowing his family's weakness. Maybe he saw his home, his history, whole centuries disappearing in a single fiery cloud. Maybe he saw a vault that couldn't withstand all this.

I saw a room bursting with dreams. Karsen Ballenger's dreams, Vairlyn's, Montegue's. Different dreams that had all gone very wrong.

"Let's get busy," Jase finally said, and began pouring the kerosene on the floor. I pulled the fuel-soaked cording from a skin in my pack and began laying it between a row of casks, then carefully ran it through the passage door. Jase poured more kerosene partway into the tunnel. I extended the cording about another thirty feet past it.

And then I turned around. "Jase," I whispered. "Put the kerosene down." He spun to face the other end of the tunnel with me. A soldier stood there, his launcher aimed at us. He seemed to know he didn't dare shoot it or we'd all go up. Behind him our crew was pinched between six very sharp halberds.

"Come out," the soldier called to us.

Jase didn't move. Neither did I. "That would be a mistake on our part," Jase answered, his gaze stone cold. "Why don't you come in and get us?"

The soldiers' eyes blazed with anger. "Come out of there!" he ordered.

Jase remained unflustered. "No."

"Then I'll send someone else instead," he called back, stepping aside.

Another man moved into his place, the same handler I had seen just days ago, the same yellow-eyed demons straining at the end of leashes he held. Their thick black fur stood on end around their necks.

"Last warning," the handler called.

I held on to the wall, a dizzy wave of sickness hitting me, and then he let them go. The dogs raced toward us.

Jase stepped in front of me, and just before the dogs reached him, he shouted, "*Vaster itza!*"

The dogs stopped immediately. They whined and sat in front of him.

Air shuddered through my chest.

They knew the voice of their master.

Jase leaned over, scratched their ears, then pointed at the soldiers, his gaze still ice, specifically calling them out to the dogs. "*Hinta! Hinta! Hinta!*" Jase stood. "*Yah!*" His hand flew forward with the last command.

And now the dogs were running in the other direction.

It was unexpected chaos, gruesome and bloody, soldiers stumbling backward. Whoever wasn't targeted by the dogs was overcome in the jostling melee, one of them losing his head to Wren's *ziethe*. In only seconds, all six soldiers and the handler lay dead. But the ruckus aroused the attention of the guards on the fortess wall. We heard them yelling for backups.

"Now!" I said to Synové. She stepped forward and began showering the guards atop the walls with a volley of arrows. Three fell to the ground, dead. One jumped for cover behind the workshop.

The rest of us rushed to gather up our weapons while Jase lit the tinder. There was no creeping back across the grounds now. We were running for our lives.

"Go!" Jase ordered. "Don't bother with the lock!" he told Mason. "Blow it out!"

"*Hinta, yah!*" Jase yelled again, sending the dogs after the guard behind the workshop.

The others started across the grounds heading to the vault. Jase went back into the tunnel with the flaming tinder. His face was tight, filled with emotions I could only guess at. He was about to destroy his own home. "Go, Kazi!" he called before he stooped to light the cording.

"Not without you, *Patrei*. We leave together."

He lit the cording and we ran.

Mason, Priya, and Samuel stood at the tunnel entrance, shooting their launchers and shouting for us to hurry, providing cover as more guards flooded in from the road through the back entrance. Dirt and grass exploded into the air near us, and Jase and I were both thrown to the ground.

"Run!" Priya yelled, and we did. We scrambled back to our feet and kept moving. Every second mattered. We weren't sure how much time we actually had. The cording was improvised, and this was not something any of us had ever done before. How fast would it burn? A minute? Two? More explosions rattled the air, but they were shots fired by our crew. Soldiers ran for cover behind the fortress wall.

We made it to the entrance, and Jase whistled for the dogs to follow. They came bounding across the grounds toward us. He shouted more commands to them and they heeled at his side. "They won't hurt you now, Kazi," he said. "You don't need to worry." With Tor's Watch about to explode, I had no time to worry. I would save that for later. Imara, Wren, and Synové led the way with the extra launchers from the dead guards slung over their shoulders. Partway in, Mason, Priya, and Samuel stopped to reload. Our precious ammo was already dwindling. Jase and I brought up the rear, guarding our backs, looking over our shoulders as we ran, firing several times when soldiers appeared.

Samuel slowed at the curve of the tunnel, looking for soldiers coming from the other end. Surely they had heard the explosions in Cave's

End and were coming to investigate by now. He peeked around the curve. "It's clear!" he called, and we ran again. The tunnel seemed twice as long as when I had walked through it. Where was the intersection to the vault?

"We're almost there," Jase said, reading my thoughts. But just as we reached the T that led to the vault, we heard the heavy stampede of steps.

"Hurry!" Jase yelled. "The code!"

Priya and Imara ran ahead of us. It would take time to get the enormous door open. We heard her pounding the code against the door, the rumble of footsteps getting louder. The rest of us walked backward, our weapons aimed.

A squad of soldiers rounded the corner, and Jase fired, the single shot in the short tunnel nearly shattering our ears. Even the soldiers who weren't hit were momentarily stunned. They fell to their knees, grabbing their heads, and searched for their fallen weapons.

"It's open!" Priya called.

I turned. Gunner, Aleski, Titus, and Aram stood shoulder to shoulder with their launchers aimed.

"Go!" Jase ordered. "Go!" He waved them all past us, including the dogs, while he covered their backs. But I had counted Jase's shots. He was out of ammo, and so was I. There wasn't time to reload.

The others ran into the vault as more soldiers flooded in from the other direction. They had launchers.

"Down!" Gunner shouted.

I pulled Jase to the floor with me, and the tunnel flashed with light. A boom like a bolt of thunder ripped over our heads. I shook my head, trying to get my bearings, and saw the soldiers on the ground. Gunner and the rest had fired over our heads, taking them down, but we heard more pounding footsteps coming. Jase and I ran, yelling for them to close the door, diving in through the small crack before it shut. The wheel spun, and the lock clicked, but as we tried to get to our feet, we were knocked to the ground again. The vault rocked violently, the ground beneath us shaking like we were in the fist of a furious giant.

CHAPTER SIXTY

JASE

The floor pitched. Screams bounced off walls and lights flickered. The earth growled and grated like a monster sharpening its teeth and knocked me to the ground again and again. Bodies bounced into mine, and then finally . . . the shaking stopped. I couldn't see. Gray dust choked the air, but I heard moans. That meant some were still alive.

"Kazi!" I yelled.

I felt a hand on mine. "I'm here," she answered. "I'm okay."

I heard Synové cursing. "You oaf! You landed on my bow! It's broken!"

Gunner coughed. Someone else grunted.

That shaking hadn't been from soldiers firing on the vault. It came from someplace deeper—from thousands of pounds of ammunition blowing up in the Darkcottage cellar.

I got to my feet. As the dust cleared, the first thing I looked at was the vault door. It was intact, not a single bend or buckle. I turned and looked down the tunnel entrance. There were no fallen rocks, no cave-ins. Others were beginning to stand, the same shocked wonder I was feeling showing in their faces, their eyes wide as they looked around. I ran to the bunk room, then the study, sickroom, kitchen—things were strewn everywhere, but the walls and ceilings had held. Rhea was already moving through the rooms checking on everyone. They all seemed to be okay.

It held.

The damn vault held.

I leaned over, my hands on my knees, and blessed the Ancients and Aaron Ballenger with every prayer inside me.

The horses whinnied from the hall where they had been stabled, and Tamryn and Kwan went in to tend and calm them. Others were beginning to set order back to the vault too. I found my mother in the kitchen just as she was getting to her feet along with Judith. "We're all right," she said. She put her hand on her belly. "The baby too. You all made it back?"

"All of us."

<hr />

The wonder was followed by elation, and then by sobering silence. All noise beyond the vault had ceased. The quiet was unsettling. It seemed we had done what we set out to do, but now the question sank in: What was left out there, if anything? We listened for a few minutes. The vault door blocked out most sound anyway, but there weren't even the muffled vibrations that sometimes hummed against the door. Nothing.

I felt my father nudging my shoulder. *Stop doubting. Go with your gut, Jase.*

"We have to go," I said. "Before they have a chance to regroup. We need to get to town and finish this."

More plans were set. Remaining ammo counted, weapons reloaded, and launchers aimed as we opened the vault door once again. It yawned wide, growling over small stones, like an old man waking from sleep.

We were met with more eerie silence. I went out first. Soldiers' bodies lay sprawled through the tunnel, covered with a thick layer of grit and ash. They almost looked like macabre, twisted pieces of stone themselves. I stopped at the T and looked in both directions. The king's mercenaries were strewn as far as I could see. Apparently they'd swarmed the tunnel in the last seconds in their effort to overtake and kill us. Not one of them stirred. Blood trickled from some of their noses, like the blast had shaken their insides loose.

I looked at Gunner and nodded. *Let them come.* If the mercenaries who were in the protection of the tunnel had died from the blast, I didn't expect to encounter trouble outside of it.

Gunner posted the dogs at the door as protection for those who had to stay behind, and waved the others to follow. There was no hesitation. They streamed out, refusing to be sequestered anymore, maybe needing to feel the sun on their gray faces. Maybe just needing to see what was left. Grit crunched beneath our boots, and the sharp smell of smoke hung in the air. As we neared the end of the tunnel, Kazi slipped her hand into mine and squeezed it as if trying to bolster me for what lay ahead.

We turned at the last juncture and walked toward the end of the tunnel, but most of it wasn't there. Anything that had extended past the mountain was blown away. We stepped around giant blocks of stone that had been tossed like bales of hay. We hadn't even reached the end yet, but through the stony opening I hardly recognized what I saw. The landscape was transformed. Cave's End was gone. Completely gone. All of it except for one jagged piece of the cave roof that looked like a sharp fang biting the sky. The back fortress wall. Gone. The grounds that had still borne some wintery green just minutes ago were completely gray with grit just like the mercenaries. At first I thought it was snow floating to the ground, but then I realized it was ash. A few tendrils of smoke rose from the rubble.

We stepped all the way out of the tunnel and then I saw the rest of Tor's Watch and what had happened to it.

"*Patrei?* You all right?" Wren and Synové asked almost simultaneously. How long had I been staring?

I took in the randomness of the destruction.

Kazi stepped forward as if she was confused herself. With the giant sloping roof of Cave's End gone, we had an open view of all of Tor's Watch.

Darkcottage, the very first Ballenger home, was gone. Thousands of tons of heavy black granite were completely and wholly gone, as if the whole structure had been plucked into the air by a giant hand. A deep crater where the cellar had once been churned with dust.

Above it all, a dark cloud rose into the sky, straight up hundreds of feet like the thick trunk of a tembris, and then the cloud branched outward, still curling, reeling, blocking out the sun.

Next to the crater Greycastle still stood, at least part of it. It was as if it had been sheared in half by a cleaver, the rooms exposed, naked, some of them still filled with furniture, which made no sense at all. Just past it, Riverbend appeared untouched except for shattered windows.

And then my attention turned to the main house, and I heard Titus sobbing behind me. And then others. There was laughter. And more sobbing. Emotions were as shattered as the landscape.

The main house still stood. It was the first time I had seen the tear through the middle of the house in the light of day, but compared to everything else, it seemed like a miracle it was standing at all. Raehouse, like Riverbend, appeared untouched except for shattered windows.

Some trees were only serrated stumps now, while others still had foliage. Random mercies were sprinkled about as if a drunken angel had passed overhead.

Mercenaries were draped over walls or lay motionless on the ground.

"Count up the bodies," I called. "We need to know how many of them are left. And gather the weapons."

I couldn't dwell on what remained and what didn't. I would have to absorb it later. Our battle wasn't over. The worst might still lie ahead. One thing I knew, we were going to take the offense this time. We weren't going to wait for them to descend on Tor's Watch again and run us back into the vault. While they were still scrambling and trying to make sense of what had happened, we would descend on them.

Everyone got to work, grabbing anything that was useful. Two hundred dead mercenaries were found. That meant we still faced an army of three hundred. All of the launchers gathered were too damaged and too dangerous to use, but then someone came running from Greyson Tunnel. A whole stash of them had been found.

"Forty," Mason confirmed. "But they're empty. No ammo."

"Bring them," I said. "Montegue and Banques won't know they're empty, just like we didn't."

<hr />

"Go!"

"Over there!"

"This one!"

Gunner, Priya, and Kazi pulled weapons from the back of the wagon and hurried to shove them into everyone's hands. Synové, Wren, and Samuel helped move them into positions, the strongest in the front.

Ash continued to fall from the sky, dusting our hair and shoulders. The towering cloud cast an uncanny orange light over the landscape.

We had ninety-two in our ranks who could reasonably carry some kind of weapon, or just insisted on carrying one—like Judith. She would be in the rear guard. The very rear guard. Tiago swore his arms were as strong as ever, and he drove the wagon piled with swords, halberds, shovels, and axes—and empty launchers.

On our quick descent from the mountain, at every switchback I paused to look at the town. The tembris blocked most of it from view, but I couldn't see any activity. Kazi and I exchanged a glance. I saw the concern in her eyes. Were they regrouping, just as we had feared? We had to hurry.

We knew they had heard and seen the explosion at Tor's Watch. Their supplies were limited now, maybe less than ours, but we didn't want Montegue's soldiers blocking the inroads, concentrating every bit of their firepower on us as we marched in.

"Over there!" Aram raised his launcher, and ninety-one other weapons were raised simultaneously. Nerves were tight and ready.

"Wait!" I said.

A small group headed toward us.

I cursed. "It's Caemus. What's he doing here?" One of their group broke loose from the rest and ran to us. It was Kerry.

"*Patrei!* We're here to help!"

"Now's not a good time, Kerry," I called back.

Caemus caught up with him.

"Lydia and Nash?" Kazi asked immediately. "They're all right?"

Caemus assured her they were safe and fine back at the settlement. Before I could say anything else, Caemus began explaining they were just leaving town when the whole sky exploded. He guessed it was Tor's Watch. "And then, not much later, a whole swarm of those devils came flying past us."

"Slow down, Caemus. What devils?"

"Those soldiers. They had all kinds of things on the backs of their horses. Bolts of silk. Candlesticks. Sacks of food. Anything they could grab and carry."

"I saw one with a squealing piglet!" Kerry shouted.

"Everyone was running and screaming," Jurga added.

The mercenaries had ransacked the town and left.

"How many?" I asked.

Caemus wasn't sure. "At least two hundred."

"They'd been grumbling about payment," Paxton said. "The explosion at Tor's Watch may have been the final straw. They cut their losses and ran."

"Were any of the other soldiers shooting at them?"

"I only heard a few shots."

They couldn't even quash a mutiny? Did the mercenaries not have it in them to shoot their own? Or were they out of ammunition?

The only way to know for sure was to draw their fire.

CHAPTER SIXTY-ONE

KAZI

"THEY'RE HERE," I WHISPERED. "I CAN FEEL IT."

We huddled behind a ruin near one of the main avenues into town. The streets were deserted, or at least appeared to be.

"The trough," I said, not because they were there, but they would all see it.

Jase nodded and pulled back the lever of his launcher. Across the way, behind the trunk of a tembris, Gunner did the same. I raised my fingers. One. Two. Three.

A simultaneous blast exploded the trough, splinters and water spraying through the air, the boom shaking the street and surrounding buildings. A rapid fire was returned—four shots—uncertain where ours had come from. A shower of leaves fell. At least two of the shooters randomly fired into the high branches of the tembris. Jase and I smiled. They were still nervous about a death angel who lurked up there. We changed our positions, moving to a low wall that adjoined the ruin. One. Two. Three.

This time the side of a toolshed disappeared.

Two shots were returned. Shattered stone from a nearby well pelted the wall we hid behind like a fierce hailstorm, and a giant limb of the tembris crashed down, narrowly missing us.

The next time only one shot was returned.

Gunner motioned to me. He was out of ammo. Jase had two shots left.

He fired, taking out the north wall of the smithy. One shot returned.

He fired again, this time taking out the wall of the lumberyard. Pieces of timber flew into the air, spinning madly upward like a startled flock of birds, and then rained down again in a loud, clattering storm. Two mercenaries staggered out, both impaled with long pieces of timber. They fell to the ground, dead. No shots had been returned. We checked their launchers.

They were out of ammo, but so were we.

Jase signaled our small army. It was time to move in. When we looked back, our forces had grown. Citizens who had fled were coming back, hoes, pitchforks, and clubs in hand.

"Go back with the rear guard," Jase said to me. "Make sure they—"

"Nice try," I replied, remaining in step with him.

"You're a stubborn-ass ambassador," he grumbled, looking straight ahead as he scanned the street for threats.

"I love you too, *Patrei*."

Our eyes constantly moved from skywalks to rooftops to alleyways. They all seemed deserted, but we kept whatever weapons we carried gripped in our hands, ready to use. Synové complained that she felt naked without her bow, thanks to some clumsy oaf who had fallen on it. Mason rolled his eyes, and I gathered he was the clumsy oaf. But other than

Wren, none of us had a weapon we were familiar with. We had to make do. The sword I carried was longer and heavier than what I was used to. I made mental adjustments in how I would swing and weight my stance. I rolled my shoulder back when Jase looked the other way. It was still stiff from when it had come out of joint.

"Do you think the rest of them have fled too?" Priya asked, eyeing the empty streets.

"The mercenaries maybe," Paxton answered. "They had no loyalty to the king. The only stake they had in this was a salary, and they saw that go up in smoke with Tor's Watch. Plus they have homes to return to. But those from here who switched sides—they have nowhere else to go."

Like the king. Hell's Mouth was his gateway to the universe—proof that he was not a nothing king like the father he had murdered. The gods had given all this to him, after all. He would never let it go. It was a legacy he was owed.

As we watched for dangers, we saw a new kind of damage. Windows were broken and businesses pillaged. The mercenaries had squeezed their promised money from the king in another way.

"Montegue!" Jase yelled.

There was no answer.

When we approached the plaza, we braced ourselves for an ambush, but there was none. Only more of the disquieting silence. The plaza was empty. What game was the king playing now?

From an opposite avenue I saw Aleski and Titus leading more citizens with weapons in hand. Our forces had just doubled.

But then from behind me I heard a muffled scream and turned. It was Imara. She was looking up. I followed her gaze into the tembris.

A woman hung from a noose. Her blue dress rippled in the breeze. Her long silver braid shimmered in the sun.

Oleez.

Hot needles burned beneath my skin. I shook my head and dug my fist into my chest like I could stop the pain clawing inside me. *No!* Groans and cries rose from our army. Curses. Weeping.

A different kind of scream ripped from Jase's chest. Feral and frightening. *"Montegue!"* His eyes were fire as he walked forward. His pace was burning rage.

"The inn," Paxton said. "They must be hiding at the inn."

A crazed energy ran through all of us now. Fear and caution had been snuffed out. We passed the mercantile. Like all the other businesses, it was deserted. Its striped awnings had been slashed in the ransacking melee, and the remnants snapped in the wind. Crates of strewn potatoes covered the ground beneath them.

We rounded the curve of the street, and the Ballenger Inn came into view. I had expected the street to be empty. Instead, Banques stood in the middle of it, facing us with twenty soldiers behind him. Three of them, No Neck, Divot Head, and Black Teeth, stood close together and looked like an impassable wall made of brick—but none held launchers. Just as Jase had anticipated, they had sent their strongest firepower to the entrance of town hoping to eliminate or at least cripple us. Those remaining only had weapons that were equal to ours, and our ranks outnumbered them by far.

Zane, Garvin, and Truko stood to the right of Banques, and off to his left were a dozen of the king's other collaborators, traitors to Hell's Mouth. In front of them three archers knelt, arrows drawn, aimed at our crowd. They could kill some of us, but they couldn't take us all down before they were overwhelmed by our numbers. Of course, we did have launchers aimed at them, and they didn't know the chambers were empty.

"I've been expecting you, Ballenger," Banques called. "Zane guessed it was you. Your childhood antics were legend. He was right. Not dead after all." He stared at Paxton and shook his head like he was scolding a child. "You picked the wrong side to betray, my friend."

"Shut up, asshole!" Priya yelled. "Your last seconds on this earth are numbered."

Jase stepped forward. "Where's Montegue?" he called. "Bring him out! Now!"

"Oh, he'll be here," Banques replied. "Don't worry about that. In the meantime, put your weapon down and order everyone behind you to do the same. We're taking you into custody, Ballenger. You're under arrest. It is the king's duty to maintain order."

Jase was beyond raging now. He was incredulous.

"It's over, Banques. You're done. The king's done. Do you not have eyes? You have nothing but a few halfhearted soldiers who are ready to run if they're smart."

Banques nodded, his lower lip pursed, looking exactly like his patronizing brother. "Yes, I see that launcher in your hand. And all those behind you. You do paint a formidable picture. Nevertheless, you are still a convicted criminal of the realm, and the king does have some powers of persuasion."

"They're both as mad as bats," Gunner whispered.

Zane stared straight at me, his chin lifting, confident, like he was sizing me up. Like soon I would be back in his grip and he would be whispering unspeakable atrocities in my ear again. Zane was not stupid. He could see our numbers. Why was he not worried?

My attention darted between the soldiers, the rooftops, and back to Zane.

My heart sped. Something was wrong.

Very wrong.

The vial? Had Montegue found the vial?

Jase raised his launcher.

Banques nodded to the soldiers standing by the inn's front doors and they pulled them open.

Montegue stood in the shadows within. He held something in his arms. *Maybe I'm a bit of a gambler after all, and the best gamblers always hold back a bit of negotiating gold.*

He stepped out into the light.

No, he didn't hold something.

He held *someone*.

Gold.

Negotiating gold.

I couldn't breathe.

My head throbbed with each step Montegue took. The only sound was the boardwalk creaking under his weight. There were no whispers. No one moved.

He stepped down into the street. "She's alive, Ballenger," he called. "Barely. She needs a healer." His brows rose. "We'll make a trade. You for her. You'd do that, right? She's called for you several times. And her mother. She really should be with her. It's your decision. I'm an honorable man. Are you?"

Jalaine lay draped across his arms, thin, pale, half dead. Maybe fully dead. I couldn't see her chest moving.

I looked at Jase. His mouth hung open like he was trying to find words.

"Give her over, Montegue," he called. His voice was weak. The agony in it ripped through me.

"A trade," Montegue repeated.

"You spawn of the devil!" Priya screamed. "Give her to us!"

Gunner shook his head like he didn't believe what he was seeing.

"What do we do?"

"Jalaine!"

She didn't respond.

"He's a monster!"

"We have to get her!"

"We can't trade!"

Jalaine's head turned toward us. She was alive.

Everyone's shouts were hushed.

"Well, Ballenger?"

Jase drew in a heavy breath. He was contemplating it.

I grabbed his arm. "Jase, no! You can't—"

"She's my sister, Kazi. I need to—"

I saw it in his eyes. He had already made up his mind.

"No!" I turned to Montegue. "You want a prisoner? Take me!" I stepped toward him, but Jase grabbed my wrist and pulled me back.

Montegue's eyes dug into mine, a ravenous hunger in them, as if he was considering my proposal—or maybe he just loved watching me beg. *You could have had everything.* He shook his head. "You're worthless to me now," he called. "The *Patrei* is the far greater prize."

"I found the papers!" I yelled, frantically trying to convince him. "I'll give them to you! The magic! It's all yours!"

He smiled. "You'll have to lie better than that. Desperation does not become you, soldier. And being a fool twice definitely does not become a king. Maybe this moment will finally convince you that I am the greater leader." He looked back at Jase. "Time is fleeting. Soon my offer will vanish."

"I'm coming," Jase called.

"No!" I said. "You won't even make it to the noose! He'll—"

Jase grabbed my arms. His eyes glistened. "Kazi, she's my sister. I don't want the last thing she sees on this earth to be his face. Would you really want me to be the man who doesn't go to her?"

The answer was a knife in my heart. There had to be another way.

"Jase—" My chest shook. "Please—"

He nodded to Titus and Gunner, and they grabbed my arms, pulling me away from him.

They called out the arrangements of the trade. The promises.

Jase dropped his sword and daggers to the ground and was ordered to unload his launcher as well. No ammunition fell out. Banques smiled, knowing we were out of ammo too. He waved Jase forward.

I watched him walk away, keeping his promise, Mason a few steps behind him. *But Montegue won't keep his promises, Jase! You know that!* Panic overtook me. A path reeling out of control. *We had a plan, Patrei. Remember? Things that you would do. Things that I would do. And things we would do together. This was not part of our plan! Jase! Stop! Please.*

"Montegue!" I screamed. "I will kill you! I will use your own magic to kill you! I—"

Shhh, Kazi.

The world bobbed. Blurred. The madness slowed. My heart slowed.

There is magic in everything, only you must watch for it. It does not come from spells or potions or the sky, nor by special delivery of the gods. It is all around you.

I searched, but I couldn't see magic. Only a monster winning.

Shhh.

You must find the magic that curls in your gut with fierce power and will not let you give up.

Hear the language that isn't spoken, Kazi, the breaths, the pauses, the fisted hands, the vacant stares, the twitches and tears . . .

I scanned the street, like I was in the *jehendra*, desperate and hungry and searching for opportunity, gauging every twitch, every glance—the mercenaries shifting on their feet, either eager to fight or eager to run; the archers, their eyes jumping from one side of the crowd to the other, nervous; the traitors to the left of Banques, their shoulders loose, smug, sharing easy whispers with one another; Zane on Banques's right, his hands relaxed at his sides, a satisfied smirk pulling at his mouth; Garvin the same, because it was all just a business transaction; but then Truko on the end, a step apart, his shoulders rigid, his eyes unblinking, staring at Jase. He wore two swords the way Griz did, his hand on the hilt of one of them.

. . . for everyone can hear spoken words, but only a few can hear the heart that beats behind them.

CHAPTER SIXTY-TWO

JASE

Montegue placed Jalaine in my arms. The faintest groan shook her chest as she was jostled between us. Ten steps back to Mason, that was all I was allowed.

I turned, holding her in the middle of the street, away from everyone. She was a feather in my arms, my little sister who had been the fire in our family. Her broken bones rippled against my touch.

"Jalaine," I whispered. "It's Jase."

She struggled to open her eyes, her lids heavy and rimmed with red, but then her gaze locked onto mine. Her cracked lips moved, mouthing my name, but there was no sound.

I brought my face closer to hers. "Sister. I'm taking you back to Mother. The family."

"You got my note?" she whispered.

"Yes," I answered. "I came as soon as I could."

"I knew you would. The family is safe?"

I nodded, not trusting myself to speak.

"Good." Her eyes briefly closed. "Jase?"

"I'm here."

"Bury me next to Sylvey."

My throat ached like a fist had twisted it into a knot.

How could she know? I pulled her close, my chest shaking. *Stop talking like that, sister. You're going to be fine! Fine!*

Her eyes remained fixed on me, waiting for an answer. I couldn't lie. Not this time. I finally nodded and cleared my throat. "I will. I love you, Jalaine."

"I know, brother." Her voice was as fragile as a cobweb, like a gust of wind would steal it away from me at any moment.

"That's enough, Ballenger," Montegue called. "Pass her over and walk back."

I kissed her forehead, my lips lingering, then handed her to Mason and watched him walk away with her. I wiped my eyes. My nose.

You're going to be fine. Maybe some lies, maybe most of them, were lies we only told ourselves.

My gaze shifted to Kazi. Her eyes were wild, scanning the soldiers, rooftops, Banques, everything, like she was searching for something.

Once Mason had Jalaine safely back with the others, I turned. The archers' arrows were all trained on me to make sure I kept my part of the bargain. A guard stood next to the king with shackles ready.

"*Patrei!*" Kazi called out. I looked back over my shoulder. She craned her neck, and her chest rose in heavy breaths. I waited. "Blink last!" she finally said and tucked her chin toward her chest.

I nodded uncertainly, still eyeing her, and then turned back to face Montegue.

CHAPTER SIXTY-THREE

KAZI

"Put your hands behind your back," the king ordered.

Jase's eyes locked on Montegue. With Jalaine out of the king's grip, the game had changed. The brokenness and love that had filled Jase's face just seconds ago when he held Jalaine had vanished. It was replaced with something burning and dangerous, like a beast had come alive inside of him.

"Now," Montegue repeated. His chest puffed out. He was breathing in this moment like the air was made of honey and gold. Jase challenging him only made it better. *This* was what Montegue had always wanted, as much as control over any continent. This was the consummate moment he had waited for—the *Patrei* answering to him.

The rage in Jase only fueled him. I watched him savor it like sweet nectar served up in a goblet. I imagined it was all part of the story he had constructed. His bitter battle and shining victory delivered by the gods. Or maybe Montegue was one of those gods by now.

"We're going to kill that bastard," Priya whispered. Her chest still shuddered from sobbing over Jalaine as Mason rushed her to the back lines, where she would be safer. Now Priya stood on the front line next to me, fingering one of Imara's throwing knives tucked behind her back, vengeance blazing in her eyes.

Synové noticed. "Twenty yards. Out of range," she whispered. "Besides, the *Patrei* is in the way." We each had two of Imara's small knives tucked in our belts. One rule of a throwing knife was you only threw it if you were certain it would hit its target. Otherwise you were giving the enemy another weapon to use against you.

"The archers," I said, because right now their eyes were on Jase and they were closer to us.

Wren sighed. "Fifteen yards. Still a stretch."

Synové sucked on her teeth, thinking. "But not impossible."

"There is always a way to make the impossible, possible," Priya whispered, reciting a piece of Ballenger history. "We will find that way."

In unison, we all edged imperceptibly closer.

The guard grabbed one of Jase's wrists and secured a shackle onto it. Jase turned his head slightly, looking sideways at me. He tucked his chin close to his chest. Our gazes burned into each other's like a lit fuse connected us. Did he get my message?

"Wait," I whispered to the others.

The guard reached for Jase's other wrist, but in that same moment Jase twisted away and a sword was flying through the air.

JASE

Blink last. Her chin tucked. *Watch. Be ready.* I got Kazi's message. I was so focused on Montegue I wouldn't have looked at Truko at all. But his eyes were locked on mine and then he blinked and I knew. The bastard blinked for the first time in memory.

There was a moment of confusion when the sword he threw flew through the air and landed firmly in my hand. I whirled, swiping it behind me, making the guard stumble back, as Truko vaulted out of their reach, over to my side.

The archers stood, stepping forward, poised to shoot, but Montegue waved them back. His eyes were wild, like a dog who had caught the scent of a rabbit. "You fancy yourself a swordsman, Ballenger? You're only a two-bit trader at best, with no training as a soldier. You really want to take this on? Let everyone watch the *Patrei* get cut into little pieces in the middle of the street by a true swordsman and soldier? Would that put an end to this?"

"Yeah, that's what I want, Montegue," I answered. "Let's not shed everyone's blood. Just mine and—" I surveyed the soldiers behind him. "Who's going to do this cutting?" I cast a mocking eye at his polished breastplate and pauldrons and smiled. "*You?*"

He bristled, like I had thrown a gauntlet across his face—which I had. His hand flew to his sword and he pulled it free, his chest swelling and his nostrils flaring as if the battle had already begun.

Banques stepped forward, forbidding it. "Absolutely not! You're the king. You will not parry in the street with a common criminal—"

"I am the king and the best swordsman on this continent. I say who I parry with! Step back!" Montegue ordered.

KAZI

I remembered Montegue boasting about Banques's tutelage. *I think it's fair to say that the student has surpassed the master.*

Was this what he had trained for? That moment when he would extinguish the last *Patrei* himself and take his place in history?

Montegue and Jase circled, their swords bobbing with threat, their gazes fixed on each other like wolves waiting to pounce.

Jase struck first. A test. Feeling for his enemy's strength. Montegue was strong. But his deflection was clumsy and his push-off slow, his return loud but ungraceful, unmindful of his stance.

Jase backed off. He knew what he needed to know. They circled again.

Banques looked on, terrified—the master caught in a lie.

Montegue came at Jase first this time, his blows unrelenting, hammering Jase backward. His face and neck were blotched with red, his mad desire driving him and flushing through every part of his body.

And then Jase whirled, ducking low, and Montegue's strike was unmet. He stumbled forward, and Jase swung again, his sword hitting the heavy pauldron on Montegue's shoulder, shoving it upward, and the tip of Jase's sword struck Montegue's forehead—the first blood of the battle.

Montegue was stunned for a moment, staggering back, wiping the trickle of blood from his brow, appearing shocked that it was even there. He looked back at Jase, no longer a king but a fierce wounded animal.

Banques drew his sword.

"Now!" I yelled. Our throwing knives whistled in a straight furious line toward the archers and then we drew our swords.

JASE

For a few seconds, I was battling both Montegue and Banques. Montegue was as incensed with Banques as he was with me, yelling for him to back off. He wanted no help.

And then the street exploded with a roar. The archers were down, and I heard the thunder of footsteps behind me.

Wren, Synové, Kazi, and Priya were at my side, fighting back Banques and the soldiers who had rushed forward to help the king. Truko, Gunner, and Paxton were on my other side, fighting back Garvin and more soldiers. Citizens flooded past us, taking on mercenaries and traitors alike.

Montegue came at me again and again, wielding his sword like it was an ax, rage more than skill driving him. Juddering blows burned in my shoulder, every sinew on fire as I met strike after strike, but he was easy to predict. Left, right, left, right. Whatever training he'd had, it was obliterated by his anger. Before he could pull back with his next strike, I slid my blade along his, unbalancing him, then swept low. My blow across his chest barely cut through his breastplate, but it knocked the air from him. He stumbled back, weaving from side to side, stunned, then tripped over his feet and fell.

I stepped toward him. I wanted to kill him, almost more than I had ever wanted anything. Preferably with my bare hands, so I could watch his life seep away as he looked at me, choking it from him breath by breath as he had done to so many I loved. I wanted to watch him suffer. But I remembered the papers I had signed. *If circumstances allow, you must offer the enemy the chance to surrender.*

"Submit to arrest, Montegue, and maybe I won't kill you. That is the law of the Alliance, and Tor's Watch is poised to be one of its kingdoms. And in case you haven't heard, I am the named head of that kingdom, as I have always been."

He gulped in a hoarse breath and struggled to his feet. "I am the king," he answered. "The only king. The gods have ordained it." His eyes were molten, like everything inside of him was consumed with fire.

The cords in his neck stood out like sharp, hot blades and his chest shook with rage, but then a loud scream bellowed from his lungs, his eyes shining with triumph, and he charged toward me.

KAZI

Priya's back was to my back, Wren's to Synové's, all of us shoulder to shoulder. No Neck's blows were bone-crunching as Synové and I took him on together. He was like a tree, his stumpish body planted in the earth, unfazed by our strikes against him. I thought his steel blade would fail before he did. Synové and I were only getting worn down—and he wasn't. This was the kind of unstoppable army Montegue intended to create with more of his magical stardust. No Neck had no armor though, and even a raging bull has a soft underside—if I could just get to it. He was backing us up against the wall. I had to move soon. "Breaking," I said to Synové, warning her she would have to take his next strikes alone, and I rolled. He was not prepared for this and my sword sliced his exposed underarm while my dagger stabbed his kneecap. He staggered, screaming in pain as he turned and aimed a blow at me, but I rolled again and his sword rang against the cobble. He limped toward me, raising his sword again, but now Synové was in position to finish him. Her sword plunged into his back and out through his sternum. He swayed, looking down at the river of blood seeping from his chest, and I moved out of the way as he fell forward, like a massive fallen tree.

But there was no time to relish victory. A scream behind us made us both turn. It was Priya. Blood gushed from her upper arm, and Black Teeth was about to strike again. Wren was already spinning, closer to Priya than us, and she planted her razor-sharp *ziethe* deep in Black Teeth's gut, but now Divot Head was advancing on Wren from behind. Syn and I leapt to stop him, her sword stabbing low and mine high, his spine crunching beneath our blades. He teetered for a moment, as if unaffected, but then tipped backward. He was dead before his enormous body thundered to the ground.

The street was a swirling mass of bodies, swords, and axes, the chaos loud and frenzied. The *ping* of every kind of metal clashed around us. The smell of sweat, blood, and terror permeated the air. Nowhere in the bedlam did I see Zane. I was separated from the others, and suddenly I was facing Banques again, the true swordsman and master. Blood spattered his face like a macabre lacy mask, and the victories he'd already claimed glowed in his eyes. Anticipation of another win glimmered in them when he looked at me. He swung, his thrusts fast and calculated, and unlike the tree stump soldiers, his feet were swift. I met his attacks, but I only had one good shoulder. The other was on fire with strain. I tried to undercut him, feint, set him off balance, but he was relentless and anticipated my moves, pushing me back again and again.

"Still think Montegue is going to make all your dreams come true?" I asked, trying to distract him.

"We'll rebuild our arsenal. We will come back stronger than before. It's not over."

"He killed his own father. You deserve each other."

"He's a man who knows what he wants. So do I." He smiled as he landed three heavy strikes against me, my sword quivering beneath his blows, my blade being forced closer to my face each time. "You're getting winded, soldier," he chided. "I think I should just end this—"

And then a loud, savage scream curdled the air. Montegue's scream. It was the sound of dreams shattering.

Banques glanced away, only for a split second, but it was enough for me to knock his sword off-center before I plunged mine into his chest.

His eyes were on me again, disbelieving.

"I warned you," I said, as I pulled my sword free, "that one day he would kill you."

JASE

Montegue's scream as he charged toward me seemed to give him flight. His sword was slashing the air before he reached me, as if he were fighting winged demons in his path. His movements were frenetic. I didn't feel like I was fighting a man anymore, but a creature driven by crazed, feverish instinct.

"*Ballenger!*" he yelled, his sword slicing straight down where my head had been. He turned, confused, looking to see where I had gone, snarling when he saw me behind him. He charged again, and this time I lunged, swinging my sword with both hands, low to high, crashing against his, sending it flying from his grasp over his shoulder.

Before I could regain my balance he dove at me, knocking me hard on my back, and my sword slipped from my grip. We rolled on the ground, his fingers tearing at my flesh. My fist smashed into his jaw, and his fist into my chin. My head snapped backward, and for a moment light blinked around me. I pulled back my arm to punch him again, but he flipped me and we were rolling again. When I was on top, I pressed down, one hand on his throat, and I almost had him pinned when he began fumbling for the dagger at his side. I reached down, squeezing my hand around his as we fought for its control. He struggled to pull the dagger from its scabbard and I struggled to keep it there, our hands shaking against each other.

"Give it up, Ballenger." His voice shook with the strain. "The gods have ordained—"

"You?" I rasped. "Prepare to meet them, Montegue. That's all they've ordained. You're through terrorizing my wife, my family, my town. You're done."

But his strength was not that of a country farmer or even a soldier. It was made of iron, obsession, and rage. And maybe stardust too. I wasn't sure if I could stop him, except that I was also full of rage. My arm burned as his hand pressed upward against mine, trying to pull his dagger free. Our hands were hot and sweaty, my grip slipping, but then I shifted my weight, maneuvering myself higher, and I let his hand fly upward, the dagger free at last. Triumph shone in his eyes, but before he could rebound, I pushed forward again, his hand still clutched beneath mine, using all of my weight to swiftly force the dagger down. It crunched past bone, through his chest, and into his heart.

He gasped, surprised, his eyes wide.

I pulled my hand away but his fingers remained grasped around the hilt. Blood pulsed from the wound in rapid bursts. He looked at me, the fire in his eyes receding. I sat back on my heels, staring at him. A grimace creased his mouth. Kazi came and stood at my side, her hand on my shoulder, the battle over.

His eyes moved between us as if he was uncertain where to look.

"They love me," he whispered. "You loved me. They will remember. I was a great—"

His last word lay frozen on his tongue.

Man? Leader? King? Whatever it was, he died believing it.

KAZI

Jase and I held each other, checking each other for wounds. None of the blood on us was our own, as least as far as we knew. Jase's lips pressed against my forehead, breathing relief.

We looked at our battleground. It was over. Some of the mercenaries had run. As Jase said, their hearts were not in this, especially with the promise of reward gone. Others lay dead.

Our wounded were being treated. Paxton ripped rags to wrap Priya's arm. He stumbled over his words as he told her to hold still, and I was sure he was consciously trying not to spit on her. Mason had been stabbed in the side by a halberd, a flesh wound, he claimed. Synové went to him to see if she could help, but he waved her off brusquely. "Gunner is taking care of it." Her lips pulled tight as she turned away.

Titus knelt, holding Aleski in his arms. Aleski was the most severely injured, and Titus talked him through it, whispering soothing words, telling him to hold on while Imara stuffed his bleeding side with cloth and someone ran to the apothecary for medicine and someone else searched for a healer.

Truko had received a blow to the head. Aram was wrapping it.

Jase walked over to him. "Never thought I'd see the day."

"Me either," Truko answered.

Jase extended his hand, and Truko shook it.

"Your head?" Jase asked.

"Just a scratch. I'm still a hardheaded bastard. Don't go thinking this means I'll be cutting you any deals. But I choose the sides I play on, and no one tells me how high to jump—at least not for long."

"We'll make sure you get back home," Jase promised.

Truko nodded, blinking, his mouth twisting. The new dynamic between him and Jase was unfurling as awkwardly as a newborn lamb rising on shaky legs.

A fallen mercenary started to revive, reaching for a sword, and Judith hit his ribs with a hoe. He collapsed back to the ground. "Get up again, and I'll make it permanent," she warned.

I looked around at the carnage. Someone was missing. I knew how cowards could escape, running in the heat of combat so their absence wouldn't be noticed. This one wouldn't escape. Not this time. While Jase went to check on the rest of the injured, I went to check on someone else.

CHAPTER SIXTY-FOUR

KAZI

THE BARN BEHIND THE INN WAS DARK. MOST OF THE STALLS were empty, the gates left haphazardly open by the ransacking mercenaries when they left on their rampage. The mournful coo of a dove floated down from the rafters as if still recovering from the riotous disturbance. Other than that, the barn was silent. A single lantern lit the interior with a flickering golden light, a beacon waving me forward.

He was here. Somewhere.

I pulled my dagger from its sheath.

My heart pounded more strongly than it had in the height of battle when I had taken on unnatural soldiers twice my size. Then again, I was about to confront a greater monster.

I heard the nicker of a horse. The heavy thunk of a saddle.

I crept forward. Dim slivers of light spilled across my path.

Come out, I wanted to say. *Where are you?* I wanted him to know I was the one coming for him this time. But I remained silent, a ghost floating across the floor, the shadow I had become, because of him.

He was in a large double stall at the end, his back to me. He rushed to buckle a saddlebag to the pack on his horse. He was in a hurry. Of course he was. His weapons were still piled on the floor waiting to be loaded.

"Going somewhere?"

Zane whirled and hissed, shaking his head when he realized it was me. "You just don't give up, do you?"

"Give them to me," I ordered, holding out my hand.

He looked at me, confused. "What?"

"The papers," I answered.

He smiled. "I don't know anything about any papers," he said. "You here about your mother? Want more answers? Let's talk about her." He took a step toward me.

I lifted my dagger. I didn't need to tell him I knew how to use it. He saw the archers go down, though the long hilted dagger was not meant for throwing, but for gutting.

"The papers," I said again, firmly. "I know you have them. Probably in that saddlebag."

He glanced from my dagger to the bag, his eyes doing a slight nervous circle in their sockets. *Yes, that is where they are.*

"I figured it out after I spoke to Gunner," I told him. "The timing. It all added up. When you escaped that night, the first place you went was back to Cave's End. No one would have looked for you there, and you were the only one who knew those papers were of any value at all. You were the king's go-between. What I'm curious about is why you didn't hand them over to him. It would have brought you great favor. You might have even displaced Banques as his right-hand man."

"Favor?" Zane laughed. "These papers are worth far more than that. I plan to have them copied—many times over. I already have several interested buyers. Do you have any idea what every kingdom on the continent would pay for these? The *magic* of the stars? There's plenty more Montegues out there." He rocked on his feet, edging closer like I wouldn't notice. "And not just kingdoms. When I was a Previzi driver, I met power-hungry lords in every town I visited, hundreds of them, and every one of those lords would pay a king's sum for a chance to control the wind, rain, and one another. While they're figuring out formulas and fighting among themselves, I'll be in my own hilltop fortress counting my fortune, richer than them all. As our dear departed king would say, imagine the possibilities." He shrugged. "So no, the papers are mine, and they're going to stay mine. But I will tell you about your mother. What *details* would you like to know? I have a lot."

His tone was vulgar, insinuating, and he studied me, gauging my reaction. He wanted to destroy my focus, watch me unravel.

"Now," I said, "by order of the Queen of Venda and Alliance of Kingdoms."

He laughed and brushed his stringy hair from his eyes. "You think your Rahtan credentials impress me? It doesn't change what you really are. The kind of filthy illiterate trash I used to pick up all the time in Venda. Your mother was relieved the day I showed up. Happy to be rid of you, for one thing. She told me—"

He lunged and I spun, the tip of my dagger slashing across his middle as I moved to the other side of the stall. The slash wasn't deep enough to cut anything vital, but it got his attention. He staggered back against the wall, holding his stomach, and then looked in disbelief at his bloody hand. His eyes darted back to me. "You stupid bitch!"

"Step aside. I have orders to secure the papers. I intend to do just that."

He grabbed a hay hook from the post beside him and slashed the air, stepping closer to me with every swipe, backing me into the corner. His reach was longer than mine. "This? This what you want, girl?" he taunted, stabbing the hook toward me. "I gave you a chance. You could have walked away."

I looked at his hand jabbing the air, the hair on his knuckles, the mole on his wrist, his face distorted in the shadows, his voice thick with smugness and threat, all of it like it was eleven years ago. Except I wasn't six years old anymore. He swiped again, clumsy in his steps, the sharp hook whirring close to my head. I ducked and dove past him, tumbling to the ground, but as I passed, my dagger slashed again, this time deeply into his thigh. He screamed, then looked down at me, his eyes wild, incredulous. I was fighting back, and I was winning. Blood streamed down his leg, his trousers already soaked, and then he charged, stumbling forward, the hook raised, but I rose up first and we met face-to-face. His eyes widened, his pupils shrinking to pinpoints. The hook clattered to the floor. He stood there, frozen, my long dagger thrust upward, deep into his belly. I pulled it free, and he slipped to the floor like he had no bones at all.

He lay on his back panting, his breaths small, and his hand trembled, searching for his wound. "What have you done?" he cried.

What I wish I could have done eleven years ago.

"Where is she?" I asked. "Where did you take my mother?"

His chest jumped with what seemed like a laugh.

"Tell me," I pleaded, knowing he only had seconds left.

"The old king's farm—in the highlands. That's where she is now—" He coughed, a weak grin tugging at his mouth. "But you'll never get there in time."

CHAPTER SIXTY-FIVE

KAZI

"SHE'S OVER THIS WAY."

A woman with sun-worn wrinkles guided us through knee-high grass on a trail that meandered away from the farmhouse. I stared at the braids that neatly circled the back of the woman's head as I absorbed the certainty. Her eyes had given me my answer. I knew as soon as I asked, "Where is my mother?" She had looked down, confirming what I had always known. Jase walked beside me. He was quiet, unsettled by the truth even though he never knew my mother.

On a bluff that overlooked the valley far below, the woman stopped at a large, flat white stone.

Jase looked down at the plain marker. "This is it?"

She nodded.

"How long ago did it happen?" I asked.

"Years ago. Before I came." She estimated that it had been about ten years, not long after my mother had arrived. The old cook had told her the story and made her promise to keep the grave marked.

"How did she die?"

"A brief illness, but the old cook said it was really a broken heart that took her. She knew the girl was fiercely unhappy, but she didn't speak the tongue of the land and no one on the farm spoke hers. She had fits of tears and rage. It wasn't until years later, after the girl had died, that the cook learned the king had procured his new wife from a Previzi driver."

"New *wife*?" Jase said.

"That's why she was brought here. The old king was an awkward, quiet man, but he wanted more sons. He believed a farmer needed sons. His wife had died, and he was disappointed with the son he had."

She told us that the younger Montegue had no interest in farming and had never even set foot on the highlands farm in all the years she had worked there.

"Did he know what his father had done?" Jase asked.

She shook her head. "I think it was intended to remain a discreet arrangement until another heir was produced, but that never happened."

That was why Zane had chosen my mother. He knew she already had one child and could likely have more.

"I'm sorry for your loss," the woman said and looked down at the stone. "I know it's plain. Would you like me to mark it with her name? We have some dye we use to mark the sheep."

I nodded. "I'll do it." She left to get a paint pot and brush. Jase left with her, saying he would give me some time alone.

I looked down at the mound of earth and plain stone. I never got to say good-bye. I never wept for her loss. Even if my gut said she was dead, I never knew for sure. Without facts, there was always doubt. Wondering. What if?

It was settled now.

I turned and looked out over the valley, the view from her final resting place. It was beautiful. Something she would have liked.

"But you never rested, did you, Mama?" I whispered to the wind.

I knelt beside the grave and brushed my palm over the small mound. *She had fits of tears and rage.* "It was you, wasn't it? Not letting go." I spoke as if she could hear me, because I was certain she could. "Did you make a bargain with Death? Rage against him? Twist his arm? Make him watch over me? Make him push me to stay alive?"

As much agony as I had suffered, how much more had she endured? Her life had been about protecting me, and then suddenly she couldn't.

I picked some of the tall prairie grass and began weaving it together the way she had taught me.

Like this, Kazi, one strand over another. She leaned over me.

Let's weave a wish stalk in too.

Do wishes really come true, Mama?

Of course they do.

Make a wish now, Kazi, one for tomorrow, the next day, and the next. One will always come true.

I tied off the grass, shaping it into a crown, and laid it on her grave.

"I wish you rest, Mama."

When Jase came back with the brush and dye, I marked her gravestone.

Mama
My chiadrah
My beloved

It would be months before the temple was rebuilt. But Vairlyn insisted on another ceremony, just as Jase had said she would. Not because a Vendan ceremony wasn't good enough, but because a celebration was due.

We had a ribbon.

We had a priest.

We had a town full of witnesses.

Even with all the rubble around us and a ceiling of sky, the temple altar still stood.

The priest had finished his part. Now it was our turn.

"You remember the words?" I asked.

"Every single one."

"You aren't going to go getting all choked up again, are you?"

Jase smiled. "Nah. I'm experienced at this now."

But as he began wrapping the ribbon around my wrist and helping me tie it off, he swallowed hard, and when he began speaking, his voice broke just as it had the first time. I squeezed his hand. "We've got this, *Patrei*," I whispered. "And remember, we have a hundred more times to go."

He nodded and leaned forward to kiss me, but Wren's hand darted out and swatted him away. "That comes after," she scolded. Our other witnesses who stood beside us, Synové and the entire Ballenger clan, rumbled agreement.

Jase's eyes locked onto mine and he began again.

> *"Kazi of Brightmist . . . you are the love I didn't know*
> *I needed.*
> *You are the hand pulling me through the wilderness,*
> *The sun warming my face.*
> *You make me stronger, smarter, wiser.*
> *You are the compass that makes me a better man.*
> *With you by my side, no challenge will be too great.*

> *I vow to honor you, Kazi, and do all I can to be worthy*
> > *of your love.*
> *I will never stumble in my devotion to you, and I vow*
> > *to keep you safe always.*
> *My family is now your family, and your family, mine.*
> *You have not stolen my heart, but I give it freely,*
> *And in the presence of these witnesses, I take you to be*
> > *my wife."*

He squeezed my hand. His brown eyes danced, just as they had the first time he spoke his vows to me. It was my turn now. I took a deep breath. Were any words enough? But I said the ones closest to my heart, the ones I had said in the wilderness and repeated almost daily when I lay in a dark cell, uncertain where he was but needing to believe I would see him again.

> *"I love you, Jase Ballenger, and I will for all of my days.*
> *You have brought me fullness where there was only hunger,*
> *You have given me a universe of stars and stories,*
> *Where there was emptiness.*
> *You've unlocked a part of me I was afraid to believe in,*
> *And made the magic of wish stalks come true.*
> *I vow to care for you, to protect you and everything that*
> > *is yours.*
> *Your home is now my home, your family, my family.*
> *I will stand by you as a partner in all things.*
> *With you by my side, I will never lack for joy.*
> *I know life is full of twists and turns, and sometimes loss,*
> *but whatever paths we go down, I want every step to be*
> > *with you.*
> *I want to grow old with you, Jase.*

Every one of my tomorrows is yours,
And in the presence of these witnesses,
I take you to be my husband."

We turned, lifting our hands to the sky, the ribbon fluttering between us in the wind, our gazes meeting the cheers of witnesses. Synové sniffled, dabbing her eyes, and Lydia and Nash beamed beside Vairlyn. The rest of the Ballenger brood, including Paxton, clapped even as they conspired, exchanging whispers with one another, probably planning to dunk Jase in the plaza fountain, which I heard was a Hell's Mouth tradition. We clearly wouldn't be slipping into a quiet ruin of our own anytime soon. At least life with a large family would never be dull.

We looked out at the other witnesses who stood beyond the broken walls of the temple, still cheering, needing this celebration just as Vairlyn had said. I saw the butcher, the chandler, Beata, and Imara. And then I saw two other witnesses skirting the edge of the crowd, watching, witnesses I was sure no one else could see. The taller one pointed his bony finger at me and said, *Not yet. Not today.* He turned to the woman whose arm circled his. She wore a crown woven of prairie grass. She smiled, her own last good-bye. I memorized her face, the lines fanning from her amber eyes, her thick lashes, the warmth of her skin, the ease in her expression, *rest*, but mostly what I saw in her face was love. She nodded, and they both turned and were gone.

Good-bye, Mama.

Good-bye.

The celebration continued with mountains of feastcake, just as Jase had promised. Everyone brought some, all of them different, with their own taste surprises, none quite like Vendan feastcake, but maybe that made it better. We celebrated in a hundred different ways. And when the last cake was eaten and the last jig was danced, we each picked up a fallen stone and together began the work of rebuilding.

We pile rocks where my grandfather died. His bones are long gone, maybe carried away by a beast. But this is where he pressed the map into my hands and drew his last breath.

> *Tor's Watch. It is up to you now. Protect them.*

So far I have kept my promise to him.

I stand back and look at the memorial. We will make sure it always stands.

When Fujiko says a prayer to honor my grandfather and his last act as commander—giving up his life to save ours— Emi tries to repeat the prayer but cannot say the long word *president*, and twists it into something else. She squeezes my hand and says it again. Miandre nods approval, and thereafter, as leader of Tor's Watch, I am known as *Patrei*.

—Greyson Ballenger, 23

CHAPTER SIXTY-SIX

JASE

One and a Half Years Later

THE CANDORAN AMBASSADOR'S BELLY HAD GROWN, HIS RED tunic rising over the table like a high tide. His buckles and jeweled chains shimmered in the flickering light of the bronze oil lamp and rattled every time he wheezed. His *straza* stood behind him, and ours behind us.

It seemed like nothing had changed—but everything had. The ambassador, in spite of evidence to the contrary, had just finished a long tirade complaining bitterly about the hard times that had come upon him because of our new business practices.

"It's been a year and half. It's hardly new, and you seem to be doing quite well."

He *was* doing well. He never seemed to remember that we processed all the incoming and outgoing inventory.

Lukas toddled around the low table, fascinated with the ambassador and all his shiny buckles and chains. He pressed his tiny finger into the ambassador's belly like it was a tempting jelly pastry.

The ambassador's wiry brows twitched. "And what is this?" he grumbled, twirling his finger toward Lukas. "You bring a baby to a meeting?"

"My brother needs to learn the business."

"He's only a pup!"

"It's never too early to learn."

The ambassador pulled hard on his water pipe, his scowl deepening, even as he slipped a shiny bauble from his pocket and gave it to Lukas to play with.

"There are other places to trade, you know?"

Gunner tensed. I nudged him beneath the table to keep his mouth shut. Some things about Gunner would never change.

"I have important business elsewhere," I said. "Take our offer or leave it. We're breaking ground on a new addition to the settlement today, and we have special guests coming."

"More special than a Candoran ambassador?"

"Very much."

His thick fingers wove together across his belly. "Kazimyrah! You know that is a Candoran name. Maybe I should be negotiating with your wife!"

"You probably should be. She'd strike a harder deal than me. Lucky for you, she's not here." I stood and gathered Lukas into my arms. "Ready, brothers?"

"Oh, sit down!" the ambassador yapped.

I raised my brows, waiting. His puffy lips rolled over his teeth. "Your father always sweetened the pot. Are you not your father's son?"

I stared at him, letting the time tick by just as my father would have. Yes, I was, in many ways. And in this way too. The Candorans were good neighbors and customers. "A new barn in the back pasture to accommodate your new dray mares."

He choked on his pipe and stood, a rare toothy smile creasing his face. I probably overshot it a bit.

"*Patrei*, always good to do business with you." He ruffled Lukas's hair. "And this little one too."

Once we were outside of his apartments, Titus threw his hands up in the air. "A new barn? Why didn't you just offer him a new palace?"

"Stop counting coppers, Titus." I reminded him that we had plenty of lumber. In the rebuilding of the town we had kept our mill working nonstop. Our warehouses were overflowing with lumber. "Plus, our drays up in the lumber camps are aging. When it comes time for us to negotiate with Candora for more, we'll use the warm barn we so generously gave them as a negotiating tool."

Gunner nodded, approving of my strategy.

Titus grunted. "If he remembers."

"He will." He was a sly dog who remembered every detail, including Kazi's full name.

I missed her desperately. I hadn't seen her in two weeks. We had put all our efforts into rebuilding the town first, and now we were making the final repairs on Tor's Watch, which required a lot of last-minute decisions on my part. I had to stay behind while she went on to the settlement to prepare for the caravan's arrival. It was more complicated this time, and there was a lot to do before we broke ground.

At Tor's Watch the remaining half of Greycastle had been mostly salvageable, and the other half was repaired with some of the black granite from Darkcottage. Blocks of it had been found as far as a mile away. Greycastle was now a house of two colors, which Lydia and Nash had already started calling it.

The main house was done, though the interior still needed extensive work—except for Kazi's and my new suite. I had rushed it along while she was away to surprise her when she returned. The walls and floor were dark, the way Kazi liked it, and I had the ceiling painted with constellations so there would always be stars above us. I was grateful that my library was mostly intact. Kerry had come to help me sort through the mess, and I had already read books to him as I had promised I would. Our suite had plenty of empty shelves that would be filled with more of our history. I guessed these last months alone would fill volumes. Priya's library, on the other hand, the one she had transcribed from the time she was a child, just like me, was entirely gone. She took it hard, but then discovered Jalaine's library was still all neatly shelved. She took it as her own, and it brought her comfort.

I buried Jalaine next to Sylvey just as she had asked. The family knew this time, but we kept it a secret from everyone else. Burial in the woods was not the custom in these parts—it was an oddity—and we didn't want their place of rest to become a curiosity that brought onlookers and disturbed the peace of the mountain. So after Jalaine's "entombment," we had another ceremony with just the family at the base of Breda's Tears. I still didn't know how Jalaine knew about Sylvey. Kazi said that messages sometimes had a way of finding people, and Jalaine had straddled a line between life and death for weeks before she finally died.

"There a fire I don't know about?" Gunner teased, trying to keep pace with me. "Someone would think you were eager."

"Not trying to hide it, brother. I haven't seen my wife in two weeks."

He opened the door to our apartments, and we went in to change and get ready. Most of the family was staying here until the main house was finished. All traces of Montegue's presence had been wiped clean.

"Where have you been?" Mason asked as soon as I walked in.

"Had to settle our deal with Candora," I answered, handing Lukas off to Aunt Dolise. She had recovered, and Trey and Bradach had returned home, but Lukas was a godsend, helping her through her grief, because Uncle Cazwin didn't make it.

Gunner saw Mason following on my heels and said under his breath, "Someone else is eager too."

Mason trailed after me all the way into my bedchambers. "We're going to be late."

"What are you so eager about?" I asked.

"They're expecting us."

"Kazi sent a message," I told him. "Wren and Synové will be there. That's something to be eager about. I've missed them. How about you?" They had been called back to Venda months ago to help escort the new caravan of settlers.

He shrugged if off. "I was talking about the queen."

Maybe.

He pulled a shirt from my wardrobe and tossed it to me, trying to hurry me along. "It's hard to believe she's finally coming," he said. "And the king. I wish Father were here to see this."

"Maybe he knows," I answered. "The Keep's coming too."

"Who's the Keep?"

"According to Kazi, he's the most powerful man in Venda, the queen's right-hand man. He used to be the Komizar's Assassin. I'd be nice to him."

"What else would I be?"

"I don't know, brother. Sometimes you can be a little harsh. Just be nice to everyone. It won't cost you anything but maybe a little of your pride."

CHAPTER SIXTY-SEVEN

KAZI

"Breathe," I whispered to Jase. "He's not an assassin anymore." But I was nervous too. I hadn't seen Kaden in over two years. I felt like a young pledge awaiting inspection.

Kaden swung down from his horse, then helped Pauline down from hers. Their three children rode in a wagon behind them. Griz lifted them down, holding the eldest, Rhys, upside down, pretending he couldn't tell his head from his feet in spite of Rhys's protests.

Lydia and Nash squealed with delight but didn't break ranks. The entire Ballenger clan stood in a line, ready to greet the Keep of Venda, his family, and the rest of the caravan that was still arriving.

Kaden walked over, looking taller and more imposing than I remembered, or maybe it was just the stern expression on his face. He glanced at me and then Jase. "So, you're the troublemaker who stole her from us."

"I knew I couldn't trust that fellow the moment I laid eyes on him," Griz added as he stepped up beside Kaden. The two of them began exchanging banter about Jase like he wasn't there.

"It's those shifty eyes."

Griz clucked his tongue. "She should have arrested him the first time she saw him."

"Looks to me like she did. He's—"

Pauline jabbed Kaden in the ribs with her elbow.

Kaden winced. "Just having a little fun." A warm smile filled his eyes, and no one's eyes smiled quite like the Keep's. Anything good in his life he had fought and scratched for, and his joy came from a deep place of understanding the lack of it. He reached out and shook Jase's hand. "Congratulations, *Patrei*." He ushered his children forward, Rhys, Cataryn, and Kit, all of them towheads like Kaden, and he told them to pay their respects to the *Patrei* of the newest nation, Tor's Watch. He and Pauline both glowed with pride as the children stepped forward. It was clear they had practiced this moment. Jase knelt, shaking each of their small hands, accepting their well wishes, and whispering to them that treats awaited them at the end of the line. The *Patrei* was instantly a favorite with them.

Then the Keep raised his hand to me, a greeting from soldier to soldier. I clapped my hand into his and he squeezed it. "Good job, *kadravé*. You make us proud. Or maybe I should call you ambassador now?"

"Forever a Rahtan," I answered. "I am still your comrade. I always will be."

Pauline stepped up next and threw her arms around me, her grip fierce. "I've missed my best student."

A warm tug pulled inside me. I had missed her too, cherishing her stubbornness like I never had before—and all the times she wouldn't let me give up when the scribbles on the page frustrated me to distraction. "I thought Wren was your best student."

She laughed. "You all were."

"Thank you, Pauline," I said. "I'm not sure I ever said it. In fact, I'm sure I was horrible most of the time, but I write every day now and actually love it."

"That is all the thanks I need." She kissed my cheek and followed Kaden down the line. I heard all the Ballengers offering their welcomes and gratitude. I heard the wonder in their voices. So much had been lost, but today so much was regained.

"Well, look who's here," Jase said, nudging me. "My cooks have arrived."

It was Eben and Natiya.

Natiya swaggered up, Eben just behind her. Her dark eyes danced as she looked at both of us. "Married," she said, shaking her head.

"Twice married," Jase replied. "Ballenger and Vendan wedding. There's no undoing it now."

"Oh, there's ways," Eben said, his black eyes full of mischief.

"So, what's on the menu tonight?" Natiya asked, patting her stomach.

Jase laughed. "Eating for two again?"

She and Eben exchanged a glance and then I noticed that her waist had grown wider. She looked back at me and Jase. "Actually . . ."

"Really?" I asked.

"Really," Eben confirmed.

We hugged and congratulated them and then Natiya gave us a small package that held sage cakes, saying now we could have an official Vagabond wedding too. As soon as I opened the package and the pungent aroma escaped, Natiya clapped her hand over her mouth and scurried away. Eben explained she was still having some nausea and hurried after her.

"At least we don't have to share," Jase mused as he took a big bite of the cake.

A sudden hush descended on the camp and we turned. The Queen of Venda and the King of Dalbreck had arrived. We watched them dismount from their horses. Vairlyn cleared her throat. So did Gunner and Priya. It sounded like they were all choking on something, or maybe trying to hold something back. The emotion of the moment swelled in me too. This day was wrapped up in so much history, both old and recent.

Make her come.

Jase had told me his father's last wishes, for Tor's Watch to be recognized by the most powerful queen on the continent. And now she was here, on Tor's Watch soil—here not just to break ground on an expanding settlement but to have Jase sign the final papers that would make Tor's Watch an official new kingdom.

"Kazimyrah," the queen said, hugging me first. If the Keep's smiles were singular, so were the queen's hugs. You felt them all the way into your bones. She raised a discerning brow and nodded toward Jase. "You keeping him in line?"

"She absolutely is, Your Majesty. She's a brutal taskmaster," Jase answered, catching on that this was not going to be a formal occasion but more like a family affair.

"Good!" she answered and gave him a warm hug too before greeting the rest of the family and pulling presents from her pockets for Lydia and Nash, small wooden flutes carved by artisans in Venda.

King Jaxon carried a sleeping Aster on his shoulder, the toddler's legs and arms dangling loosely in a deep sleep. He spoke quietly so as not to wake his daughter, telling Jase that no kingdom had opposed Tor's Watch admission into the Alliance, with the exception of Eislandia, which hadn't weighed in at all because there was still no ruler to succeed Montegue. It was being managed by custodians until a new one was chosen. He whispered his congratulations too, and shook Jase's hand.

Kerry ran up, eager to meet the king, and Jase introduced him. "This is Kerry of Fogswallow. He's good at cracking kneecaps. Maybe there's a place for him in your army?"

"We always need some good knee-crackers," King Jaxon agreed.

Jase pulled Kerry close to his side. "He's also the young man who helped save my life. Without him, I wouldn't be here."

"Honored to meet you, Kerry of Fogswallow," the king said, shaking his hand. "Keep the Dalbreck army in mind."

Kerry nodded, staring at the king in awe.

When all the greetings were finished, the papers were signed and cheers erupted. The sound echoed through the valley, pure and holy and joyous, almost like music in a temple. The repeating refrain hummed in my veins, and the look in Jase's eyes, the way he swallowed and nodded, taking it all in, melted something deep inside me. It was a moment I would never forget. The cheers were followed by laughter, tears, prayers, and countless embraces, and then we all spread out, welcoming the new settlers.

Caemus smiled as they jumped out of wagons and turned in circles, soaking in the beauty of their new home. Their faces were filled with as much wonder as his had been when he first arrived in the valley. The queen was given a tour of the settlement and the fields that continued to be bountiful. Children of the newcomers swarmed the giant oak tree in the center, taking turns on the swing.

These last months swept past me, the lowest lows, the highest highs, and the hope that had kept me going, the hope that was crushed, but rose up again and again, the hope of Lydia, Nash, Jase, the hope of a vault full of people, the hope that so often only hung on by a tenuous thread.

"Mistress Brightmist! What a wondrous day, is it not?"

It was Mustafier, the merchant from the arena. He had brought gifts and clothing for the newcomers and had volunteered to help with the details of getting them settled.

"Yes, Mustafier, exquisitely splendiferous," I agreed.

He cackled, happy that I remembered his flowery words.

"So, have you crafted a riddle to commemorate this stupendous day?" His long thick brows twitched, eager.

I smiled, listening to the sounds of beginnings, of saws cutting wood, of hammers pounding nails, of imaginations blooming.

"I think I might," I answered.

I eased down on a pile of lumber and watched the busyness of the camp, excitement pattering through it like a welcome summer shower. Mustafier waited patiently. "How about this one?" I asked and began.

> *"My heart is undying,*
> *my wings spread wide,*
> *When I'm set free,*
> *I soar, I glide.*
>
> *I tame tomorrows,*
> *I offer shade,*
> *I make the fearful,*
> *Unafraid.*
>
> *I'm a rope with no end,*
> *A sword and a shield,*
> *No army can match,*
> *The power I wield.*
>
> *On occasion I'm lost,*
> *Or tossed in the fight,*
> *Downtrodden, beat,*
> *My hands bound tight.*

But a shout, a stand,
A smile, a jest,
A meal, a drink,
A good night's rest,

A swing on a tree,
an orange, a kind deed.
How little it takes,
for me to be freed."

The wordy merchant was unexpectedly quiet. He looked out at the busy camp with me, watching the children playing, watching Jase eagerly talking with settlers, and he wiped his eye. "Splendiferous," he finally whispered.

———◦◦◦———

Jase left to stake out the new homes with Caemus and Leanndra, the representative of the settlers. He was eager and animated. He had great plans for this expansion. Besides building ten more homes, he had sent enough lumber for two more barns, a work shed, a mill, and a large schoolhouse.

In the first months after all the destruction, funds had been tight for the Ballengers, but the settlers had rolled up their sleeves and pitched in. They'd had a bountiful harvest and cooked and served food for all the workers Jase had hired to help rebuild the town. All the Ballengers were grateful to them. But during Jase's weeks in the root cellar as the settlers nursed him back from the brink of death, his bonds with them had deepened in a whole new way. They were family. He wore a tether of bones at his side now, just like they did. *Meunter ijotande.* Never forgotten. This settlement was in his blood now, and he had a passion to see it thrive.

I sighed as Jase disappeared from view behind a knoll. We hadn't had two minutes together to even talk today before he was whisked away by duty, and I wondered if I'd be able to steal a moment with him at all.

I noticed Mason, first looking at the horses, and then skimming heads as if searching for something.

"Looking for someone?" I asked.

"Jase said Wren and Synové were coming. Priya was looking for them."

"Priya? I saw her over by the food tent. I'll go—"

"I'm going that way. I can tell her," he said, waiting expectantly.

"Wren and Synové will be along. They were riding rear guard on the caravan. A wheel broke on one of the wagons. They're staying behind until they get it rolling again."

"Should we send someone to help them?"

"Like you?"

"No," he said quickly. "I've got things to do here. But there are some hands—"

"They have it covered, brother, thank you."

Brother. They were all so infuriatingly different. But alike too. Mason had so much pride. Gunner, on the other hand, the brother I had thought I would always hate, had grown on me. *Yeah, the way a tick grows on a dog,* Synové had said before she left. She hadn't quite developed the same fondness for him yet, but she had at least stopped calling him the nasty one. I missed her and Wren terribly. They had left six months ago and would only be here for a week before they were off again, escorting the queen and king's entourage to Morrighan to attend her brother's wedding.

The sun dropped closer to the spiked tops of the forest trees, its golden light beginning to shimmer with shades of twilight. Evening would soon tiptoe in. I told the camp cooks to ring everyone for dinner. We had a lot to feed. Between the thirty-five newcomers, the queen's entourage, and the Ballenger crew, we had well over a hundred—double our last groundbreaking. I made sure dinner was beef stew—not venison and leek—and that there were plenty of potatoes for Priya.

I headed to the river to wash up, breathing in the smell of meadow and forest, of camp stoves bubbling, and of fields ripe with wheat ready to harvest. I soaked in the sultry summer air and the hum of distant voices. It was an entrancing balm, circling the valley. My footsteps slowed, easing into a rare leisurely pace.

For over a year our days had been nonstop and filled with vigorous work. The town was repaired and thriving again, and with news of Tor's Watch becoming a recognized nation, the arena had rebounded and was busier than ever. There was still work to do on the family home. Vairlyn had said good riddance to Darkcottage, that she wouldn't miss it and that she rather liked the openness created by the elimination of Cave's End. Vairlyn always looked forward, and I tried to learn from her. Trees were planted in the new open space, and a lower garden was created that included a greenhouse, because Jalaine had loved to garden. The arrival of Lukas had created fullness in all of our lives, but he didn't replace the hole that Jalaine had left. We talked about her often as if she were still there. We talked about her sacrifice trying to save the family, because whatever mistakes Jalaine had made, we had all made them, moments and decisions we couldn't take back.

I destroyed Phineas's papers that had been in Zane's saddlebag, burning them before I ever went in search of my mother. *It will never be over. Not now. A door has been unlocked.* Beaufort had been executed, but his words still haunted me. For now at least, the door was locked again. I never did find the vial I had hidden in the canyon. It was a worry, but in the explosion at Tor's Watch, the rocks in the canyon had shifted, the crevice widened, and I assumed the vial had fallen into the dark depths of the earth, maybe all the way into hell, swallowed by tons of solid rock.

Someone like Phineas only comes along once every few generations.

And someone like Montegue.

I prayed it would be even longer than that.

I prayed that hungry dragon would stay in his dark den forever.

———◦◦◦◦———

"There you are! Hiding from us?"

I turned to see Wren and Synové walking down the embankment to the river. I jumped from the water and ran up the slope, throwing my arms around them. They were both flushed with the summer sun, and smelled of trails and heather and wheel grease.

"Okay, enough," Wren said, pushing me away and sizing me up. She nodded approvingly. "*Patrei's* been covering your back?"

"Always," I answered.

She shrugged. "Should be us."

"Well?" Synové asked. "Did she tell you?"

"Did who tell me what?"

Wren and Synové looked at each other. "She doesn't know," they said almost simultaneously.

"What?" I demanded.

They both shrugged nonchalantly, like it was suddenly unimportant. "The queen will tell you when she's ready."

"I'm ready."

We all spun and looked at the top of the bank. The queen stood there—with Berdi.

I squealed and stumbled to the top of the bank, pulling Berdi into my arms. Everything about her was soft and warm, and even though she had been on the trail, she still smelled of bread and sweet fish stew—or maybe it was just all the memories I was breathing in.

"Surprise," Synové said.

"Well, look at you!" Berdi chuckled, then felt her sides and pockets. Her brow wrinkled with mock confusion. "Hmm, still have all my spoons," she said. She turned my chin from side to side. "What did you do with Ten?"

We laughed. Hugging had not been part of my repertoire.

Berdi had been patient with me like no other when I first arrived at the Sanctum. The kitchen was her domain, and no one dared trespass without her permission, so of course I did endlessly, rearranging her pots and stealing her wooden spoons just to annoy her. She began laying her spoons out in plain sight to make it easy for me, which of course took away all the fun. And then on nights when I refused to come to dinner she left a small meal out for me on the tiny table in the kitchen. She understood my head when I didn't even understand it myself.

She stared at me now, probably most surprised by my overt affection. That was not something I had ever been generous with. At all. Ever. Not even with Wren and Synové. Affection, like love, was best tucked away so you didn't become accustomed to it. At least that was what I used to think.

Berdi told me she was going to Morrighan for the wedding and then on to Terravin to check in on her tavern. She had a longing to see it one more time. The years were rolling by, and she was slowing down, and she wasn't sure if she'd be able to make the long journey again.

The queen scoffed, saying Berdi would outlive us all and that the true reason they were going on to Terravin was that King Jaxon had promised he would take her back there one day, and she was holding him to it. Now was the perfect time. "It will be a romantic getaway, reliving our days together when we first fell in love." Her eyes still glowed with that love. "And of course, we miss the tavern too. It's where it all started."

I looked back at Berdi. Years. They were adding up for her. She had aged since I had seen her last. Time could run out. But it could run out for us all, at any time, no matter our age. Maybe that was why—

I hugged her again. "Come on, I'll walk you to the cook's tent. They could use your expertise—"

"Wait!" Synové said. "That's not what the queen had to tell you."

The queen smiled. "I'll leave them to tell you about it." She left with Berdi, who was now eager to get to the cook's tent and lend her expertise.

Wren and Synové took turns telling me the news, finishing each other's sentences.

"We have a new assignment."

"At least for the next several months."

"But it might be permanent."

"We're going to be staying on here as liaisons."

"Because of the new settlers and all."

"Well, maybe not exactly here. Maybe in town."

"And with Parsuss still up in the air, the custodians need help."

"The queen says she can't put it all on you."

"And with us—"

"Well—"

Finally their chatter slowed. "I think the queen mostly knew we were missing it here," Synové said.

"Missing you," Wren added.

"And some of those Ballengers," Synové said. "But not the nasty one."

I suspected "the nasty one" now referred to Mason.

My heart soared as I walked with my bowl of stew and rye, like I was a Valsprey in the clouds carrying the best kind of message. I was afraid to even think it. Wren and Synové. Here. *A perfect day.* Would the gods hear?

I looked up into the heavens and shook off the thought.

When I reached the gathering beneath the oak trees, there was no longer the Ballenger-Vendan divide. Everyone was spread out, finishing their dinners, perched on whatever seat they could find, stacks of lumber, sides of wagons, overturned buckets, and the few benches we had brought along. Lydia and Nash had already gobbled up their dinners and huddled near the center oak with Kerry, their flutes in hand as he tried to teach them the tune of "Wolf Moon." Gunner sat off from the crowd—with Jurga—slowly eating his stew, his eyes mostly on her. I searched for Jase and spotted him sitting on a crate in deep conversation with King Jaxon, both of them with sleeves rolled up, their boots thick with dust. Kerry said they had all been digging post holes together.

I watched Jase's face as I ate my stew, his expression animated, his hands moving as he explained something, the king nodding in return. I smiled. I remembered his hands moving just as passionately when I refused to sign the letter to the queen until he agreed to reparations. I had believed in Jase, but I had never thought a day like this would come. The twists and turns were always surprising.

Wren, Synové, Priya, and a Vendan newcomer sat on a bench together finishing their meal, all of them leaning in close like they were old friends. And then Mason approached them, talking mostly to Priya. Synové looked down, fiddling with her persimmon braid, pretending he wasn't there, but I saw his dark eyes glance her way again and again.

An older boy joined Lydia, Nash, and Kerry, and led them in the tune. The wistful melody of their flutes floated through the camp like a soft hypnotizing smoke. Heads turned.

The king pulled the queen to her feet to dance.

Kaden and Pauline followed, their children holding on to Pauline's skirt and Kaden's trousers, Kaden kissing Pauline over their heads, before Kit reached up, wanting to be held in her father's arms.

Several of the newcomers joined hands, pulling in Paxton, Titus, Priya, and Aleski, showing them the simple swaying Vendan dance.

Eridine and Hélder circled their arms through Vairlyn's, and Aram and Samuel grabbed Wren's hands, pulling her over to join them.

Caemus sat on a stump, nodding and tapping his foot in time to the tune.

Watch for the magic, Kazi. It is all around you.

"Dance?"

I whirled and warm brown eyes met mine. "*Patrei*, I was beginning to think we would never get a moment alone."

"Then you don't know me very well, do you?"

"Oh, I know you, all right. I can see your kind coming a mile away. This is all for show, isn't it?"

"Absolutely."

Jase pulled me into his arms.

I laid my head on his shoulder, feeling his muscled chest beneath my cheek, breathing in his scent, the smell of fresh-sawn lumber still on his clothes. "Tell me the riddle again, Jase," I whispered.

"You just want to make wrong guesses so you can kiss me."

I clucked my tongue. "You're onto me, *Patrei*."

He pulled me closer. "Happy to oblige, Ambassador," he said, and then whispered the riddle, his voice like a soft warm blanket around my shoulders. I was lost in its magic.

Lost in wonder.

Lost in gratitude.

Utterly lost, but completely found,

Captured, taken . . . a prisoner bound.

I made wrong guesses as he knew I would, and he kissed me between each one. A wilderness sprang up around us, wish stalks filled our pockets, and a chain jingled between our ankles. The twists and turns I never could have foreseen, the steps that brought us from there to here, they tumbled through my head in an astonishing blur.

I happily lost track of time, but then Jase nudged me and whispered, "Look over there."

I opened my eyes and saw Mason approach Synové across the way. He appeared to speak a few words to her. She spoke a few back and then he took her hand and pulled her out to the clearing to dance. Their steps were hesitant, but slowly the space between them closed and Synové rested her head on his shoulder.

The queen once told me there were a hundred ways to fall in love. Maybe there were a hundred ways to find and give forgiveness too. I think I had already found a few of them.

I jotted a few last words down in my journal, recording every detail of the way the final papers were signed, the way Jase had looked, the way I felt, remembering the scent of campfires and meadow and hope, who was there and what they said, and I thought about the way history was made every day in small and large ways, by all kinds of people, every action creating new destinies, even the act of naming an obscure little town. New Fogswallow. The settlement name was finally decided. Caemus and Jase suggested it, and Kerry and the rest of the camp enthusiastically agreed. A bit of the past, a bit of the future. The first new city of Tor's Watch.

Jase pushed open the tent flap and walked inside. "Mije and Tigone are saddled up and ready." It was time to go home. The barn and mill were done. The houses were well underway, the stonemasons now laying their foundations.

Jase leaned over where I worked at the desk and swept my hair aside, kissing my neck. "I have a surprise for you when we get home."

"Jase Ballenger, every day with you is a surprise."

He peeked over my shoulder. "Getting it all down?"

"Every word."

"Good," he whispered. "We have a lot of shelves to fill."

I closed the book, stuffed it in my saddlebag, and we left to go home.

Who will write our story, Jase?

We will, Kazi. You and I will write our own story.

And side by side, every day, that is what we do.

CHAPTER SIXTY-EIGHT

THE NEST WAS ABANDONED, THE JAY LONG DEAD. THE STRAW and sticks had fallen from the crook of the tree season by season. *Lowly thieves*, the crow thought, *that's all jays are.* But a glint caught the crow's attention. He circled, eyeing the prize. What had the jay stolen now? Something colorful and shiny.

It was too good to pass up. It would look impressive in his nest too. He pecked it loose from the weave of sticks, then clutched it in his claw before it could fall to the ground. As he flew away, he didn't notice the stopper was loose. It didn't really matter. He couldn't put it back anyway. Even he wasn't that clever a crow.

Dust slipped from the tiny vial, leaving a nice glittering trail behind him. Some of it floated to the ground; some caught on the wind, swirling upward into the clouds; and some whooshed away on currents traveling to places far beyond Tor's Watch.

Soon the glitter was far behind him, already forgotten by the crow. All he could think of was how magnificent his nest would be once it held his new shiny prize.

ACKNOWLEDGMENTS

First, a world of thanks to all the readers, booksellers, librarians, and more who have bought, embraced, and spread the word of the Remnant realm in countless ways. Without you, this world wouldn't exist beyond the first book. Your imaginations and enthusiasm expanded it all the way to Hell's Mouth—and then some.

My brilliant agent, Rosemary Stimola, is a one-of-a-kind wonder. Thank you, Ro, for being the indomitable *you* and also for leading the stellar Studio crew: Pete, Adriana, Allison, Erica, and Debra, who help me navigate this business.

I am grateful for the incredible team at Macmillan and Henry Holt who work their book magic: Jean Feiwel, Laura Godwin, Angus Killick, Jon Yaged, Christian Trimmer, Morgan Dubin, Brittany Pearlman, Ashley Woodfolk, Teresa Ferraiolo, Gaby Salpeter, Allison Verost, Lucy Del Priore, Katie Halata, Mariel Dawson, Robert Brown, Molly Ellis, Jennifer Gonzalez, Jennifer Edwards, Jess Brigman, Rebecca Schmidt, Mark Von Bargen, and Sofrina Hinton. Thank you also to the many more who work tirelessly behind the scenes. I'm thankful to you all for your dedication and immense talent.

I am certain that Starr Baer, Ana Deboo, and Rachel Murray are superheroes with superpowers. They read crazy early drafts of *Vow of Thieves* and somehow made sense of it all and then offered clever guidance. Thank you. I owe you all new capes.

Rich Deas did it again. How could he top the gorgeous cover of *Dance of Thieves*? I thought it impossible, but Rich always manages to up his game. Mike Burroughs's elegant touch with design details helped make the book a work of art. Tremendous thanks to you both.

I will just say it right now, because it is true: Kate Farrell, my editor, is a goddess. She is patient, encouraging, creative *beyond words*, and has special foresight matched by none. She believed in this story every step of the way, and her wise counsel helped me regain my vision when I was lost. She deserves a constellation named after her.

Thank you to all of my foreign publishers who have created such beautiful books and gotten them into the hands of readers all over the world in such spectacular style. I hope to one day thank you all personally!

I am forever grateful to fellow writers Alyson Noël, Marlene Perez, Melissa Wyatt, Jodi Meadows, Robin LaFevers, Stephanie Garber, and Jill Rubalcaba, who offer advice, laughter, cheerleading, perspective, and wisdom through all the ups and downs of this business.

Like Jase Ballenger, my family is my foundation and strength, though my family is much more well-behaved than his—most of the time. Ben, Karen, Jessica, Dan, Ava, Emily, Leah, and sweet little Riley, oh the smiles you bring. You are my inspiration and joy.

And once again, my deepest thanks to Dennis, who literally watches my back and heart at every turn. He is a warrior of his word and I am more grateful for him than the air I breathe.

ARENA

HELL'S